THE
PRIVILEGE
OF
THE
HAPPY
ENDING

THE PRIVILEGE OF THE HAPPY ENDING

SMALL
MEDIUM
&
LARGE
STORIES

KIJ JOHNSON

Small Beer Press
Easthampton, MA

Small Beer Press
150 Pleasant Street #306
Easthampton, MA 01027
smallbeerpress.com
bookmoonbooks.com
info@smallbeerpress.com

Distributed to the trade by Consortium.

Library of Congress Cataloging-in-Publication Data

Names: Johnson, Kij, author.
Title: The privilege of the happy ending : small/medium/large stories / Kij
    Johnson.
Description: First edition. | Easthampton, MA : Small Beer Press, 2023.
Identifiers: LCCN 2023024856 (print) | LCCN 2023024857 (ebook) | ISBN
    9781618732118 (paperback) | ISBN 9781618732125 (ebook)
Subjects: LCGFT: Short stories.
Classification: LCC PS3560.O379716 P75 2023 (print) | LCC PS3560.O379716
    (ebook) | DDC 813/.54--dc23/eng/20230605
LC record available at https://lccn.loc.gov/2023024856
LC ebook record available at https://lccn.loc.gov/2023024857

Also available in hardcover (9781618732163).

First edition 1 2 3 4 5 6 7 8 9

Text set in Minion. Titles in Shree Devangari 714.

Cover art by Sophia Uceda (sophiauceda.com).

Printed on 50# 30% PCW Maple Smooth Antique Cream 30 recycled paper in York, PA.

Contents

in loving memory of Jim and Ursula

THE
PRIVILEGE
OF
THE
HAPPY
ENDING

Tool-Using Mimics

The simplest explanation: Here is a picture. It is a girl, six? Seven? The 1930s, to guess by the pattern on the smocked dress she is wearing, the background of the dark studio. She is smiling and holding her hands above her head. She has short chestnut curls.

She also has a translucent membrane that cascades behind her head like a wedding veil or a cuttlefish's stabilizing fins. At the waist, she breaks into tentacles. Or is it her smock that ends like this? Two of the tentacles are playing an F chord on the ukulele at her waist. Two of them look like human legs, and wear Mary Jane shoes and mismatched socks. Or are they human legs? Pictures are so unreliable.

She smiles and smiles.

Here is a possibility.

The octopus raises her young; as with every species, the goal is to bring at least some of one's offspring to viability and the age at which they will in their own turn bear young. Her genes will move forward through time, like a soccer ball passed down the field toward the net.

This is her tried-and-true strategy, honed over millennia. She lays her teardrop eggs in jeweling clusters, tucked into a crack formed of coral and her own purling flesh. They look like quivering tender pearls, but they are edible and there are many predators and opportunists in the world. She cannot leave them for even a moment, though this means she must starve herself. As she waits to repel such devourers and destroyers of the young as come too close, she tendrils her arms through the eggs, to keep them clean and oxygenated. They tremble in her delicate currents.

Her skin shreds from her before she dies, but by this time the infants have grown strong. They press through the eggs' thin ripping walls and scatter spiraling away, each pretty as a primrose, pretty as a star. Many of the young die, but some live, grow, find concealments and craveries, develop strategies of their own.

This, then, is her boldest daughter.

They are tool-using mimics, each with her own agenda. This is my way. This is mine. They hide them from you. They change colors to blend, to startle, to convey information. They contort their bodies and legs to feign the shapes of other creatures, fiercer or less edible. They hide in beer cans. They carry coconut shells—they can move fast even burdened like this—and when they are threatened, they curl tight and pull the shells close, like a clam.

Tool-using mimics. It is no surprise that some might become women.

Or perhaps this.

A woman who has always wanted a child walks along the beach. It is Florence, Oregon. It is 1932. She has been told by her brother-in-law that it is dangerous for a woman to walk alone, but who would attack her? She is of no account: awkward, unmoneyed, unyoung. The men in town know her family too well to assault her. If someone else does? She spent her youth ignoring the violate touch of secret enemies, and now her brother-in-law. . . . This is why she walks alone.

There has been a storm so she is looking for the glass floats that appear sometimes from the strange and lovely Orient. Instead she finds an egg the size of her fingertip, with the teardrop shape and unsettling color-shift of the pearl earrings her sister wears for evening parties; but it is soft, as though an artisan with puzzling goals has fashioned a tiny bag from the tanned skin of a mouse and filled it with—something.

Through the egg's translucent skin, the lidless eyes are startling black.

She carries it cupped in her hands back to her brother-in-law's home, which froths with dark brocade and carved walnut ornamentation, like a coral reef shadowed by clouds or sharks. In her high-ceilinged bedroom she places it in a washbasin that she fills with cold water and table salt. A hundred times a day, she runs the single egg through her fingers. She does not know how to describe the stubborn resilience of this tender flesh. At night when she is not alone, she takes her mind away to the single egg: its delicacy; its softness. *You beauty*, she whispers. *You clever beautiful little thing. I will protect you.*

The eyes watch everything: patient, already learning, already uncannily knowing. When intelligence is inhuman, there is no need for neonate time.

What is eventually born has her chestnut hair and her smile, which her sister has not seen since the wedding, and her brother-in-law has never seen, for all his secret visits to her room. When she is cast out (for an illegitimate cephalopod daughter is beyond the pale) she and her child emigrate to Australia. Perth. No one knows her there. She takes a widow's name and wears a ring she purchased from a pawn shop near the wharf in San Francisco.

No many-limbed father will claim this girl; no cold-fingered kinsman will touch her.

Or.

When the blue-and-gold damselfish come hunting, she has learned a trick. She conceals herself (*just mud*, she whispers to the water; *there is nothing inside this hole in the ocean's floor*) and unfurls two tentacles, bands them yellow and black. They sidewind like a swimming sea snake, the venomous natural predator of damselfish. Such fish are bright as a Fabergé trinket and when they flee, the ocean is for a moment engemmed, bejeweled.

She folds in her serpenting arms, turns them back to the color of holes, but it is not finished. It will never be finished. They will return—and if not them, then others. Eventually her eggs, or her young, or herself, will be killed. The ocean is cold in so many senses.

I cannot raise my daughters like this, she thinks. *It must be better above the water.*

How can it be worse?

Or.

Her husband has always been a fisherman, owner and captain of a small trawler called *The Sea Snake*. He will die in the ocean, sucked low by a storm he will not have predicted, ignoring the warning she gives each time he leaves: *you'll walk out that door and you won't return.* They all die, eventually. His death-notice has been written in rime on his skin since before they met. How can she invest in such a man?

During his absences, she dreams. But not of him—nor (as another might) of his clean-limbed brother, who has his own boat and eyes brown as chestnuts; nor even of the baker who took over the ovens when his father died, who will never die shipwrecked, castaway, dragged down or drowning. Not even he, though she would not be the first to heat her hands at his oast in her husband's absence.

Her longings are secret, more complicated. When she wades into the cool water to collect kelp for salt-burning, she feels something envine her legs. Seaweed, she assumes: meristems and stipes given an illusion of intent, air-bladders plump as phalluses importuning her thighs. She cannot stop thinking of this. At night, she throws aside her quilt and shivers in darkness as she imagines tendrilling, trialing arms, a nibbling beak orgasm-sharp. But of course it was kelp. And the salt on her tongue when she wakes in the night? Tears or night-sweat. Dreams.

So how does she explain *this* when he returns—the swelling belly, after her husband has been gone so long, when the only hands that have touched her are her own and the sea's? He will never believe her, nor forgive her.

If he returns.

She wades into the ocean and calls to the father, unsure he exists. When he spreads himself across the waves and looks up at her with one vast eye (the tip of a tentacle wrapping her ankle, an embrace as delicate as a finger-brush), she makes a bargain. Her husband will fail to come home, and her daughter will not grow up trying to guess the difference between the tastes of tears, and sweat, and the sea.

And they pretend to be lionfish. To be venomous soles. To be fat, flat unfoundering flounder. Jellyfish. Yellow-banded sea snakes. Anemones. Brittle stars, mantis shrimps, nudibranchs, scallops, ambulant shells. Rays. What can't they do? They pass, and pass, and pass.

Touch them and at first they recoil then coil, enwrap and enrapture you. Their curious and unsettling overwise eyes are too close to their pursing sharp mouths.

Take them home to your three-bedroom ranch in Hopkinsville, and they unscrew all the lids, open the grilles, break the ornamental seashells. They climb into transparent boxes, into resin grottos shaped like fairyland castles and ceramic skulls with bubbling eyes. They wait until they hear the garage-door opener and your car backing out, then slip through your filters and cross your carpeted floors to eat secretly your tropical fish. Sometimes they return to their salted tanks. Sometimes they vanish entirely.

They survive, and suffer. And thrive, until they don't. They pass, and pass through, pass by and pass on. You will never understand them.

* * *

Once upon a time there was a little girl that no one called Pearl. She did all things well: laughed, danced, thought, dreamt, played.

Someone took that photograph. The laughing little girl: someone said to her, *Don't you want to look nice for the picture? Then hold still while I comb your hair*, and, *Not that dress, darling; pick the pink one*, and *Okay, young lady, can you open your eyes a little wider?*, and *Stop squirming! You're ruining the pictures.*

Guess which variety of octopus she is based on. Guess which girl. Guess what she thinks, why the ukulele, why the smile. Whose daughter was she? Was she your grandmother? The picture is old enough, anyway. She will grow up outside your ken to be everything you love and fear.

Between 1933 and 1935, she was billed on the marquees of small-town theaters across the Dust Bowl as "Pearl: The Gem of the Ocean," but was known more informally as *that little freak-girl, with the tentacles. Can you imagine?* Her performance included singing and dancing, and a comedy routine with an immense black woman pretending to be her despairing mammy, billed as Mississippi Beulah but in fact named Enid Johnson, from New York.

It always ended with a balletic swimming exhibition in a heavy-glassed tank filled with water: this, in towns where there had been no rain for a thousand days, where the youngest children had not known so much water existed in the world, except in photographs. And photographs lie.

The day after a show, the water was drained off and sold by the cup, but Pearl did not know this, already crossing the inland dust sea to the next dry town, drowsing against Enid's shoulder.

In time, her skin seamed, grew lines. How did they like her at fifteen? At thirty? The records do not tell us.

In the oceans, there is a population bloom. Climate change, overfishing: the water grows warmer, and being stripped of certain (highly edible) predators by seines and traps and rising temperatures, the cephalopods step up, filling the gaps. They start to live longer, remember more. They make plans, think through how to optimize their happiness and success as a species.

Pearl was the first Cephalopod Ambassador to the Dry Lands. They did not realize that no one would listen to her. Eight is a very great age for a squid, though, as it happens, not for a human. Plus, she's a girl, and who knew *that* would make a difference?

But we do what they want, anyway. The warming oceans are filling with tentacles. We will be gone and for a time they will remain.

In one version of the world, Pearl goes back to the ocean. She started happy—wore flowers, danced, played ukulele—but that ends, as it always does. Sober adulthood is a hood she will not wear, so she shucks its tight folds, slides off the pier's end into the foaming coastal waters. The photo is all that is left.

Does she find a male who overlooks the deformities of feet and hair? Does she live to run her fingers through her own tear-shaped eggs? Does she die surrounded by the soft ripped shells of her sea-spangling daughters? Does she fit here any better than anywhere else?

The simplest explanation: The picture is a fake. Can you trust it? Emulsion, itself an unreliable material, carefully painted over with acrylics. The colors are a tap dance that conceals the underlying sepia-tone lie. This tentacle-girl has never existed, but she is as real as anything else you have not seen with your own eyes, touched with your questioning fingers.

And even that. What do you know of your own daughter? Only what you think you know. She does her best playing when you are not there.

Mantis Wives

"As for the insects, their lives are sustained only by
intricate processes of fantastic horror."
—John Wyndham

Eventually, the mantis women discovered that killing their
husbands was not inseparable from the getting of young. Before
this, a wife devoured her lover piece by piece during the act of
coition: the head (and its shining eyes going dim as she ate);
the long green prothorax; the forelegs crisp as straws; the bitter
wings. She left for last the metathorax and its pumping legs,
the abdomen, and finally the phallus. Mantis women needed
nutrients for their pregnancies; their lovers offered this, as well
as their seed.

It was believed that mantis men would resist their deaths if
permitted to choose the manner of their mating, but the women
learned to turn elsewhere for nutrients after draining their
husbands' members. And yet the men lingered. And so their ladies
continued to kill them, but slowly, in the fashioning of difficult
arts. What else could there be between them?

The Bitter Edge: A wife may cut through her husband's exoskeletal
plates, each layer a different pattern, so that to look at a man is to
see shining, hard brocade. At the deepest level are visible pieces of

his core, the hint of internal parts bleeding out. He may suggest shapes.

The Eccentric Curve of His Thoughts: A wife may drill the tiniest hole into her lover's head and insert a fine hair. She presses carefully, striving for specific results: a seizure, a novel pheromone burst, a dance that ends in self-castration. If she replaces the hair with a wasp's narrow syringing stinger, she may blow air bubbles into his head and then he will react unpredictably. There is otherwise little he may do that will surprise her, or himself.

What is the art of the men, that they remain to die at the hands of their wives? What is the art of the wives, that they kill?

The Strength of Weight: Removing his wings, she leads him into the paths of ants.

Unready Jewels: A mantis wife may walk with her husband across the trunks of pines, until they come to a trail of sap and ascend to an insect-clustered wound. Staying to the side, she presses him down until his legs stick fast. He may grow restless as the sap sheathes his body and wings. His eyes may not dim for some time. Smaller insects may cluster upon his honeyed body like ornaments.

A mantis woman does not know why the men crave death, but she does not ask. Does she fear resistance? Does she hope for it? She has forgotten the ancient reasons for her acts, but in any case her art is more important.

The Oubliette: Or a wife may take not his life but his senses: plucking the antennae from his forehead; scouring with dust his clustered shining eyes; cracking apart his mandibles to scrape out the lining of his mouth and throat; plucking the sensing hairs from his foremost legs; excising the auditory thoracic organ; biting free the wings.

A mantis woman is not cruel. She gives her husband what he seeks. Who knows what poems he fashions in the darkness of a senseless life?

The Scent of Violets: They mate many times, until one dies.

Two Stones Grind Together: A wife collects with her forelegs small brightly colored poisonous insects, places them upon bitter green leaves, and encourages her husband to eat them. He is sometimes reluctant after the first taste but she speaks to him, or else he calms himself and eats. He may foam at the mouth and anus, or grow paralyzed and fall from the branch. In extreme cases, he may stagger along the ground until he is seen by a bird and swallowed, and then even the bird may die.

A mantis has no veins; what passes for blood flows freely within its protective shell. It does have a heart.

The Desolate Junk-land: Or a mantis wife may lay her husband gently upon a soft bed and bring to him cool drinks and silver dishes filled with sweetmeats. She may offer him games and pornography; may kneel at his feet and tell him stories of mantis men who are heroes; may dance in veils before him.

He tears off his own legs before she begins. It is unclear whether The Desolate Junk-land is her art, or his.

Shame's Uniformity: A wife may return to the First Art and, in a variant, devour her husband, but from the abdomen forward. Of all the arts this is hardest. There is no hair, no ant's bite, no sap, no intervening instrument. He asks her questions until the end. He may doubt her motives, or she may.

The Paper-folder. Lichens' Dance. The Ambition of Aphids. Civil Wars. The Secret History of Cumulus. The Lost Eyes Found. Sedges. The Unbeaked Sparrow.
There are as many arts as there are husbands and wives.

The Cruel Web: Perhaps they wish to love each other, but they cannot see a way to exist that does not involve the barb, the sticking sap, the bitter taste of poison. The Cruel Web can be performed only in the brambles of woods, and only when there has been no recent rain and the spider's webs have grown thick. Wife and husband walk together. Webs catch and cling to their carapaces, their legs, their half-opened wings. They tear free, but the webs collect. Their glowing eyes grow veiled. Their curious antennae come to a tangled halt. Their pheromones become confused; their legs struggle against the gathering webs. The spiders wait.

She is larger than he and stronger, but they often fall together.

How to Live: A mantis may dream of something else. This also may be a trap.

Butterflies of Eastern Texas

"Tickets, please," you say as you walk forward along the narrow aisle. "Ladies, gentlemen, tickets?"

It is a very modern train, with a cream ceiling and sage-green upholstery, grounded power outlets beside each seat like tiny surprised faces. Or perhaps it is much older, golden oak paneling and black iron wrought into tendrils and acanthus leaves. The narrow seats are covered in crushed burgundy brocade and Roman shades swing over the half-opened windows; you can hear a steam engine far ahead. Or it may be altogether different, streamlined aluminum brushed until it seems to glow from within and sea-foam green; old-world walnut and dusty-rose velveteen; charcoal gray and the brilliance of LED screens built into the backs of the seats. . . . It changes each time you close your eyes.

You have been on this train for a very long time.

"Ticket? Thank you, sir."

Some things never change. The view through the windows is always a bright blur of fields, towns, riverbeds defined by trees. Beyond it all, where even the swiftest movement does not change anything fast, the clouds pile into cumulus towers against the blue sky. It always seems to be mid-afternoon.

Your job stays the same. Make sure everyone has a ticket. Make sure everyone gets off the train at the right station. Rules are rules: no one rides this train without a ticket.

* * *

People get on, people get off. The seats are about half filled: men, women, children sometimes. You never see them clearly—it is as though they are video projections onto an irregular surface, a movie screened on a broken wall—but practice has taught you how to interpret what you *can* see. Sometimes it's guesswork, you admit.

Here is a man dozing, his ticket tucked into the headrest by his ear. He seems to be balding. He wears a tweed jacket that is almost the same gray as the small bristly dog curled into his lap.

An older woman with long silver-blond hair is reading a book with a green cover—or is it red? She puts it down as you approach—"Ticket?" (or blue maybe?)—to hand you a slip of stiff paper, icy white, flecked with black markings and a blue-gray blush that is the company's logo. What is the name of the company? You can't remember. "Thank you, ma'am."

A young man looks out the window, as though dreaming. He has an orange wiffle bat at his feet, though you aren't sure if it's his or whether someone long gone has left it behind. He hands you his ticket absently, without looking.

A woman with a basket of peaches at her feet is weaving cat's cradles in her fingers with her son. She looks up laughing and a little apologetic—her hands are full of green string—but their tickets are on the seat beside her. "Thank you," you say with a smile, pick them up, and move forward.

"Tickets?"

You approach a young woman who is wearing festival-red with a butterfly embroidered over her heart. The band in her dark hair is also ornamented with a silk butterfly, so real-looking that it seems about to take flight. A Cloudless Sulfur, you realize suddenly; the other is a Palomedes Swallowtail. How do you know this? You don't know anything about butterflies.

Her expression is rueful.

"Ticket, miss?"

She opens her hands: no ticket.

"I'm sorry!" she says—and from her lips tumbles a butterfly, smoky gray, blue-green, orange, and black. A Pipevine Swallowtail.

It catches itself in midair as though indignant and flits to her hair. The other butterfly moves aside: not silk, after all. The Swallowtail over her heart quivers.

You realize you are gaping, and have to remind yourself to shut your mouth. She smiles apologetically. "There was no one at the station office, and I had to catch this train. I *had* to. There wouldn't be another in forever. So I figured I could get a ticket from you?" Another Pipevine Swallowtail, a Common Snout, and two Goat Leafwings. The Leafwings are the exact orange of the wiffle bat; you glance back along the train, but the dreaming young man still gazes out the window. No one seems to notice the butterflies or this woman but you.

You're still gaping. She continues, "I'm really sorry about—this." She gestures to her lap, where a Variegated Frittelary has just fallen. The Leafwings fly up to settle at her temples; the Common Snout has tucked itself just behind one ear, as though shy about its drab coloring.

Her face is so clear to you. You look back again. She is the only one like this, as vivid as daylight. You can see where a single strand of hair has twisted itself into the collar of her bright dress.

"I'm sorry, regulations do not permit conductors to sell tickets," you tell her. "And it's not possible to travel on this train without a ticket. You'll need to leave the train at the next stop." Nothing falls from your mouth but words. "I'm sorry."

"Can I pay when I get to the destination? I mean, *all* the ticket offices can't be closed! I'll pay. I *want* to pay." Gray Hairstreak, Julia Heliconian.

You shake your head. "It's not like that. I'm really sorry. Rules are rules."

"I guess I understand," she says, a little sadly. Common Buckeye. By now she is wearing a crown of butterflies: browns and blues, silky grays and golds, orange and a surprising bright emerald, a Juniper Hairstreak. A Zebra Heliconian loops above her head, looking for a place. For a second, its stripes as it flutters make a question mark.

This brilliant crown, the festival-red dress—none of it fits her expression.

"We're coming into a station," you say gently. You know this because you can hear it in the sinking tones of the engine, the wheels on the rails. The landscape outside is slowing: a town crowds into the windows. "Can I help you with your bags, at least?"

"Oh, I don't have any," she says, with another Common Snout. She stands, braces herself as the train eases to a stop. "Well, I'll work something out. I just—" She smiles. Even sad, her smile is the most beautiful thing you have ever seen. "Thank you anyway." She reaches out, as though to shake your hand, and the new Checkered White settles onto her palm.

"Wait," you say, and carefully lift the butterfly. It is the exact shade of the tickets in your other hand, icy white flecked with black and a blue-gray blush that is the butterfly's body. "This will work." It settles itself comfortably onto the stack of tickets and strokes its front legs together.

Her eyes light up. "I can stay?"

The tickets in your hand, the passengers, the train, the things you can't see and the things you can; the things that change and the things that do not. . . .

"Well, I have a better idea," you say. "If you're interested?"

She says yes with a Tawny Emperor.

It is the work of a moment to give the tickets to the dreaming young man. He is happy enough to take on the task; he has seen what may come of it. Butterflies spiral about your heads as you and she walk along the aisle toward the door. You step down onto the platform through a cloud of wings and color and words and delight. There is a town there, entirely new to you. You laugh just as she says, "I can't wait."

Monarch. Queen.

Five Sphinxes and 56 Answers

I.

She asks riddles. A life depends on the answers. Yours, if you are wrong.

According to Apollodorus, the Sphinx has the head of a woman, the body of a lion, and the wings of an eagle. Other authorities, equally reliable, claim its tail is a snake: an asp, like the Chimera's. Sometimes her head is that of a man, though that is only an androsphinx. Often an artist takes liberties: the Sphinx has the body of a cheetah, the breasts of a notable courtesan, the tail of a housecat. Sometimes it has no wings at all. Many sphinxes do not even fly; at the end of some versions of Oedipus's tale, the Sphinx throws itself from a crag and dies of the fall.

Where does the Sphinx come from? Even its parentage is uncertain: Mother, either Chimera (lion, goat, and serpent), Echidna (half serpent, half woman), or even Ceto, human mother of monsters. Father, any of a checklist but probably Orthrus (two-headed dog) or Typhon (a giant with many snake heads springing from his shoulders). Her monstrousness was baked in at birth.

Was there a home life? Was it happy, or did her father throw bottles and pass out drunk on the couch? Was he simply absent, caught up in his day job? Or was this a single-parent home, the

Sphinx's exhausted mother bringing home takeout at the end of her long day: orphaned children as tender as veal, a man sobbing out the last of his blood from the stumps of his chewed-off legs? Or has the Sphinx always been solitary, hatched like a sea turtle, toddling alone to safety, her survival dependent on luck and circumstance? *Was* she alone? Did she wish she was?

Anyway, this story starts here:

Hera, queen of the gods, summons the Sphinx, whose name is Phix.

Laius, King of Thebes, has sinned against me, says Hera. Details emerge. Some years ago, Laius was told he would die by his son's hand, so he took what seemed to him reasonable precautions. Step One: When his wife Jocasta bore a son, Laius ordered him killed—though in fact the huntsman given this charge only staked the infant to the ground and left him to the wild animals. This child, lamed for life by the spear through his leg, is of course Oedipus. (Exactly as prophesied, many years later he will kill his father. The story shapes itself as predictably as a table from IKEA.)

Jocasta undoubtedly has feelings about her husband's treatment of her infant. Perhaps she would deny Laius her bed but it's moot because, Step Two: The King of Thebes decides no longer to sleep with women, not even his wife.

Which leads to Step Three: Laius solves the problem of his aching cock and his midlife insecurities by kidnapping and raping a boy. Chrysippus.

Hera is goddess of marriage and married women. To what exactly has she taken offense, that she curses Thebes? Is it the rape? That it was a child? That it was a male? That it is a public humiliation to Jocasta, his faithful and unfucked wife? Has Jocasta prayed for Hera's intervention, and for some reason, out of all the similar prayers, out of all the world's atrocities against children and women, this one prayer has caught Hera's attention? Do Olympian politics play a part here? Could it be that this is painfully reminiscent of Hera's own marital troubles, Zeus and the rape of Ganymede?

Punish him, says Hera, her cow-eyes implacable as stones. *Poison his wells, slaughter his animals, let no man approach or leave the walls of Thebes unless he answers a riddle you pose.*

She storms off, leaving Phix with the basics clear. Raze, ravage, ruin. Riddle.

Q: Why did Hera torment all the people of Thebes, when only Laius had committed the crime?
A: Because all men are liars. The play on Laius's name is more evident when the riddle is spoken aloud.

Q: Why did Hera let the women suffer, too?
A: Because women are used to it.

A: To get to the other side.
A: A penguin steak, or a zebra in a blender.
A: Have him walk in front with you.
A: Dogs can't read.
A: When you are a mouse.
A: The other half of a loaf of bread.
A: Wait for the elephant to leave.
A: It was stapled to the chicken.

II.

You grow up in the sort of place and time where the town whistle blows on weekdays at nine, noon, one, five, and six: *off to work, home for lunch, back to work, shift over, be home by the six o'clock whistle for dinner or you're not getting any.* In the summers, you and your brother Tim rattle around town and along the nearby gravel country roads: *Be back by six* but also, *Don't be back before six.* Your bike is bright green with gorilla handlebars and a banana seat; Tim's is smaller, blue, and doesn't have a basket. Tim is eighteen months younger than you are but just one year behind in school, your only friend. You cycle through playing together, fighting, and ignoring one another on a timeline as regular as crop rotation.

Small-town Iowa, the 1960s. There is a creek with snapping turtles and a small dam you can jump across. Behind the high school, there is a pile of field-and-track pads you can jump into from the top of a storage shed behind which the school's ladders are stored. There is the highway, which you have to cross if you want to buy candy with your fifteen-cent allowance. There is scary Mr. Tjaden's house. There is the Lutheran church that they leave open sometimes, and then you can sneak behind the altar and press your face into the openings of the giant brass vases they store there, smelling the ghosts of lilies. At the end of your street, there are corn and soybean fields threaded with grassy drainage ditches that you pretend are entrances to a labyrinth, though none ever lead to anything but dead-ends spangled with insects and pollen. There is a one-room library, but you are only permitted three books at a time and if you want to keep one for more than two weeks, you have to bring it back in person so they can check it out to you again. But only twice.

The library is where you first learn about the Sphinx, in a big book of Greek mythology. A week later, you check out *Bennett Cerf's Book of Riddles* and *Bennett Cerf's Book of Animal Riddles*, though they're little-kid books and you are ten. You begin to waylay your brother every night, crouching at the garage door. He can't leave his bike outside: Mom will kill him if he does. If you stall him until the exact moment of the six o'clock whistle, you can rush inside and be in your seat on time, but Tim will be late for supper and get in trouble.

"'What kind of animal eats with its tail?'" you ask. Through the screened kitchen door, you smell pork chops and boiling sweet corn.

"Kariiiii," Tim whines.

"You have to guess," you insist.

Tim is starting to cry. "No, you have to let me go in!"

You squeeze your hand into a snake shape. "No, you must guess!" it hisses. "Pick anything," you add in your normal voice.

"Earthworm," he says.

"Wrong!" says your snake. "Now you must die, mortal man!"

Your snake lunges at him, and he trips and falls backward in the driveway, gets tangled with his bike. Just as the six o'clock whistle blows, his crying turns to screams. There's blood.

Q: Kari Ann Ellingson, what exactly do you think you're doing?

—your mother, from the kitchen door

A riddle is designed to mislead. The question has a double meaning or a confusing meaning. Sometimes, no meaning at all.

Some riddles pivot on wordplay, puns, and homonyms. Bough, bow. Coffin, coughin'. Black and white and re(a)d all over.

Conundrums.

Others speak with forked tongues. Look for allegory. Who carries their house on their back? Look for sleight of hand: The tyrannosaur can't clap because it is extinct.

The third cheats by being nonsense, or even by lying. Roosters can't lay eggs. Elephants are never two-dimensional. Apples don't talk.

You're not meant to get the answer right. You are meant to fail.

A: Friday was the name of the horse.

A: An egg.

A: One, but the light bulb has to want to change.

A: Shark-infested custard.

A: String, or nothing.

A: They both have bills on them.

A: A spider.

A: She has taken a picture of him and developed it in her darkroom.

III.

Imagine Grecian Thebes as a walled city on a hill rising in the middle of a narrow valley. The valley is rococo with stone gorges and crags. It was once well populated, flanked to the north with sunny fields of whatever is grown in Boeotia—olives? goats? wheat?—but the people and the fields are all gone now. The herd animals are dead in the fields, clustered with vultures, ravens, hyenas, and busy flies. The tilled fields and orchards are scored deep with claw marks. Poisoned black circles spangle the ground, caused by the venom spat by the Sphinx's asp-tail.

Imagine Thebes behind a tall wall that girdles a hill rising from the center of the valley. The hill's crest is visible above the wall, beaded with temples and sacred groves. Depending on your reading or viewing, this may have the crumbled, icy imperfection of the Parthenon or resemble the castle in a Disney movie. There are a few secret side-doors, the permeable membrane of any walled city: even in sieges, women slip out at night to wash menstrual rags and diapers in the river, or to make uncomfortable bargains for food, or even just a moment away from the horror and tedium of a city besieged.

Imagine that the main entrance to Thebes is along a raised road wide enough for five horsemen to ride abreast, fashioned of bleached gold stone. Imagine a huge column to one side of the causeway. It is tall enough that from its capital you could see all seven approaches to Thebes.

This is not the way it really was. Thebes is a real place on Google Maps, with a website and everything. No city could or would be laid out like this *except* in a Disney movie. But a writer has limited control over what you see when you read her words, and this—town, hill, wall, raised roadway, pillar—is an accessible shorthand we can agree upon.

Imagine atop the column at the entrance to the causeway: the Sphinx. On the red-clay krater you saw on the Wikipedia page, she has been painted as a pretty thing the size of a small panther, with an elegant profile and ideal breasts, her hair elaborately looped and dressed with jewels. Here, now, the Sphinx is the size of a lion. She is not beautiful. Her face is dirty. There is dried blood on her mouth. Drying viscera cakes her breasts. Her hair is a tangled and gummy mess.

She looks down at you and asks you a question.

It's no wonder so many die. Who could keep their head at such a moment?

A: Onion, or penis.
A: A flock of jackdaws. Or swallows. Or gnats.
A: A teapot.
A: Rain, or a siren, or water.
A: A fox burying his mother under a holly bush.
A: Courtship.
A: A needle stabbed in the sand.
A: Ten chickens.

IV.

What the Sphinx is not:
- male
- interested in your problems
- an answerer of questions

This list intersects exactly with what your mother is not.

It is no surprise that you grow up obsessed with trying to find answers to unanswerable questions, questions designed to deceive. You read *Stranger Than That!* and murder mysteries and Russian novels you do not understand. You tear through the self-directed units in eighth-grade science class so fast that your teacher makes you do them again. You're the Elephant's Child: there are not enough answers in the world, and often enough you find your nose bitten off.

* * *

A: Water and ice.
A: The letter O.
A: Only halfway; after that it is running *out* of the woods.
A: Blue.
A: Just one.
A: The German owns the fish.
A: A school.
A: A horse.

V.

Phix looks about her. This is her home now: this pillar, this valley, this city, this sky. The pillar is broad enough to sleep on if she curls up tightly. Rain and wind do not bother her, though when it is cold, the asp that is her tail will bury itself in the fur of her haunch, looking for warmth.

Hera said to Phix, *Let no man approach or leave the walls of Thebes,* but she didn't seem to mention this to anyone else. At first, the seven approaches remain crowded: herders leading bullocks or flocks of sheep, carts arriving with wheat, cheeses, amphorae of wine; leaving with fine-woven woolens, loom-weights, spools, and new carpentry tools. There are messengers, horsemen or fleet-footed runners. There are slaves on errands, beggars, merchants, flaneurs.

Phix keeps busy. She circles into the sky and drops from above, flaring her wings at the last moment with the snapping sound of a flag in a windstorm. She tumbles the men from their horses and carts, presses them to the ground with her lion's paws. She gives them a chance—or rather, a "chance." Answer this riddle and I will not kill you.

Once the news gets out, men learn to flee Thebes on moonless nights or low-skyed, rainy days. Dressed in the colors of dirt, they slink like spies. Dead, and dead. Riderless horses stray across the ravaged fields until Phix hunts them down.

The rules—raze, ravage, ruin, riddle—have become apparent to all. Poor men still hazard their lives because they have no choice, and now they are joined by well-armed men walking alone, aspiring heroes who stand at the base of the pillar and call up to the Sphinx. *Monster, ask your riddle.*

Dead, and dead.

After a while, whole days go by in which no one approaches.

Phix ends up with a lot of time to herself. She swims on updrafts until the city is only a bit of dirty clutter on the ground below her, high enough that she sees all the lands claimed by Thebes: to the north, fields and orchards extending to a far-off lake, and the smoke from distant farms and smithies. Nearer Thebes, a cautious margin that is turning to wasteland. In all other directions, the city is cradled by the Cithæron mountains, colored russet, gold, and the violet of shadows. She can see the marks of her dedication to her task: the venom-leached fields, the spattered stones. Vultures and hyenas settle like dust on the fragmented remains of answerless men.

But the razing of Thebes is her day job. At night, Phix rests on her pillar. A mile to the south, the city's torches leave dirty stains on the night, blots she can ignore. In moonlight, the shadows are dark as ink, but on moonless nights, she sees a misty, foaming river of stars between spangled black-sand banks. The land turns dim silver.

She has a monster's senses. She sees and feels things you cannot understand. Starlight pringling her upturned face. The rosemary bite of cold air, the amber taste of darkness.

Is she lonely? Does she make poems in the fastnesses of her mind? Does she share them with the asp? Does she sometimes cut off a new poem suddenly to say, *look, O look!* as a meteor burns a rusty line across the sky? Do they tip their faces up to watch miracles together, snake-face and woman-face?

* * *

Phix parses Hera's words. *Let no man approach or leave.* Angry spittle had flecked from the goddess's mouth, settling to earth as basil plants around the pillar's base. Did she mean exactly what she said? Does she still mean it? The weeks stretch on. Do the rules still hold?

Phix lives through her mouth: the asking of questions, the devouring of men. The languages of the world jostle in that red cavern. She builds her riddles behind her teeth, releases them on breath that reeks of the previous failures.

But what of the women of Thebes? Do they, some nights, slip out through secret passages? Does Phix see them move silently across her wasteland, gleaning what they can, picking through the rags of yet another dead hero in hopes of something to eat? Do some of them, thinking she sleeps (she never sleeps), approach her pillar to collect the holy basil, the only thing still growing in all this ruin?

Do some of them, already familiar with the nature of monsters, linger? The nights are cold. The women huddle in woolen shawls, leaning back against the stone of the pillar's base. The fresh scent of crushed basil surrounds them, like food, like comfort. Perhaps they are visible to the men pacing the city's defenses, but what are *they* going to do about it? There is no stopping the women without leaving the walls. And who knows which woman is which, or cares? All cats are gray in the dark.

Do the women of Thebes tell their secrets here, gathered at the pillar of Phix, the Sphinx? The wandering husband, the cruel lover, the heedless son—the loneliness of lying unalone in your bed—the tensed shoulders and dropped eyes of entering a room leaden with male breath?

Phix listens. Are all the men of Thebes bad, or are the women who come to her pillar outliers? She thinks it through. A woman with a good husband—one who does not beat her—would be content in her bed, would have no desire to risk rape or death to slip at midnight through the dark streets and out the river gate.

Does Phix drop, effortless as a cat from a table, onto the ground beside them? Do the women comb out her tangled hair and wash her breasts clean? Does she turn her face away to protect them from her breath? Does she make promises from her averted lips?

And Jocasta the queen, married to a pederast, kidnapper, and rapist, father and murderer of her child: Does the Queen come to Phix in the night, tell her secrets as well? Does she love her husband in spite of all this, or beg for his death, or both?

It is ironic that one of the few men to escape Thebes successfully will be its king. Laius sneaks off with five attendants to find someone willing to fix his problem for him. Down the road a way, he meets a limping stranger at a crossroads. There's a standoff, neither willing to grant right of way to the other. The prophecy is fulfilled: Laius is killed by his son—for this is Oedipus, of course. Do you see how his story creaks toward its final, inevitable, confusing answer?

A single servant escapes to flee back to Thebes, blood-spattered and exhausted. Phix has grown bored of killing slaves and poor men—they always seem so resigned and never have even a chance of answering her riddles—but her duty is clear. She drops halfheartedly, but she is not disappointed when he slips past her. She shrugs her lion's shoulders: what possible difference can it make if one slave gets through?

Oedipus is following the slave, but his limp makes him slow. In time he approaches Thebes, the causeway, the pillar. The Sphinx.

Q: What's brown, has a hump, lives in the desert, and sings like a bird?
A: . . . I give up.
Q: A camel.
A: Camels don't sing!
Q: I put that in to make it harder.
A: Kari, that's not fair!
Q: So what?

VI.

By your senior year, you have two jobs, working at a family restaurant until ten and then taking money at the front door of a strip bar until two. This is not what you tell your parents you are doing. Your mother thinks you stay late to close out the restaurant's kitchen, and your father seems not even to be aware that you're no longer at supper.

Some nights, when the bar closes and the well and the coolers have been refilled, the staff all drive thirty miles to the nearest Perkins Restaurant for sour coffee and pancakes the size and texture of Frisbees. You always go, grateful for the invitation—just as though you are a peer and not ten years younger than anyone else, leaving in a few months for college.

You use one of the two family cars to shuttle between these. The miles add up. There are fights until you learn.

A: Leave the tank filled.
A: Even if you think your mother won't notice that you were not home when you said you would be, she will. Have your excuse ready.
A: Tim will cover up for you.
A: When you start having sex with Mac, do your own laundry.
A: If you decide to go back to Mac's house for sex after your shift, go home first and write an entirely fallacious note outlining an impromptu sleepover with Linda. Your mother will not believe you, but she hates these fights as much as you do, so she will pretend.

The silences will stretch on for days.

Five years later, you take an internship in Phoenix, your first time away from Iowa, your first attempt at adulthood. Two weeks in, you are leaving your apartment complex on your way to work when you get in a bicycle accident and break your foot. You call your mother from the emergency room, terrified and in pain.

A: What do you think I can do about it from here?

This is when you finally accept that you are on your own. When you are much, much older, you will also realize this was her way of telling you that she was concerned for you.

A: Six months.
A: Seltzer water and paper towels.
A: Every six thousand miles, three thousand for older cars.
A: Distilled white vinegar.
A: 2000 for a woman, 2500 for a man. These are guidelines only.
A Keep hydrated and if at all possible, stay awake until your normal
   bedtime.
A: Ideally, within 72 hours of the event.
A: Caring communication.
A: Use a rubber band.
A: Turn them inside out and wash in cold water. Do not use the
   dryer. When the time comes to freshen the black, use iDye for
   natural and poly fabrics.

VII.

Could Phix leave? The women in the night have whispered that Laius is dead, killed at a crossroad by a stranger. This must have been the news brought by the slave who slipped into Thebes a day or two back. Queen Jocasta's brother has announced that anyone who kills the Sphinx will win for himself rulership of Thebes and the new widow as bride. Phix sharpens her claws on a dead olive tree, preparation for the next wave of men who won't have answers.

Now that Laius is no longer alive to watch his subjects suffer (if that was the point), Phix thinks that Hera might end the curse on Thebes. But perhaps she's forgotten about all this? Hera's a busy woman. How is she supposed to keep track of everything? Or maybe there's something else about the city that bothers her, something she does not care to admit, and the sins of Laius were only her excuse for something she wanted to do anyway. Did they disrespect her altar? Did they come in late for supper? Some things just can't be forgiven.

But if Phix leaves, who will she find to comb out the tangles of her hair, to wash her breasts clean of gore? Who will stroke the cool strong muscles of her snake? And she knows she is useful here. She has heard what the women of Thebes say about its men. Eventually she will lose her riddle contest and the story's creaking mechanism will push her from its workings—but meanwhile? At least she is helping the women of Thebes.

She is not human, so realizing that she is doing this from compassion comes as a surprise to her.

While most stories emphasize the first, there are actually two riddles Oedipus is required to answer.

The first: *I have one voice, yet walk on four legs in the morning, two at noon, and three in the evening. What am I?* There are variations, depending on which source you read, and a number of overlapping answers: "this riddle"; a man; humanity; Oedipus in particular.

Oedipus answers correctly, limps forward onto the raised roadway.

Not so fast, says the Sphinx.

Q: Two sisters give birth to each other. Who are they?

But Oedipus gets this one right, as well: Day and Night, each in turn cracking open the hinge of her pelvis to release the other and dying in the act. Women bearing women infinitely, their roles simultaneous and slippery: mother/daughter/sister/murderer/victim.

And, riddles solved, Phix kills herself. She has served her purpose in advancing the hero's story, and now she is extraneous, a potential plotline complication down the road when sex with his mother, his blinding, and his ignominious death should be driving the story; and so she is hustled offstage. She throws herself from the column and dies.

A life depends on the answers to the Sphinx's riddles: yours, if you are wrong—but hers, if you are not.

Accounts vary. There may have been a third riddle. There may have been many riddles.

In other versions of the tale, the Sphinx does not leap to her death but devours herself: poetic justice, perhaps a little too on the nose, the biter bitten.

In most versions, she has been eating the men who failed to answer her questions. She must have used her lion's claws to tear them to gobbets soft enough for her human teeth to chew, small enough for her woman's throat to swallow. Bones, sinews, and cartilage would be beyond her delicate jaw's capacity. She is likely a messy eater.

But it is one thing to shred someone else. To devour herself, she must use her own lion's paws to tear past her hide into the soft parts of her body, her belly and groin. She must not flinch; if she does, she must try again. The blood will make her claws slippery.

This is all covered in a phrase, *devours herself.*

Does the snake's head that is her tail go first? Does it ask questions?

* * *

VIII.

After your first band concert:
Q. It was pretty awful, but fifth graders are never going to be any
      good, are they?

After you started dating Jeff in tenth grade:
Q: You aren't sleeping with him, are you?

Every other time that you told your mother you were seeing
someone:
Q: Why didn't you settle down with Jeff?

When you told your mother about the rape:
Q: What were you wearing?

When you told her about the divorce:
Q: Don't you think your father and I sometimes wanted to split up?

When you admitted yourself to the hospital for repeated suicidal
ideations:
Q: Do you have health insurance?

When you visited home for the holidays with your new husband:
Q: Don't you think that wearing black washes you out?

When, after much discussion with your therapist, your husband,
your brother, and your best friend, you told your mother you
loved her:
Q: Why would you say that?

When you said it again:
A: I never really wanted children.

IX.

If you are Oedipus:

Consider your luck. You answer some riddles, which ends up being all you need to defeat the boss monster. The camera pulls back; a dramatic cut scene replays the Sphinx dying, though with better production values than you remember from the actual event. The music is triumphant. From here on, it's just epilogue. You limp forward into a world where everything is about to go your way: power and wealth, kingship, hot (if older) wife. King of Thebes! Game over! No further questions.

And then the world bites you on the ass. You got what you got at the expense of so many others: your slaughtered father/rival, your dishonored mother/wife. All the people who died because of Hera's anger and the Sphinx's siege of Thebes. The Sphinx herself, dead. And all for nothing. Because this is where you were always meant to be and would have been without all this pain, if only your parent had not decided you were a threat and cast you out. You're here now but you got here the wrong way.

Your blindness joins your limp. Eventually you die.

If you are the Sphinx:

The goal is self-awareness, not existence. Phix is fortunate. She can look into her own eyes, lion-woman to asp, asp to woman. Even her thoughts are dialogues.

There are so many versions of this story: plays, fragments; works that have been lost, tales told by women or slaves that never got written down at all.

Is there a version of this story from the perspective of the women of Thebes, where Hera, goddess of marriage, has set Phix to destroy the unfaithful and abusive men, and Laius is only one of a series; where Oedipus is the villain who drives women back into fear and servitude?

Is there a version of this story where Phix stands at the center: *her* yearnings, *her* deeds, *her* hubris? Or would she even have hubris, daughter of monsters with her faces tipped to feel the spangling touch of starlight?

There is a version where Phix does not die meeting Hera's demands. It is mine:

Phix knows Laius is dead. She wants out of this pointless chore, so she throws Oedipus a softball question or two. Not: *Who the fuck do you think you are?* Not: *Why do you think you deserve the air you breathe?* Not: *Who am I?*

He answers.

She looks down from her pillar's height and says, *The city's that way*. He is now someone else's problem.

She lifts on her eagle's wings, curling her paws under as she spirals up the dirty updraft over Thebes. Receding below her: the city, the venom stains, the wasteland, the farms, the mountains. The Anatolian steppes are a day's flight across the Aegean to the east. Or she can go south, crossing the great sea to the Sahara, a desert so large that no god can find her. There are androsphinxes there. She need not be alone; she could have cubs, or stalk the oases and learn the taste of camel. If she goes north and flies long enough, she will find ice deserts where woman-head and asp-head can watch the sky ripple and shift in colors only monster-eyes can see.

What do you think? she asks the asp, and it gives her an answer they both like.

Q: How long does a sphinx live?
A: Same as you, a lifetime.

If you are your mother:

She sends you checks, she sends you pictures of cute t-shirts clipped out of catalogues, she sends you *Economist* articles that she thinks you might be interested in. She tells your brother Tim about your accomplishments, even though she knows that he already knows, that you and he talk all the time. If you don't call her every week, she tells him that you never call. If you call her at work, she puts down her task to chat, even though she hates when people take personal calls at work. Pursuing a flawed strategy for mitigating loss, she picks fights with you the day before you leave after a visit. She does not know how to say I love you, or even to open a space where the words can live. Does she love you? Do you love her?

You have come to accept that she is who she is because of her own confusing and critical mother, and the cycle goes back through forever, it seems: women unhinging their pelvises to bear other women and then getting started on the hard work of dying, back and back and back, mothers and daughters and mothers of monsters.

Mixed messages, riddles you can't solve. You stand at the entrance to a great city, the world. Your mother waits astride the rock that bars your way. The first riddle ends in your adulthood. It is unlikely she will be alive for you in your three-legged stage, though perhaps she is counting on you being there for hers.

The second riddle is existential, and there is no answer. Night and Day. Living 'til night or waking up in the morning is always a matter of faith. In the end, both women die.

Your mother is Jocasta, trapped in a no-win situation.

Your mother is also Hera, angry and vengeful and punishing the wrong people.

Your mother is also what you have tried hard not to grow up to be. Have you succeeded? Could she have done better? Have you?

There are other versions of this story, as well.

If you are you:

A:

Ratatoskr

When Lila is ten, she wakes up one night. Her bed is next to the window facing the alley that runs behind her dad's church. At night in the summertime, it is a shadowy tunnel overhung with elms. This is back when elms dominate every small American town, before disease destroys the great Gothic arches that make cathedrals of the streets. This is also before air-conditioning is common in Iowa houses: let's say the 1960s. She's the daughter of a Lutheran pastor and a librarian. She is bookish and observant. This is Ray Bradbury country.

It is July. There are thunderstorms every third night, the ratcheting clockwork of Great Plains summer weather still somewhat reliable. Storms are so regular that Lila can sleep through rolling thunder and even lightning. Not this time, though.

Her white curtains are shut but her window is open, so they billow. When she was six, practically a baby, this scared her and she screamed one night until her father ran into the room, comforted her, and showed her that the terrifying ghosts were just her normal curtains, unlined poplin with a border of black pom-pom fringe, sewn by Mom for her fifth birthday. When they blow open, she sees the shadowy elms shaken by the wind, and through them, flickers of sickly light from the streetlamp at the alley's end. She's seen all this before.

She pulls her sheets up to her nose and shifts her head on the pillow so that she can look out more easily. Silent summer lightning heaves behind the trees, now outlining their crowns in precise silhouette, now gone, leaving only darkness and scraps of streetlight. The blowing trees make a sound like waves on a stony beach, a noise she knows from last summer's vacation to Oregon. Lightning, trees, surf-sound, streetlight, curtains. None of this frightens her.

—Until the lightning collects into a form taller than the trees. For a moment, the curtains slap shut, concealing it; but they blow back open and it's still there, so she screams for her father, though she is careful not to move, not to draw its pale eye.

And Dad, reliably, comes in. He wears pajamas and his glasses. He's barefoot. "What is it?" he asks. He's a little impatient: he has an early service in the morning; this is Saturday night. Lila is too terrified to care.

"Out . . . the window," she gasps, then bursts into tears.

Lila doesn't have nightmares very often. With an inward sigh, Dad sits on the bed beside her, and she throws herself into his arms. "A . . . monster," she pants. "Outside the window! It was . . . bigger than the house. . . ." She starts to cry again.

He gets it out of her eventually. She saw a shape behind the elms, titanic, glowing dimly, with a tail of fire and shining white eyes. Her description sounds like a squirrel to him, but he doesn't laugh—though he will tomorrow, when he tells his wife about it as they dress for church. Cradling Lila in one arm, he leans across the bed, pulls the curtain open. Elms, streetlamps, lightning. "No monster," he says. "See? Just the trees in the wind." She seems calmer now, so he adds, "I think you might have been dreaming, bunny."

"No," she says flatly. Lila can be very stubborn. "It was *there*."

"Look." He points with a finger. "See? Maybe that was the tail you saw—that streak there—and this part might be the head?"

"It *saw* me," she says. "It was coming toward the house."

He doesn't say: *That was just the wind moving the trees, bunny.* Lila's entirely capable of turning a situation like this into a tantrum or at least an all-night conversation, and his alarm is going to go off at six-thirty. He strokes her back, like a kitten's. "Well, it's gone now. I promise you're safe."

He gets out after only nine questions, dodged with the skill of experience. Bedtime prayers once more, another good-night kiss.

For her part, Lila knows what she saw. Dad closed the window, but once he is gone, she kneels at the foot of her bed and pushes the curtains aside again. She saw exactly what he was pointing at—tail, head—but she *knows* the monster was real. More even than she knows that Jesus is real, because she's never seen him outside of pictures in Dad's church, and this . . . It was right *there*.

She never forgets this.

Later that summer, she figures it out.

The library in her very small town is one room, with rotating metal fans under a high plaster ceiling deeply carved (later, she'll learn to say *sculpted*) with floral garlands and baskets of fruit. Honey-colored oaken bookcases line the walls. There is a desk by the door. It all smells delicious, of glue dried to dust and the sunburnt-grass scent of old paper.

She is allowed to check out three books at a time. She is way past CHILDREN's by now, up to the *K*s in SCIENCE FICTION: two bookcases' worth of rocket-ship stickers that she is reading systematically with the utter focus of Summer Book Club. Come Labor Day, no one but her parents will believe how many books she read or what they were.

Still, sometimes she goes back to CHILDREN's, slumming, and today there's something new: *D'Aulaires' Book of Norse Myths*. She can tell already it's a Perfect Book: oversize, mythology, pictures, decent number of words. Best of all, she is the very first person to check it out. She writes her name, *Lila Maurtveit*, extra neatly on the top line of its crisp, unstained checkout card.

Her mom has insisted she spend the day outside—*I don't want to see you back here before six o'clock*—so Lila bikes to the little park across the street from her house and flops facedown on a shaded picnic table. On page 32, she reads about Ratatosk. He's a squirrel that runs up and down the world tree, Yggdrasil, carrying news between the eagle on the top of the tree and the dragon at its roots. There's a picture on the next page, but it's just an ordinary cute squirrel with tufted ears and bright eyes, and it doesn't look any bigger than a real squirrel.

Lila knows better, because Ratatosk is what she saw that night. Ratatosk, taller than the elms, glowing, looking at her with his white eyes.

She climbs off the picnic table and walks to one of the park's many oaks. She's careful to look for anthills before lying back on the cool grass with the top of her head just touching the tree trunk. It goes up for a long way without branches before it radiates into a silent summer-long firework. Other trees reach up and into her line of vision, greens and greens and greens, their trunks all pointing toward a clump of dead leaves exactly overhead. She wishes it were an eagle. She imagines Ratatosk running down the trunk, from outer space all the way down to where she is. He's got something to tell the dragon, whose name is Nidhogg. The hard roots behind her head are Nidhogg's tail—but that gets a little scary, so she sits up, pulls grass from her hair.

"Ratatosk," she tries the word aloud. *Rat* and *tusk*. Cool.

There's one other book about Norse myths in the library, something called the *Elder Edda*. It's shelved in CLASSICS and it is ancient—it says 1889 on the title page—covered in faded blue fabric with gold writing on the spine. Lila has to get special permission from her parents to check it out, even though it's on the regular shelves.

She slogs through, understanding very little and mixing the names up in a way that will confuse her about Norse mythology for the rest of her life. In the end, there isn't any more here than in the d'Aulaires' book, except that *this* book says *gossip* instead of *news*, and spells his name *Ratatoskr*. This sounds better to Lila: fancier, more monstery, more godlike.

* * *

In the summer, every day is the same except Sunday. And even that. As soon as church is over and Sunday dinner eaten, the rest of the week, all the way to next Sunday morning at nine a.m., stretches like hot taffy, drooping in the middle. So it's hard to say when exactly she sees her first squirrel ghost. School's still a long way off, anyway.

Lila's riding back and forth on the street by her house, on her new emerald-green bike with the gorilla handlebars and white banana seat, and she notices the dead squirrel on the pavement. There's always one somewhere, sometimes scarily flat, with strange smears that darken over days until they wash away in the next rainstorm. This one looks unsmashed, just curled into a gray comma on the street—except for the dried trickle of blood under its open mouth and its one visible eye, still open, still shiny black.

She drops her bike into the grass by the sidewalk, checks for grown-ups and cars, then crouches in the street. The sun shines through the fan vaulting of the elms, a shivering blend of light and dark.

And this is the first time Lila sees a squirrel's ghost. In the shadows, it's only a thickening of the shade. In sunlight it's a *something*, like the cellophane discarded from a pack of cigarettes. Maybe it's because she saw Ratatoskr, or maybe the ghosts have always been there and she just never noticed. Advertising was like that: suddenly one day she realized all those pictures and words everywhere were about things you were supposed to buy.

The ghost is nosing at its body, confused.

"You can't stay here," Lila says. She leans back on her heels, thinking. She can't pick the corpse up with her hands. Mom has been very specific about touching dead animals, and in any case: fleas, ticks, maybe pieces falling off. If she *did* try to pick it up, maybe it would be saggy or rigid. There might be maggots. "Don't be scared," she says to the ghost. "Wait for me—I'll be right back."

Five minutes later she has snuck inside and retrieved a shoebox she usually stores under her bed, all the Barbie clothes dumped onto her pillow. She crouches down again beside the squirrel, realizes she will need a sturdy stick, stands again. Fifty years from now she won't remember how effortless this all was: Lila with knee surgery coming up, steady aches in her right hip and the sprained ankle from three years ago that never recovered.

She uses a stick from the park to roll the body into the shoebox. The underside eye is skim-milk white, and it reminds her of Ratatoskr's pale eyes in the darkness and wind. "I'm sorry," she says to the eye. The ghost frets, away and then close again, and then she feels a swarming electrical zap that starts in her ankle and writhes up her body, settling like the buzzing of a honeybee into the space between her shoulder blades. It is the squirrel-ghost, along for the ride.

Lila carries the box to the alley behind Dad's church, careful, as though it's an offertory plate. Her bike stays where it is: no one steals bikes in this town, in this decade. Under the low branches of the lilac bush, she makes a nest of branches covered with red leaves pulled from a scarlet maple in the church's side yard, carefully rolls the squirrel into it. A little splash of electricity shimmers through her shoulders and dissolves, and the ghost reappears.

"Hang on," she says to the little squirrel-ghost. Five minutes later she returns from a kitchen raid with a juice glass filled with Wheat Chex and Planters peanuts. She will forget the juice glass here, and after this there will always be only five in the set.

Milky-eyed, the body lies cradled in its shady nest. The first questing ants have found it; she uses a twig to brush them away. The ghost is still there, sitting on its hind legs with its front paws curled under. She thinks it looks anxious. "It's okay," she says, and pours the food onto a piece of bark. "There, I got you something."

The little ghost seems to see the food, tips down to inspect it with its narrow face, hips high and front paws close together. It still looks anxious. Does it need her to bury the body? She doesn't like the thought of that. It was raining a day ago, which means there will be worms. "You don't want to be with worms," she tells it. "You like trees." It seems to agree.

That's the first one.

* * *

After a while she realizes that she doesn't need to retrieve their bodies or leave food. The ghosts are willing enough to leave their shattered bodies, if offered an alternative.

She invites them in, little electric shivers that swim up through her body and wait quivering inside her shoulders until she finds safe places for them: wasteland forests, county parks, random clumps of trees. She doesn't know what they do next, but she never sees one again after she has brought it to a woodland. Perhaps Ratatoskr claims them. Perhaps he is their god. Maybe this is why there was so little about him in the *Edda*, in d'Aulaire: he's not for humans. Maybe he takes the squirrels who died violently off to some squirrel Valhalla, where they wait until Ragnarok, until the moment the world is meant to end, when they will return and—

—and fight? That seems unlikely. They didn't pick fights with the cars that killed them. Perhaps, unlike the dead warriors of Valhalla, there *is* no end to their heaven. Ratatoskr gives them a forest free of feral cats and coyotes, where walnuts fall from every tree and bird feeders are interesting puzzles that can always, eventually, be solved. Or maybe it's not quite that easy? Nothing in life is simple, so why would death be?

She will see squirrel-ghosts for the rest of her life. When she turns thirty-six, she will marry a vet tech with big, careful hands and a slow laugh, Jamie from Spokane. They will share everything—concerns about their parents as they age, grief and dread as the world grows simultaneously hotter and colder. If anyone would understand, it would be Jamie. Does he see the ghosts of Scotties and tortoiseshell cats? But in the end, she will say nothing to him. Ultimately, how we see death is a private matter.

Five years after her marriage to Jamie, her father will die, and ten after that, her mother. Jamie's parents will die in their eighties, and then Lila and Jamie will be alone. Eventually it will just be Lila, Lila and the squirrels and the memory of Ratatoskr.

Lila does see Ratatoskr a second time. Eight years after the first, she has graduated to a decent dirt bike and spends her free afternoons riding the gravel roads around town. In the fall, she leaves for college in Oregon. By spring, her parents will have moved to Wisconsin. She will never come back.

She's on one of the overpasses where a county road crosses the railroad tracks that arrow east–west across the world, like an infinite snake stretched out in the sun. August, late afternoon, the sort of day people say is too hot to bike unless you are eighteen, not going with anyone, and bored.

For years, she's biked these roads. Except for the overpasses, it's all flat: fields of black dirt or snow in the winters, corn and soybeans in the summers. Tangled hedgerows thread between them, with wandering woodlands of cottonwood tracing the creeks and runoffs. Towns are small forests, just their water towers and steeples visible above the canopy. Scattered across the landscape: old corncribs and ruined barns turned silver with time, blue-and-white silos clustered like cans on a shelf in farmyards otherwise hidden behind poplar windbreaks. The stop sign where T63 meets 188 is miles away, a single fleck of startling red in all this green and gold. Lina is seeing 130 square miles of the world, pinned down by the sky.

And up, of course, an infinity. To the west and north, attended by smaller cumuli like acolytes, a thunderhead the size of a mountain advances inexorably toward her, indigo at its base and pushing a cold wind. Or will it pass just to the north? She drinks tepid water from the metal canteen her family used to take camping and she waits, though she doesn't know why yet. For the rain to cool her on her way home, she thinks. For something.

She sees Ratatoskr suddenly, mysterious as a message on crumpled cellophane. But she knows how to read the scattered light: he is miles high and scarcely a field away, clinging head-down to a pillar of air just ahead of the thunderhead. She stands immobile, afraid to breathe, afraid to move. His white eye is bigger than she is; if he were to look at her, she would—

And he does.

For the rest of her life, she will try to make sense of all this: Ratatoskr in the trees, the ghosts, Ratatoskr climbing down the pillar of the sky. At the end, she gets her answer, but just too late to share it with us.

Coyote Invents the Land of the Dead

She was there, that is Dee, and her three sisters, who were Tierce, Chena, and Wren, Dee being a coyote or rather Coyote, and her sisters not unlike in their Being, though only a falcon, a dog, and a wren. So there they stood on the cliff, making up their minds how to get down to the nightbeach where the dead unbreathe, a deep steep dark bitch slither it was, though manageable Dee hoped.

The cliff was a high sandy sharpness, but you, O my darlings, might not remember what it means to pass down that narrow dark, your own lives being so past and the dead so quick to forget. Standing on the cliffs what Dee sought was her own ghost love, named Jace and dead a year but still so recent to her mind that she could sniff her fingers or they might be paws and by a year-gone remembered smell see him longlegged goldeyed and lowvoiced with big hands—and the sisters going along with her because they did not wish to see her do it alone, plus each sought something else that she didn't explain, not then or not to Dee anyway.

They had no death-permit for climbing down, but there was no law against trying some of the narrow paths the dead might use. They could try to climb straight down the rawslither rocks or along the arroyo Dee and sisters saw off to one side, or one or two other possibilities that might give them a skinny slight weak chance of finding the beachy sand and all its dead and massy seashells beneath their feet.

Or they could find the beach the faster way: throw themselves from the cliff's edge and hit the sand with permit in hand, as the saying is. And that was what they were discussing on the cliff.

"Well, fuck, and I'll have to do it the hard way," said Dee. "I might be just that bit late coming back." Her quick runrumble voice rippled out from her mouth and plashed against Wren's pinhole wren ears and Chena's great tufted dog ears and the fluffed falcon feathers where Tierce's ears were. All four were what they were, and women also, and more. They were fashioned of myth. That is the way of this story.

"Or never," Wren said highsharp as the whistle from a dry teakettle. "The dead say that too, and then they go down the cliffs and they never come back"—featherlight on a brokenwood sapless and unlifed tree, and hopping from foot to foot, so angry as she was. "It's the dead down there, sister. Go and you are dead."

Above and behind them were stars and clouds and the moon sliding upward, the long calm rise of it. But there was no sky over the nightbeach and the strange ocean beyond. The skystarsmoon dayworld ended abruptly just overhead at the brink of the cliff leaving a curled lip like poor and unfinished knitting, and beyond that just nothing but the sights secret inside an undreamer's eyelids. Chena reached up and touched a thread trailing from the sky's raveling edge with one clawed toe (that may for purposes of this story and your own comfort be seen as a woman's hand, if it seems she must be either woman or beast but cannot be both; which shows your folly, O my dears). It tingled like electricity. A sequining star slipped loose and came resting onto her dark muzzle, leaving tracer lines when she moved her mouth and low in her throat said, "She's dead already, Wren. It's what Dees that are Coyotes do, is die."

"—And come back." Dee hoping it was true. Ears had heard tales of other Coyotes that made the long climb down that cliff—though stories said they had *their* permits: killed by jealous lovers

by gods by revenging victims by falling from trees or into deep
water by folly or stubbornness or selfishness or the ten thousand
ways that Dees could fuck up. Down the cliff—but back too, and
bringing back heaving and snapping with them fire for humankind
or jewelsome girdles for bragging rights. Or perhaps she was that
same Coyote but unremembering, or else it might be a different
cliff; Dee did not know.

"You better hope tales are right," Tierce said all beaksharp
snap. "You're a fool to long for the lost when they're on the
nightbeach. But you'll go anyway, I know you," and Wren agreed
most chirpingly.

Dee was toenails-close to the cliff, and dirt and little rocks
scrabbled away from her feet and over the edge but making no
noise as they dropped. The others were behind a bit, and lookback
Dee saw the outlines of her sisters black against the starbusy
dayworld nightsky. Their faces were invisible until she lit a match
and then a cigarette and held it between her toes or maybe it was
fingers. And then the hawk- and wren- and dogeyes all glowed
gold, worriedlike and sad too, and they were right to be so. Dee
had never long longed for anything lost before this, not even her
own mother. Only Jace. And Dee was the center of things; bullseye
on the target, the twenty-one on the felt, the tight-binding chord
of the arc of Everything. Touch Dee and the world shivered.

Turning, Dee, and she stared down. The only light on the
nightbeach came from the sky behind them, with the cliff's
shadow stretched halfway to the ocean's edge; plus past that, faint
shifting lines like dirty yarn being rolled, that was surf that went
nowhere and not strong; and also a phosphorescence the bitter hue
of sodium, vapored and trapped inside lamps. Down: hundreds
of feet or miles or something else, Dee (knowing as all do who
approach the nightbeach) that it would change as she went.

"Well, this is me, then. I'm going," she said, and dropped her
furl-ash cigarette.

The path was a narrow winding of rocks and dirt crushed to
dust. She slid slipped and soon fell, thrashing through sourscent

thornprickle brush until she slammed against a rock that left her unbreath'd for a while and then she realized she wasn't breathing anyway. Mist rose from her muzzle but did not inandout just slid steadily free, collecting into a shape at first indefinable; only, she walked down and down and its form clarified and completed, and it was a Coyote like her, curled as though motherscruffed and hovering a few feet out from the cliff at eye-height.

Dee not a thinker thus not wondering what this shadow-Coyote meant, whether ghost ka lost soul child unborn or something unknown: "The fuck do you want?" Dee said though not wanting the answer, and it said nothing and turned and advanced ahead, soundless and then invisible and gone maybe so that she was relieved and worried both, though never otherwise the worrying sort.

Of a sudden, a great light started up on the cliff high behind Dee, a surprising blaze of a bonfire, set by her sisters she figured but arcbright as welding or lighthouses. Dee was not the only one with gifts and Being, and Tierce could use the sharp of talon and eye to set great fires. But Tierce would lose vision from this. Love costs for anyone, hawk woman god and all.

Twistingback Dee's long foot touched a rock and it cascading took its fellows lavanching along and Dee with it too. The path: a startlestart, and a slipstumble long middle, and then a dead end; just like life.

The nightbeach where Dee landed was of sand. It and foamstained water hissed together and whispered; Dee folded her ears back to block the sussury but it came through anyway, screeping in through the cracks of her. The wet cold air felt thin, though Dee stood at sea level for the lowest sea of all—if air there was; no telling without lungs' inandout. Her shadow was a severaled blurthing that did not have her shape, shivery by the light of Tierce's eyes and the demimoon in the semisky behind, halved now that it had risen to the dayworld's ceasing, and sloppy with dangling and glowing threads.

The sand around her was heaped everywhere with mounded massy dark shells, pyramiding into black piles as high as her waist, and over the sand- and waterwhisper the piles chirked when a crawling wave touched them. Dee stooping saw they looked just like dayworld shells, shaped like ears or trumpets or vulvas, but they had no light nor sheen to their curves and they felt colder than they ought. Dee pushed the shells aside with her feet as she walked, and they chunkled against one another.

A sudden falling crash off a short distance: a small blurshadow thing heaved upright and shook itself, and said with Wren's chirp, "The air stopped carrying me." She sounded indignant, betrayed by her natural element and peevish in any case because of Dee's as she saw it stupidity. But here she was: love costs a price, as she knew as well as Tierce (and you, O my darlings), and she was hoping this would not in this case be true but suspected that it would. "I was flying down and it just gave up."

"You weren't supposed to follow," Dee snapsaid. "This is mine to do. Not yours."

"Since when do you say what is what for me?" Wren hopped to Dee's side, and stopped being a blurred shadow and became herself, drab gray and brown but her eyes the bright precise points they always were.

"At least Chena's not coming down, is she?" Dee glanced up at the cliff, to the fire Tierce had set. Pushed by the wind, it gustled and vanished and rose again in sheets of flame the colors of brass, of gold bronze copper and blue sapphires.

Wren opened her beaking mouth and then shut it not saying anything.

Dee closed her eyes for a moment. "Fuck." Now that she looked, she could see the sturdy dark shape downscrabbling the cliff. Instead of picking out the safe path, Chena was running straight in a great tumbling of noise and rocks and torn bushes: which ended in Chena landing with a sound that might have been a yelp or might have been a laugh. She loped toward them, kicking shells aside with chirping skrankles of sound.

"That was fun." Chena smiling, her tongue lollhanging out. "I wouldn't want to go back up, though."

"You can't," angry Dee said. "And now we're *all* dead."

"Not *yet*," Chena said.

"Not ever it was supposed to be. Tell me Tierce isn't coming down."

"Nope," shakinghead Chena; as Wren "When did you become the grownup?" asked.

Dee thinking, *When I lost Jace* and it stabbed through her again like losing a leg, and every time waking jumping up maybe to run somewhere, and being reminded again when she fell: no leg. Jace, who had been laughing air in her lungs, longstorying talemaking lover of Dee; and all the sun there was, for her.

Chena shaking her head in any case: "Tierce keeps the fire for us. Have you found your Jace yet? I just see this"—pointing.

Dee looked down at the shells all everywhere, the cerith whelk natica coils of them. Some were smaller than her toenail, others broad as cradling hands might carry. She picked one up, phone-size and black and smoothly curved like a tulip, and held it to her ear. But nothing inside it, not even the sound of her own pounding blood echoing back, though maybe that was no surprise if her pulse was as gone as her breath.

Chena picked one up too, the size of clasped hands and scrolled tight as a flemished rope, and absenteyed held the tiny opening to her ear: listening to her own lack of pulse, Dee reckoned though maybe not, so intent was she; and then dropped it chirkling back. "These are the dead."

Dee's Coyote-self knowing, saying: "Yes," and seeing it was truth even as the word slid from her mouth.

Chena: "He's a shell. Still you want him?"

And Dee nodded.

Wren added, practical she: "Good thing it's forevernight, because it will take all night to find him, huh."

Uncertain they stood looking this and that way: shells everywhere and the ravel-lorn waves, and, beyond Tierce's light, all otherwise as dark as a cave. Wren speaking at last, quick-eyed as all birds: "There;" and they looked a way along the long beach, and there were rocks pinnacled even higher than the shells. "A tide pool."

"Is there tide here?" Chena asked knowing No. No moon, so no tide.

On the nightbeach, distance was mutable or even irrelevant. Still, crossing took time and they walked for a while and a second while and more whiles still, to the rocky place Wren saw, the pinnacled untided pool.

Waning light from Tierce's fire, as they shuffled through the shells of the chirpling, chattering dead, speaking perhaps to one another though not to Dee as she leaned low and listened; nor to Wren, tipping her head close to the largest she saw, a whelk the size of a sleeping hound, and hearing nothing, no thing at all—yet she would not step inside the shell's curling lip: no fool Wren. It was hard to see the pillaring rocks clearly, scarce lit to one side by the strange ocean's glow, and to the other by Tierce's fire and the half of the sky that still held stars: the dayworld's moon long gone by now.

Wren could not fly in the unair of the nightbeach, but she was smaller than the others and not so careful with stepping on the shells, and so Wren sandpipering down to the water: "No tide," she said. "The water just moves, doesn't go anywhere, is all."

Dee slower followed, for she kept picking up shells and listening for Jace, and Chena slowest of all though she listened only once: lifted a cowrie folded pretty as a cunt, to which she harked for a time and then shook her head and replaced it carefully, and thereafter would not step upon even the smallest but pushed them aside as she passed.

Wren walking: "This is all they do, the dead? Heap up like this?"

Dee thought of Jace alive runrunning along a suncrusted canyon, laughing and his black eyes agleam, and the bright taste of flesh and blood and the matings and the sleeping together coiled, and roiling about in a fight and the all all all of it. Hated being bored, Jace when he was alive.

Why was Jace so special, my dears, O my darlings? What man, what walker on legs and laugher at jokes, is worth all this? And Jace is not, of course, nor any man, all flesh and imperfect unminding; or rather say all men are, and all women. Dee loved Jace and the loving was enough, for Dee anyway.

And for the others? Chena longed for her own sweet Linnerl; that is her hiddenmost reason for being on the nightbeach that she would not share with Dee (but I share with you, O my dead darlings; a teller of stories knows all secrets). And Wren and her vast chattering family, aunts and sisters and brothers and bickering uncles back in the daylands; and also Tierce now forever behind them, squinting through wearying eyes into the skyless dark above the nightbeach, but thinking of her nestlings asleep—Is Jace worth such love? Or is Dee?

After all the whiles they walked, they came at last to the rocks.

Wren always with questions: "What exactly are we looking for? What shell-shape? What markings?"

"Fuck if I know," Dee said, tired for once and realizing suddenly that she was cold and getting colder. The breath not coming from her mouth (she noticing this again) scared her a little. "Just anything," and they split up a bit.

Hard walking, or scribscrabbling rather, among rocks raw as new lava, pockmarked Dee felt through her long fingers and toes, and the holes each filled with water. Stepped forward and sank to her knee. Bent-head she tasted and got salt, but sterile: no flesh-shred shit microlife broth. In a pool, she saw a small fringing glowness and touched it, and it snapped shut anemone-quick, only there was no life to it, she could tell from the touch, just cold light and this movement. *Jace*, she thought. What can he chase and what does he eat when a shell? And where in this ocean of shells?

A thing flashed by her face, and herself automatic in her hunting she caught it, felt muscle and quick coilings thrown over her hand (or paw), a sensation she knew well from the desert:

snakes but boneless this time and beaky, biting her palm without effect. She held the thing up and its wet surface gleamed under Tierce's soft fading flare of a flame.

It was an octopus, so small that its head fit her cupped hand but it writhing rippled down, hydrostat legs yearning toward the pool until she caught the small beak and pinched it in her fingers and then the creature stopped. "Where is he?" she asked and shook it. "Jace."

Tentacled her ankle now: another octopus roiling itself up her leg, and suckers this time like cold angry kisses, so she dropped the little one. Was a splash.

The new one was bigger, its head like her head and clearly too big for the pool. So many legs meant many things held, and it clutched her and also the rock, and also a whelk with an unfurling lip and a hole broken through. *What's inside?* Dee wondered, and then chilled as she thought it: Nothing. In the dayworld, living-sea cephalopods drilled through shells and sucked the insides to inside themselves: food, and nothing left over but a hollowedout hush.

So, here: there was death and that was nothing, a shell on a shore; but even that could be taken by these nightbeach monsters, and then there was nothinger nothing.

Raging Dee did not bite at wrapping legs; but she called out and in a flash, Chena with her, they tore at the suckered coils—without effect, until Wren.

One copper nail pounded poisons a tree is the story, and maybe as well a many-branched beast. There were no nails but Wren gave it a penny she had carried onto the beach for no reason except that she had it, and perhaps had heard tales. The octopus brought it with the tip of a tendrilling leg to its beak and then everything loosed and was lost beneath the pool's surface, the whelk and Dee freed.

She grabbed at the shell as it sank. As she listened this time, a sound, fluteshrilling whistling of the unbreathing breeze through the hole. Dead, and then deader than dead. But not Jace. She knew he was somewhere here still, lost and bored, and someday bored out unless she could find him.

"Let's not do that again," Chena said. Blood on her leg collecting where she had torn it on rock but not flowing, not here where the heart drove no pulse.

On a pumicey pillar beside, Wren: "We can't find him and then this. What now, Dee?"

"Fuck," said Dee. "We'll have to do a thing."

Suspicious Chena, closest sister to Dee and thus knowing the ways of Coyotes too well for her own comfort: "Do what? This is the nightbeach, the end of all evers."

"But beyond that?" and Dee pointed across the phorescing fluorescing sea.

Nodding, Chena: "One shore means another."

"But no boat to get there," Wren said. "And how will going there, if There is—how will this change things, Dee? Jace is dead."

"Is dead gone?" Dee. "I'll cross and find out if There is a place, and come back with an answer maybe."

"*Maybe* answer, or *maybe* back, or more likely neither." Wren, tart. "Shells are dead and then deader than dead, and no coming back. So. There's a nightbeach and maybe a beach nighter than night, and maybe no coming back from there, either—not even to here."

Chena sighing: "Wren, it's what Dees do that are Coyotes, is do. Foolish or not. Can *you* stop her?"

"I am not the thing that stops Dees. But no boat . . . ? *That* will," Wren said.

Dee said, "We will swim."

Chena: "The There there is, is maybe too far. We'll drown."

"Why would we drown?" Wren, askance. "We do not breathe here; why would unbreathing be a thing?"

"We will find out about drowning, I guess," said Dee.

But. Back on the cliff in the dayworld, and the sun rising at last though invisible from the nightbeach: fading, ember-eyed Tierce. She stood and looked down, and the light of her eyes still shone on cliff ocean and shells. And she saw the pinnacled rocks and the tentacled things; and dark Dee and bright Chena and the flicker of Wren. Read their lips from so highdistant a place; and knew they were gone, gone and lost; and blinked her charcoaling eyes.

The water was black, thick as oil, and viscid it slid up their legs as they walked into the untided surf. The dirty pale seafoam clung to their hands like the ropes of saliva from a sunburnt dog's mouth, and smelled not unlike. Wren fastidious turned her beak away, and then, "Oh!" said she, smallest: lost her footing and came resting upon the water's face, unbreaking the surface tension. Dee and Chena could not float, slipped beneath.

There were no shells under the water, but a steady long shelf of sand the color of a deer dead beside a road. Chena curled her lip in distaste. It was not dark beneath the water, no more than above. There being no moon nor stars nor glasscased hotflaming filament meant that no place was lighter than any other down here, but also no darker.

Wren was right that they did not drown. Still, there was no satisfaction in this; the water crawled everywhere thick and cold along all their inches as they shoveshouldered through it. For a time and before she went too deep, Chena could reach up and touch Wren's feet overhead; but Dee paid no mind, only pressed forward and on, the broken whelk in her hand.

For a while and then another while, Dee felt small coilings along the ocean's floor as she walked. She knew them for the tentacled things that killed the shells of the dead. One wrapped around her ankle, but she bent down and tore it free and that was the last of them.

A third while: eels with hands and no eyes.

There were other things, and clouded bittercold blood stained the sea. For a time.

* * *

I say to you, O my darlings, *for a time*, as though time was. The steps collected infinitely until the sea's floor shelved up again and *for a time* ended, and they came free of the sucking surface, and found Wren landed already and scraping her beak on the shore.

"That was exciting," Chena said when the cold salt sea had drained from her mouth. "I saw a thing like a ray, and a forest of black kelp, and a car that wept, and a shark. What did you see?" she asked Wren; but what Wren saw or had done as she stalked the surface between unsea and unsky, and what it was that she scraped so carefully from her beak, she said nothing about, then or ever.

Dee dropped the holed hollowedout whelk to the ground: looking-'round Dee. And this was the other shore. Sand. Behind them all the ocean, untiding water rocking but not crawling. Ahead ramping dunes of pale sanddrift, and past that tufty grass and harsh-husked hollow sedges, and a hissing that would have been wind if wind would have been. And beyond that rising, a plant-fringed ridge where notched dunes slanted into grass and unberried bushes. And after that the dun unsky only.

No life, of course. No footprints or pawprints or clawprints or shells, save the whelk.

They looked back (breathless no longer a surprise except remembering that it once had been different); and back past the slipping thick slippery ocean, the beach and the cliff, and nearly beyond sight was the ravelhalved world of the brightbreathing alive. But no fire nor Tierce: she had watched them walk deep and then deeper, and as they sank closed her scorched eyes: saltstung for a time. Then they opened again, and reduced but alive she turned and returned to the living, lightwinging her way to her children her nest her mate and the taste of mice bright on her tongue. Home. For a time. Her story ends here for you, unless someday as fringed murex or peaked conch she tells it herself.

I do not know what secrets the shells of the dead share among themselves. I listen and hear hissing; but it is enough.

"Well," said Wren when her beak was scrubbed clean. "Now we're here. Where *is* here?"

Chena loped up to the ridge and back down. "There's nothing. Beyond the ridge? More hills and grass is all, and maybe for all ways."

Dee kicked at the untoed untouched and rippleless sand. "No shells on this side. But no octopus either." Pausing she: "They would be safe here, all the shells."

Cunning Coyote-Dee, and clever sister Dog-Chena as well, and Wren Queen of the Birds sharp enough though attending only half what was said: always her eyes scanning the unsky. They thought it all through: the long sloping sandfloored ocean. But no waves to move shells, no tide to make waves, no moon to make tides.

"So we need a moon," said Chena. "A moon to bring the shells."

Headtipping Wren: "Let me see what I can do."

"This is mine to do," Dee said. "For Jace."

Practical Wren, and a little tired of Dee: "Can *you* fly?"

Dee, shaking head.

"Then it's not."

The rules for the unliving lands are not what you thought when you walked under sunlight, O my dears. There was no more thickness of air on this side of the ocean—and yet Wren up featherlight flew. The unsky was a flat textured hard curve like the inside of an eggshell, but fluttering Wren seeing a scuff in the surface no deeper than gravelscratched shoe leather, for long flitting whiles picked at the flaw. Flakes of unsky curled free and fell, and dissolved into brass-tasting mist on the upturned faces of Dee and Chena. The scuff became a dent, a pocket, a niche—and now Wren hoverclung to its lip as she worked—and at last made a Wren-sized hollow. She came down, and with her a drift of bitter drab skyscrape that made Chena cough. "There's that."

"But no moon," said Dee.

"No moon yet, no. Now's when you help. I need fur."

Chena: "For a moon?"

Wren: "Also twigs."

They looked: sedges ocean grass bushes sand slopes and unsky. "No trees means no twigs," Chena said.

"This is mine to do," said Dee. "Finally."

Dee biting bones free from her feet with her long bloodied teeth, slim fine phalanges for clever Wren's craft—for you forgot, O my darlings, that they are each woman god and creature folded together in skin and desire. But so they are: mysteries as great as yourselves and your once-stories. But Chena did not see that the metatarsals of Dee's feet grew back then or ever, however godlike she might be. Perhaps that is another way that the dunes beyond the ocean are different from the dayworld and its myths where Coyotes retrofit rekit and retool, bones and blood renewed on demand as the stories require.

Wren carried each skinnystick bone to the niche in the unsky, and she wove. It was not the tight tidy basket she would have entwined in the dayworld for her gawkish and featherless nestlings, but a shaggy ragged tangle: coyote bones and dog fur, and down plucked from her own breast, each feather shaft tipped in her unwelling blood.

And that nest was the moon of the dead: dun and unshining, the great gravitational well of untime and unspace.

Then a pause. And nothing.

Wren sighing. "Well, then, there is another thing, I guess:" and she laid an egg and another and a third: airfathered, Wrenwilled and windfilled.

And then nothing again.

They three watched, Wren high in her nest and her sisters on the sand: a whileslong time.

And a wave and another, then long rolling coils repeating along the sands, each stronger as the newbuilt moon learned its role. With tide comes time, and now static unnumbered whiles became waves and moments and *soons* and *thens*.

"Soon," said Wren.

And then.

Chena soft: "Listen."

The first small shells came in a foaming wavecurl that withdrew and left whisperlight augurs and ceriths and wentletraps trinkling together. They burrowed into the hissing wet sand, to leave only holes. And larger shells later, the great conchs, the syrinxes and the sheening nautili, and always the waves. Imagine it, O my darlings—or do not, but remember instead, if you can—your whispering shellselves pulled along the sandy floor, past the sights Chena saw, and the longtendrilled things that Dee fought, and all the wonders and terrors they did not meet. Perhaps you did not all make it, but many and many of you did, and found yourselves here, on the far beach.

And among the dragged massy shells at last, Chena heard the thing she was dreaming of: a whisper, a hush. A whelk washed to her feet, as long as her hand and smooth as an egg: rested and did not dig. She caught it up with a sob and pressed it against her ear and heard her name like a breath: *Chena.* Linnerl, her own dear Linnerl dead and lost and now found in a massy rose-colored limecalcium twist. Because Chenas love as deeply and foreverly as Dees do, only they talk less about it.

But no Jace. Not then, nor in the *then*s after, as each shell rolled up and found its own place on the shore, until holes spangled the sand and waterfilled reflected the secret-egged moon of Wren's making. And poor Dee running stumblefoot, bittenpaw clumsy, desperately across the tiny dim unmoons holing the dun sandy under-unsky. No Jace.

The shells rolling in but fewer now and all only newest-dead: each cockle ark augur and bittersweet clam fallen to the nightbeach in the last little whiles, but soon moved on in moonsummoned tiding through the oleic oilthick sea to this shore; and quick digging down into the sand and thus: safe.

But no Jace.

No Jace among all the shells: so, either holed out or holding out on the nightbeach. Or something else, that Dee could not guess, but you perhaps may.

Dee stumbled to a halt: "He's not here. He's not coming."

Chena's voice like a gentlesoft growl: "Those we love do not come when *we* will it, but when *they* do. Death does not change this."

"But I *loved* him."

Wren snorted. "As though that were enough."

Startlesharp face turned up to the moon: Dee, all id and hot eyes on herself, self-tricking trickster surprised by the truth—but despair does not sit long in Coyote/Dees. Lessons are learned, just not the right ones. A snapping nod: "I'll go back for him. We all will."

"Not I," rumbled Chena, cupping the cradled whorl of Linnerl; and eyes-rolling Wren: "Try, if you must."

Dee, a-limp to the shore where the tide swashed: stepped forward and pressed paw (that was hand) to the thick viscid ocean. She could not break the meniscus, nor skate Wren-light on its surface. Stepped forward and forward. And just nothing: Dee still where she stood, unadvanced. "We cannot go back?"

"No:" Wren and Chena together, and Wren: "That's what we *told* you."

And Dee, eyes turned for the first time to others, and knowing at last: "I've killed you."

Again, "No," Chena said. "We are here for you. But not just for you." And she smiled, the Linnerl-whelk in her hand-that-is-paw. "We had our own reasons, as well."

"What reasons? You never said anything," said Dee.

"When was there space?" Wren snapsaid. "Your needs always fill you. Where was there room for Chena to long for Linnerl—or for me to do what I did, and for why?"

Dee said, "What is your reason, then?"

"I was curious, that's all."

This was a lie. Wren's heart is her own, and her wishes too; Wren if she chooses may speak to you somewhile of her reasons for coming to this far beach, and for her in the sky that holds three unhatching eggs. Do not forget: Wren is god, bird, and woman. The power of Wrens is to speak and build nests. Wren invents as cleverly as any Coyote: builds homes of shreds, creates children of air and bone. But her secrets are not mine to share, my chirkling dears, any more than are yours.

* * *

Coyotes or rather Coyote must always be doing. Dee waited for
Jace, until she didn't: lightminded long longing but restless too,
too restless to linger long on the beach. For many whiles, she
paced the shore looking back nightbeachward (but beyond sight),
and then for more whiles she walked the long sandy hills. In the
end she peeked over the ridge's edge and saw beyond: more hills
more grass and farther than far a dark line along the horizon,
which might be trees or something else—different, anyway, than
sand and sedge. But Dee thought: trees, and if trees there might
be more trees, a beyond to the beyond, and even some something
past them: mountain or lake or a city or a staircase. They couldn't
go back, but maybe they could go forward, and maybe on the back
side of nothing was all.

She returned to where Chena sat with her own dear Linnerl
and her circle of curious chirkling shells, and Wren, so far above
in her nest but tipping one feathered pinhole ear to hear; and said
to them: "I can see a way out of this. I can get us home."

"This is home," Wren said chirping sharp: "See my nest? See
my eggs?"; but Dee unheeding as ever: "Think of it! Dayworld sun
and insects hazing the sky at dusk, the taste of sweet water. Home,
or at least an adventure."

Wren again: "*This* is home. It's not the home we had, but what
is?"

"And you?" Dee asking Chena, but Chena only held Linnerl
close, and looked down at you, dear ones, all her heeding shells,
and said at last: "I have work here, sister."

"Well fuck," said Dee; "so I'll do this alone." Dee silent a
moment, then: "I'm sorry." This was the first time she said that
word, to any. And perhaps only.

And she left. She has not returned, though Wren thinks she
cannot, but must always be on and on. Tricksters are not reliable to
love in any case, not even Dee. Or perhaps she was right: perhaps
there is a way back to the dayworld and around and through that

place, and thus back down to the nightbeach someday, and that she will in time return across or under the sandfloored sea. Or not.

And so you are here, O my darlings, and this is to the credit of Wren and of Chena and even Dee. Here you are dead on the beachgrassy shore beneath a nestmoon and birdstars, but at least you are not deader than dead. There is for you no way back to the dayworld lands or even the nightbeach. But there never was, and here are no beaked and tentacled things to unmake you.

There are always more of you, always new shells, massy and dark on the nightbeach, and some tidedrawn come sooner and some later: shells lingering on that nightbeach shore waiting for their own loves Dee-like or like Chena to come searching for them—only none do. No one makes the tumble to the beach of her own will. Or only a few.

Over us is Wren's tightwoven moon and her dark-winged fledglings, that have scattered like shadowstars across the dun sky; and who is the father of them I may guess. Do the dead overlap? I do not know: only that she is content enough, and as whiles have collected, so have the shells that were once her vast chattering family, aunts and sisters and brothers and bickering uncles, all come to her at last; and so she did not leave them forever, after all.

Jace remains lost but tides bring shells with each wave. Some scallop or slipper may contain him or may not. For Dee's sake I ask you each if you have seen him, but your chirtle and skankling speech is all for one another; to me you do not answer, though you listen I know. If he is found in the hard lacy curl of a murex, I will tell him that Dee has gone on. He may follow or not: he has other kin here, other loves. Love is no one-thing but many. We are never alone.

Or perhaps he is deader than dead. That is a way that things are, too.

Dee did what Coyotes do that are creator and creature: rush and long and drag a train of chaos behind them and then leave others behind to build what they will from whatever remains. But I that am Chena am dog, god, and girl, and what Chenas do is love and watch over—and here I am not alone, with sister Wren singing above, and the whorl of whelk-Linnerl in my hand to murmur in my ear. And you all, O my darlings, to tell this tale to—so perhaps you are not so dead after all. What is life but stories, and love?

This is the why of the Land of the Dead.

The Ghastly Spectre of Toad Hall

"Toad Hall has a ghost," said a voice.

The Toad, the Mole, the Water Rat, Beryl (the Mole's sister), and the Rabbit were all gathered in the stately Blue drawing room of Toad Hall. It was Christmas and the Toad had put together a party of great magnificence for his friends, sending for fancy holiday crackers from Town and ordering a succession of lavish meals from the Hall's temperamental master-chef, M. Grouffle. When the clock struck midnight on Christmas Eve the double doors into the Great Hall would part to reveal the TREE: candlelit and ringed with heaps of brightly wrapped packages peeping out like chicks from a hen's skirts. In the morning, those gifts would be opened and there would be yet more food. By midafternoon, the guests would return to their homes (only just across the river, after all), to sit beside their own comfortable hearths, digest, and open their Christmas mail.

The friends were currently suffering the slight longeur inevitable to the gap between dinner and the revelation of the Tree. The Toad was asleep on a velvet-covered divan with crocodiles' feet and, since no one was inclined to anything so athletic as moving furniture or rolling up carpets (for Musical Bumps), or even thinking of a word that begins with W, they had fallen instead into idle chat. They had exhausted their discussion of all the benefits attendant on a Christmas spent with friends, instead of (for instance) returning to one's childhood home to be judged by one set of relatives whilst sleeping on the narrow bunk beds from which another set had been ousted; then moved on to books (for several were great readers, and as a Novelist, Beryl of course had strong opinions, even about books she had not read); and then (inevitably, for it *was* Christmas) to ghosts, and that was when—

"Toad Hall has a ghost," said a voice.

It was the Toad, awake after all. The response was a clamor of questions and exclamations, but the Toad paid no heed, only heaved himself upright and looked around hopefully. The kindly Rabbit ran across to the tea table and poured out a cup, giving it to him. "Thank you, Rabbit!" he said gratefully, taking a sip. "O, *tea*," said he, as though he had expected something else. He put down the cup on a pie-crust table at his elbow before he raised a magisterial paw, quelling the havoc. "A ghost," he explained. "That haunts Toad Hall," he added, clarifying things.

"A ghost!" Still standing beside him, the Rabbit was clasping her paws in delight, for she was a great lover of ghost stories.

"R," said the Toad, with a small bow.

"You never said anything about ghosts before this!" said the Water Rat plaintively. "One right here on the River Bank, and you never bothered to tell us?"

"It never came up," said the Toad. "I was barely a tadpole, you know."

The Rabbit gasped. "You've *seen* it?"

"Certainly not," said the Toad with dignity. "I was a healthy lad and sleeping soundly, just as I ought. But! Two of the maids saw a ghostly Toad lady draped in tatters, wringing her paws and moaning." He demonstrated.

The Water Rat looked about, as though expecting a spectral form to pop through the wallpaper. "Where was she seen?"

"The first night, they said, she just floated around the Portrait Gallery and the halls."

The Mole asked, "She materialized more than once?" He had snabbled the paper crowns from everyone's holiday crackers and was wearing them all together, which gave rather a festive effect.

"*Two* nights," responded the Toad. "The very *next* night, two of the footmen were patrolling the house—to reassure the maids, you know—and *they* saw the ghost, too. They all followed it as it floated through the halls, until it floated through the wall into my father's room."

"And what did *he* see?" asked the Rabbit breathlessly.

"He never told us," the Toad said, heaving a sigh. "He died that very night."

They stared at him speechlessly and he continued. "A surfeit of eels, my mother always said. But the maids overreacted utterly, because there'd been some sort of nonsense about a ghost and my grandfather's death—and, come to think of it, my great-grandfather, as well."

Beryl leaned forward. "Let me be sure I have this correctly. The night before your father died, you had a ghostly visitation. And then, the next night, she returned and entered your father's bedroom. And he died that night?"

The Toad nodded.

Beryl continued. "The same night?"

The Toad nodded again.

"And she was there for the deaths of your grandfather and great-grandfather, as well?"

The Toad nodded a third time. "Though it's hard to imagine they *all* ate too many eels. I know that my grandfather died in November, and everyone knows you should not eat eels caught in November. Unless *that's* why he died? Or perhaps he ate pickled eels?"

"Toad, I know what she is!" said the Rabbit, her eyes very large indeed. "She is a FETCH."

The Toad shook his head. "The maids were very clear that it was a ghost."

"A fetch is a sort of ghost, Toad, dear," explained the Rabbit. "When she comes, she *fetches* someone into the afterlife, do you see? Though your ghost is *also* a death omen, for when she comes the first night, she is warning the master of the house of his imminent Doom!"

"Why warn him?" asked the practical Water Rat. "Wouldn't it be better to catch him unawares?"

The Rabbit replied, "Ghosts always have Reasons. Perhaps she is required to give the master of the house time to revise his will?"

The Toad frowned in concentration. "You're telling me that my father was killed by a ghost and *not* by too many eels?"

The Rabbit said, "Well, eels might have been part of it—I don't know how many he ate—but the ghost's Reason for being there was to usher him into Death!"

Beryl said suddenly, "Toad, your father's bedroom—that's the same room you sleep in, isn't it?"

"Of course," said the Toad, indignant. "It is where the master of Toad Hall always sleeps."

The Mole said, "But that's the very same room the fetch materialized in! Aren't you nervous?"

The Toad scoffed, "Why would I be? We Toads are very sound sleepers, and we had no eels at dinner. And anyway—"

But they were not to learn what the Toad would have said, for the clock began to chime midnight and the doors to the Great Hall swung open (assisted not by spectral forces but by two footmen) to reveal the TREE.

Later that night, Beryl awoke suddenly and groped for her little pocket watch, which she always kept beneath her pillow whenever she was away from home. It was 2:37, and what had awakened her, she knew, was a sound somewhere in the house.

"Beryl?" whispered the Rabbit from the other bed. "You're up? Did you hear it, too?"

"*Something* woke me," said Beryl cautiously.

"It was a moan!" said the Rabbit. "*oooOOOooo—*"

Beryl stopped her. "Shh! Someone is moving about downstairs!"

"You don't suppose—"

"It must be servants, needing to do something or other."

"But why would they moan?" asked the Rabbit, reasonably enough.

"Or burglars," said Beryl, grasping at straws.

"Or a *ghost*!" countered the Rabbit. "In any case, we must find out more, don't you agree?"

And of course Beryl did agree, so they wrapped themselves in their dressing gowns (a friendly scarlet for Beryl, periwinkle for the Rabbit) and left their room, where they met the Mole and the Water Rat just leaving *their* room on the same mission. The Mole was in a sensible but very attractive grey-plush dressing gown (an early gift from the Water Rat, as his old one was deemed too shabby for house parties), but the Water Rat wore a banyan of startling splendor, ornamented with peacocks on a gold-and-maroon ground, which had once belonged to his great-great-great-grand-uncle and was brought out only for special occasions.

"Did you hear it, too?" said the Mole and the Rabbit to one another, and the Water Rat and Beryl whispered, "Shhh!"

"*oooOOOooo . . . oooOOOooo . . .*"

The Water Rat swiveled his ears. "It's coming from downstairs."

"Servants," said Beryl again, a little desperately.

"But we're going to make sure," added the Rabbit.

"Too right we are!" said the Water Rat.

They crept down the stairs in single file, each with a paw outstretched so as not to stumble into any inconveniently placed suits of armor (as ought you, if ever you creep about someone else's house in the middle of the night): Beryl first (since, she reasoned, if you are going to be a fool you might as well do it properly), then the Rabbit and the Mole. The Water Rat, that sensible fellow, kept to the rear, just in case the moaning *was* bandits, after all, and any were inclined to sneak up behind them.

The sounds were clearer now, obviously coming from the Portrait Gallery, which opened out from the Great Hall. Hardly daring to breathe, they padded across the Hall, established themselves on either side of the archway, and peeked in.

Even by day, the Portrait Gallery was slightly spooky. The Toad's great-great grandfather had refurbished it, and the fashions of that time had demanded a dark, disturbingly foliate wallpaper that seemed to shift slightly whenever one took one's eye off it. To the left was a row of tall windows and to the right were scores and scores of portraits: paintings large and small on canvas and on ivory; oils, water-colours, and even marble busts—and every portrait a member of the Toad family, Toads in military uniforms and fancy-dress togas, frock-coats and robes *à la Polonaise*, Toads going back and back to the time of Queen Anne and even before.

At night, it was all so much worse. Heavy draperies heaved and shivered in the drafts that pushed past the windows they concealed. The wallpaper, illuminated by a single dim fairy-light at the gallery's far end, seethed ominously, the vines appearing to reach out from the walls as though seeking victims. And as for the portraits! To a Toad, they seemed to bow and sneer, and even to turn slightly so as to better eye askance the clustered River Bankers.

This is all very interesting to recount, but the perspicacious Reader will not have lost sight of the main concern: *What about that moaning?* And for all the room's unsettling nature, every eye was focused, not on the wallpaper, the portraits, or the shifting curtains, but upon—

—a spectral form! In fact, a GHOST: the pale, glowing figure of a Toad lady clad in the shreds of a pale gown of the Regency period (unless it was a nightgown, and then it might be any era) and wringing her paws, all exactly as described by the maids so many years ago. She was midway along the Portrait Gallery, and they could see right through her.

"*oooOOOooo,*" she moaned, but now they could discern words: "*ToooOOOooad! Alaaas, the HoooOOOuse of ToooOOOooad!*" Evidently the maids had not stuck around for the full experience.

Beryl had stepped forward into the room, the Rabbit beside her, and the Mole and the Water Rat as well.

"There *is* a ghost!" said Beryl just as the Rabbit said, "A fetch!"

Perhaps the ghost heard them, for she moaned again, "*Alaaas! ToooOOOooad!*" and dissipated like smoke.

"Toad!" exclaimed the Mole and the Water Rat, and they all turned and bolted up the stairs.

* * *

When the four friends burst through the door of the Toad's bedroom, they found no sign of him. His magnificent bed, its canopy held high by wingèd plaster Toadlets, was a rumpled sea of quilt and burgundy satin coverlet. It hardly seemed possible that he should not have responded as they shouted his name and rushed from bathroom to dressing room, turning every light switch (for Toad Hall had electricity).

"Where is he?" cried the Rabbit at last, and sat down with a plump on the side of the enormous bed.

"Argh," said the bed, and the quilt-sea heaved back like a receding wave to reveal the tousled Toad, in pyjamas of a virulent coquelicot. "Wha—what? My dear chaps, it's much too early for visits." He yawned hugely.

They tumbled over themselves to tell him of the ghost.

He yawned again. "The Toad Hall ghost? How nice for you to have seen her, since you all seemed so interested. Here, you say?"

"Well, downstairs in the Portrait Gallery," said the Rabbit. "But indeed, it was her! What will you do?"

He groped for his dressing gown and pulled it on (it was purple brocade, and almost as magnificent as the Water Rat's banyan). Looking more alert, he said, "What time is it? Not even three? I am always happy to see you, dear chaps—but *after* the servants are up, if you don't mind?"

The Rabbit cried, "Dear Toad, are you not afraid?"

"Afraid? *I?* Of what?"

"Of the ghost!" explained the Rabbit.

"Faugh!" said the Toad scornfully. "A Toad does not cower, a Toad does not cringe and tremble and recoil!"

There was a moment's silence as the friends recalled the many, many occasions when the Toad had in fact done all these things, in series and in parallel, until the Rabbit said, "But, Toad, she is a *fetch*, you know! She is here to take you to your Doom!"

Astonishingly, the Toad's response was a giggle. "He-he! I see! You woke me up because you were *worried*? For me?"

They nodded.

"But there's nothing to be afraid of, you know! I've thought it all out. Last night, as I was washing for bed, it suddenly came to me. Even if she is a—whatever you keep calling her . . ."

"A fetch," supplied the Rabbit.

The Toad waved a paw. "One of those—she can't touch me! I shall just stay away from eels—"

"It's not *about* eels specifically," Beryl said.

"The main thing is that I have found a Loophole!" said the Toad triumphantly. "Last night, I summoned Hampson—" (Hampson was the butler) "—because I thought he might know more. And he did: he said the same thing happened for my grandfather and great-grandfather as for my father—the Ghost floated around the house on Night One, and then on Night Two, she entered my room—only it was theirs back then—one at a time, I mean, not all at once, and— Anyway, she entered their bedroom—my bedroom, I mean—and they died that night."

The Rabbit shivered and reached for his paw, but he waved her away, starting to giggle again: "So, don't you see? HE-HE—All I have to do to be safe from her is NOT BE HERE!"

They gaped at him. "That seems rather a large Loophole!" said Beryl finally. "Do you mean that if you leave, you won't die?"

"He-he! Hampson told me. My great-*great* grandfather also saw her drifting through the halls that first night—but he left *immediately* on the Grand Tour that very night, and didn't return for more than a year, and by that time she had given up, I suppose. Anyway, it wasn't until years later that he died, of gout. It's all written in the records in the muniment room. That's where Hampson found it."

Beryl asked, "If that worked, why didn't your other predecessors—your father and grandfather and such—leave?"

"We Toads are not really readers," said the Toad. "Except my grandfather"—he laid a paw on his breast—"but he preferred the Classics, you know."

The Rabbit said decisively, "It's clear then. You must leave immediately!"

He waved a dismissive paw. "And ruin Christmas? Certainly not! There's plenty of time. We'll open our presents in the morning—well, in a few hours—and we will lunch, and then, *after* you all go home, there will still be *plenty* of time for me to catch a train to Town. Perhaps a little shopping, a jaunt to the Continent, then home when the coast is clear!"

"What if she tries when you get back?" the Water Rat asked.

The Toad chortled. "Then I'll just leave again. It's foolproof!"

Beryl shook her head. "If it's that easy, she doesn't seem very effective as a fetch, does she?"

"More of a semi-fetch," agreed the Rabbit.

At Toad Hall, it was the job of the juniormost maid to enter each bedroom at seven, deliver a tray, make up the fire, and open the draperies. This habit (humane for all but the juniormost maid), was intended to tease the sleeper into consciousness with the pleasant scents of coffee and croissants and the natural, gentle increase of morning's light. But that day, nothing worked as it ought. For one thing, it was Christmas morning and the servants had been up late the night before. For another, the maids had somehow learned about the ghostly visitation, and they refused to be alone, so that it took two maids to perform these simple tasks—plus a footman to escort them, holding a cudgel and looking about ferociously— and everything therefore went more slowly and was much noisier than usual. And for a third, there simply *was* no daylight, only a glooming gray that did not lighten with the advancing hours.

In fact, it was snowing, a blizzard so thick and fierce that it would have done justice to the works of Jack London. When Beryl and the Rabbit awakened at last, at the advanced hour of nine-fifteen, they noted the cheerless light and the snow and hurried downstairs in rather a thoughtful frame of mind.

Before they had retired for the second time, the friends had agreed that they should be ready to leave as soon as possible, so they came down to breakfast in their everyday clothes. The Toad seemed not to notice, but rushed over to each of them and clasped their paws, crying, "A Happy Christmas to you all! Breakfast, then PRESENTS."

Beryl and the Mole exchanged a glance, and the Mole said, "Toad, it's snowing."

The Toad danced a caper. "It is! Lashings of it! So, after presents, sledding—ice skates on the River—snowtoads! Snow forts! Snow—"

"Toad, no!" said the Rabbit. "You have to go to Town today, remember?"

"I do?" said the Toad, then: "Oh, I do. But . . . PRESENTS!"

Beryl said tactfully, "Toad, dear, it would be hard to feel festive when we are all so worried for you."

But grinning broadly, the Toad had waved for a footman. "Nothing to be worried about! Remember my Plan? If it makes you all feel better, the chauffeur can start readying the car right now to take me to the station. Plenty of time for breakfast, and we can open the presents in no time at all. And then perhaps there will be time for one little tiny snowtoad?"

"No snowtoad!" they all said. But in the end, Toad's *entire* plan had to be set aside (except for the breakfast), for the news came back quickly: the snow was too deep to drive in. In fact, the door to the garage could not even be forced open against the rising drifts.

"Nonsense!" said the Toad, and hopped from his seat. "Hampson!"

The butler materialized. "Sir?"

"Open the front door!" ordered the Toad.

"I very much fear—" said Hampson.

"The DOOR!" said the Toad imperiously.

The entire party trooped out into the entrance hall, along with such household staff as were in earshot. The butler shot the bolts and stepped back, and the largest of the footmen placed his hands on the latch and pushed.

The door wouldn't open.

"Try again," said the Toad.

Footmen leaned their shoulders against the door and heaved: at first just the largest, then the second-largest beside him, then as many as could get a shoulder against the carved walnut.

Nothing.

"Try again!" said the Toad, sounding strained. "Try the other doors. Try *all* the doors!"

The household staff (and the guests) ran about as though participating in a party game of some sort, rattling every door and peeping from every window—but to no avail. England, having decided on a Christmas blizzard, was doing the thing thoroughly. Since midnight, the snow had been falling as though dumped from baskets, and by now there were simply *feet* of it, which the rising wind was packing into drifts the size of cottages. The windows revealed nothing but an irregular pale-grey wall of blowing snow, except where an encroaching drift had begun to creep its stealthy way up the glass. At this point, the chauffeur returned to the Hall, soaked through and crusted over with ice, to announce that there was simply no way nohow that the car could get out of the garage, let alone start, let alone drive anywhere—and that even the horses, normally so useful around the grounds for mowing and such, could not get out of their stable.

Trapped? *Trapped*?" said the Toad.

Half an hour later, the friends were re-collected in the blue drawing room, with the Toad once again supine on the divan with crocodiles' feet. The Toad was famous for his fits, but this one had been more than ordinarily passionate; now he lay inert, damp from tears and weak from thrashing about, and the Rabbit knelt beside him, chafing his enervated paw between her own, with smelling salts on the floor beside her. Beryl, the Mole, and the Water Rat stood a little aside from this touching tableau, looking anxiously at the Toad. Hampson hovered in that peculiar semi-transparent way that is a trade secret of butlers.

"So what *can* we do?" said the Mole. "We can't drive him out by horse or in a motor-car. The train station in the Village is too long a walk for old Toad even in good weather—even if the trains were running in this weather."

"And even if *anyone* could get there," said the Water Rat. He loved wintry tramps, but *he* would not have gone out in this weather for any but the direst of reasons.

Beryl was thinking. "Do I have this correctly, Hampson? Toad has to not be *here*, in Toad Hall."

Hampson advanced, apparently without moving, and said, "Madam, Hall records imply Toad Hall *and its estate*."

"So we can't move him to the stables or anything?" said the Water Rat.

Hampson looked mournful. "No, sir. Nor to the gamekeeper's cottage nor the homes of any of the tenants."

"I have an idea," said the Mole diffidently. "What about *my* place? Would that work?" Mostly, the Mole shared the Water Rat's pleasant little waterfront residence just across the River, but he had a home of his own, a cozy hole quite close to Toad Hall but off the estate's grounds. He had loaned it for the winter to a cousin, an aspiring painter of landscapes, but young Stanley had returned to the Hills for the holiday, and the house was quite empty.

"Mole, what a clever idea!" said Beryl warmly.

"Are we sure the"—the Water Rat stopped himself and looked warily in the Toad's direction, then lowered his voice—"g, h, o, s, t—won't follow Toad to Mole's house?"

Hampson said, "I do not believe it can, sir. As far as I can ascertain from Hall records, it has never left the grounds."

"We have to chance it," said Beryl. "What choice do we have?"

And so it was decided. Assisted by the two largest gardeners, the Mole and the Water Rat would escort the Toad across the fields to the Mole's house. The gardeners would return to let everyone know they had gotten there safely, but the Mole and the Water Rat would remain with the Toad until the weather broke and he could be hustled off by train to Town. Beryl wanted to accompany them because she knew that everything seemed to go better when she was there, and the Rabbit wanted to accompany them because she loved adventures—but they were sensible animals and acknowledged that they were unnecessary to the expedition. They, therefore, would remain guests at Toad Hall until the roads were clear and they could return to their home, Sunflower Cottage.

As soon as the plan was revealed to him, the Toad leapt from the divan. "Yes. Why, yes! A spectacular escape! I see it now—I flee across the tundra into the teeth of the gale, where even a ghoul fears to follow! Wolves howling as they pursue us—the river ice cracking beneath our very paws! He-he! A Mole breaks through and sinks beneath the icy waves—"

"I say!" said the Mole and his sister indignantly, but the Toad only waved a dismissive paw.

"—only to be saved by the quick thinking of—THE TOAD! A Water Rat—"

"Toad!" interrupted the Water Rat. "We are *not* crossing the River. There *are* no wolves—"

"There might be wolves," said the Toad mulishly.

"No wolves," repeated the Water Rat. "And we are only going through the rose garden, then across the East Lawn, through a few hedgerows, and across a hayfield or two. No tundra at all! But it's not going to be pleasant, so let's get it over with before the snow gets even deeper."

It took quite an hour to get the Toad ready, and for M. Grouffle to throw together a basket of food to tide the evacuees over, since there was no telling what might be in the Mole's larder, given that it was being maintained by a struggling *plein air* artist. The Water Rat and the Mole had not brought their heaviest tweeds or woolly mufflers for what was supposed to be a three-day house visit; but Toad Hall had many attics, and it was the work of a moment to locate and bring down some trunks from Toad's grandfather's day. That gentletoad had been a great explorer, and here was everything needed to equip an expedition for the Polar wastes. It was only with effort that the friends dissuaded the Toad from bringing a rifle for polar bears, a six-person tent with a patented entrance flap, and a portable stove guaranteed to light in any weather. As the Water Rat and the Mole outfitted themselves, Beryl and the Rabbit sheathed the Toad in layers of coats, scarves, woollen trousers, and mittens, the whole surmounted by a sealskin parka that left him looking a bit like a novelty pen-wiper. At last the expedition set off, stepping out through a window in the blue drawing room, for Toad Hall's doors were all drifted shut. A footman pushed the window closed and effaced himself, leaving Beryl and the Rabbit alone at last.

"He's off!" said the Rabbit with a sigh of relief. She flopped down on the divan with crocodiles' feet.

Beryl went to look out the window, but already the snow concealed any sign of the party. "I hope they will be safe! I wish I had gone with them."

The Rabbit nodded. "And I! I am sure I could have been most useful in dissuading wolves and polar bears!"

Beryl pulled closed the draperies and turned away from the window. "Lottie, dear, the Toad was wrong. There are no polar bears in England! Or wolves."

"Well then, I am sure they will be fine. I wonder when the gardeners will return to tell us how it went?"

"I suppose a few hours, anyway. I admit I'll feel much better when I know that Toad is safely—"

There was a knock on the window.

The expedition had ended poorly.

Wading through the drifts with the intrepidity of voyageurs discovering yet another muskeg, the party had crossed the veranda and descended a flight of stairs into the rose garden. As they left the shelter of the house, the wind grew stronger still, and they pushed through hissing, howling snow so thick they could only see a few feet in any direction. The head gardener had wrapped his beloved rose bushes with padded burlap against the cold, and now, thickly caked with snow, they loomed rather. The Toad, seeing a misshapen white form suddenly materialize mere feet away, gave a scream worthy of Drury Lane and leapt to one side. He landed in the snow-filled basin of one of the garden's fountains, where he found himself surrounded by *other* grotesque forms, all reaching out with hideous paws: in fact, snow-caked marble Toadlets proferring shells from which, in the more clement months, water would pour. During the subsequent thrashing, he fell and knocked his head against a Toadlet. The evacuation party had carried the unconscious Toad back to the house, removed his winter garb, and arranged him on the divan with crocodiles' feet, with a thick bandage around his head and one thicker still around his paw. His ankle was swelling ominously. There was no way to summon the doctor, as the telephone wires had fallen, but it stood to reason that if no one could get out, a doctor couldn't get in, either.

"So now what?" said the Water Rat. He had shucked off his outer raiment, but he was still wet through, and steamed gently as he stood with his back to the fire. "He can't walk, that's certain."

Beryl asked, "You don't think he is, ah, dramatizing his state?"

"Faking it, you mean?" said the Water Rat, who called things as he saw them. "Not this time. That ankle looks pretty bad."

"Could he be carried?" asked Beryl, tapping a paw on her chin, as she often did when thinking. "A litter perhaps . . ."

"No," sobbed the Toad, recovered from his latest swoon and listening in from the divan. "No, dear friends, there's no use! I am doomed—DOOMED!"

The friends exchanged a glance as if to say, "Whose turn is it *this* time?" and the Mole went to sit beside him, speaking in a soothing tone that seemed to do nothing, for the Toad's voice grew ever louder and higher, like a whistling teakettle settling in for a good boil. The other three stepped farther away and lowered their voices.

"We have to do *something* to save him!" said the Rabbit.

"We will," said Beryl with decision. "We just have to think it through."

And so they thought throughout the day, coming together from time to time in low-voiced clumps to exchange their ideas.

Could they fight the ghost? But of course mere physical violence would have no effect on a spectre.

What about disguising the Toad? "—As an aged nurse, or a sweeny or something," the Water Rat said; "We could put him by the kitchen fire with his face wrapped as though he has the toothache, and call him—oh, Sadie or Sally."

"Would a ghost be tricked by that?" asked the Mole. "He doesn't look much like a Sadie or Sally, you know."

They thought.

The Rabbit said, "One of *us* could disguise ourselves as the Toad!"

The Mole objected, "But then the ghost might kill *you*, you know."

"No," explained the Rabbit, "because when she comes close, we would reveal the trick, sending her off covered in shame and ignominy—or we might even Pounce at her and drive her away forever!"

"Or she might kill all of us," said the Water Rat in his plain way.

The Rabbit looked disappointed but brightened immediately. "What if one of us disguises herself as *another* ghost? And explains that the *old* ghost's services are no longer required and I, the new ghost I mean, is assigned to take her place?"

But somehow this also did not receive the positive response that the Rabbit had expected.

At luncheon (which they had *al fresco* in the blue drawing room to keep the Toad company, for he flatly refused to be taken to his bedroom), they were still thinking.

Could they lay the ghost? Only, none of them were religious, and Toad Hall's library seemed quite devoid of books offering schemes for dealing with the undead. Even Beryl had no useful information. "But there may be something useful in the muniment room, you know," said she; "Hampson says there are all sorts of records stored there, going back centuries, so perhaps I'll find something."

The Water Rat said with approval, "That's clever, Beryl! If you can find out *who* she was, then we'll know *why* she is doing this.

What is her *motive* in haunting Toad Hall?" (The Rat was partial to crime novels.)

"I imagine it's because she's a ghost," said the Mole.

After lunch, the despondent Toad agreed at last to be taken upstairs and put to bed. He was having a wretched time of it. Ordinarily a situation like this—injured, trapped, in pain, and doomed—would have brought out all sorts of histrionics, but the pain in his ankle and head left him genuinely miserable, which made weeping and thrashing most unpleasant. The housekeeper gave him two aspirins, and the friends took it in turns to sit with the Toad.

Tea was served early, while the Rabbit was upstairs.

"I've been thinking," said the Water Rat. "We'll just have to try and reason with the ghost."

The Mole said, "Only you can't reason with ghosts, not that I've ever heard. Beryl, have you found anything useful in the muniments room?"

Beryl shook her head. "Nothing useful, I am afraid, though there's so much it's hard to say. Rent rolls, game records, crop rotation schedules, diaries . . . I did find an excellent recipe for a syrup of hyssop—against coughs, you know."

"Only, the ghost doesn't have a cough," pointed out the Mole.

"And this, of all things!" She pulled a slim green volume from a pocket and showed it to Rat and the Mole. "It's entirely filled with verse, written by some past Toad or other."

"How's the poetry?" the Water Rat asked curiously, for he was a poet himself.

"See for yourself!" Beryl passed it across.

The Water Rat flipped through the little volume, pausing in places.

> *O! Mighty elm! O! Stocky oak!*
> *How green thy boughs; how brown thy bark!*
> *How like dear Father—save that he,*
> *Sleeps in the Hall and you, the park.*

"Is it all like this?"

"Some of it is worse," said Beryl. "Still, for a Toad to write even bad poetry is a wonder, I should think."

The Water Rat passed it back to her. "Though I don't see that this helps, unless maybe the ghost likes being read to?"

She stuffed the volume back into her pocket, but it was a little too large and peeped out in the most rakish way. "Well, join me in the muniments room, and we'll see if we can find anything of more immediate application."

Night fell all too soon for the desperate River Bankers. All that thinking, all that fretting and *what-if-we*-ing—for naught! The Toad was doomed.

Still, they agreed that they must try, and since nothing seemed more likely to work than anything else, they decided they might as well try it all. Thus it was that, by the earliest time a ghost might reasonably be expected (certainly not before ten-thirty, they agreed), the friends were waiting in the Portrait Gallery: the Mole and the Water Rat, heavily armed, crouching behind a statue of that famous Enlightenment beauty, Lady Georgianna de Toad (as Artemis); the Rabbit, draped in a sheet with eye-holes cut out with her embroidery scissors, rehearsing ghostly moans in an undertone; and Beryl, who carried a copy of the *Book of Common Prayer*, in case it might turn out to be useful somehow. The Toad remained upstairs with his foot elevated on a pillow, under the watchful eyes of the housekeeper and his burliest footmen.

The ghost was no early riser. Eleven came and went, and eleven-thirty. "Midnight, then," said Beryl with a certain satisfaction: that is what she would have done if she had written this story.

At 11:46 by Beryl's little watch, there was a sudden flurry of noise—but it was out in the Great Hall, the opposite direction from which they were expecting the spectre to arrive. It was the Toad.

Alone in his bedroom (for one could not count the housekeeper, the footmen, and the continual visits of his friends), he had thought his hardest, as well; but the only solution that had occurred to him was to burn down Toad Hall. Surely, if there were no Toad Hall, there would be nothing for her to haunt! Genius! But if he did? Then there would be no Hall for the distraught world to convert into a shrine after his untimely, his tragic death. There would be no cenotaph, no charabanc-tours from Town for his grieving fans, no annual visit by a minor Royal to lay a wreath upon his tomb. And when he mentioned this option (it had been Beryl sitting with him just then), she had squelched it with vigor: it was Toad Hall *and its estates*, and the ground wasn't flammable, particularly in a snowstorm. "And if burning down Toad Hall *did* work," added Beryl, "there would be no cenotaph or tours, because you wouldn't be dead, you know."

True, all true. But it bothered the Toad to know his friends were trying so very hard, and all for him. He was often a silly Toad and even a cowardly Toad, but he loved his friends, and he simply couldn't let them risk their lives for him. And so at 11:46, he limped downstairs, footmen supporting him on either side, trailed by the housekeeper carrying a cushion for his foot and such members of the staff as were not otherwise occupied in hiding beneath their beds with wax in their ears. "I am Here," he said with dignity, as he entered the archway.

They all exclaimed, and the Rabbit and the Mole, in the most gratifying way, rushed to his side, urging him to return to his bedroom, but—

"A Toad . . . will not shirk," said he, presenting his profile in rather a noble way. "If it is my fate to"—he choked—"die tonight, I will not cower in my bed! I will confront my Fate here, with my friends. I will not let you risk yourselves for . . . Me!"

Beryl said, "But *we're* not at risk, you know. She wants *you*, not us."

"And we *have* to try, you know," said the Rabbit, squeezing his paw.

"I suppose," said the Toad, a bit less nobly. "But! If it comes, I hope I shall know how to face my Destiny!"

And so it was that the divan with crocodiles' feet was brought in from the blue drawing room and placed by the archway that led to the Great Hall, and the Toad settled there. The household staff retreated to what was generally agreed was a safe distance, and the River Bankers returned to their posts.

The Great Hall's clock chimed midnight, and a sudden cold wind rushed along the Gallery, causing the draperies to heave as though possessed and blowing out all the candles (for the electricity had been out since midday). In the sudden gloom, they saw a ethereal shape drift toward them, the same spectral Toad lady of the night before. Its thin voice wafted along the Gallery as it approached. *"ToooOOOooad . . . Alaaas the Hoouse of ToooOOOooad! DooOOOooomed!"*

As the ghost passed Lady Frances as Artemis, the Water Rat and the Mole leapt forth to bar the way, cutlasses and pistols in paw. "Stop!" cried the Mole but she continued to drift forward until she gave them no choice save to leap aside or attack. The Water Rat slashed boldly but his cutlass had no effect upon her diaphanous form. The Mole, emptying his pistol, achieved nothing but to drill several holes in a minor Van der Hooch immediately behind her, and to blow the nose off a marble bust. She slipped past them with no more than a reproachful look, still groaning, *"ToooOOOooaad . . ."*

The Rabbit fared no better, though she tiptoed forward in her best imitation of the spectre's steady glide, fluttering the hem of her sheet and intoning the groans she had been practicing. The spectre did not slow, only gave a sidelong glance that might have been disapproval. *"ToooOOOooad . . . thy doooOOOooom is niiigh. . . ."*

The spectre was nearly to the archway where the Toad was seated. Only Beryl still stood in its way. *"DoooOOOooo—My boook!"*

"Excuse me?" said Beryl.

"My boook! Where did yooou find it?"

It took Beryl a moment to understand. The ghost was pointing with one eerie paw at the slim green volume peeking out from her pocket. She pulled it free and raised it. "This? I found it in the muniments room."

"*I thooought it was looost!*"

"It's *yours?*" said Beryl.

The ghost blushed. "*A few thoooughts, scribbled dooown to fill my idle hooours. Did yooou . . . reeead it?*"

"I didn't like to, but you were threatening my friend, you know. I must say, you're very good," said Beryl.

The ghost said anxiously. "*Yooou think sooo?*"

"Admirable," averred Beryl, carefully not meeting the Water Rat's eye. "Really, these should be published."

"*ReeEEEeeally?*"

"O yes," said Beryl, perjuring herself without hesitation.

"*But—hooow . . .*" She trailed off, wringing her spectral paws.

Beryl had been thinking quickly. "It happens that my publisher might be interested, but—"

"*Yooou are an auuuthor?*" the spectre gasped.

Beryl nodded.

"*But . . . my duuuties,*" moaned the ghost with a sudden return to form. "*ToooOOOOooad, alaaas TooOOOooad—*"

"You *could* fetch Toad—" said Beryl ("I say!" said the Toad indignantly); "—but publishing is very expensive these days, and he is the only person I know who could afford to see your book into press. *If* he's alive."

The ghost looked hopefully at the Toad.

"Of course!" said the Toad, picking up his cue. "A Poetess in the Toad family? I would be delighted to do whatever I can to support your booook—I mean, book."

Later, the members of the house party agreed that this was the third or possibly fourth strangest Christmas they ever had.

They opened their gifts at last on the morning of the twenty-sixth: Beryl got a fountain pen and a glass bottle of purple ink, a lilac-coloured parasol, and a very pretty shawl knit in secret by the

Rabbit. The Rabbit received a perch, bird seed, and accoutrements for the lovebirds she had wanted since forever and was to pick out for herself in Town when she and Beryl next went. The Water Rat got embroidered slippers, a stack of crime novels (selected by the Mole), and a cunning implement that peeled and cored apples with the twist of a crank. The Mole was thrilled with his gifts, red mittens and a box of tulip bulbs guaranteed to be from Holland.

The Toad? It was always difficult to think of anything for the Toad, for if he wanted a thing, he purchased it immediately in quantity and at immense expense. And they had to be careful about bringing new things to his attention, for one never knew what might set him off on another of his mad capers. In the end, the friends had pooled their resources and settled on the collected works of Sir Walter Scott, for it was agreed that nothing could be less dangerous and more improving than reading.

And as for the ghost: *Pensées,* available for 2/6 at booksellers or by application directly to The Dustcough Press, has been a runaway success. Miss Anthea V. Toad (decd.) has found herself on a whirlwind tour of the major cities of England and America, where she is a passionate advocate for the rights of women, also ghosts.

The Apartment Dweller's Bestiary

The Aincolo

You're showing your boyfriend what to put in a smoothie and you open a cupboard because he told you he had toasted coconut somewhere and you figure sure, coconut, why not; and that's where his aincolo is, squatting in the yellow serving bowl his mom gave him last year for Christmas. That's cool. You have lots of friends with aincolos. They get in everywhere. But he was so weird about it, picked up the bowl with the aincolo hunched down now, nothing visible but two eyes in a cloud of cream-colored fur, and took it out to the living room and hid it somewhere. Why? Why.

But this got you wondering what else there was: what numbers in his Contacts lists, what porn on his hard drive, what texts, what friends, what memories; and you realized you really don't know anything about him—and, more, that you don't really want to. You have your own secrets, one of them that you aren't over your last boyfriend yet, and that his is still the only name in your Favorites list.

The Alafossi

The bathroom in your new apartment is problematic. Right after you moved, you noticed the fan made weird noises after you turned the shower off—rustling and little rippling squeaks, almost as though there were a bird up there. After a few days, you realized there really *was* a bird up there, or maybe a couple. And after a couple of weeks spent contemplating the matter while hot water poured on your head during your hangover showers, you decided that they were probably alafossi. You've seen them in the neighborhood, pulling at bits of trash they find or just hanging out in the trees in front of your place.

You thought about telling your landlord, not caring except you thought one might fall into the bathroom fan, and then you realized there's a screen up there to prevent exactly this sort of thing, so you just dropped it. Anyway, it was winter and you were worried they might not find another place, and the noises were nice, like having a pretty upstairs neighbor and you pretending that she's maybe putting on her makeup at the exact time you're shaving, or maybe even sharing your bathroom and leaning in to your mirror with that look they get when they're doing their eyes.

So everyone's getting along fine and now it's spring, and all of a sudden there are new noises, and you're like: babies. And it kind of pisses you off, because there's a thing you can't ever tell your friends because they would give you endless shit: you want all that. You're kind of tired of drinking at the Harbor on weeknights. You want a girlfriend who turns into a wife, and then babies and even the hard job and the rest of it. You've only told one person, your dad, and he said, Don't rush it; but you're ready, you are fucking *ready*.

Anyway, in the meantime, you stop smoking in the bathroom, because it's bad for human babies so probably alafossi babies, too.

The Begitte

Your grandmother told you, "It's good luck to have a begitte in the house," and they *are* generally pretty great to have. It's written into your lease, like renter's insurance and no waterbeds, that a begitte is okay. Your begitte, which you got from a buddy when he moved in with his girlfriend, is a spotted one with crazy long white whiskers. It sleeps on the couch most of the time, looking like a novelty throw pillow. It grooms itself and it does not shed.

Your begitte eats the things that you do not want: dead pens, wire hangers, empty Kleenex boxes, old running shoes, crumpled Coke cans, toothpaste tubes, the dead double-A batteries at the back of the junk drawer, the needle you lost in the carpet, your neckties from when you had the shitty job at Clement & Neleman, the jpegs from other peoples' weddings, the breakup playlists an ex-girlfriend sent you, some porn that got downloaded back in December.

It also ate that one picture of your old girlfriend from, what is it, ten years ago now? The one at the beach where it was pouring rain and she was freezing her ass off but then she got hit by that huge wave and even though she was soaked to the skin she started laughing and couldn't stop, and that was pretty much the moment you fell in love with her.

The begitte was right about that one, too.

The Bergdis

There's a black-and-white picture of your mom with a bergdis, back when she was a librarian in St. Paul, before she met your dad and they moved to Iowa. It's hard to tell what color it is, but you can tell from the photo that it's a beautiful one, its long tail wrapped down her arm and around her wrist for balance, and its diamond-shaped face half-buried in her dark hair. She's looking at whoever is taking the picture and laughing so hard.

Bergdises live anything from thirty to fifty years, but you don't remember seeing it, or her ever talking about it. You don't know who is taking the picture. You don't remember seeing your mom laughing like that, ever. There's actually a lot you don't know about the sorts of people that own bergdises, like her.

* * *

The Crestone

One of your friends got a crestone a few months back. It's cute, a small reddish male with a black tail that she braids with a little yellow ribbon securing the end. It licks crumbs off the kitchen floor. It kills spiders. It helps with zippers up the backs of dresses. If she is hanging a picture, it stands on the couch and lets her know how to straighten it by tipping its head one way or the other. When she choked on a piece of takeout chicken tikka masala last week, it dialed 911, though she managed to clear her throat before the EMT people showed up.

"You could call *me*," you say. "For stuff like that. You didn't need to get a crestone."

"Not the nine-one-one call," she says. "And I can't keep getting you to come over and kill spiders. Look, it's always there when I get home. What's wrong with wanting that?"

You understand, and you're tempted. A crestone would have your back, too. But maybe you would get a terrible crestone. Maybe it wouldn't tell you when your hem was down or remember your birthday. Plus, your boyfriend left; why wouldn't your crestone?

The Deliper

You still remember that last night. You were both crying, so why was this even happening? If neither of you wanted it, then why could neither of you seem to stop it? And if one of you did, then why wasn't it already over? And then it was, and you drove to your friend Korbin's house to stay, and that was that. But you hated it, even after you got this apartment, even after you got the new furniture, the unsprung mattress, the silverware with the fake patina. You smacked the console table against the wall a little, just so that it had some dents. You hung some family pictures.

Getting the deliper was supposed to help, but it hasn't worked that way. Now there are two of you alone together, and the deliper hates this life just as much as you do.

The Hapsod

You find the hapsod behind the bed when you move it to vacuum,
a task you generally avoid; only, last night your girlfriend brought a
little jar of powdered honey over, promising to brush it all over you
with a feathery cat toy shaped like a bird (which she also brought)
and then to lick it off: something she had found online, or maybe
one of her friends had. You have to admit that it felt pretty good
until she inhaled some, went off in a coughing fit, and dropped the
jar. The powder went everywhere. And so, not generally the sort
of person who vacuums but aware of the possibility of ants, you
get out the hoover, pull the bed away from the wall, and find the
hapsod.

It is quite small for a hapsod—which you have seen in
an occasional YouTube video, plus some of your friends have
admitted to encountering one: clearly an adolescent, crouched
over the pale scattering of powder on the carpet, next to a golf ball
that has rolled under the bed even though you don't play golf and
don't know anyone who does.

You are pretty sure your girlfriend would swoon over the blunt
little antlers, the rabbit-soft gray fur, the immense eyes. Your phone
is in your pocket. You could call her. She would be here in no time.
She would rush in and coo over your hapsod. She would puzzle
over what to feed it, and the words *we* and *us* would turn up a lot
in that conversation. She might stay for the night; but really, who
needs that? You and your hapsod are fine together. It's probably
easier just to break up now and get it over with.

The Hericy

You pretty much stopped using your kitchen once you started
that huge project at work, but now you're going to a dinner party
hosted by your ex-boyfriend and his new girlfriend, mostly
because you don't want to look like you're not over him. You

figure that hand-baked cheese crackers should fulfill your host-gift responsibilities nicely.

The oven is set to Warm, though you're pretty sure the last time you used it was the last time you made cheese crackers for a dinner party. You pull open the door and peer in. Six sets of shiny black eyes peer out. It's your hericy, which vanished three months ago and you never could find, and you must have cried for weeks about it—only now there's another hericy too, a largeish good-looking striped brown one, also some babies rolling around in a pile of shredded parchment paper on one of the racks. They've got a crumpled aluminum-foil dish full of dried apricots and a small cast-iron skillet you're pretty sure is not yours, filled with water. Really, you had no idea hericies were so resourceful.

You pick one of the cuter ones and tuck it into the red Chinese take out box you were going to use for the crackers. You know what's going to happen now. The new girfriend is going to squeal and cuddle it, and hold it up to your ex-boyfriend for him to cuddle it, too. The ex-boyfriend is going to look a little nervous, as though the hericy-bearing ex-girlfriend might make a scene. You know this because this is *exactly* how you ended up with *your* hericy.

Still, a hericy is pretty cool, so when he dumps her, too, at least she'll have that.

The Kein

You are not always sure, and neither, it seems, is your kein. More than once, your kein has scuttered across the living room to squat in the entry, staring back at you with what might be defiance shining in its small, pale eyes. You walked to your front door and you opened it, night air coming in and light pouring out. Your kein glared up at you, a stocky little thing, twin tails tucked close. "Well, go on," you said and waggled the door a bit. "If you want to be somewhere else. Feel free." But it did not go, which makes it different than your last boyfriend.

You're glad it didn't. It doesn't mind that you sleep in your dirty socks or play *Age of Heroes* 'til three every night. It keeps your secrets. A cat might fill the same space, but the kein's already here, so you make the best of it.

The Lopi

When you move into the apartment on Vermont Street, the lopi are already there, two or three of them fluttering in the corners of each room, just where the walls and ceilings meet. What exactly do they look like? Like bats, like insects, like tiny silent birds the color of smoke? They never seem to rest. And what do they eat? Do they chew on your soap, lick the residue from the bottles in the bathroom? Or late at night, when you are trying but unable to sleep, do they swoop down to eat whatever has fallen into the aluminum liners under the stove's burners? Wikipedia is of limited assistance here.

Before you moved in, your landlord promised to replace the old windows and repaint the dirty walls, and also to take care of the lopi problem. The windows are done, the walls now a tasteful eggshell color, but the lopi remain, and really, it's not worth calling the landlord about them. They're not that bad. They replace the pictures you don't hang. The whirring of their wings is a white noise that conceals the silence.

And there are nights when you are alone in the full-size bed in the single bedroom in the new apartment, everything so much smaller than your old life, and just as you fall asleep, you feel their feet on your face, delicate as antennae or memories.

The Louet

No one wants a louet, and yet, here you are with one. It has no great love of incense. It eats cantaloupe and corn germ, which it painstakingly chews from the kernels with its tiny scooplike teeth. It likes being read to, especially Henry James's lesser works. It frowns intelligently at certain places in his travel writing, but you are pretty sure it is faking it; your own appreciation of Henry James is shaky; how can something the size of a kitten be more esthetically enlightened than you?

And yet, it is the louet that suggested you not get the retro haircut; the louet that suggested you stay away from Cheever's later work; the louet that argued against hot pants and the crazy guy from the gym. The louet is always right, and you are always wrong, and it is the despair of the louet that you never seem to figure this out until it's too late.

The Mume

On the other hand, the great thing about your mume is how it never makes you feel bad about *anything*. It loves the food you eat, the movies you watch, the clothes you wear. Feathers eternally ruffled in excitement, it sits on your shoulder when you play computer games. It never gets bored. It never has needs. You're never wrong. You get the feeling that if the mume could speak, everything would end with an exclamation point. How many things in life make you feel as though you just won a trophy for general awesomeness?

It also doesn't care in the least that you were kind of an asshole to your last boyfriend. He didn't care at first either, but by the end he would call you on your shit, which you didn't want to hear, which is maybe the reason why he is gone and you have a mume instead.

The Orco

Most nights, you fall asleep while reading, and your book and your glasses end up in bed beside you, along with your phone (just in case), and your orco. You were always someone who liked to sleep touching, so sometimes in the night you reach across and feel the wand of an earpiece, the book's hard spine, the ruffle of the orco's hair, its breath on your hand. As long as you don't wake up entirely, it's like all the pieces of someone.

The Phildar

You have this mutual friend who tells you about seeing your ex and her new partner at what used to be *your* donut place, and that's the day you run out to the Humane Society to look for a phildar. Phildars are high-maintenance: they need a special diet and lots of attention. They cannot be trained to use a litterbox or to walk on a lead. They need their claws trimmed regularly or they'll scratch you. Still, they're beautiful and you've always wanted one, and there one is, in a small pen in the room with the parakeets and the rats and the little corn snake. You pick it up in the palm of your hand, and feel its tiny, scaly weight, observe its swiveling amber eyes. Is it judging you?

It's not like you have any excuse to feel she abandoned you without reason. It's not like *you* weren't the problem: the one who was never quite ready to shelve your books together, the one who never quite wanted her to meet your family, the one who could never quite say I love you. You always wondered why she put up with it, and yet there she was. Until she wasn't.

You've been brooding about this and realized that the irrevocable, unspeakable truth that had flavored everything was that you withheld all these things because you didn't actually respect her that much. Or, at all. But then, why were you with her? Maybe *she* wasn't the one you despised.

Anyway, she never liked phildars. Getting this one will probably keep you from asking the next question.

* * *

The Hooded Quilliot

You bring your new hooded quilliot home in a cardboard carrier and let it out in the living room. At first you see only the top of its head and then its eyes glaring up, and then the quilliot leaps out of the carrier and onto your coffee table.

Your hooded quilliot has lived better places than this, with nicer people who made more money and they all adored, *adored* it. It had its own room. It ate oysters flown in from the coast. A professional groomer came every two weeks to trim its nails. *This*—the cute teak coffee table you got for fifteen bucks at an *amazing* garage sale last year, and the rest of it, too: your friends bringing homemade salsa and crab dip for card parties that last 'til four, and the shoes piled by the back door because everyone here goes barefoot—*this* is not what your quilliot is used to and, to be frank, it is all very, very disappointing.

But then, *you're* not the one who was in a little steel cage back at the shelter, with a yellow sheet of paper clipped to the bars that said Abandoned.

The Ravock

There's all sorts of information about it online, post-mortem predation. First they eat your lips, your ears. The tip of your nose. Your eyelids. The flare of your nostrils. Fingertips. All the places a girlfriend would kiss you first.

Their weak paws and small teeth cannot make a way into your body until you are already dissolving. When is that, like a week after death? Would someone find you before then, and why? Would your absence be noted? When your friend Jason got dumped by his boyfriend, it was almost a week before you realized you hadn't seen any texts from him lately. You assumed he was talking to other people, and anyway, you're always getting busy or distracted, and so is everyone else.

You imagine it: a stroke, maybe, since you're not the overdose type; you, slumped over your dead laptop. Would there be shit? You look down at your ravock, curled into a tight ball on the rug by your feet where it's sleeping off dinner. It's making that little dreaming growling noise it does sometimes. How long would it wait?

The Gray Regia

Your regia hated your old boyfriend, the one who came over after you had your surgery to read children's books to you when you couldn't sleep. He used funny voices for the different animals and you would start laughing and then it would start hurting and you would tell him to stop. And he *would* stop, that was the amazing part. Most guys would have kept on reading, just for a moment or two, teasing maybe or just that little streak of meanness that men have. He was even really nice to your regia, though it was pretty obvious what it thought of him.

But it didn't work out. You talked about moving in together but then there was an amicable sort of breakup, neither of you quite sure what was happening but both pretty sure it was the right thing. Maybe one of you just lost interest? Anyway, you have the new boyfriend. *He* would have kept reading, but your regia likes him better, and maybe your regia knows what you deserve.

The Sandnes Garn

You knew you had a Sandnes garn at your old place, but it didn't bug you or anything. It's a pest, sure, but you learned to make some noise when you walked into your bedroom to give it time to hide. Under the bed? In the closet? Who knew? The occasional glimpses were kind of cute, little furry horns and beady eyes peeping from behind the dresser you got from IKEA.

When you decided to move in with your girlfriend, your friends offered to help with the lifting. "Does your apartment still have that Sandnes garn?" one said. You nodded. "You need to set some traps or fumigate or something, 'cause otherwise you'll spread them to her place. I'll take that dresser if you're not going to want it," he added.

He did take the dresser but you *didn't* fumigate, and when you get settled in you realize he was right. You see it sometimes, after she's fallen asleep half spooned against you, her hair a grapefruit-scented tickle in your face. The Sandnes garn sits on the chest of drawers that came from her mother's house, next to the picture of all her brothers. Its eyes gleam in the hall light.

Your Sandnes garn is patient. It can wait. You'll fuck this one up, too.

The Skacel

There are close to a hundred species of skacel. While some can be easily distinguished by the casual observer, others may only be differentiated behaviorally or through DNA analysis. People, it seems, make a hobby of identifying their skacels, and a surprising number get the test, which costs between sixty-nine and just under two hundred dollars.

You're not willing to go that far, but you have spent some Friday nights clicking through the internet looking for your skacel, which is small, short-beaked, and rose-colored. The Short-beaked Skacel is a sandy-olive color with a burgundy head and green eye markings. The Roseate Skacel has a narrow beak with a slightly hooked tip. The Lesser Skacel eats roaches, spiders, and other vermin but is neither roseate nor short-beaked; plus, your skacel tends not to eat them so much as kill them and leave them in the bathtub.

The Eastern Skacel drinks cold coffee from a saucer on the floor, which your skacel does not. The Kansas Skacel can eat and digest styrofoam take out containers. The Blue-faced Skacel nests most often in linen closets. Given short walks outside and plenty of toys, the Norway Skacel can live happily in even the smallest apartment. The King Skacel can be trained to retrieve items but resents neglect. Burney's Skacel would prefer it if you stopped bringing girls over. So would the Noro (a variety of skacel), plus it has some feelings about post-modernism.

Your old girlfriend probably wishes you had spent this sort of time on her. She has a skacel too, with an unmemorable beak but vivid yellow markings along the wingtips. You haven't been able to find that one, either.

The Smerle

You could take your smerle outside and people were always very impressed—an actual smerle, with all the feet and the outrageous crest and everything. Where did you get it? Was it imported? If you didn't mind telling, how much did it cost? It was like having a good beard or driving a boattail Buick: there was a lot of upkeep but it was worth it.

But then things changed. It started to droop, and its colors faded. "Get another smerle," one of your friends advised. "Smerles love company."

"*I'm* company," you said, but you got another one anyway, this one chestnut-colored. Your smerle perked up and now you had *two* to walk on matching leashes: two smerles that played together, twined about one another; a pair that pretty much ignored you.

The Tatamy

"One tatamy grows lonely," your grandmother always says, like, "Troubles come in threes," and you figure that's about right. You started with the one. You were getting dressed for work one morning and there it was, curled tight into a gladiator sandal you'd almost forgotten you had. A week later, there was one in the other sandal, and then a few days later, two more peeked from your Uggs from college, and then there were what seemed like dozens, tucked into all the pairs of out-of-date shoes and boots you'd meant to take to Goodwill. They leave your sensible shoes, the work pumps and trainers, alone. You're not sure whether this is a judgment.

You have no idea what they eat, and you're not sure what they do with themselves when they are not tucked into your shoes like hermit crabs. All night you hear them rustling in your closet, often making small rhythmic bumps, as though they're mating or dancing to house. Mostly you don't mind that you are the only one in the apartment who is going to bed early or sleeping alone. But there are times when you imagine turning on the light, stepping into your old shoes, and dancing.

The Urna

The first couple of times you stayed out all night, you worried about your urna, all by itself in the apartment; but urnas are supposed to be pretty self-reliant as long as you leave out food and water, and that seemed to be true. You came home in the morning and found it sleeping in your bed, a rounded hillock under the comforter and, hilariously, the tip of a tail peeking out. That's always been a thing, no urnas on the bed, but you were feeling guilty and that tail really was pretty cute, so you let it ride. And it's not like there's an easy way to prevent it when you're not home. Crumpled aluminum foil? Doublestick tape? You're pretty sure the urna would be past that in about ten minutes.

Things started changing in your absence. This one picture fell off the wall; you assumed the urna had been prowling around the apartment or something. Your toothbrush vanished, ditto;

but then there was a new toothbrush, and where did *that* come from? And then you had a new Spotify channel, smooth jazz. And after that, an actual paper newspaper subscription. How did your urna turn out to be such a codger? You suppose you should do something to maybe bring it a little bit up to the times, but that would mean staying home more.

Anyway, it seems to be doing all right for itself: there's a second toothbrush, a little red one. It's seeing someone—which is a little distressing. Why is it so hard for you, if even an urna has someone to love?

The Wolle

It's hard to pull the trigger on an apartment. The one-bedroom on Massachusetts Street has a southern exposure and tall windows that look down onto cute shops and busy sidewalks, though you wonder whether that would get on your nerves. It's small. If someone came, they wouldn't have anywhere to sleep except the floor or, hypothetically, your bed. There's no pet deposit if you get a begitte, which maybe would be okay later. Right now you can't see making a commitment like that.

On the other hand, the two-bedroom out on California is cool and shady. It's in a beautiful neighborhood, right next to a park with a really good disc-golf course. There is nothing on the hardwood floors and no curtains in the windows, so the rooms echo. Guests could stay in the second bedroom, if you bought a bed—but the rest of the time? You think you'd have a hard time filling that space. There are probably lopi.

Or you could just keep sleeping on the couch in Cortney's living room in her place on Vermont Street, and then you don't have to choose anything at all. It's a comfortable couch. She says she doesn't mind, says you're a great houseguest, says you're not a pain in the ass the way some people are. You take out the trash. If you borrow her car, you fill the tank. The two of you order takeout and watch television shows a season at a time. Her wolle curls up between you, dozing.

It occurs to you that in another life, *you* might very well be the begitte, the lopi, the quilliot.

The Apartment Dweller's Stavebook

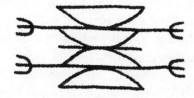

A Stave Against the Ill-Will of Others

You are probably not actually that important, but if it comforts you to imagine that you are the center of this story, sure. Make a round medallion of white oak as broad across as your hand, and sand it until it is smooth to the touch. Carve this rune using the boning knife from that set of five Henckels you bought during your gourmet cooking phase—this is the purpose of that knife; you never used it for anything else, did you?—and color it with the black powder from a toner cartridge.

The fight, the scene, the mingled shame and resentment and anger: if you didn't love the drama of all this, it would evaporate in a week or two, anyway.

* * *

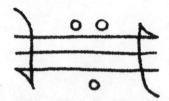

A Stave Against Roaches, Mice, and Your Mother's Ill-Will

Carve this in the alphabet of coffee shops on the handle of a broom purchased from a big-box superstore, in the hours when there are no customers and the aisles are filled with plastic-sheathed pallets of cheap desiderata. Sweep each corner of your house, always toward the center of the room.

How many brooms did your mother have? What did *her* rituals look like? Did they succeed? No, or you would not still be here.

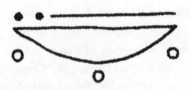

The Seal of Wet Boots and Slush

February trickles on, bitter and endless and grimy. The rubber floor mats in the car are stained. You wish you had children; if you have them, then you wish you did not. When did this become your world?

Most credit card companies don't really care what your signature looks like, or even if it is consistent. Instead of your name, you might inscribe this symbol with blue-black ink beside the X, and it might be for anything: five days at Disney World, a

Coach bag, the 300SL, the spa day, the Final Four tickets, the grill. But it will still be February, and your front hall will still be rimed with grit and the ghosts of dirty water.

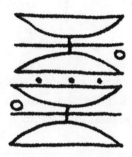

A Stave to Save Your Marriage

Everything operates in failure mode: the business you work for, your lower back, your car. You just didn't notice. Why would you? Noncritical failures can be recovered from, compensated for. They accumulate like October leaves or dead skin and dust mites, then are swept away or ignored. The windshield wiper blade that only smeared the rain was a small annoyance but it was dealt with: a visit to the auto parts place instead of lunch, and a dry-cleaning bill from where you leaned across the hood and got dirt on your coat. But when the transmission blows, don't act surprised, as though nothing has ever gone wrong with this car before.

Your marriage.

Find a Number 2 pencil. Sharpen it to a point. Break the lead off, and pinch the tiny cone of graphite between your fingernails, to write this stave on the inside of a frying pan with a loose handle. Most likely, there have been too many noncritical failures already, but it's worth a shot.

* * *

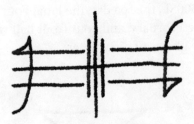

The Ghost Stave

On a Friday night when you cannot reach your best friend, trace this symbol on the back of your left hand in mingled bourbon and blood. You will sleep, at least for a while.

The Seal of Wind

For when he is always talking and he does not listen: after the inconclusive sex, when you tried to tell him what wasn't working but he kept touching you harder as though that would fix it; after the restless night and his arm heavy across you until you threw it off, sweating, and he mumbled your name and cupped one sweaty breast and pulled you closer; after he brushed his teeth, gargled, and spat in the shower; after reading aloud tidbits from his newsfeed as you counted the minutes until he would look at his phone, say, *welp, that salt isn't going to mine itself*, stand, pull on his coat, and grab his messenger bag and his keys; after the quick kiss on the side of your mouth and *see you tonight, baby*; after he is gone at last.

Collect the remainder of the cold coffee from his cup and, mingling the coffee and your own spit, draw this seal on the screen of your computer. There are no words to this spell; why would there be? More words are the *last* thing this situation needs.

The Seal of Betrayal and Loss

By the way? She lied when she left, when she told you it wasn't anyone else. She erroneously thought that this would hurt less. The notion of slipping from one man to the next was not one that she could reconcile with the way she wants you to think of her. Even now, she courts your opinion.

You are already carving this stave into the insides of your eyelids, though you are not yet aware of it.

A Cross for Pet Owners

Use salt to write this symbol in the middle of the kitchen floor. Within minutes, it will be scattered; this will in no way alter its effectiveness.

Don't get comfortable. There is always a built-in expiration date.

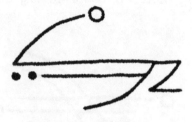

Greater Day Job Stave

You can be simultaneously burnt to the socket and bored.

You have dozens of cheap ballpoint pens at your workstation. Their sticky blue ink clots and smears: stains desk drawers, the bottoms of pencil cups, the carpet behind your desk. Break one of these pens open and use the remaining ink to inscribe this symbol upon a sheet of 20-pound 8½" x 11" paper. Fold the paper tightly and press it into the dirt of the seedy-looking parlor palm in the reception area. It will be found, a week from now or a month from now, by the Plant Services person your company hires. She will keep your secret: she doesn't like her job, either.

The Stave Not to Fuck This Up Too

Scratch this symbol upon the enameled curve of a chipped thermos, and color it using blood drawn from your left earlobe.

Say nothing. You can hide anything behind silence.

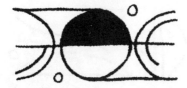

A Stave in Preparation for Knee Surgery

Using blood from the web between your right index finger and thumb, draw this upon that medal from the track meet in eleventh grade. This is the first real proof that your body is already starting to refuse the hard work of keeping you alive.

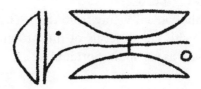

Stave to Defend Against Unwanted Memories

In the night, in the shower, in the car at the stoplight on Third, at the Tuesday meeting, when you check your account balance online and their name is still there, when you decide yes or no to the movie, when you see a pocket watch in a thrift store like the ones they used to collect and maybe still do, when you sign up to bring the yams to Thanksgiving, when you put on a scarf, when you buy gin instead of bourbon, when you are kissing your new lover, when you are eating bacon, when you breathe, when you breathe, when you breathe.

Draw this stave in black Sharpie on your forehead. You might as well.

* * *

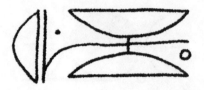

Lesser Dream Stave

Go back to college? Learn how to restore cars? Sign up on Tinder? Take up a sport? Ask your friends for an idea for a story you might want to write? Try contra dancing? Cut your hair? Grow your hair? Watch pornos? Knit a scarf? Update your LinkedIn? What about Unitarianism? A book club? Shave? Piano lessons. Wines. Home brewing. Quilts, caucuses, tattoos, CrossFit, classic jazz, witty socks. Whatever it takes.

Paint this symbol on a TV tray from the 1960s. It is best if it is avocado green, with faded decals of mushrooms in garlands, though the paint you use is not important.

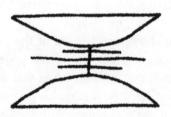

Greater Dream Stave

You will perform this spell alone, because, no matter who is in the room, that is how you do everything in your life.

You are like everyone else. You think you can save yourself. You think you can be happy, but death is inevitable. How do you wake up and move forward in the face of that? What do you expect that will mean to you? Will you at last be able to rest? Heaven and hell both seem exhausting. Maybe death will be like dreaming, or ticking off everything on your to-do list and seeing what the empty page looks like.

The Apartment Dweller's Alphabetical Dreambook

An **abalone** shell in a dream signifies a new home.

To be **afraid** in a dream signifies strife along with danger, which seems obvious enough.

Clear **air** in a dream signifies success in one's business affairs.

If the **air** is polluted, it signifies a disagreement between you and your mother: a common enough condition, though you usually know better than to respond to her ancient, flaking criticisms. Still, there are days when you are tired, or just tired of it all. Tomorrow will be one of those days, and you will find yourself yet again tasting rusted metal and sulfur.

To sit in an **Audi** signifies great strife and financial disaster. It is hard not to connect this to the fact that your ex left you for someone who owned an Audi.

To dream that one is **awake** signifies a death.

To be stung by a **bee** in a dream signifies weight loss. Anyway, according to humanity's many attempts to map meaning in dreams, this *is* one of the possibilities and the one of most immediate interest to you.

To see **birds** in dreams signifies that one will hear bad news that is nevertheless of no immediate relevance to their own life.

To snare **birds** in a dream signifies a poorly told lie in the next day, a lie that nevertheless convinces. Which lie? Large or small? There are so many possibilities in a normal day. Are you the liar or the lied-to, the fool or the villain?

For **birds** to take something from you signifies hearing loss. This should not worry you: you know you've been losing the higher pitches already. Maybe the world will be calmer when you are missing more of it.

To pluck the first **blueberry** of the season, filled with anticipation and the sweet, grainy memory of how blueberries taste, to place it (in her dream) upon her tongue, and to realize by that angry little snap of sourness that it is not yet quite ripe, signifies a financial loss.

To handle someone's **bones** signifies hatred. The knob of the femur is a fist. The ribs are an argument. Finger bones are needling, slanted gossip. The skull like a stoneware bowl in one's hands is the end of it all.

To hold a **book** in a dream signifies a sudden discovery. Can you open it? What is its title? Are the pages blank? Is there writing on them? Print? Is there a store from which these books come?

If you awaken remembering a **book** from your dream—the loveliest story, but lost now: Remembering what you cannot remember will ruin the day. But you *will* forget, eventually. Do we need to spell this one out for you?

If dreaming, he sees his **brother or sister**, he will develop a cold sore.

To dream of a **calendar** signifies a sudden interest in football, charitable donations, sports cars, cloud-watching, tango, the prints of Hiroshige, cosplay, or sharks. Is this true because you have dreamt of a calendar and then read this list, or would it have happened anyway?

A **car** approaching at a great speed, so close that he feels the wind of its passage, signifies a text that he will misinterpret.

To be in the back seat of a **car** with no one in the front, even as the car is rolling along the highway, and to stretch across the seat for the steering wheel, desperately wondering how to reach the brakes: Nothing is as it should be.

If you dream that you are installing a crate engine into your **car**, an ATK Ford 302 long block; if in the dream you observe the throttle's choke plate, pretty as jewelry, a silver disc that pivots along its diameter to reveal an intake manifold, the sort of aluminum gullet that can speak only in growls; if you and two friends you do not recognize are washing dead leaves from it (for the crate was opened outdoors, and it is October in this dream: a fatal mistake) and water splashes into the manifold, and you are overwhelmed with dread because you might ruin the engine—such a dream signifies a personal regret.

Cats playing signifies praise in a public forum.

If one of the **cats** is striped, you are ill-advised to read the comments.

To accept new **cheese** signifies an unexpected small windfall, a check of between one and two hundred dollars.

If the **cheese** is old, you will keep forgetting to deposit the check.

A dream of **climbing** a tree signifies that she will gain honor. But how does she know what climbing a tree feels like, to have dreamt it: her hands on rough bark, the complicated exchange of information between muscle groups, bones, and tendons? Has she *ever* climbed a tree, or is this somehow embedded into the genomes of this body she alternately ignores and obsesses over?

To **climb** a mountain, but looking up, to realize that you will never get to the top, signifies that your future is coming, and you are not ready. You have faked it before this, sure. This time won't be harder, will it? And it never is—until you fall. Or worse, until the moment your right posterior talofibular ligament finally betrays you while you're stepping off a curb maybe, or into a car. The orthopedic surgeon will tell you that this is the result of all that running and working out when you were younger, that your other ankle—that, in fact, all your joints—are just as damaged, primed to go as easily as this one did. The takeaway from this dream: You're fucked.

To suddenly realize in a dream that one is not wearing **clothes** is the human condition.

New **clothes** in a dream signifies new love. Why are you having this dream? You *have* your spouse; you have already made all these compromises. Maybe it only means that you are sick of those jeans with the coffee stain on the thigh that has never quite gone away. Surely, that's at least equally likely.

To speak with a **dead** person signifies annoyance, happy news, or a change in one's fortunes.

One who sees a **dog** with a red ear will receive an email with mixed implications for the future.

Dogs barking or running free signify a show that will haunt you even at work, even when you are kissing the person you'd like to think you love. Why is *Westworld* so much realer than anything else in your life?

To dream that you are **dreaming** signifies a death. Yours, eventually.

To **drink** wine, a gaffe.

To **drink** vinegar, it is time to renew your driver's license.

To be **driving** along a remote country road; the gas gauge says E, and there is nothing nearby; this signifies trouble with money.

If in a dream, he is in a gray **elevator:** One corner is thick with shadows that the light does not dispel, which he realizes are a creature that means him no good, though it does not attack. When the elevator's door opens, he steps into a gray room with a very high ceiling. There is a corridor. He is holding a knife. The shadow is beside him now, and he suddenly knows this is an adventure, not a dream. He feels a slight sense of loss about the world he is no longer part of—the job, the partner, the kid, the hobby, and the car payments—but here he and the shadow have an important mission, enemies, allies. How is he supposed to get up when the alarm goes off at 6:30, shave himself, read his emails, drink his coffee? His life will never be this strange, this frightening and empowering and exciting. This dream signifies nothing at all. If it did it would break his heart.

To physically **fight** in a dream signifies a problem with your taxes.

If the **fights** follow one upon the next, until the night is filled with battles, this signifies the sort of decision that has no good options. It does not matter whether the battles are hand-to-hand, or with weapons.

* * *

If one sees **fire** in any place, that signifies a reorganization of one's place of business. One will escape the layoffs, but will be asked to select which of one's staff is to go.

To book a **flight** signifies a mistake. It is $328 through Expedia; $422 with Southwest, but then you don't have to pay for your bag—but you still will have to drive through rush hour to get to the airport, and then TSA, and how long will *that* take? The possibilities for failure in your day to come are endless.

To see in a dream your great-aunt's **glassware** standing on a card table at an estate sale, with a sticker that says 8 RED 8 WHITE 8 SHERRY 8 WATER 8 TUMBLERS $40 THE SET, signifies a sudden change in your situation.

To handle some **grain** signifies illness. This must be another dream from your deep memory, for when have *you* ever handled grain, to know what that feels like?

To hold a **gun** in a dream signifies a thunderstorm, or perhaps self-delusion.

If the **gun** is an HK VP9, you may expect an email from overseas. It has news that will seem good; later you will realize that the email brought you only sorrow.

If one sees oneself accept **honey,** it signifies that one should be careful not to be deceived by another. But really, so what? It would be so much more pleasant to believe what she says, and knowing it is lies ahead of time changes nothing, after all.

To see **horses** running loose, or to be attacked by them, signifies trouble at work.

To **kiss** a dead person signifies one's child is at risk; otherwise, that tomorrow will be stormy.

If, in one's dream, one sees a creature, an inarticulate **lemur**-thing: Its eyes are a pale violet, and the fingers of its paws are very long. It makes garbling sounds at you, and you can't help but feel it is trying to communicate, but you are fully occupied with some small tedious task: counting nails or writing status reports or sorting receipts. It remains with you throughout the dream, a weight on your shoulder so slight that you forget it for short periods. Every so often you suddenly remember it with a jolt of panic: Where has it gone? You must not lose it! It is critical! But it is still right there, still garbling, still staring at you with its violet eyes, and so you return to your pointless dreamtime counting or compiling. Your therapist would have a field day sorting this out, but you do not tell her. You feel protective of this lemur-thing. Your secrets are your own. Such a dream signifies, you are pretty sure, nothing worth discussion.

To receive a **letter** in the mail, in a handwritten envelope with a stamp on it, signifies a personal regret.

To see the **moon** signifies a happy surprise.

To see two **moons**, her cholesterol levels are slightly higher and she will need to alter her diet.

To see a crescent **moon**, it is September in her dream.

To see a white **moon** signifies nothing at all. Why do we assume everything means something?

If her **period** starts in a dream, it signifies a meeting at work.

To check one's **phone** signifies that your bladder needs relief. Anxieties are all the same anxiety.

To dream of standing offstage waiting for one's entrance in the third act of a **play**, a play one has not even read, let alone memorized, signifies strife at the holidays related to the in-laws.

If she sees her front door opened by a **rabbit-butler**, and knows his name is Montgomery, and steps into a Palladian entry hall painted the blue of robins' eggs, where she shakes the rain from her great red umbrella; if her rabbit-butler takes her wet things and offers tea in the library and a crime novel she has never read; and then she awakes, she will look around her bedroom—her yoga pants on the floor and tomorrow's work clothes neatly on the dresser—and then she will call in sick and spend the rest of the day trying to get back there.

A **radio** turned on and chattering signifies bad news, but there's nothing dream-specific to this.

To **rejoice** in a dream signifies sadness.

A **river** flowing through her house—she will remember nothing of this dream.

To have **sex** in a dream signifies anything but sex, if your therapist is correct. Or is it that she's just tired of people distracting themselves from the hard work of humanity?

To have **sex** with one's spouse signifies strife.

One who opens his mouth in a dream to **shout** a warning and finds he can make no sound—he will realize that he has lied but that no one seemed to notice; is that because he was good at it, or because no one cared enough to do more than find ways to step around him and his inadequate lie?

If the **sky** is in flames, this signifies an evil that has its bitter advantages: your senile father's death, the chlamydia that brought the affair to light.

To make a **speech** one has carefully prepared signifies a happy situation at home. All that therapy has paid off.

In a dream, if one walks beside a low concrete retaining wall and hears a voice in one's ear, and turns to see a **spider** the size of a small dog sitting upon one's right shoulder; if in the dream it has taken a great bite (which was not felt) and the ragged remaining flesh of the shoulder is turning gray—it signifies . . . Hmm. It would be easier to know what this signified if one could remember what was said by the spider and by you. This exchange was the answer to all your questions, then and now. This dream will haunt you for the rest of your life.

To see a butternut **squash** in a dream signifies self-doubt, or else a good report from your child's school.

Driving an **SUV**—you will realize you are in a dream, and yet you will be unable to awaken. Who selected this vehicle, anyway? What production designer makes the decisions about your dreams?

To be turned to **stone** in a dream signifies that your fifty-ninth birthday is coming.

To eat **sweets** signifies that tomorrow your child will surprise you with a flicker of maturity you never suspected, followed immediately by an action so spectacularly immature that you will wonder whether that bedroom can ever be converted into a workout room.

To **taste** something in a dream signifies news. One may draw all sorts of obvious connections between what that taste is and what sort of news it indicates. Milk chocolate = cheerful news. Pickles = sour news. Coffee = bitter news, or eye-opening news, or warming news. Bacon = news that is not healthy and may be cruel but which is nevertheless almost irresistibly attractive—such as learning that your ex's new lover totaled the car, or is still sleeping with their own ex.

One's **teeth** falling out signifies that the water heater in your home is about to go.

Recollecting in dream the vivid smell of the dusty **theatre** where one's high-school plays were performed signifies that, if in the morning one were to walk slowly enough into one's place of work, a crow would offer advice of some importance. But of course you'll be running late and you'll ignore this dream. It's wildly improbable, anyway.

To be caught up by a **tornado** in a dream signifies new love.

To **wash** dishes by hand signifies a sudden memory.

To be stung by a **wasp** signifies angry gossip. You must stop.

To wind a very old **watch** you do not recognize, and see that you are only turning the hour and minute hands around and around, signifies that you will receive a year-end bonus of between two and ten percent of your current income. You will imagine this changes something in your life, but will spend this money almost immediately on a new transmission.

To see **water** on the boil in a dream signifies strife with an enemy. Is it Rick from work? Your oldest son, nineteen now and accusing you of not understanding him? Your mother?
To eat dry **wax** signifies a wedding in the family.

To **yawn** in one's dream signifies confusion. Are you even asleep? You are in your bed; there is light creeping in through the door to the hall. But surely that blurred face in the mirror on the bedroom wall is a dream?

Later, as you stare into a sky the color of aging **zinc**, you will wonder whether there is a way back into last night: the garden of sapphire leaves, the fountain of car exhaust and roses, the man who told you a secret.

The Dream-Quest of Vellitt Boe

Vellitt Boe was dreaming of a highway and ten million birds in an empty sky of featureless blue. The highway, broad and black as a tar pit. The birds, a cloud of them, like a mist writhing, like gnats pillaring over the dark marshes of Lomar or flickering shoals of silver fish in the crystal seas beyond Oriab. The sky: empty, untextured, flat. A great black beast crouching beside her growled steadily, but the birds were louder. One called with a high sweet voice, and it was saying, "Professor Boe? Professor Boe!"

Reality returned in rapid stages: the never-absent pain in her back; the softness against her face of sheets worn satin-smooth in the College's laundry; the cold air; the moonlight graphed by the casemented windows onto the broad bare floor of her dark bedroom; the percussion of urgent fists; and the voice, soprano but strong, one of the students and afraid, so afraid: "Professor! Please, O gods, please, you *must* wake up!"

And she was awake. Vellitt pushed herself upright in her narrow bed. "Wait!" she called, caught her robe from where it lay across the foot of the bed, and stepped into her slippers. She went to open the door.

It was Derysk Oure, the third-year Chymical Studies scholar, one hand still raised from the knocking. In the sallow light of the hallway's single gas-jet, her face was the color of drying mud, and more anxious than Vellitt had ever seen it. She was dressed in a pyjama suit—quite daring, really—but with a country shawl around her shoulders, and she was weeping. "Professor Boe! Please, please come right away! I don't— It's Jurat."

Food poisoning in the Hall, scandal, suicide. There were a thousand ways a women's college might find itself destroyed. Clarie Jurat was third-year, reading Mathematics with Vellitt, and her best student in twenty years of teaching at Ulthar Women's College: a brilliant girl, strong-willed, charismatic and beautiful, with long laughing eyes and thick black hair she wore always in a heavy fishtail braid half down her back.

"Lead me." Vellitt followed Oure down the stairwell. The girl was still sobbing. "What about Jurat? Calm *down*, Oure, or I'll have you on my hands, as well. This is not the way an Ulthar woman behaves."

Oure paused, pressed her palms against her eyes. "I know, I'm sorry, professor. You're right. I was on my way to bed, and Hust burst out of their suite just as I was going past, and she said, *She's gone, she's run away with him*, so Martveit ran to get the Dean, and I came to get you. I don't know anything else."

"Jurat takes exams in three months. When did she have *time* to meet anyone?"

Oure turned back down the stairs. "I don't know, I'm sure." It was a lie, of course, but the girl said no more.

They exited Fellow's Stair and crossed the quad. Only one set of lights shone out, from Jurat's windows. Good; the fewer awake in the first uncontrolled moments of this situation—whatever it was—the better. The shadows were all moving as the moon visibly shifted phase, drifting southward on some god's whim. The cold night air was filled with the sharp scents of chrysanthemums and the first fallen leaves, and so quiet that she could hear cats wailing outside the College wall. A clowder had congregated within the quad, as well. They ceased whatever was their business and watched as Vellitt and Oure passed, and one, a small black cat, separated itself from the rest and followed them into Jurat's stairwell. The cold light streaming in through the windows vanished suddenly as the moon passed behind the dining hall's tower, and they were left in the flickering amber of the weak gas jets on each landing.

A handful of young women had clustered near Jurat's door, wrapped in bathrobes or shawls or the blankets from their beds, for the College did not waste its funds heating the stairwells. Their voices burst around Vellitt, high and nervous. She snapped out, "Women!" with the authority of long experience, and they fell silent, their anxious, sleep-worn faces tracking her ascent like poppies following the sun: the old women they would become for a moment showing through their youth.

There was a circle of space around Jurat's door, the women's curiosity in equipoise with their unwillingness to be associated with whatever crimes she turned out to have committed. Only Therine Angoli had crossed, weeping soundlessly as she held Raba Hust, the Ancient Sarnathian scholar, a heavyset girl with warm brown skin turned the color of ashes and dust in the dim hall light. Hust was Jurat's roommate. Angoli, Hust, and Jurat had been close, the Three Inseparables.

Vellitt announced to the assembled women, "It remains past curfew. Return to your rooms before the Dean arrives and finds herself obliged to take notice. I need not remind you that discretion is and must always be a byword of Ulthar women. Do not speak of this even among yourselves, until we know more—especially to no one outside the College. Miss Hust, I must detain you for another moment."

Without waiting to see her order followed, she disengaged Hust from Angoli's clinging arms and thrust her into the room, to close the door.

Jurat and Hust's sitting room was disordered, the wardrobe doors ajar and clothing distributed over every flat surface. Open-faced books teetered in irregular stacks on the paper-strewn floor, and a tray of dirty crockery from the buttery had been shoved halfway beneath one of the two unmade beds. Even the framed prints on the walls, scenic photographic views of the Naraxa Valley from a generation ago, were crooked. The room looked as though it had been ransacked during a particularly violent abduction, but all the women students' rooms did these days—as though there were a fad among them of being as sloppy personally as they were disciplined in their studies.

Hust fell into a padded armchair and with the heedless flexibility of the young, pulled her feet up, wrapping her arms around her knees and hugging them close to her chest. She was still sobbing.

As Vellitt moved piles of old Articulations from the two wooden study chairs, there was a brisk knock, followed immediately by the entrance of a small woman with short, grizzled hair and the clever eye of a hunting bird: Gnesa Petso, the Dean of Ulthar Women's College. She was dressed in a soft woolen robe, once red but a decade old and dimmed by age and laundering. Without preliminaries, she seated herself on one of the cleared chairs and said briskly, "Hust, every moment is important. What has happened?"

Hust gave her a piece of notepaper, folded twice. The Dean read as Hust said, "When I came back from the library tonight, Jurat wasn't here. That was nine o'clock, I think. She hadn't said anything to me about being out late, but I assumed she had a late pass to be at a lecture or a reading party, or—" But she was flushed, lying.

The Dean, casting a bright black eye up from the note, said, "—or that she slipped out to be with a man. Miss Hust, do not disgrace yourself trying to sustain someone else's lie."

Hust ducked her head. "I found her letter under my blankets. I've been working on Articulations, so she knew I wouldn't see it until late."

The Dean passed the note to Vellitt. Clarie Jurat's handwriting was as beautiful as everything else about her.

> *Raba, dear—*
>
> *Do not be distressed! You know what this says already, don't you—You always see everything so clearly. I go to be with Stephan—I know it is shocking, but there is such an enormous world, and I cannot see it here. He says there are millions of stars, Raba. Millions. Please show this to Therine. I am sorry for the people who will be hurt, but how could I*

ever explain this to dear old Prof Boe? To the Dean? To my
father? It is impossible—they could not understand—and
Stephan tells me it must be tonight or never—and so I go!
The greatest adventure, yes? Be happy for me.
      Your loving,
         Clarie.

The story was soon told. Clarie Jurat had met Stephan Heller
when the Three Inseparables had attended a Union debate four
weeks ago. He had struck up a conversation outside the Hall, buying
them all coffee at the Crévie. He had been captivated by Jurat: no
surprise, Hust said—a little wistfully, for of the Inseparables, she
was the plainest. What *was* a surprise was that Jurat found him
equally attractive. He was good-looking, tawny-skinned and dark
eyed with excellent teeth, and very tall (Hust sighed), but it wasn't
any of *that*. There was just something *about* him.

The next afternoon, it had been tea for Hust and Jurat—
Therine Angoli had been unable to join them because of her
Maritime Economic History tutorial—and then it had been Jurat
and Stephan, Stephan and Jurat, weeks and weeks of high teas
and low teas and tiffins, of walks through Ulthar's quaint narrow
streets and punting upon the Aëdl; of after-hour bottles of wine
shared in the sorts of public places where the kellarkips did not ask
about the University status of young women. That Jurat's studies
had not suffered during this month was more a sign of her innate
brilliance than of any devotion to her work.

And now this.

The Dean said, "We need to bring her back before this
becomes a known thing. Is he a student?" No, Hust rather thought
he seemed older than that. "Well, where does he stay? You must
know that, yes? She must have said *something*."

Hust hesitated, biting a cuticle.

Vellitt snapped, "I know you have no wish to break silence,
Hust, but believe me: This is the right thing to do. We *must* find
her. Do you know who her father is?"

"She never talks about her family. What does it matter, anyway?" Hust dropped her hand and looked up a little defiantly.

The Dean explained, "Jurat's father is one of the College's trustees, and he reports to the University's board."

Hust said, "She's an adult, and she's in love. She is permitted to plan her own life, surely? What's wrong with that?"

Vellitt snapped, "What's wrong is that her father might have the College shut down—"

Hust looked aghast. "Oh, surely not!"

"—and perhaps get women banned from the University altogether," said Vellitt. "*This* is why we must find her quickly and bring her back. Where does he live?"

Hust bit her lip. "I know Heller has been staying at the Speared Hart. He's not from Ulthar. I thought I said: he was special. He's from the waking world. That's where he's taking her."

"That *fool*," snarled Vellitt Boe to Gnesa Petso.

It was ten minutes later. The Dean had ordered Hust to return to bed, but Vellitt saw a flicker of a bright shawl above them as they descended the stairwell: Angoli, lurking on the landing. Never mind. Hust would need comfort, and Angoli as well: the Inseparables separated forever now, and for such a reason.

Gnesa and Vellitt had come to Vellitt's rooms as being closer; and she had turned up the gas jets and poured whiskey for them both. The Fellows of Ulthar's Women's College were expected to live disciplined lives free of the indulgences the male Fellows of the other colleges might enjoy, but this was honored rather in the breach, even at the best of times. Just now, Vellitt thought they needed the whiskey's bite, but she barely tasted it before she put it down and began pacing.

Gnesa looked up at Vellitt from her seat in one of the worn brocaded settees. "Sit *down*, Vellitt. We must think, and this is not productive."

Vellitt dropped into the facing seat. "I know, but—ah, this is infuriating. I thought we trained our women to think clearly, and this, this elopement— We're always walking a fine line anyway. How could she not see that? She could get women banned from the University—and for *what*? For a personal whim?" It was impossible to stay still; she stood to pace again.

"For love," Gnesa said.

Vellitt shook her head. "She is too intelligent not to see the damage—not for her, but for the others, the ones who won't marry, who don't have that option, perhaps. It was selfish. Jurat should be better than that."

"When are young people in love anything but selfish?" said Gnesa. "Were you any better?"

"I harmed no one but myself when I was young," said Vellitt. "And my parents were dead. But—" She bit off the words, took a breath, then a second. "I do see what you are saying, Gnesa. I apologize."

"Accepted," Gnesa said. "So we must find out, *primus*, whether any part of this is true—"

"Jurat may be a fool, but she is no liar."

Gnesa continued, "—*secundus*, whether they have left Ulthar yet, and if so, *tertius*—the waking world? How does one get there?" Vellitt opened her mouth but Gnesa raised a finger. "*Primus* first. Go wake up Daekkson and send him to the Speared Hart to see whether they are by some mad chance still there. If so, he can drag her back by the ear and this may be over before dawn. We'll figure out the rest while he's gone."

"I'll rouse him," Vellitt said. "I may as well use some of this energy for *something*."

It took rather less than five minutes to cross the quad, awaken the porter in his rooms behind the main gate, and explain the situation. When Vellitt returned, she found Gnesa had moved to her desk and pushed aside the Articulations stacked there.

"Done," Vellitt said when Gnesa looked up from what she was writing. "He'll report to us here as soon as he returns."

Gnesa nodded. "Excellent. If he does bring her back, there will be little harm done. Provided she's not pregnant, anyway. If she's gone—" She picked up the page before her. "Here's my thinking."

It was a list. Gnesa read it to her, voice raised slightly to be heard in the bedroom as Vellitt dressed. The other Professors and Fellows of Ulthar Women's College would need to be awakened, collected, and told—which meant the scouts would need to be awakened, which meant the College housekeeper, who would handle all that. There would have to be an emergency assembly for the students, enjoining silence for all their sakes—they could not count on the news remaining secret; best to take the ram by the horns—and it would have to be before anyone left for lectures and classes. At Matins, then, though there were plenty of students who skipped the rituals. The scouts would need to be told to rouse late-risers to make sure they were there. The kitchen staff would need to be warned that the entire College would be at breakfast in a body right afterward, instead of arriving in their more usual dribs and drabs or skipping it altogether.

Gnesa would need to write to Davell Jurat and tell him the College had lost his daughter—"and ask him, *Please, kind sir, do not shut us down,*" she said sourly. There would be a different letter to the other Trustees, stating that Jurat had been taken away by a man of the waking world: hinting at unknown sorceries (though certainly not lying directly), and so perhaps the College might not seem so culpable. If everything were handled carefully, and so long as the whole thing could be hushed up, and provided there was no possibility of recurrence, the Trustees might be convinced not to close the College

Vellitt walked out to the sitting room buttoning her walking skirt, as Gnesa ended, "If they *were* at the inn but are gone now, find her somehow." Gnesa looked up. "This is all assuming that he is what he says he is, a dreamer, and not just some smooth-talking Thran man, here to seduce University girls."

Vellitt sat to lace her shoes. "I don't think so. Jurat has read Maths with me for three years now. The students tell their tutors things—you know how they do. I know she's ignored men who were much more handsome than this Stephan Heller sounds. Hust said he was special, and I think he is. There's a . . . sheen to waking-world men. A dark charisma. If you spend more than an hour or two with one, it's obvious. *That's* what Jurat was responding to."

The Dean put down the pen and leaned back, eyeing the painting of Utnar Vehi above the desk. "Too bad. It would be better for us if he *is* a charlatan: then we could track him, eventually anyway. Otherwise . . . What if he has taken her back to his world already, Vellitt? I know dreamers can leave our lands from anywhere: They vanish here when they awaken in their own world. I saw it once, a few years back. A man walking along Dubv Lane, and then he was gone."

Vellitt said, "Stephan Heller could do that, but Clarie can't. *This* is her world; she's awake already. I think they'll have to pass through a Gate. There's one on Hatheg-Kla. Dreamers call it the Gate of Deeper Slumber but it just looks ordinary, just wrought iron and moss. There are supposed to be stairs behind it that lead to a temple serving the Flame, and another Gate, and then the waking world."

Gnesa was eying her, surprised.

Vellitt added, reluctantly, "I knew a dreamer, a long time ago. Let me show you something, Gnesa." She picked up *Aldrovandi on Theoretical Geometry* from the seat under the gabled window, and riffled the monograph's pages until she found what she sought and handed it to the Dean.

It was a piece of cardstock a little larger than her hand, printed with a vivid photographic image of an unfamiliar town square: pale stone buildings and slate flagstones, white umbrellas, glowing green trees, crowds of people dressed in bright colors. Where the sky should be was a flat blueness.

Gnesa looked up. "Is this somewhere in Carcassone?"

"Not Carcassone. He always said our Carcassone was named for a place in his own world, but it's not that, either. Look: different buildings, and the colors everyone is wearing. This is the waking world. It's a place there." She pointed to words along the bottom: AVIGNON, LA PLACE DE L'HORLOGE.

"Where is the sky?" Gnesa touched the blueness with one small fingertip.

"That blue *is* their sky."

"There is no patterning, no mass? What is it made of?" Gnesa's field was Material Studies. She turned the card over and fell silent. The back was simpler: CARTE POSTALE printed in dark blue on plain white; precise, crabbed handwriting in ink that had faded from black to the color of old blood.

Veline, you always wish for proofs—R.

"'Veline'?"

"Me." Vellitt looked down at the little photograph, the tiny bright women, the specks on the piazza's flagstones: birds, or debris. "I didn't believe him when he told me about the sky, so he brought this to me. Gnesa, I can follow Jurat and Stephan Heller to Hatheg-Kla. I know the way. I've crossed the forest and I've seen the Gate."

Gnesa frowned. "Too dangerous. I'll send Daekkson."

"It has to be me."

"No. He is twenty years younger than you—and, not inconsequentially, male. The west . . . that is rough country, Vellitt."

Vellitt snorted. "The Skai plains? Not so very rough! No, I do take your point, but consider. Which of us is more likely to bring her back? I'm her tutor, Arbitrix for her exams. We need her to *listen*, to understand what is at risk if she clings to this folly. If Daekkson comes up with them on the road to the Gate, she will not listen to him, and it will be hard for him to retrieve her without a scandal. And if they have passed it? He has no options."

"Would *you* have options?" said Gnesa.

"More than Daekkson anyway. Trust me, Gnesa. I will find a way."

Gnesa stared into the flames for a moment. "Your point is valid, and I accede. But—can you travel fast enough?"

"I'll have to, won't I?"

They were interrupted by a knock at the door. Daekkson, back from the Speared Hart: Stephan Heller had departed that very afternoon in the company of an extraordinarily beautiful woman: obviously Jurat, from the nightkip's dazzled description. They had asked about the west.

Gnesa dismissed Daekkson and turned to Vellitt. "That's that, then. Are you sure you want to do this?"

"Does it matter?" Vellitt said, tired of it all suddenly. "It's what I do: teach women not to be fools. I have spent the last twenty years of my life here—making a place for women who don't fit anywhere else. She can't be allowed to ruin it for the others."

"All right. How soon will you depart?"

"Immediately. Professor Freser at Thanes-College can take my lectures and students. Can you let everyone else know who needs to?"

"Done." Gnesa jotted it down and stood. "I'll get the Bursar to pull together some funds for you. Bring Jurat back to us, Vellitt. And yourself." Gnesa embraced her, a sudden surprising touch, then was gone.

It was not quite an immediate departure, but it was quick for all that. Vellitt Boe unearthed from the recesses of her closet a small leather pack, crumpled and smelling slightly, pleasingly, of ancient rains and distant soil. She found her old walking boots and her walking stick of gnurled black wood.

When Vellitt Boe was young, she had been a far-traveler, a great walker of the Six Kingdoms, which waking-world men called the dream lands. She had seen Irem, that pillared ruin, and she knew that it was not the fantasia of the Academician's pretty painting above her desk but—like the rest of the world—dirtier and infinitely more interesting.

She had been born in the harbor town of Jaren where the frigid Xari spilled into the northern reaches of the Cerenarian Sea, but in her nineteenth year she left, and for years after that she had voyaged: crossed plains and forests and fenlands, ascended mountains and walked in the belly of the under-realms, sailed in strange-hulled boats across unfamiliar oceans under the low sky. She had traveled until she realized that this yearning life could not be sustained, that time would eventually erode away her strength and courage; and so she stopped. She applied to the Women's College of the University of Celephaïs and settled into rooms there, a perfect student, brilliant and disciplined. She received her Physical Studies degree in Mathematics and came to Ulthar, to stay and grow old and teach other young women more rational responses to their restlessness. It had been sensible, a reasonable end to her far-traveling youth.

Packing came to her automatically, a memory stained not into her mind but into the muscles of her hands. The tricks came back: how to fold her spare socks and where the tin box of medical supplies best fit. She stowed a sweater, a blouse, heavy gloves, her flat steel canteen, comb and toothbrush, soap in a small bottle, whetstone and oil, matches—all the oddments of traveling finding their places in the pack as though they knew their way. She added her electric torch, but such torches had existed only as expensive, temperamental fripperies thirty years ago, so she also found her old tinderbox. She tested the flint: satisfied, for her hand had preserved the precise, economical flick that sent blue-white sparks spattering across her leather deskpad. Dropping the tinderbox into its little interior pocket, she lifted the rucksack by its shoulder straps. It was lighter than it would have been, for she no longer had rope and grapnel, nor her blanket roll, nor the compact little cooking kit she had carried—but it was heavy enough, for all that.

She carried it out to the sitting room and dropped it on the settee. She still had the machete she had carried so long ago, so she unearthed it from the back of a drawer and strapped the ancient sheath in its place. It nestled gently into the cradle it had worn for itself, just beneath the top flap.

It was only a few days' travel, in any case. She would be crossing the plains of the Skai, going through Nir and Hatheg-town—small but civilized enough. Later, when she approached the wastelands of the Stony Desert, there would be roadside inns, or a farmer could be paid for a night in an unused or hastily vacated bedroom. It would be more dangerous when she entered the forest that girdled Hatheg-Kla, for it was inhabited by the zoogs, strange, sinuous, and untrustworthy. But she would be less than a day under those trees, and she had been there before. As for the waking world (if it should come to that), she had no idea what to expect, so there was no knowing what would be needed.

She took up her old knife from where it had rested for twenty years, a combination paperweight and letter opener half-buried beneath the papers cluttering her desk. It made a tiny sound as she unsheathed it. The edge was still sharp. She returned it to its sheath, and slipped it beneath her jacket.

She laced on her walking boots, and stood, and for a moment looked about herself, at the dark, crooked gables and slanting ceilings of her rooms, the cluttery wallpaper and soft furniture. She had been in these rooms for twenty years and everything was as known as her own reflection: more, for in recent years she had not lingered on that aging stranger in the silvered glass.

On an impulse, she walked into the bedroom and looked at herself in the pier mirror. A stranger infinitely familiar stared back: a stern-eyed woman in walking tweeds, with heavy laced boots and black-and-silver hair pulled away from her lined face. An old woman but not soft—or, she thought with a sudden inward wry laugh, perhaps not quite *old*, but also softer than she had been.

She was interrupted by a soft knock: the College's Bursar, with academic robes tossed over her seafoam-green nightdress and her hair a tangled braid, looking quite mad. She had things for Vellitt: letters of credit, an oiled-leather purse filled with coins, a small parcel of weight-stamped gold lozenges, and a little notebook ruled for bookkeeping. She did not speak of Vellitt's task, only said a quick farewell and a stern enjoinder to record all expenditures, for the University's Accountancies. As the Bursar left, a sleepy scullery maid appeared, bringing sandwiches from the kitchen for the first day's travel. Typical of Gnesa to think of this, even in the middle of so much else to do.

And so Vellitt Boe left Ulthar Women's College, walking silent and alone across the quad and through the postern gate: Daeksson at his post in the porter's hutch, looking uncommonly weary. "Good luck," he said as she passed; and, "No ill thing," she replied. Stepping through the postern gate, she let the heavy door fall shut behind her.

She paused and looked about herself. A narrow slice of sky overhead showed as pitch darkness, for the lane was narrow here, ancient and kenneled and crowded close by stone walls pierced by many-paned windows, dark now.

This was Tierce Lane, but she knew them all, every mews and alley. For twenty years she had paced Ulthar's bounds, traversed its parks and ancient greens, crossed squares, passed fountains. And the people: her colleagues and Fellows and friends—and a thousand lesser connections, with kellarkips and shopkips, the girl who served sardines and cream-tea at Gulseren's and the cheerful delivery boy from Patles's Books. These were Home, or something that passed for home.

She was brought back to herself by a sudden movement at her feet. It was the small black cat that had followed her to Clarie Jurat's rooms, or another like it. It wreathed her ankles, gazing upward, and its eyes shone with light reflected from the lamp over the postern gate. "I have nothing for you," Vellitt said. "Go back inside, little one."

It did not. Vellitt walked to where the lane met the High and turned west, and the cat trotted beside her. This was the old part of town: half-timbered buildings with overhung second stories and peaked roofs, the occasional shrine or public building of heavy granite. The air smelled of ancient mold, but also of herbs, of rue and basil and catmint, for every window had a hanging basket bright with greenery. When she crossed Affleur Road, a single lamp shone in the Weeping Tower of New College—a student in his rooms, cramming for exams as Clarie Jurat should have been. Later, on the Mercü, a light beamed from the open back door of a bakery: the smell of fresh bread everywhere. There were few other signs of life. Even Ulthar's ubiquitous cats were scarcer, pursuing their private errantries as the night eased into dawn.

She crossed Six Corners, automatically making the Elder Sign. After this, the High widened and opened into a series of arcades and markets, and the smells changed to new-gathered greens, spices, hanging pheasants, and the pork and mutton that hung already in linen-wrapped pink slabs in front of the flescher's; for now morning was coming. The tea-seller called out a greeting to Vellitt as she unlaced her canvas shop front; they had talked often enough of tea, weather, travel. Vellitt only waved as she passed. If all went well she would be back soon. If it did not— But there was no reason to think of that.

She turned onto Nir Road, and the buildings spaced themselves out, became detached houses, then cottages with gardens. Small hornless goats eyed her through withy fences. She heard poultry chuckling in back gardens, and once through the open window of an ivy-wrapped cottage, a woman's voice singing: "*Sarnath, Sarkomand, Khem and Toldees; Always say, 'Thank you!' and, 'Sir, if you please.'*"

Vellitt paused when she came to the top of Never-rye Hill, panting a little from the long ascent. Ulthar behind her was achingly beautiful in the rose-pink rays of the new sun: the Six Hills crazed as a tumbled quilt, a random patchwork of red gabled roofs frilled with ornamental iron chimney-pots and lightning rods, and the dark gaps that were roads and gardens. Crowning the highest of the hills, the Temple: a tower surrounded by a grassy field, bright with the first tents for the great Sheep-fair which was to commence in three days. Like a garland about the hill's base were the Seven Colleges of Ulthar's University: New College, Eb'Taqar, and Meianthe School and the others; ancient, cool, and palladian structures of pale stone blushing the sunrise-pink of cherry blossoms, their quadrangles turned trapezoidal by perspective; hints of lush garden. Newest and humblest of them, the Women's College was a clutter of buildings scarce fancier than the town, but she gazed hungrily until she identified the bell tower and the slate roof of the new dining hall.

Never-rye Hill was capped with a little shrine, knee-high and fashioned of porphyry so worn that it was impossible to know what god it honored, whether Great One or Other or some being altogether different. It was traditional to leave a nut when one left Ulthar, and the shrine was half-buried in hazels and almonds, walnuts and acorns, everything much picked over by squirrels. She had forgotten to bring an offering, but a century ago, some thoughtful traveler had planted a walnut tree close by. It took but a moment to find a fallen nut in the long grasses and lay it among the others.

The small black cat from the College had seated itself upon the shrine's stained offering-slab (for it was not always nuts that were offered here) and was cleaning its ears with complete absorption. It was unlike cats to travel like this, but she also knew that cats lived according to their own schemes and agendas. "It grows harder from here," she warned the cat, but it dropped to the path and walked forward as though to say, *You are wasting time.*

Vellitt came to the great stone bridge that crossed the River Skai and paid the penny toll to cross. She inquired of the money-taker whether she remembered two people from the night before, but the girl only shook her head. Her brother had managed the booth; she had only begun her shift an hour ago. "People mostly don't cross at night, any case," she added with a melodramatic shiver. "On account of the ghost!"—set to launch into the story of the man buried alive in the bridge's masonry. But Vellitt had heard it before and moved on, leaving the girl to relate it to the reluctant ox-driver behind her.

Her plan was to follow the Lhosk-Hatheg road past Hatheg-town, to the great curve where it approached the zoogs' forest, just before it plunged into the Stony Desert to meet the caravan road. For now, she was still on the plains of the Skai: open country threaded through with hedges, pretty rolling farmland, and pasturage the dusty green of late summer, scattered with white-fleeced sheep. She stopped for lunch at an inn well past the Bridge, and afterward, she repacked her rucksack, to remove everything that four hours' walk made less imperative, arranging to have the excess shipped back to College. The black cat watched with interest, and when Vellitt at last shrugged back into the straps, it leapt easily onto the top flap and settled there. It almost exactly countered the weight she had just removed, but its breath was pleasant on her ear. It seemed a fair trade.

The afternoon was slower. She had always been a great walker, but it had been years since she had gone so far. Being sensible about her age, she had called it—but in fact there had been no drive to work harder when she was only traversing the mannerly Karthian Hills or the pleasant garden-lands of the Skai. Her muscles stretched and grew warm, began to ache and then grew numb: all usual enough for the first day out, she remembered.

The air was misted with pollen from ripening fields. Across a valley, she saw (and heard) a tractor trundling across a pasture, a glossy, violent red against all the green. But mechanical vehicles were still a recent and rare thing in these regions, and mostly it was oxen or zebras pulling carts and threshers, and the voices of the drivers calling out, *Chirac, chirac, hai!* The sun blanked the sky to a pale blue, the titanic swellings faded to no more than slight differences in tint and texture.

She stopped for the night just past the little town of Nir, at a road-inn called the Lost Lamb. No one there had seen Jurat and Stephan Heller. The only other travelers were three young traders with cinnamon and sandalwood from distant Oonai, on their way to the thousand gilded spires of Thran. They smelled of their sweet wares and she could not help but breathe deeply, but they, seeing only an old woman in sturdy shoes, did not speak to her.

Vellitt Boe awoke aching in every joint. For the first miles, all she could think of were hot baths and her research desk back at the University library, no doubt baking in the sunlight that came through the clerestory windows; but in time her stiffness eased with movement, and she began to walk as the far-traveler she had once been. Certainly, the morning was beautiful, the sun bright and the seething sky faded to faint basket-weaves. As she left the plains and ascended into the hills, the farmhouses and cottages became less frequent, and their fences had the look of being constructed to keep things *out* as much as *in*. The hedgerows grew wild, and sometimes she caught hints of a green glow in their tangled hearts.

She came to the top of a ridge and saw the country spread around her, the Lhosk-Hatheg Road a pale line across the tangled green and gold countryside, and the peaks: the green wooded slopes of Mount Lerion to her north, white-capped Mount Thurai to the northwest; and to the west, hazy with distance and so much larger than she ever remembered, the great mountain Hatheg-Kla, its snowy peak fading into the shifting sky, so that she could not be sure of its final heights.

She stopped at a remote house and bought bread, tomatoes, and slices of smoked goat's belly. Vellitt asked about Jurat and Stephan Heller, but the farm woman had seen nothing, only took the money unsmiling and returned inside, shutting the door firmly against the slight midday breeze. Vellitt lunched alone a mile later on the parapet of a stone bridge across the sun-spangled Reffle. Knowing the stream's reputation, she did not refill her canteen, and when the cat ambled down to investigate the water's edge, she called it back. A moment later her caution proved justified. A bird alighting on a willow-wand that overhung the Reffle dropped suddenly, as though dead or drugged, and a red-scaled carp the size of a wild boar rose from the shadows of the stream's bottom and sucked the bird in.

The afternoon was less pleasant, hotter and dusty. Her shoulders under the straps felt raw, and her thighs burned. Just before dusk she stopped at a farmhouse to rent a room from an unsmiling man who answered direct questions but offered nothing more. Yeh, Hatheg was just aways along t'road. Yeh, he saw a couple walking that way this very morn: the girl swart-haired and the man tall. Yeh, he might've been a dreamer (he made the Elder Sign); he had that look on 'm; but he wa'n't paying no attention, he had his own work to do, not idle like some. That night in the little attic room, Vellitt wrote Gnesa Petso: *I'm relieved, I suppose*, she ended. *I might have been wrong and Jurat on a dhow down the Skai, halfway to the coast.*

The third day started worse still: everything sore and a new, searing pain in her right heel where a blister had broken. When she came to Hatheg-town, she posted her letter and purchased food but did not tarry, and by midmorning she had come far enough that she saw a faint viridian glow on the scattered clouds in the north, light reflected from the glowing fungi of the zoogs' forest.

Past Hatheg, the road became a mere track. There were no people and no roadhouses or farms, but many tangled, shrubby copses; rangeland a-haze with pollen and insects; weed fields that cast up guerdons of flame-red blooms as high as her head. The green in the clouds grew brighter, and coming over a hill in the early afternoon, she saw the forest's edge to the north. The line between the rangeland and the glowing woodland looked so precise that it seemed almost to have been ruled by the Elder Ones.

She turned onto the next track that headed north. It was wide enough for carts but had fallen into disuse, and it ended a few miles later in the weed-choked yard of a ruined, crumbling grange, home only to dust and spiders. Vellitt walked to the grange well but the reservoir was dry, and she thought better of trying the rusted iron pump. It would, she suspected, be shriekingly loud in this silent place. After a short search, she found a narrow path leading toward the forest and followed it.

Zoogs were small, essentially cowards that would not threaten humans unless they felt they could get away with it. But she had no wish to find the limits of their cowardice, so in late afternoon she stopped a half-mile from the forest's edge at what must once have been a shepherd's close. The high, tight-folded stone walls were still largely intact, thick and taller than Vellitt, with a single narrow entrance through which sheep would have been driven. When she climbed a broken section, she found the stone remains of a shepherd's seat that overlooked the area around the close. She made a pad from her rain cloak and settled in, her flashlight and machete close at hand. It was surprisingly comfortable.

Cats move fearlessly between the dream lands, the moon, and the waking world—and to other, unknowable places—but this cat was no fool. It stayed close to Vellitt, and as night deepened it climbed into her lap and would not leave. "You should have considered all this before you came," Vellitt said. Her voice surprised her. It had been midmorning since she had heard any human sound.

She could not tell if it understood her. In her far travelling days, Vellitt had known a dreamer who claimed to understand the speech of cats, but of all the cats she had ever met in Ulthar—a town crammed with them—none had ever spoken to her, nor to anyone else, that she knew anyway. The dreamer had been a serious-minded man and dishonesty had not been his besetting flaw, so perhaps it was a waking-world thing.

Time passed. As night fell, the forest's viridian glow grew stronger, but this was the darkest sky she had seen in decades. She could see every constellation, every star. As well as she could recall from her schoolgirl lessons, she recited their names: Algol, Gemma, Arcturus, Mizar; the blue spark of Polaris; green-mantled Venus; the red disk of Mars, large enough that her outstretched thumb just covered it. Ninety-seven stars in the dream realms sky; six constellations.

Clarie Jurat had written, *He says there are millions of stars.* Vellitt had heard this before about the waking world, but she could not imagine it. Where would they all fit? The sky was hardly infinite. She could see its pendulous, titanic folds, its shifting patterns, black on black. And if each planet or star had its own buffeting, fretful, whimsical god, how could the waking world survive?

And so the night passed and always Vellitt's face turned to the scant stars and the moonless, massy sky beyond. Once she heard sounds, so faint that she wondered at first whether they were real, of long-toed paws pushing through grass and fluttering whispers. She turned on her flashlight and cast the homely yellow beam down into the grasses around the close. Silence fell suddenly. She was not disturbed again.

* * *

Vellitt Boe did sleep though she had not intended it, and awoke to a coruscating sky turned rose-pink by the sunrise. She continued along the narrow path. The cat remained with her, hunched on her pack so that she felt the tickle of its whiskers against her jaw. When she turned her face, she saw its eyes glowing leaf-green and intent.

The wall of underbrush that marked the forest margins thinned and was replaced by a thick mold underfoot, the rotting remains of the dead leaves that had fallen from the towering oaks crowding everywhere. Young oaks pushed through the mold, as did ferns of surprising size and pale-domed mushrooms several feet across. The tree trunks were wound with ivy, or ruffled with shelf-like fungi climbing as high as she could see, to where the oaks' groping boughs tangled into a canopy. The leaves blocked the sun except as a mottled glow, but the forest was light enough, from the green shadowless luminescence emitted by the fungi. The air was clammy and smelled of decay.

She remembered how to read the patterns the fungi made, and found her way to what passed for a zoog highway. She had a password she had learned long ago and she spoke it at intervals, though the fluttering noises did not come easily to her tongue, and she was not sure it would work after so many years. Though she did not see the zoogs, she heard them sometimes, just at the edges of what she could detect: the pattering of their narrow paws among the ferns, or a rustling that might have been mistaken for a breeze (save that there was none), and several times, the fluttering sounds of their whispered speech. The black cat crouched tight-muscled and unmoving on her pack. The zoogs would not have frightened her much when she was younger, but now. . . . And yet, why? *They* were not changed and, while she was older, neither had she altered in any fundamental way. Perhaps she was grown wiser with age.

After a time the highway branched. Recognizing her location, she took the right-hand path, coming at last to a clearing around a mighty slab of stone set into the forest floor: an access point to the under-realms fashioned by gugs in eons past. The zoogs feared it and would not approach, which made it a safe place to pause—provided the great slab did not lift.

Vellitt knew something of the under-realms from her far-traveling youth. It had been an accidental horror to fall through a sinkhole in the Mnar swamps with her companion. At first she would not have survived it without his knowledge, for he had alliances among the ghouls—slumping canine-faced creatures that ate the dead and were said to have secret routes into all worlds. He enlisted their aid in returning to the surface, and taught Vellitt bits of their glibbering, meeping speech as they traveled. But the party was attacked by ghasts—scabrous, humped, and horse-like, with flat faces and unsettling, intelligent eyes—and they had been separated. After endless dark whiles finding her way alone, she came to a city of gugs: enormous, oily-furred, and six-pawed monsters with vertical mouths that bisected their heads, framed by shining red eyes on stalks. Eventually she found a party of ghouls to whom she spoke in her limited way, and they brought her back to her companion. When they at last emerged, the sun was very bright. She had been underground for nearly a month.

Vellitt ate and rested beside the great slab, and resumed her long walk through the high-ceilinged tunnels of twisted wood. The zoogs returned to haunt her steps, and now she felt as though there were an intentionality to their stalking. The password had not worked after all: too old, or perhaps the zoogs no longer cared what might happen if they failed to honor it. They paced her beneath the ferns and mushrooms and in the branches overhead. At times, small loathsome paws reached out to brush her ankles or back. Their flutterings sounded excited, even to her unaccustomed ears.

Feeling like a fool, she drew the machete from its sheath. But perhaps she did not look like one, for the zoogs pulled back. Beyond the canopy daylight was ending, but she was too far into the forest to retreat. It never grew truly dark, though the viridian glow was like corpse-light, faint and slightly sickening to her eyes. Her electric torch's batteries would not last the night, so she fashioned a torch from a fallen branch and the contents of a small bottle of pitch she carried, relieved to find the skill remained.

She walked. The zoogs began pressing her again, but with sweeps of the torch she kept pushing them back. There seemed to be scores of them, never fully to be seen: glimpses of brown fur among the ferns, a prehensile tail zipping from sight, yellow eyes gleaming out at her from hidden places. Her arms grew tired. The cat growled steadily, barely audible.

A young zoog, bolder than its fellows, crept close and nipped her ankle. Unthinking, she swung the machete, connected with a meaty sensation that ran from her hand into her shoulder. The zoog fell back with a panicking, quavering howl entirely unlike their fluttering language. Again, the zoogs retreated, and she pressed forward. Again, they overcame their fear and crowded close. They were hunting her.

And Vellitt found that, despite her exhaustion and her age, she could run. She threw the torch toward a zoog that approached too nearly, and fled forward by the green light: the cat afoot and running, a fluid shadow just ahead. She knew where she was, for she passed a standing stone she remembered from years past, ancient, hexagonal, and pierced. She was close now. The zoogs seemed to know her goal as well, for several had climbed into the trees ahead of her and were waiting to drop on her. She shouted, "Go on then, you!"—her voice breathless and hoarse with anger—and as she ran beneath them, she raised the machete over her head. They chose instead to drop behind her and join the pursuing band.

The overhanging trees opened out as she ran into a clearing: a quarter-moon and the looming shadow of the mountain Hatheg-Kla against the black starred sky—and on moss-thick flagstones stood the gates, a basalt trilithon framing paired portals of black iron. For the first time she doubted herself, for only once before had she seen the Gate of Deeper Slumber, and then it had been ajar, and now the gates were closed and might be locked.

The zoogs poured into the clearing behind her and for the first time she could see them clearly: scores of brown, shadowy forms with long, articulate limbs, knee-high as they loped on all fours. Their forward-looking hunters' eyes shone as they raced toward her.

The cat streaked through a gap in the ironwork of the gate; and Vellitt following slammed into it with a deep ringing noise, as though someone had struck a gong the size of a city. At the immense sound the zoogs stopped short and with cries of fear, tumbled backward into the trees. Vellitt tore open a gate—unlocked after all—and passed onto a broad staircase of pale moss-covered stone. She ran to the first landing and there halted at last. The zoogs did not follow her. She was, perhaps, safe.

It took a long while to catch her breath. Before her heart had stopped pounding, her sweat had turned icy on her face and under her breasts and arms. The cat crouched beside her, panting in its small-lunged way, so she poured water into the canteen's cap, and the cat lapped it dry while she drained the rest. Her right ankle hurt viciously, and she bled in a dozen places from scratches caused by tearing through the branches. She had not known she could run so far—or at all—but as a young woman she had been quick and strong, and some of that remained.

She looked about. The zoogs' forest was not visible except as a glow that seemed to come from a great distance, much farther below than the steps she had ascended. From this side, the trilithon was the same rough-cut basalt, but the gates were not iron: one, carved of a single piece of ivory cut from some unknown but mammoth beast; the other, woven of broad strips of translucent horn. If she walked through those gates, would she find herself in yet another place, *her* dream lands? Did women have dream lands? In all her far-traveling, she had never seen a woman of the waking world nor heard of one, but she thought of the little picture card of AVIGNON, LA PLACE DE L'HORLOGE, the town square and all its women in their bright summer dresses. There were as many women as men in that image. Was that even possible?

Finally her exhaustion caught up with her: days of walking and only an hour or two of sleep in the past two. Vellitt dropped into something that was nearly a coma. If she dreamed, she remembered nothing of it.

She woke to full daylight. Her arms hurt from holding the torch and machete, and her ankle had swollen, but otherwise she felt amazingly well, alive as she had not in years. She smiled, remembering something a traveling companion had said long ago: *Nothing like not dying to make you feel alive.* Hungry as she was, she ate nothing, for she would have no more water until she came to the temple.

Curled close beside Vellitt's pack, the cat slept on. It had found its own meal, for there were bloody paw-prints upon the railing, and tufts of fur the greasy brown of a young zoog's pelt: impressive, for she would not have thought the cat was large enough for such prey. Only when Vellitt shouldered her pack did the cat stretch lengthily, blinking its vivid eyes against the morning sun. "Would you like a ride?" she asked and bent low, but it leapt to the railing and trotted upward.

It was said that the stairs between the Gate and the temple of Flame were seven hundred in number, but she quickly lost count. They hairpinned up forested crags so steep that she could reach out and touch the rock as she ascended. The stairs soon became no more than irregular granite ledges interposed with steep pitches of trail. She climbed beyond the tree line until there were no living things but Vellitt and the cat, which, against the nature and character of its kind, was systematically picking its way straight up the mountain. She still could not see Hatheg-Kla's uppermost reaches, only soaring cliffs fading into the pale patterns of the heavy-swelling sky.

Her muscles were aflame, and she labored for each wheezing breath. The air was thinner here, and it smelled different, as though spiced by strange seas and ice fields immeasurably distant. She wondered whether this was the smell of the waking world, or whether the scent was from space itself. Was she still *in* her world? When she paused for breath, as she often found herself forced to do, she saw behind her only an ocean of clouds eye-achingly bright in the sunlight, and overhead, the sky's faint, coruscating anthemions.

Not seven hundred steps but what seemed thousands; yet there was eventually an end to them. It had been a long time since she had looked up; her head was bent to watch her feet, focused on the next step and the next and the next, running with sweat until she ran out of moisture and it dried to salt on her skin. And suddenly there were no more steps and she raised her head.

She stood on a granite ledge some twenty paces across and twice that long, smooth as a lecture-hall floor and glittering with quartzite. To one side the world fell away into the cloud-fields she had climbed through, and above, the moiréed sky, so close it seemed she might reach out and touch some coil of that mutable substance. To the other side was a concave rock-face pierced everywhere with windows and doors and little balconies carved of living rock. A hundred feet over her head, the rock face bulged out, sheltering the ledge from the sun.

She was still catching her breath when she saw a man in one of the upper windows. Perceiving her, he vanished, reappearing a moment later upon a stone balcony to descend a ladder, which he managed nimbly despite the voluminous draperies of his violet-colored robes and the laced sandals upon his feet. He was civil to the cat but disdainful to her, though he could not do less than the ancient laws of the temple demanded, showing her to a guest cave and sending for food, water, and wine. She asked for news of the dreamer Stephan Heller and his companion: whether they lingered here or had passed already into the waking world—or had, perhaps, not yet arrived. He would say nothing. He could not disregard her application for an audience with the temple's priests, but he heard her with little courtesy and left immediately.

She drank water until sweat finally broke out, then ate. Her cave was cold, and glaring with light that streamed through a large opening high in one wall, but she slept as well as ever she had in her gabled rooms in Ulthar.

For the next two days, she waited in growing frustration. She sent messages to the high priests Nasht and Kaman-Thah via the disdainful acolyte assigned to attend her, and by every other violet-robed man she saw, priest or proselyte. She gave her name but did not speak of the College, nor of her status as a professor of the University, for she knew that away from the garden-lands of the world there was often little notion of educating women. Otherwise there was nothing she could do. She learned on the first day that she was the only guest.

She filled her hours. She paced on the polished ledge watching the sky shift, picotage blurring into strange foliation and congeries of fracturing cubes; trying, as she always did, to understand the underlying rules. Since it was not forbidden, she also explored the honeycombed caves of the temple. Many of the corridors and rooms were torch lit, smelling of pitch and sweet resins, but there were deeper, less travelled tunnels illuminated only by lichens that glowed a dull, cool brown; and once, a sickly pink that caused an immediate and intense headache which lasted for hours.

Late the first afternoon, she found a long room lit by a row of windows high upon one wall. There were dark paintings on the walls, glass-faced cabinets, and tall shelves stacked with scrolls and handbooks. She took down a small scroll, written in a script she recognized as Ib'n, which meant it was unimaginably ancient; and indeed the vellum (if that is what it was) cracked as she held it, merely from the pressure of her fingers. She replaced it carefully, and took instead a handbook bound in dun-colored buckram with strange words upon its cover: *Daniel Defoe Moll Flanders*. They meant nothing, so she flipped the book open—it was her own language; the strange words were names—and she realized it was a book from the waking world. She looked more carefully. Many of the books were similarly alien, and inside the cabinets were unfamiliar objects of steel or brass or a bright glossy substance like lacquer. She reopened the book and began to read, but an aged man in violet robes so old they had faded to lavender entered the room, and castigated her for touching the books. Despite the obvious differences in language, age, and sex, his tone was a mirror of that of Uneshyl Pos, Librarian at the Women's College; for all librarians are the same librarian.

On the second day, Vellitt found herself near the cavern of Flame itself—she could hear a rich, roaring crackling and see firelight of an inconstant bloody red flickering at the far end of a tunnel—but she was turned aside by a severe-looking man with a great forked red beard, who had something of grandness in his manner and bore beaded crimson gloves upon his hands. He turned away, but she laid her hand on his arm and spoke, "Please. I am seeking two people, a dreamer from the waking world, and one of our own, a young woman of Ulthar. Can you at least tell me whether they passed this way?" The priest looked at her hand as though deciding whether to push it off, but said nothing, and she persisted: "I have a duty to retrieve my charge, Clarie Jurat. I cannot go without knowing whether she has passed through here."

She thought he gave a start at the name, but he replied only, "I will tell you this: no one of the temple has opened the Gate, not in many years."

She was not unaccustomed to rhetorical evasions, so she asked a little tartly, "Then, has anyone else?"

But the man said only, "This part of the temple is forbidden," and left her. She watched his receding back, rigid with disapproval. She toyed with the notion of defying him—and indeed, the young woman she had been might have done this, trusting she would not be caught; at the worst, that the priests would not kill her—but she was older and could no longer trust to youth or beauty to get her out of trouble. And wiser: There was no point to such defiance.

She turned at random down another corridor and found herself in a high-ceilinged chamber filled with a gentle white light. The lovely cavern had all the appearance of a secret garden, for upon its floor were green mosses like grass, spangled with colonies of mold like starry white flowers; it was these that illuminated the space. Tall, heavy-stiped fungoids trailed hyphae, elegant as willow-wands, and beneath them were things that looked like bright hostas, though as she approached she saw that they were fungi as well. The scent reminded her of lilies but was not. The slight strangeness was not unpleasant.

A broad pillar rose at the cavern's center, pierced with a gate caked so thickly with lichens that she could not identify the figures wrought into the iron, except that they were creatures. Inside the pillar was a staircase of white stone, circling upward into shadow. The cat (which had accompanied her for its own inscrutable reasons) loped forward, squeezed through the gate, and trotted up the stairs. Vellitt placed her hand on the iron, but the metal burned as though it had been newly pulled from a fire, and she stepped back quickly.

She was returning to her rooms when a purple-robed boy found her, panting like a dog in summertime from running. "Nasht has called for you," he gasped, and all but dragged her by the hand. She followed him, wondering whether she was to be cast from the temple at last. The boy trotted ahead, looking back every few feet, but she refused to rush. She would not meet the high priest Nasht sweaty and breathless.

They came to tall doors of white wood bound in iron. The boy effaced himself; wordlessly the two acolytes standing sentry opened the doors. She stepped forward and found herself in a long, narrow audience room, lined with statues of unsettling configuration and dimly illuminated by sconced torches burning every shade of red: crimson, scarlet, and carmine. Raised on a many-stepped dais of polished basalt at the room's far end were two seats as grand as thrones, and over each hung an immense boulder of black granite that glittered with reflected flames. The left-hand seat was empty, but a black-bearded man sat on the other, wearing heavy robes of indigo and violet, and a pshent studded with opals. She stepped forward.

The High Priest looked down at her and exclaimed, "Veline!" in a voice that summoned a memory she could not quite grasp.

She looked curiously up at him. "Not for many years. I am Vellitt Boe of Ulthar. I come for news of Clarie Jurat, and to retrieve her if I can."

The man stood, so that his pshent brushed the overhanging boulder. Something in the manner of his movement plucked at that lost memory.

"Reon?" she said hesitantly.

Recognition changed things. The High Priest Nasht, who once had been Reon Atescre, led her from the red-lit audience room through a door behind the thrones to a small windowless cave, stone-walled, low-ceilinged, and furnished with surprising attention to comfort. Spots of light from the many pierced-work lanterns spangled across the plush wall tapestries, the heavy padded furniture, and the shelves stacked with novels and pastoral poetry: a room at odds with the severity of the temple as a whole.

He poured glasses of the sweet green wine of Hap, and they sat looking at each another for a moment. Reon Atescre of Sona Nyl had been slim and laughing-eyed, a lighthearted, fearless man who was not attracted to women, seeing her for what she was and not what he wanted her to be, and therefore an easy companion to her. They had parted ways in the infamous demon-city Thalarion for no reason but the restlessness that is in the young. In all the years since, she had heard nothing of how he fared. Now, so changed, and heavier altogether: his face nearly hidden behind his black, spade-shaped beard, so that she could not see his mobile mouth. His light step had turned ponderous with weight and authority. Even his voice seemed heavier, its humor silted away.

"I have had a vision, but first I'll answer the question you've been asking for two days. The dreamer Stephan Heller came to the temple of Flame three days ago at dusk, with a woman of our world, though he did not give her name."

She came to her feet. "So I was hours behind them! You—"

But Nasht interrupted, "*Listen*," and in a more natural voice, added, "I see you are still as hasty as ever you were, Veline. Leaving our lands is always easy for dreamers, but Stephan Heller wanted his companion to cross, and he had one of the silver keys that opens the Upper Gate. But people of our world may not pass into the waking world, so we barred their passage. That night, he prayed to the Flame, and my fellow priest Kaman-Thah had a vision. It was an edict from an Elder One, demanding that she be allowed to pass. So we stepped aside."

Vellitt turned from her pacing. "I could have overtaken them! You've wasted *days*, Reon."

"Sit *down*, Veline. You're giving me a headache," Nasht said, sounding in that moment so like the friend of her youth that she did so, leaving unspoken all the hot words that warmed her mouth. "We didn't know she was followed, but we couldn't have refused the edict in any case. But this afternoon, the Flame spoke to me. It was a single piece of information only, like a thunderclap in my mind: that Clarie Jurat is the granddaughter of a god."

Vellitt shook her head. "No. Her father is a burgher of Ulthar. She was born there. He owns shares in the Woolmarket."

Nasht said, "Actually, I should have guessed when I saw her— she has the look of the people of Leng."

"Hypothetical Leng . . ." Vellitt had grown up on stories of that icy and inhumane plateau bounded to the north by the great mountain Kadath, where the gods half-slept in blind, muttering madness, under the malicious eyes of their divine keepers.

"*Not* hypothetical," he said. "I've been there. But some of the stories we learned as children are true. At times, a god escapes from Kadath, takes human form, and lives in Leng. For a while he thinks a little as we do: he loves, he dreams, he drinks wine and laughs at jokes and picks fights in taverns. Clarie Jurat's grandfather escaped and fell in love with a local woman, and after a year or two he returned to Kadath, and his lady bore a daughter."

"Leaving her alone," Vellitt said.

"Not by choice, I expect. But there's no real escape from Kadath, even for the gods. Their keepers find them and drag them back. They became mad and forgetful again; but sometimes they dimly recall their freedom and their lost loves, and if they can, they watch over the children of their children."

"Like Jurat. So was it her grandfather that commanded her passage?"

Nasht frowned. "No. And that troubles me. It can't have been him. I know the wheres and wherefores of many gods. The Elder One that is Clarie Jurat's grandfather sleeps deranged and dreaming on his silk-draped couch on Kadath, and he has slept like that for many years."

Vellitt rubbed her eyes. "But why would another god care?"

"What if Clarie Jurat's loving grandfather awakens and finds her gone out of this world? Rage, vengeance, reprisal and annihilation. I think *that* is the intention of the god that sent the vision."

"Ulthar." Of course. The gods of the dream realms were petty, angry and small. History was filled with tales of their irrational rages and disproportionate vengeances, of cities buried in poisonous ash, of garden-lands laid waste. Annihilation. In her far-traveling days, she had walked in these god-blasted wastelands. Once, she had found a child's gold anklet, half-melted and still encircling a small, charred bone. Ulthar's narrow streets and pretty squares, its houses and halls and temples: all blasted by god-fire and melted to slag, to glass; and its people—the students and wool merchants, the grocers and stable masters and dressmakers and every one of them—all food for carrion beasts and ghouls.

The grandfather of Clarie Jurat would do it, because it is what gods did: destroy things and people. She set down her glass carefully with fingers grown suddenly nerveless.

Nasht had been silent, watching her expressions. Now he replied. "Ulthar and more. Nir and Hatheg, and all the plains of the River Skai, even. Who knows why? Perhaps the Old Ones play latrunculi, and Clarie Jurat is a coin in their game, and Ulthar would be an incidental loss. Or perhaps Ulthar and the rest are just ants under the feet of fighting drunkards. Or perhaps a hate-filled god revels in destruction and pain, and causes it however he may. Veline, I've served them for twenty years, and I know little more than you."

She said with a tight laugh, "I was taught to worship them, but how can I? How can any reasonable person? Mathematics does no harm, at least."

"Worship? Is *that* what we do?" Nasht tipped his glass, watching the lamp light spangle through the wine. "We placate them, that's all."

"All right." Vellitt heard the tremble in her voice; and then, taking a breath, repeated more strongly, "All right. So. I must— *must*—go after her and bring her home. Reon, will you let me through the Upper Gate?"

Nasht said slowly, "It's forbidden, but I think I would anyway. If I had the means. I have not been able to leave Hatheg-Kla for all these years, but I remember the Skai plains—the fields. The sunlight on the wheat fields. How beautiful it all was. But only dreamers have keys, and not even all of them."

"So there are other keys?"

There were, but only five of which Nasht had certain information: Stephan Heller's, gone into the waking world. One, with a dreamer who had gone questing for the pillar-city Wenč of legend; it could not be guessed where he was, nor even whether he yet lived. Another, in the pocket of a waking-world man grown addicted to ghenty and wandering somewhere in the Six Kingdoms—unless he had pawned it for the silver. And one lost into remote Zobna, when the dreamer Adrian Fulton had been seized by shantak birds and carried screaming away.

The fifth belonged to Randolph Carter, who reigned as king in distant Ilek-Vad. Vellitt nearly dropped her glass.

"*Carter?*"

Nasht paused at her tone. "You know him?"

"I did," and she started laughing, surprising them both. "He is a king now? Of course, he would be. Always a man with ambition. We traveled together, after you and I parted."

Nasht tipped his head with such a quizzical expression that she added dryly, "Yes, Reon, *just* like that."

"Is that a problem?" he asked. "Love complicates everything."

She said only, "For my part, no. It will have to be him, anyway— Ulthar's need would outweigh all the rest. But I haven't seen him for thirty years—water long lost to the sea. And there are no other routes?"

"Undoubtedly, but I don't know them. I'm sure they're all of them very dangerous."

"Ilek-Vad." Vellitt tipped her head, listening to the crackling behind her ears. "That is—very far. Months. And Carter. But there's no choice, is there? I'll leave at dawn."

Nasht arranged for meats and breads to be prepared for her journey, sighing a little as he did so. "I wish . . . but I've gotten heavy and slow," he said, slapping his belly with a rueful laugh that was filled with the Reon Atescre that was. "I don't know how you've stayed in the same place for so long without growing mortar and moss as I have."

It was still early. There was much wine, though Vellitt had barely one glass to every three Nasht drank and he did not seem to grow drunk. Perhaps in this manner he had found the means to reconcile his heart to his lot. They dined together, speaking as friends do, long-parted and soon to part again: of their lives as they were now and as they had once been, sliding without pause between memory and present preoccupations. Reon Atescre had been a impish man, light-footed and merry, and Veline Boe scarcely less so, and they had laughed often then, and now as well, as they retraced their travels together through Sarrub and Parg, Zar and Xura.

They spoke less of the subsequent years. After leaving Thalarion, Vellitt Boe had continued to far-travel and, meeting Randolph Carter a year later, journeyed with him for a time. A year or two after they had parted, she stopped her wayfaring, attended the Women's College at the University in Celephaïs, and accepted a post in Ulthar: a sensible decision, undoubtedly the right one. But speaking with Reon, she realized suddenly that her life in Ulthar had never seemed quite real. She had not bothered to relocate from her chaotically gabled rooms on the Fellow's Stair because it hadn't mattered to her. She had pretended, and even convinced herself, but Ulthar had never been home.

Nasht's story was shorter than hers. After he and Vellitt had parted ways, he sailed to the harbor city of Lelag-Leng in the far north, ascending the plateau of frozen Leng itself. "The men of Leng were as beautiful as I'd been told." He raised his glass in a silent toast, though his face was somber. "But it was cold and always dark, and the people were suspicious of me. They don't see strangers often, except the gods who escape to walk among them, and I certainly wasn't that. But there was one house that welcomed me and fed me. They drugged my food and tied me to a stone to be burnt alive as a sacrifice. The Elder Ones accepted me, but not as my hosts intended, maybe. I didn't burn. When I awoke, I was lying on a slab of smoking basalt, my clothes charred to ash, and a ukase in my head like a pounding brown noise: *Reon Atescre is dead. Nameless go to Hatheg-Kla and become Nasht.* My host's fields and flocks had been blasted to ash. I have been here since."

"And your family?" Vellitt said softly. Reon had always been full of sunny stories about his brothers and sisters, and she had gone with him once, to stay with his parents for the Turfilae festival, when they had welcomed her with laughter and home-brewed ale: a loving home, and joy-filled.

His voice was empty. "Reon Atescre is dead. I hope they forgot him quickly."

He did not smile again that night.

Before they separated, he led her to the library and took from a shelf a small flat object of black enamel ornamented with silver bosses and black cabochons. He spoke prayers over it that caused shadows to move through his eyes, and left him looking pale and drawn behind his black beard. "There," he said finally, and handed it to her. "If you make it to the waking world, this box will bring you to Clarie Jurat."

"What is it like, the waking world?" she said, turning the box over in her hands. It was surprisingly heavy and cool to the touch.

The question had been idle, but he answered, in a voice of visions: "Filled with strangeness and monsters. The sky never ends. The night has a million million stars. There are no gods." He had no recollection of his words a moment later, even when she repeated them to him; only laughed and said, "Well, you can tell me the truth of it all when you return."

"Of course," she had said. "When I return."

Back in her guest-cave after their farewells, she wrote to Gnesa of everything she had learned and of her plans to go to Ilek-Vad and ask Carter for his key, return, and charm or force her way past the keepers of the cavern of Flame to the Upper Gate. She did not see the cat all that night, but when the first light through the high window was cold lavender with approaching dawn, it returned, its whiskers spattered with the gore of some tiny beast, and groomed itself contentedly, cleaning blood and flecks of matter from its face. So it also was stronger than it had been in Ulthar, lean with muscle though still small, and when it followed her onto the white ledge and back down the stairs, she did not seek to dissuade it.

Dawn departures. How many of these had there been in those years of far-traveling? And now, again.

Down was as wearying as *up* had been, but more quickly traversed. She looked out on what seemed an eternal, creamy sheet of clouds and above them the tesselate shell-forms and shingling scrolls of the louring sky, but eventually she descended into the clouds and saw nothing, emerging to observe that what had been an featureless sheet of cirrus from above was, from this side, no more than a single cumulus cloud capping Hatheg-Kla's apparent heights. Passing through the horn and ivory gates in late morning, she encountered no zoogs. But she had no wish to tempt her luck and left the forest by the most direct route. By the time she crossed its margin, the westward sun was settling into a cloud the color of dried blood. She moved out quickly onto a dry wasteland of stones and sand, scattered with patches of thorny shrub and dry grasses that scraped any exposed bare skin, raising tiny, stinging red lines.

Just before dark, she found a place of trilithons and shadowy statues of inhuman form: a ruined temple complex to some unknown god, blasted by its jealous master, razed by some divine enemy, or trampled by great beasts, time, or circumstance. She settled on a ruined pavement cradled in the corner of a crumbling shrine wall and built a fire from the branches of a dead thorn tree. The wood was dry and resinous, burning quickly with sweet-smelling green flames. Vellitt laid out her blanket, sighing a little, for her bones ached already in expectation of the hard bed, but when she laid back, it was with relief. The temple's beds had been soft and the food excellent—the priests were not of an ascetic order—but the air seemed purer down here.

She looked up. The gibbous moon seemed very low tonight—as though, were she still the young woman who had scaled Noton, it would be no great task to swing herself up onto its shining surface—but as she watched, it began to move, rounding to full as it sailed to the east.

She thought of Carter. Not a tall man but dark and handsome with excellent teeth: attractive in the way of all dreamers, but always with an essential, solitary coldness. In her far-traveling years, she had met five waking-world men that she knew of, and they had all seemed to share this.

She had never met a woman from the waking world. Once she asked Carter about it.

"Women don't dream large dreams," he had said dismissively. "It is all babies and housework. Tiny dreams."

Men said stupid things all the time, and it was perhaps no surprise that men of the waking world might do so as well, yet she was disappointed in Carter. *Her* dreams were large, of trains a mile long and ships that climbed to the stars, of learning the languages of squids and slime-molds, of crossing a chessboard the size of a city. That night and for years afterward, she had envisioned another dreamland, built from the imaginings of powerful women dreamers. Perhaps it would have fewer gods, she thought as she watched the moon vanish over the horizon, leaving her in the darkness of the ninety-seven stars.

From where she lay there were several routes to Ilek-Vad. The fastest would be to go north by northeast and meet the Oonai-Sinara caravan road, which would take her to the headwaters of the Xari. She could follow the river, take passage in Sinara on a dhow to the Cerenarian Sea, and there find a ship sailing east to the twilit ocean at the foot of the glass cliffs of Ilek-Vad. Between now and then, there would be weather: this was Sextilis, but with Septiver, autumn could come, and by Octaver there would be the start of the winter seas. And beyond all that, distance in the dream lands shifted according to laws not the wisest geographer could understand, subject to the whims of the bickering gods. In all, it would take weeks—months. So much time lost—and to be lost—and not even on a certainty.

She fell asleep on her plans. She awoke once to an animal noise heard afar, and felt the black cat's paw touching her face. The air was the deep cold of desert nights, and she had curled into a ball to preserve her warmth. She made a small opening and the cat crept into the blanket and pressed its chilled body to her, where it warmed quickly. She laid her hand on its fur. It smelled of killing, for it had been hunting.

She traveled more quickly this time. Her aches changed each day, but she was growing stronger, and the tricks of the road came back to her: how to tend her feet at the end of a long day; how to shape a hollow for sleeping in sandy soil; how to build a protective perimeter of shifting stones and noisy shrubs. Some skills had improved with age. She was silent now in ways she never had been at twenty-five, as though her bones themselves had grown lighter.

Though she had matches and the electric torch still retained some charge, she took pleasure in using flint and tinder to start her nightly fires.

The caravan road was not so busy as it had been before the Five Oases had been turned to venom, but she saw occasional bands of traders on camel-back, and she was passed once by a courier riding his zebra fast toward Oonai, leading two backup mounts. Wild places are emptier of large predators than any town-dweller imagines, and she saw nothing larger than an adolescent rock-cat with the spots of infancy still fading from its flanks; but she heard the coughs of a red-footed wamp, and once, far away, the howling of a pack of the long-legged gray dogs that dwell in the deserts. The black cat of Ulthar grew still leaner and dustier. It hunted for its own food now, though it was happy to take bits of dried duck meat from her fingers when they paused in the middle of the day. It walked as much as it rode on her pack.

The desert changed, sandy soil and shrubs to a dirty white sand flecked with low, flat succulents, then red-gold rocks and waist-high sagebrush. She climbed into woodland and junipers, and eventually came to the icy headwaters of the Xari, cradled in a cirque of quartzite that glittered in the midday sun. She followed the river as it danced northward down a succession of waterfalls and rapids past the first remote homesteads. She slept for the first time in a week upon a mattress, in a hamlet that had no name— no name, for they had decided centuries before that anonymity would make it harder for Elder Ones (or tax men) to find them; except that everyone came to call them the Unnamed Village and so their plan failed, after all. Everyone seemed to chatter endlessly: talkative innkips, voluble bakers, garrulous farmers. She had grown silent in her days in the desert.

She came to Sinara, where the Xari descended in a final sparkling cascade before settling into sedate middle age and a mannered progression down the Valley of Narthos. She booked passage on a dhow leaving in the morning. The trip to Xari-mouth would take between three and nine days—depending, the shipkip told her with a sour look as he made the Elder Sign: depending on wind and weather; depending on the ways the inconstant land might alter as they crossed it; depending on whether the attentions of the whimsical gods were drawn to the slim-hulled white dhow.

It was barely midday, so she took a room in an inn and called for a bath. As she undressed, she saw a stranger, taller-seeming (because leaner) than the woman in her mirror back in Ulthar; the coppery skin of her face and arms grown darker; her black and silver hair tangled into the elf-locks of a mad visionary. She looked—not younger than she had in Ulthar; but wilder, more powerful: more like the Veline Boe who had traveled in her clear-eyed youth as far as Narath, as far as Rinar. She ruefully shook her head and bathed, and walked into Sinara's main town, to find a place that might clean the sand from her clothing and blankets, and into a shop where a woman did things to her hair until it fell in many tiny shining silver-black ropes about her face, and she looked less mad and more visionary. Also, it would be much easier to take care of, now that her quest had grown so much longer. But it was a slow process, and it was nearly dark when she emerged at last from the woman's door.

The dhow left at dawn. Because there were no other women, the shipkip had with reluctance given her a room to herself, a tiny berth behind the galley that smelled of onions and garlic, for the cook was from Asagehon. On the first day, the shipkip tried to have the black cat cast overboard. Vellitt objected, and the cat vanished into some hidden recess of the dhow. The contretemps left her friendless, so she spent her days on deck, watching the Valley of Narthos unspool itself, bright and heartbreakingly beautiful.

Summer was ending, and the first gingkos flared brilliant yellow against the green of those garden-lands. This was gentle country, comparatively free of great beasts, so the farms and orchards were large. The air that blew across the deck was rich with the smells of ripening fruit and grain. She had not come this way in years, but the landmarks came back to her: now a red-tiled riverside inn, now the acres of reedy backwater called Bakken, now the hillside orchards, a boatyard, a silver-walled temple, a misshapen oak tree isolated in a ploughed field and bound tightly in chains. But there were also differences. A swath of fields had been burnt to the ground, the soil scarred the dark blue that indicated divine fire, and the water downstream was for many miles stained black as tea.

The passing of days concerned her, but in the end it was a quick sail. On the morning of the fourth day, the dhow docked at Cydathria's riverside wharves. When she disembarked, the small black cat appeared as though conjured by a stage magician, and preceded her down the gangway. It was hard not to see the flick of its tail as an insolent farewell to the shipkip.

Vellitt Boe went immediately to the office of the harbormaster, who eyed her with contempt and tried to serve the man standing behind her first. But she had taught just such young men in her Topology lectures back at the University: it was an annoyance but no more to check his insolence and collect the information she needed. There were (he told her, his consonants as clipped as he could make them) five ships in Xari-mouth scheduled to set off in the next few days. Two were sailing to Ilek-Vad, with stops: a southern trireme without a name, and a three-masted thoti, the *Medje Löic*. Or (added the harbormaster, uninterested) she might wait: another would come soon enough. Cydathria was always busy in the autumn, as ships came for the products of the Narthos orchards.

She walked along the great jetty to where she could see the ocean-going ships, some busy at the granite wharfs and others at anchor in the Throat, awaiting their turn. It was a sunlit day with a light wind that breathed salted air into her face.

The trireme was loading, a black-hulled vessel with a single towering mast. She recognized its type, and knew better than to take passage.

She fell in love with the *Medje Löic* the minute she identified it, out in the Throat. The unladen ship rode high, and the perfect proportions of its rigging and hull were clear. In an earlier decade, she would have taken passage on so graceful a ship without regard to destination; she would willingly have sailed off the world's edge into the abyssal chaos if she could do so cradled among these flowing shapes. Beauty, true beauty, had that power.

She tracked down the *Medje Löic*'s captain in a dockside office, irrationally afraid that the man in line ahead of her might take the last berth, or even that the captain might for some reason refuse her; but there were still berths, and her money was of course good. "The cat as well?" the captain asked, for it had followed her and was absorbed in examining the corners of the office. "We've a cat already, so yours'll have to work it out with Finellio, but *Medje*'s a big boat. We're scheduled into dock tomorrow night for loading. Stay at the Red Dog, and we'll contact you there."

The rest of the day was spent in errands. She exchanged two of the letters of credit for more gold, grateful for the Bursar's foresight, and walked up to Cydathria's High Town to purchase the things she would need for a journey that had stretched from days to months. She showed her credentials at the scholarium and was admitted to their library, where she wrote to Gnesa. She found a narrow shop she knew of old and bought a quire of paper and new pens for the voyage, and returned late to the Red Dog.

The next day, she took a ferry across Xari-mouth to Jaren, to see the home of her childhood. The town did not appear to have changed much, everything a smaller, stodgier version of Cydathria: the short granite wharfs for such boats as could brave the shallows on this side of the harbor; the warehouses, shops, and inns of Jaren-bas, crammed between the waterfront and the rosy cliff; the zigzag road and clever zebra-propelled funicular up to Jaren-haut; the smell, omnipresent, of the sea. In Jaren-haut, she walked along the High Street, past the shop where her mother had had her shoes made and the arcade where they had bought milk and vegetables and meat. The flescher was gone, replaced by a man that sold green-and blue-veined cheeses. The confectionary was still there, and still smelled of buttercream and sugar and baking. Nothing inside had changed, not even the order in which the sweets were arranged, but she did not recognize the woman behind the counter.

She took the right turn onto Lebië, a lane too steep for wheels. It had been possible to see Jaren's wharves from the top of the maple tree at the end of Lebië, and each day, she and her brother had watched the ferries from Cydathria, to look for the tiny, dark, upright figure of their father. They knew to the minute how long it took for him to get to Jaren-haut, so they met him when he came off the funicular. He solemnly paid them a penny each to carry home his folio and any parcels there were.

When she had been small, Vellitt had indulged the fantasy all children had, that these were not her parents, that someday an Elder One, kindly, wise, and handsome, would reclaim her. It had not been until after her father's death that she realized the father-god of her imaginings was exactly like him.

Their mother's absences were harder to predict, for she had been a sometime sailor even after her marriage. This happened whenever she could find a ship that took women as crew, though there were few, mostly just hoppers shuttling between Cydathria and Hlanith; but occasionally an ocean-going xebec. She had not returned from one of her rare blue-water trips, when her ship had been pulled underwater by something immeasurably vast and hungry. The news had come to Jaren in Vellitt's sixteenth summer. Her father made her promise never to sail, but when he died in her nineteenth year (pneumonia; it had been a terrible winter), she bought passage on the first ship to leave after the funeral—a schooner running to Sarkmouth, where the dark marshes of Lomar met the Cerenarian Sea's icy western reaches. Lomar was at all times grim, and in the month of Gamel it was also bitterly cold and windy, the air laced with acrid snow. She responded to its bleakness as a reflection of her own sorrow. She did not come back to Jaren for five years. Her brother had in that time married a humorless woman and grown stern. He was gone now as well.

Their house was still there, a tall, narrow structure still painted blue-gray, but the shutters were vermillion now instead of green, and beneath the windows, the small pine trees in urns had been replaced by pots of ceramic nightflowers. After a time, she walked back down through Jaren, returning to Cydathria just as the sun set.

There was a message awaiting her at the Red Dog: the *Medje Löic* was at the Sea-Eel Wharf, taking in cargo and supplies. Passengers were advised to report to the thoti in the morning.

The College had a triannual tradition of presenting a University play during Somar-term and Vellitt had occasionally assisted behind the scenes. The frenzied activity on the *Medje Löic* reminded her a little of that, the decks crammed with sailors and shore workers racing in interleaving patterns without collisions as they loaded the last cargo and stores.

She watched from the upstairs parlor of the tavern at the end of the wharf—also called the Sea-Eel—where the passengers had been sent to keep them out of the way. They clustered at the windows or sat writing final letters: mostly solitary men in the carefully inconspicuous clothing that marked experienced travelers, but also a party of traders from Kled unafraid to mark their wealth with the excellence of their jackets, a courier and his guard in green and yellow livery, and a chatty man who introduced himself to everyone, even her, claiming to be from Rinar. His accent and ornate layered tunics were not quite perfect, and she pegged him for the commoner sort of shipboard grifter. She was surprised that the captain had not seen through him and barred passage. He must have paid well.

One of the solitary men had the look to her of a far-traveller. She knew that expression, that posture: She had seen it in herself for years and learned to recognize it in others. When he looked at her, did he see it as well? No, she was settled: Professor of Maths at Ulthar: friends, a hobby of botany, her rooms. This cat, currently curled beneath one of the chairs watching everyone's feet with an engaged, assessing air.

She was the only woman, of course, but she was used to that. In her years of far-traveling, she had met a few others like her, though they usually wayfared with a husband—legal or common-law or false—for too many men misunderstood a woman who traveled alone. Sometimes she and Reon Atescre had pretended to be married as being easier for them both. So had she and Randolph Carter, though in that case there *had* been love, she thought. As a young woman, when she had been beautiful and had worn her hair short and her clothes loose to conceal that fact, she had known all the signs of men and read them well enough that she had been successfully robbed only three times and raped once, but none of those had burned from her the hunger for empty spaces, strange cities, new oceans.

Final embarkation was in late afternoon. Her cabin was a near-perfect cube of teakwood scarce taller than she, with a built-in bunk, clipping hooks for clothing, a little folding desk, and, to her delight, a porthole, though it would not open. Vellitt unpacked quickly. Following her into the room, the cat assumed immediate possession of a yak-wool scarf she tossed for a moment upon the bunk. "I need that, cat," she warned, but it only curled tighter and gazed up with bright eyes. In the end, the scarf remained there for the rest of the voyage.

She visited the two public cabins assigned to passengers. The dining cabin's single table was not quite large enough for them all to eat together—they were thirteen—and so, she was told, people might if they chose take their meals in the main cabin, apart from the others. The Kled traders had already claimed for themselves one of the main cabin's tables, and had laid out the first arrangement of tiles for a game that she knew from experience would take days to complete. There were other tables and chairs, a selection of small stringed instruments, and a single cabinet crammed with the sorts of books people read on long voyages: lengthy biographies, mountaineering sagas, popular page-turners from twenty years back, a few classics of the sort that go unread unless there are no alternatives.

The *Medje Löic* left the wharf at dusk, picking its way to an anchorage in the Throat. Vellitt stood on deck for a time, watching the torch lights of Jaren and the gas-jet glow of Cydathria, then slept soundly in her narrow, rocking bed. She did not dream, nor did she feel the first living swell of the sea along the thoti's hull as it weighed anchor and began its voyage.

The *Medje Löic* was a beautiful sailor; and with the wind in a fair quarter, the air cool, and the days Septiver-bright, Vellitt spent much of her time on the aft deck, watching the land pass, or else gazing up through the layered, complex geometries of the wine-colored lateen and settee sails to the foliant sky beyond. The man she had identified as another far-traveler also preferred the aft deck, and they spoke occasionally, as when he pointed out the flying city Serranian, so far to port and so high that she could barely see the pink-marble towers against the pillaring cumulus clouds. Tir Lesh Witren was his name.

This was shore-hopping, the land always in sight to starboard. They passed the jungles of Kled, league after league of rolling hills above rocky shoreline, cloaked entirely in a surprising lush green, for the trees of Kled did not lose their leaves in winter. The air was rich with spices and flowers, and she took in great lungsful. At night she saw scatterings of light ashore, as of towns lit by gaslight or even electricity.

At first, she ate in the crowded dining cabin, but the other passengers had little to say to her, and she found their conversation (all of trade and card-games) dull, so she began to take her meals in the main cabin, reading books she found on the crowded shelves, or content in her thoughts. She was joined sometimes by Tir Lesh Witren, or one or two of the others. The most frequent was the youngest of the Klethi traders, who eyed her with a certain awed fascination and spoke with her as though she were eighty instead of fifty-five, asking questions about events of ancient history as though she might have been a witness, loudly, slowly, and with great courtesy.

On the fourth day, they rounded a cape and there was a single pinnacle of pure labradorite rising a hundred feet above the waves. In the Septiver midafternoon sun, it was striated purple and gray and blue, like the wing of a grackle. But her memories of other voyages overlaid the view: a stormy midmorning a year after her father's death, when the stone had seemed to shine with an inner violet light; a summer afternoon when the pinnacle looked nearly lavender; a night when she stood on the ship's deck with a man and the pinnacle had been a spear of platinum aimed at the full moon resting overhead. But that one, she remembered the kiss more than the rock.

On the morning of the eighth day, the thoti coasted into the port of Hlanith. Passengers and cargo were to be exchanged, but the captain was eager for a fast return to the sea. "Twenty-four hours," he told Vellitt: "I'll sail with or without you."

Hlanith had much the look of Ulthar but sturdier—as indeed it had to be, a port town facing north. Contact was frequent between the two, along a pikeway through the Karthian Hills; and since becoming a professor, she had visited more than once in her ramblings. It took no time to locate the last few oddments she decided she needed for the voyage. She stopped for tiffin at a little tea house she remembered from years past, for it would be weeks before she ate greens again. She wrote and posted yet another letter to the Dean. It felt repetitive, tedious to write—*on my way, still going; yes, indeed, another day traveling*—but it needed to be done to keep Gnesa and the College informed. But more than that, it anchored her to her mission and her home; for as the miles of her journey multiplied, Ulthar was becoming a bit remote, distant, in the past.

She was wandering toward the harbor and considering Clarie Jurat, wondering whether she was also walking along a busy street and where, when she felt herself jostled. She did not think anything, only spun on her heel and grasped the arm of the man who had touched her, and found his hand just leaving the outer pocket of her jacket, empty. He twisted away and fled: a tall man, pale as winter hay. She leaned against a wall waiting for her sudden shaking to subside. It was good to know she was still no easy prey, but it took a long time to calm her hurried heartbeat.

Of the passengers, only the four traders from Kled and Tir Lesh Witren remained. The five new passengers were tough-looking men: couriers, an accomptant with documents for Ilek-Vad, and a reeve representing a man with international interests. There was a harder edge to the crew as well, for after this they would leave the comparative safety of the coast and it would be blue-water sailing until they got to the Eastlands.

Two priests came aboard as the *Medje Loïc* prepared to cast off from Hlanith, attired in layered robes of blue and black wool richly embroidered with silver thread so that even their faces were concealed behind panels of silver mesh. They moved clumsily, bulkily; and water pooled beneath them on the scoured teakwood deck. Since the rituals were forbidden to landsmen, Vellitt found herself banned to her cabin. When she came on deck again, the thoti was at sea. By morning they were out of sight of land.

Distance in the dream lands was never a constant, and the seas were even less stable. Randolph Carter had once made the passage from Hlanith to Celephaïs in three days—a feat that was legend—but three weeks' sailing between the two was more usual and even six weeks or more not uncommon; and their destination, Ograthan, was farther than Celephaïs. And then back, if all went well and Randolph Carter gave her the key. She counted the days over in her mind, an unhappy arithmetic. Could the College conceal Clarie Jurat's absence so long? Did the University know yet? Were steps being taken to suspend or close the College? Or had the mad, mindless god that was her grandfather already awakened, found her gone, and lashed out—Ulthar a dark poisoned rubble across the ground? It was hundreds of leagues, but sometimes she couldn't help but scan the southern horizon for fire and smoke.

Septiver turned to Octaver. The days grew colder until she lamented the yak-wool scarf on her bunk. Vellitt paced the decks and distracted herself with the complex topologies of the wind-filled sails and the sky, so low that it seemed the mainmast might snag on its vague ungeometries, weighty as a tent roof pregnant with captured rain on the brink of squeezing through the canvas. There was little else to see. The *Medje Löic* sailed alone in a circle of sea twenty leagues across. Only once did they see another ship, a caravel that revealed itself as a pirate when it pursued them for an entire light-winded day in a leisurely chase that ended at dusk. Another day, there was whale spume on the horizon, and once, miles to the north, a calm gall on the water as long as the *Medje Löic*, which was (she was told) a kraken's tentacle-club floating just beneath the surface.

There were nights when the elapsing time chewed at her and she could not sleep. Tir Lesh Witren and the reeve who had boarded in Hlanith were often awake into the late watches, so she joined them sometimes in the main cabin, stepping into their endless games of chess, but neither of them were a match for her. And Tir Lesh made her uncomfortable. He watched her, his eyes too steady. He asked too many questions: about her past, about her destination. Had she been twenty instead of fifty-five, she might have assumed it was desire, or a mere opportunistic gauging of his chances, or even imagined, illusory love. But there were twenty-five years between them and it was impossible to suppose any of these drove him. So perhaps it was only curiosity; but she avoided him when she could, and when she could not, she offered a bland, damping, slightly chilling civility she had honed across a lifetime.

Many nights she chose instead to walk on deck: the lowered voices of the watch at their work, the softly glowing wake. The moon was often gone, so she watched the seething sky behind the ninety-seven stars, daytime's blues replaced with a thousand blacks touched with red, with brown, with a poisonous green so dark it was almost undetectable, all tumbled together in churning boils the size of planets

When she had been younger and her eyes fresher, she had seen it better. Randolph Carter had told her once that the waking world's sky was not like this. "It's just empty," he had said. "No patterns, no changing, except what is clouds and the time of day."

They had been camped in Implan's bonny hills that night, three days out from Oonai along the trade route that led to Hathegtown. They had set no fire.

She shook her head, a little impatient. "I know, you showed me that picture. But *beyond* the atmosphere. *Behind* the air."

"Nothing," he said. "After the atmosphere of Earth, you are in space, which is vacuum. Well, there *are* stars—billions, I suppose—and nebulae and gas clouds—but they exist in the infinity of space. I'm no astronomer."

"So many stars," she mused. "Do they all have gods? How do they not annihilate one another?"

"It's not the same in the real world." By *real*, he meant *Earth*.

She tried to picture it. "If the sky is infinite, why would you come here? With so many stars of your own?"

"Our world has no sweep, no scale," Carter said. "No dark poetry. We can't get to the stars. Even the moon is hundreds of thousands of miles away. There's no meaning to any of it."

"Do stars have to mean anything?" she asked, but he reached across and kissed her, and that had ended that conversation as it had ended so many others.

She remembered Clarie Jurat's letter: *He says there are millions of stars.* She was presumably on Earth by now, with her waking-world lover. She would have seen his sky. Perhaps he had taken her to his home. Stephan Heller was a great dreamer here, so he must be as powerful in his own place. He would have a palace, an estate of some sort. And she, with the charm of a god's granddaughter—he could hardly fail to love her utterly. He would marry her and she would become chatelaine of whatever lands were his: rich, respected, and adored. It was a pity she could not be left there.

But at other times, Vellitt thought of Clarie's father, Davell Jurat. She had met him often enough; the trustees of Ulthar Women's

College were invited to Incepts and Last-nights, holiday dinners, the College's annual report, and the alumnae Moot, and Davell took his duties seriously. He was already a widower when Vellitt first came to teach, but Senior Day Room gossip said that his wife had been truly beautiful—"a Ling'troh sculpture," Gnesa Petso had once said with a sigh, for her tastes ran to such. Some people had wondered at their marriage, for Davell was a short man with a crooked jaw and a pugged nose, but Davell's humor and glowing charm were extraordinary, even shadowed by the loss of his wife and the accumulating weight of years. Vellitt saw Davell and Clarie Jurat together at her Incept. His expression as he watched her take student robes for the first time had been a complex mixture of love, pride, and a terrible tender fear that made Vellitt look away, it was so strong. It must be ten thousand times worse for him now.

If Ulthar still stood . . . and then, frustrated with her circling thoughts, she would distract herself by watching the luminescent, wavering chevrons of their wake fade back to darkness, or by gazing at the mysterious glowing disks clustering in the ocean's depths.

The disks intrigued her, and night after night she watched them: patches of indistinct phosphorescence, roughly circular and no larger than her hand, she thought. She imagined they might be jellyfish, but when she asked a crew member, he only made the Elder Sign and spat over the railing. Later, the captain came to her where she stood at the aft rail and ordered her never to speak of them again. His voice was harsher than she had ever heard it, even to his crewmembers, so she complied and thereafter kept to herself her observations of how they moved, changed size, overlapped, and absorbed one another.

There was a half-mooned night nineteen days into the blue-water passage when she saw the little glowing circles scatter as though fleeing from some unseen predator. One grew larger and then larger still, and she realized that it was not small but had been instead very, very far away, beneath hundreds of fathoms of water so winter-clear it concealed nothing. It grew and grew, a wheeling diatom that increased in clarity and complexity until it was the size of a house; the size of a galleon; the size of a city filling the ocean beneath them from horizon to horizon. She observed details now, glowing windowless towers and five-sided structures—giant pentangular basins everywhere blazing with cold bioluminescence—the radial lines broadening until she could see countless smaller shapes streaming along them like platelets in a capillary under a microscope, or men racing in a panic along a crowded street.

It seemed certain that the *Medje Löic* would be shipwrecked, beached among whatever strange entities raced along those radial roads, but it sheared to starboard as it rose—larger and then larger still—until miles away it broke the surface with a sound like a hurricane, wheeling up into the sky, high enough to occlude the gibbous moon; and the phosphorescence died in the air, so that nothing more could be seen of the things that lived in that place.

It crashed back into the water, faster than gravity could pull. It was only then that Vellitt remembered that this diatom-city had been fleeing something. And it had not escaped; an unseen maw, immeasurably vast and hungry, had sucked it back down the way the carp had sucked the dead bird into its scarlet mouth, back on the Reffle so long ago.

It took minutes for the chaos of jumbled water to get to them, ample time for the captain and his crew to turn the thoti into the waves; and fifteen minutes for the bursting seas to settle at last.

It took much longer for Vellitt to stop thinking of her mother's death. Had her father imagined this?

Vellitt Boe awoke one day to cheers and singing and came on deck to see green shoreline far to starboard. It was the Eastlands at last, the Tanarian Hills and above them Mount Aran, green and gray, white-peaked with early-autumn snow. The *Medje Loïc* had crossed in twenty-three days with no losses. The crew celebrated with a day-long party: flutes, recorders, a cornet, fiddles, and drums; the men in their best, dancing quick-stepped hornpipes and flickering jigs. She watched and sang and drank watered grog, all barriers erased for the day. When one of the sailors, a grizzled foremast-man with waist-length braids ringing a dome of bare scalp, invited her to dance the scharplin with him, she joined him—and surprised them all, for she had learned the tricky, stumbling steps in her youth when sailing to Mnar, and they came back quickly. For the last days of the voyage, the crew treated her with delighted affection, as though she were a pet one of them had brought on board and tamed to become a mascot. Perhaps she should have danced the scharplin earlier.

After that the ship was never out of sight of shore, and the leagues spun out beneath the thoti's hull. Three days later, they landed at the nephrite wharves of Ograthan.

The docks of all towns are the same—wharves and warehouses, men shouting, wood and rope creaking: the smells of dead fish, creosote, and salt. On a promontory above all this stood Ograthan proper, fortified with titanic walls against the sea and what lived in it. But it had been long centuries since anything had threatened them. The city had grown well out into the green country beyond, and the thick walls had been pierced in a hundred places by tunnels and curious little hatchways, and entire windowless rooms dug out stone by cautious stone. The wall in its immensity did not seem affected by these invasions except that sometimes it groaned, and siftings of dust would appear in unexpected places. But someday it would fall, and Ograthan vanish beneath its stones.

The passengers dispersed for the day. Vellitt ascended a broad street, with terraces in place of stairs and shops that grew in luxury as she approached the town. She ate berries in yak's milk for breakfast, as being the thing farthest from shipboard food she could find. She had heard of the honeycombed walls of Ograthan and, deciding to explore, she penetrated further into town. The streets grew narrow and choked with trash, the houses dirtier until they vanished and were replaced by slum-like buildings fronted with grimy taverns. Hard-faced men sat on tumbled stones smoking tobacco laced with ghenty. She saw one such, asprawl in the dust of an alley, his greasy head lolling against the stained stones of the giant wall. Even vile as he was, he had the sheen that meant he was a dreamer, a man of the waking world. She tried to speak with him but he only pushed her away and folded forward as though unboned, to vomit into his lap.

At one point, she thought she saw Tir Lesh Witren duck under an archway—she recognized him by his jacket, as familiar to her as her own coat after their long passage. There was no reason he might not also be here, but for reasons she could not articulate she felt uneasy, and turned to go back the way she came. Returning to the ship, she was relieved to learn that he had in fact disembarked, and his room taken by a man hastening to Ilek-Vad on the wings of bad news, hoping to arrive before his father's death.

The *Medje Loïc* left the next day, and after that to starboard there was Hazuthkleg, Oxuhahn, the Hills of Hap. Every sight was new to her, for she had never come so far east. They were sailing into the twilight lands now, so the sky dimmed until the sun became an umber disk she could look at directly. The sea changed into something darker, though still clear. When she looked down into the shadowy water she saw walls, roads, and movement. It felt as though she were coming to the rim of reality. Her restiveness grew. She nearly wept with relief when she saw the glass cliffs of Ilek-Vad.

Vellitt Boe and the black cat left the *Medje Loïc* with regret, on Vellitt's part at least. She took a room in a portside inn and immediately wrote to the king of Ilek-Vad, the dreamer Randolph Carter, reminding him of their long acquaintance and asking for an audience. It was an awkward letter, since they had been lovers and she had no idea what he thought of that now, so she kept it as short as she in courtesy could. She hired the innkip's daughter, a fleet-footed girl of fifteen whose restless mannerisms reminded her a bit of her own young self, to take it to the castle. It would take an hour or more for the girl to climb the steep road up the cliff, and longer still before she would receive a response (if there were one) and return. Well enough: Vellitt had other things to do.

Nothing she had with her was appropriate, so she found a dressmaker to make a gown for her audience. She took great pains over the fabric and cut, and laughed at herself as she did so, for she knew that it was not for the king of Ilek-Vad she did this, nor even to please an old lover, but for her own vanity. She had not seen him in thirty years and it had been she who left him. It would not do to look shabby, or as though she regretted anything of her life since—which had, after all, led her to her current state, Professor and Fellow at a great and ancient University.

She articulated some part of this to the dressmaker, who was (in the way of such women) incomparably wise and guessed all was not spoken. The dress would be heavy silk of a rich corvine black ("Like a professor's robes, but richer," said the dressmaker), square-necked and narrow-sleeved, with the cascading, trailing skirt preferred by Ilek-Vad's aristocracy. "Elegant, intelligent, and strong—but not too young," the dressmaker said. "I will have it tomorrow at noon, if you come back tonight for a fitting. And for the audience, your cat may have a ribbon to match. Or . . . No, that would be too much. I will consider."

"It's not my cat," Vellitt said, but otherwise acceded to whatever was said. She paid the slightly shocking sum demanded of her without complaint, grateful again for the Bursar's foresight. After that, her hair—and then there were shoes to purchase, and a scarf she might use as a shawl.

It was dinnertime before she and the cat returned to the inn, and found a reply to her application: *Randolph Carter, ordained king and right ruler of Ilek-Vad—Narath—Thorabon—Octavia— Matië—*(there was quite a long list here)—*salutes Vellitt Boe, Celephaïan Doctor of Theoretics and esteemed Professor Maior at*

Ulthar's ancient and honorable University, and summons her to attend on the morrow, at five o'clock.

She went early to bed. In the night the cat tapped her face with a silent paw until she pushed it away. It repeated the gesture and a little annoyed, she sat up, awake, to hear a soft, careful snicking at her door. A lock-pick.

She slipped from her bed, reaching for the long knife beneath her pillow, but as she rose the cat cascaded to the ground with a heavy thump, and the snicking noise stopped. She crossed the room in a few strides and jerked the door open. It was too late. There was no one visible in the short corridor.

She lit the gas lamp in her room with fingers that trembled only a little. Who was it, and why? She knew somehow that it was not a burglar, nor a man with rape on his mind. Was it a kidnapping? Was this to do with the gods? With her quest to retrieve Clarie Jurat? She remembered Tir Lesh Witren, the way he had watched and mined her for information. Perhaps he had been a spy of some sort, but for whom? He had disembarked in Ograthan; it didn't seem possible that whatever information he had managed to collect might get to Ilek-Vad faster than the *Medje Loïc* had. And what did it imply for Ulthar, if there were spies set? Or was it just some court intrigue that had everything to do with a king and his politics, and nothing to do with her?

There was no sleeping with such thoughts, but Vellitt was old and wise and experienced in far-traveling. She was able eventually to eliminate the pointless circling fears and slept at last. But the cat remained awake until morning, lying at the foot of her bed, still as the pictures on the wall save for the occasional twitch of an ear or a whisker or the blinking of its green eyes.

The dress: finished, wrapped in silver paper, and laid tenderly into a box of pale-blue cardboard; her rucksack and a valise purchased to contain the clothing she had acquired in her travels, repacked; the whole sent up the cliff road on a zebra-drawn cart driven by the innkip's daughter: and finally in early afternoon, Vellitt Boe herself ascended the crystal cliffs of Ilek-Vad beneath the strange twilit sky. The cat walked beside her.

The cliffs were wind-etched to the delicate white of hoarfrost, but wherever a crag had recently sheared off, the surfaces were clear as glass, and she could see into their crystal depths: shadows cast by the higher slopes and the road itself, striations and flaws, visible caves. She looked back at the sea whenever she paused for breath. From so far above, the ruins of a great underwater maze were visible beyond the harbor, and a single fleck of red angling across it: the *Medje Loïc*, her sails filled with the offshore wind, off to the sunlit lands.

It was midafternoon when, winded and a little weary, she took a room at an inn in the many-turreted town near the palace. She arranged for the attendants that would walk with her, for no one navigated the steep streets of Upper Ilek-Vad without an escort carefully calibrated in size and formality. She bathed and dressed. There was still nearly an hour before she might present herself.

The dressmaker was as much a master of her art as any king's architect. The gown was exactly correct: severe, wise, and beautiful. Vellitt had no jewelry, but her hair shone like steel and iron, a bob of tight-twisted cords that brushed her jawline when she turned her head. She was older and her face was set into lines, though her eyes were the same as they had ever been, she thought. A matching neck-ribbon for the cat had been judged *de trop*, and the dressmaker had created instead a slim collar from a scrap of blue ribbon embroidered with silver. To Vellitt's surprise, the cat permitted it to be placed about its neck, then sat, examining itself in the room's glass.

She was going to be seen by an old lover, now a king. It was impossible to assume she would not be considered against the Veline Boe that was. She hadn't loved Randolph Carter. He had been a man like many, so wrapped and rapt in his own story that there was no room for the world around him except as it served his own tale: the black men of Parg and Kled and Sona Nyl, the gold men of Thorabon and Ophir and Rinar, and all the women invisible everywhere, except when they brought him drinks or sold him food; all walk-on parts in the play that was Randolph Carter, or even wallpaper.

But he had loved her, or thought he did, and that had brought her, sputtering and gasping, above the surface of his self-regard. The dreamers' sheen and the power of his passion had for a time attracted her, but in the end she had not wanted a life spent treading water in his story. She still did not—and yet she regarded herself in the glass a little ruefully. To have that choice made irrevocable by time and age was painful.

"Eh," she said to the cat, who at the sound looked up at her with narrowed eyes. "Let us make our curtsey to a king."

The throne room of Ilek-Vad was a space a hundred meters square, fashioned of dark opal that glittered with the brilliant colors of butterflies and jungle birds. The ceiling was lost in elaborate vaults hung with lamps that cast a sharp electric-white light. The throne was as grand as the room, fashioned of a single giant golden opal and illuminated by torchières bearing blue flames that never died.

But the king did not sit there. There was a lower throne to one side, on a Drinanese carpet of great size and beauty, alongside other seats and a round table of aloeswood. Lanterns hung above this wall-less room on chains of such length that they swung like pendula. It was to this space that Vellitt was led. A man in scarlet stood as she approached. She recognized him immediately, though she had forgotten that he was no taller than she.

But he—"Veline?" Randolph Carter said sounding a little shocked, and then more firmly, "Veline." She saw it suddenly. She was older and he had not predicted the ways it would change her. In the same moment it came to her that *he* had not aged externally, not by more than a year or two. He took her hands in his, and after an almost indiscernible instant's hesitation, saluted her upon her cheek. His guards and her escorts left them there;

and Vellitt Boe and Randolph Carter stood alone in that soaring feather-hued space.

There was no question of formal supplications. He led her to sit beside him on the divan and poured from a bottle of pale-yellow wine from Sarrub. It tasted like sunlight and home to Vellitt, for the College's cellars were filled with Sarruvi wines. She told him of her quest, the journey thus far and what was to come.

He looked at her in silence for a time, then said, "Four days ago, a vision came to the priests of the great shrine in Narath, with a message to be brought to me in secret. There is a god: foolish, mad, and sleeping. The daughter of his daughter has vanished from these lands, and the oracle spoke of the results should he awaken and find her gone—the Skai valley in fire, from Mount Lerion to Sarrub and the Karthians, and even into the zoogs' forest."

Vellitt put her head into her hands, suddenly faint.

"It was an *oracle*, not a prophecy," Randolph said. "It hasn't happened, not yet, but the vision warned that mischief-making gods are even now whispering into his ear and tickling his feet, so that he shifts restlessly upon his couch. And more: the vision cautioned that there are yet other gods who do not care either way about him, but will prevent any attempt to retrieve the girl." He sighed. "So many gods, so many factions and politics and petty resentments. So. If you are the one seeking her, then you are the one they hunt."

She recounted the attempt to break into her room and of Tir Lesh Witren on the ship, and added, "It did not seem to me that any of the usual reasons applied. For this, then, I suppose."

He said with decision, "You had better stay here tonight." Summoning an attendant, he gave orders. When the man was gone, he continued with some satisfaction, "I do not think even a god's followers will seek to harm you beneath this roof."

"Thank you." Vellitt leaned forward. "You've heard my situation. Will you give me the silver key that opens the Gate? You can see how critical it is. I'll return it myself or have it brought back to you."

But Carter was already shaking his head, and his face expressed an inward grief that seemed inapt for the situation. "I don't have it. It's gone and I don't know where, whether it was stolen, or I hid it somewhere to keep it safe from theft, or—or something else. Thus far I've been able to remain but I feel it—the real world dragging at me like gravity. I can tell that there is coming a time when I lose this fight and fall back into the waking world. Without the key, I'll be trapped there."

He pinched the bridge of his nose, a homely gesture that brought his essential nature back to her as his unchanged face and voice had not. Thirty years ago, she would have reached across the space between them, touched the frowning line between his brows with a fingertip, and kissed him. Even now she felt the impulse ground into her muscles, but she had larger concerns now.

"Then Ulthar cannot be saved?" She thought of it. Ulthar, but also Nir and Hatheg and all the little inns and farmhouses, the shepherds and the ox-drivers, Gnesa Petso and the Bursar and Derysk Oure, the toll-taker at the bridge with her practiced tale of human sacrifice, the man renting punts on the Aëdl, the Eb-Taqar Fellows with their elaborate Flittide parties, the girl in the Woolmarket who had taught her monkey to curtsey for coins—so many men and women and children. And everyone gone. She took a breath. "There must be alternatives."

They talked on. More wine was brought, and cakes and dates and little curls of an indescribably tender meat, which they ate absently as they spoke. There *were* alternatives, six that Carter knew of, all so dangerous that there was evidently no need of locks and keys.

One was a cave deep in the Tanarian Hills behind Celephaïs, where the grassy hills grow dry and turn to badlands and eventually the great Eastern desert. But that route was forbidden by ancient edicts and, while Kuranes (the king there) was Carter's once-friend and ally, he was old and would not challenge the ancient ways. If she went, she would have to enter the hills in secret.

Or, if she had money enough and did not fear treachery, she might take passage on one of the black tall-masted triremes that could sail to the moon itself. It was alleged that one might cross into the waking world by traversing its shattered regolith, but Carter did not know the details of how that might be done, nor how to descend from there to waking Earth.

The plateau of Leng under the shadow of Kadath was rumored to cross the boundaries of all worlds; but, having stated that, they considered the prospect no further, knowing that it was, of all options, the worst.

Or, there was a ghenty den in distant Rinar, a few steps from the city's great market. One entered an unnamed alley and spoke certain words into a star-shaped aperture cut into a door, and if the words were the correct ones, the door would be opened. The den was so thick with the mingled smoke of tobacco, thagweed, hemp, and ghenty that it was impossible even to cross the room unaltered. When one entered any of the curtained alcoves, it was easy to judge the eerie visions contained within as hallucinations. "But they're not," said Carter. "The fourth door to the left leads to the real world."

"That doesn't sound so hazardous."

"Then I have misspoken. There are things behind those curtains that would destroy you merely by being seen."

"I am not so weak," she said, angry.

"You could be made of steel and diamond, Veline, and it wouldn't matter. Some of the alcoves open onto the space between the stars. The Other Ones would find you there."

She sighed. "What else, then?"

Or, the cats might aid her. The small black cat in its blue collar had accompanied Vellitt to her audience and been well rewarded: Carter had saluted it with honor as a noble of its species, and it had been served with its own fine foods: mountain-clear water, minced mice, and a tiny fish still flipping its tail in a lapis dish. Now he stroked it where it lay upon his knee. Of course, he had always been wise in the ways of cats, valuing them above entire races, many men, and most women. "The cats have their own secret routes. They've saved me before this," he said.

"Would the cat aid me? Would you, little one?"

Carter consulted (so it *was* true that he could speak the language of cats), but after the colloquy, he shook his head. "She would willingly, but she tells me that it's not possible for men of the dream lands to travel thus. Or women," he added, perhaps remembering Veline Boe's ill-advised attempt in her youth to climb Mount Ngranek, of which it was said that no *man* could ascend and stay sane.

And so it came down to the secret paths of the ghouls. They both knew something of the creatures, who dwelt in decayed packs in the unlit under-realms. Scattered through those ichor-wet caverns and tunnels were their secret routes into the graveyards, deadfields, and necropolises of a hundred worlds. Carter had once had friendships among them, though their support many years earlier for a quest of his had brought the deaths of many. "So do not tell them I sent you," he ended with a wry expression; "not until you know whether they associate the name of Randolph Carter with friendship or whole-scale slaughter."

Carter gave orders for an escort and supplies to leave at dawn. Vellitt sighed inwardly: always, dawn. She showed him the glossy black object from the library of the temple of Flame, but he could make nothing of it, saying only that it might be from his future, as time between the two worlds was not constant—obvious enough, seeing Carter's unlined hands and her own, hard-knuckled and old, when she took back the object—and could even, perhaps, move backward. He offered her two additional gifts of great value: a password that should secure safe passage and the aid of any ghouls she encountered, and a carved red opal suspended from a fine black iron chain, which would allow her to see in the lightless under-realms.

It was not yet late, so they remained talking, moving to his private apartments high in one of Ilek-Vad's opal towers: cold rooms despite the fire that rose, smokeless and eternal, from a iron brazier broader than a man was tall. There was dinner and more wine, a red so soft that it flowed across her tongue like a recollection of autumns past. Beaujolais, he told her, brought in memory from a place in his world called France. The small black cat of Ulthar curled up beside him, purring in its sleep.

They had met in the marble streets of shining Celephaïs, kissed before they had spoken: Veline Boe young, clean-limbed, and radiant, and Randolph Carter with the sheen all master dreamers have. They had kissed and then spoke and then far-traveled together for nearly two years: a xebec that stopped in Sarrub, in Dylath-Leen, at the wave-swept jetties of the isles of Mtal and Dothur and Ataïl; weeks afoot exploring Thalarion and the jungles behind that demon-city; a freight barge to Sona Nyl and then Oonai and the long overland walk to Teloth and Lhosk; the pataran they had sailed to Thraa, and the flat-beamed abari that took them up the river Ai; and finally, the disastrous crossing of the swamps of Mnar, which had ended when they fell through into the under-realms.

"Such a dark place, your world," Carter said, after a lingering silence. He lifted his glass and looked at the flames through the wine. The room in the tower of Ilek-Vad had grown quiet, the servants gone and the fire low.

"Is the waking world so different?"

"You might have found out," he said softly. There had been a night when he had invited her to return with him: no talk then of it being forbidden. She had refused, not understanding why. Now she understood that it was not the waking world she had said no to, but Carter.

"No," she said suddenly weary of it all: his self-absorption and the soul-sickness that sat so uneasily on his young face. He loved who *he* was: Randolph Carter, master dreamer, adventurer. To him, she had been landscape, an articulate crag he could ascend, a face to put to this place. When were women ever anything but footnotes to men's tales?

"You were so beautiful, Veline," he said. "Beautiful, clever, bold-hearted."

In the dim light, she could see him erasing the lines on her face, and with mingled regret and affectionate contempt she recognized his expression. He would try to kiss her—or rather, what he remembered of who she had been—in spite of the difference in their years, in spite of everything. And so she claimed a fatigue she was not feeling, and left him.

Randolph Carter did not accompany Vellitt Boe on her quest, and in this also he had changed, for in the youth they had shared, he would never have refused such an adventure. He stood upon the steps of the dark opaline palace of Ilek-Vad, dressed in royal robes of red couched in silver, and bearing on his head a great crown of gold, each point ornamented with an impaled silver mouse—for he was known as the Shrike to his enemies. In spite of his smooth face and unsilvered hair, he looked old, older than she, gray and stern; and Vellitt mourned a little for the Randolph Carter she had known.

Here at last, after all these weary leagues, the small black cat of Ulthar left her: seated beside Carter, grand as a vizier in its blue collar. Vellitt knelt to stroke its head a last time, and murmured, "Be well, little one." It was better this way. No cat would abide such a foul place as the under-realms, and in any case it could not survive, too small not to be eaten (if some worse fate did not befall it); but she nevertheless wept, and wiped the tears away secretly against the back of her gloves.

Carter had assigned Vellitt an escort of twenty men. Riding-zebras and yaks awaited them at the base of the cliffs; and here also was a choice gift to be offered to the ghouls: a small ebon box, sealed with red wax and etched with runes.

The nearest access to the under-realms was through a cavern deep in a silver mine in the mountains behind the town of Eight Peaks. The mine had been worked for centuries, though always there had been strange noises heard in the deepest shaft, until the day when a rock face had collapsed inward and ghouls of unusual enterprise had swarmed out across the mine. Many miners had died. Others had been dragged screaming away, and no one knew what had happened to them. The mine had of course been abandoned, though with some regret, for the silver had been of high quality and did not oxidize.

The journey to the mine's adit would be only a few days, depending on weather and the mutability of distance. Though according to an apologetic Carter this was traveling light, Vellitt had a silk-batted tent to herself, instantly erected and warmed with braziers every time they stopped for more than a few moments. There was wine, and she could not help but smile a little when she was brought seasoned venison to eat, or cream whipped into a froth with honey and newfallen snow. The Carter she had known would have mocked such luxuries.

Nevertheless, it was an uncomfortable, not to say risky, journey. The mountains of Perinth were never safe, even in summer, even to those not hunted by the gods. The Octaver nights were very cold, and in the mornings her feet made dark silhouettes on the rock as they melted the hoarfrost. At all hours, the party saw great shapes moving across the snowfields of distant glaciers, and heard shouts like thunder echoing and reëchoing across the cirques. The moon never once appeared, though there was no telling whether that was because it had been summoned to some god's entertainment ten thousand leagues away, or whether it had been sent away to leave these crags in darkness.

On the third afternoon of their travel, the troop's captain stopped and established camp in a meadow beside an agate-graveled stream. They were within an hour of the adit, but it was too late in the day to find their way down through the mine to the ghouls' entrance into the under-realms, let alone to do so, exit, and get far enough away from the mine to ensure safety from whatever monstrosities might seethe forth with night.

The captain was a canny, angry man with eyes the color and hardness of jade, and she knew that had she been twenty she would have found a way to kiss his mouth, to see whether she might soften those hard eyes a little. She kept her thoughts to herself. She knew his anger was not for her personally but for his task. Leaving an old woman alone here went very much against the grain.

Even wary as the captain was, the attack when it came caught the party unawares. The doubled guards were alert through the night as they watched for mountain-beasts or even ghouls from the adit. But the threat came from the heights: monstrous shantak birds floating down silently on greasy wings. Vellitt was tucked into her silken-walled tent but too restless to sleep, checking and double-checking her pack. The air outside filled suddenly with shouts and screams, the sounds of huge claws sinking into flesh and armor, and the indescribable percussion of bodies being dropped onto rock from shattering heights.

She caught up her pack and tore free of her tent just as it was smashed flat by one of the shantak birds, so close that she smelled its carrion stench and felt the repulsive flick of an oily feather against her face as she stumbled away.

She had dropped over her head the pendant fire opal which granted the ability to see in darkness. It was clear that the situation was hopeless: the captain dead in pieces a yard from her feet (but his angry jade eyes still blinking up at the sky) and the rest of the troopers dead or dying, fighting against things they could not see. There was nothing she could do, and she had a task more important than the lives of these twenty, but still she was weeping as she left those terrible sights and sounds, running along the narrow path the captain had pointed out to her the night before.

She estimated that she had gone nearly half the distance when the sound behind her grew suddenly louder and more ominous. The shantak birds picking over the ruined remains of the camp had discovered her absence and rose on their clashing wings to find her; it was the flapping and their shrieks to one another that she heard. With her augmented sight, she saw the foremost of them outlined as a red throbbing shape high against the seething dark sky. Silver light was just brushing the mountaintops: whatever god had ordered this attack had also summoned the moon for the hunt, and she would not be free to move in total darkness for long.

That final hour was a game of cat and mouse, but cat and mouse with a score of flying cats the size of elephants and a single mouse with wits and broken cover. She hid beneath overhangs and behind rocks, moving only when they were flying away from her or out of sight, making it to the scree field leading to the adit just as the moon cleared the nearest mountain and shone directly down into the valley. Cold white light exposed the smooth cascade of rubble; she was obvious as she scrambled up the slope. The shantak birds, detecting her at last, tucked their wings and dove. She ran under the mine's low beam and turned to see them slam into the ground just outside. One ducked its head to reach in with its great beak, but the scree shifted, began to slide in a roaring, thundering avalanche, and it fell screaming to one side and vanished. Dust glowing white with moonlight rose and concealed the mountains and sky. Hovering shantak birds began to claw at the adit. Vellitt ran for her life.

This was the last time she saw the seething sky of the dream lands.

The mine's main tunnel was smooth-floored and broad, a steady smooth decline. Ilek-Vad's archives had included a crude map drawn by the only man to escape the disaster, and she followed its directions down tunnels and metal-runged ladders, past rock-falls and ancient, ruined equipment, along a seam of silver so shiningly pure that it looked as though it had already been smelted. The air grew warmer. Except for one place where she heard water rushing at a great distance, the mine was utterly silent. She began to wonder whether the hole at the bottom of the deepest shaft had been resealed: a new worry.

But the hole was open, a ragged maw just tall enough for a single slumping ghoul. She ducked to pass through and found herself in a rough tunnel that opened into a series of caves, each larger than the one before, until she came into a cavern some hundreds of feet high and a mile or more across, and so long that she could not see to the far end.

She threaded her way through a badland stained with lichens that shone sometimes, blue or green or orange. The opalic vision gave everything the two-dimensional feel she remembered from certain late summer afternoons. Living things (or what passed for living) glowed slightly red, even the night-gaunts crisscrossing the cavern overhead on silent batlike wings. She was still being hunted.

She paused only when fatigue left her clumsy and stumbling. The water in her canteen was lukewarm but sweet, and in its scarcity all the sweeter: not every stream would be water, and not even the water here was safe. Her pemmican would be the only food until she found ghouls, for, though she could not eat what they did, they might at least tell her which fungi or lichens were not poisonous.

Vellitt knew a little of ghouls' ways. Some lived in cities taken by guile and violence from ghasts or even gugs, others lived in nomadic troops, and still others dwelt alone, though these last did not live long. Troops tended to rove near their favorite exits into the worlds in which they fed; if she could find such a group, she might shorten her journey. In the meantime, she must avoid capture by the patrolling night gaunts—or any other creatures, for there would be ghouls eager to betray her, ghasts and gugs, and yet other, unnamed beasts.

The cavern floor descended, opening out until she was in a space so big she could not imagine how the unsupported folds and heavy blocks of the roof did not collapse and bury them all, even more so when she realized that it was running with water, and that she was immeasurable miles beneath the twilit sea she had traversed in the *Medje Loïc*. She had a flash of memory—red sails against a shifting blue sky, the smell of salt—but it seemed unreal, impossibly beautiful compared to these reeking caverns, the strange, sickening flatness of the opalic vision.

As she descended, the badlands turned to what she could only think of as woodlands, a thick forest of towering mushrooms with trunk-like stipes that dropped squirming spores the size of infant mice onto her head and arms. When the agaric forest thinned, she found herself in a maze of close-set stalagmites, where in a small clearing she saw the first sign of occupation: a seven-sided flat stone many feet across and no higher than her knee, thick with crimson lichens and tiny mushrooms like the lolling tongues of voles. She felt such a cold creeping horror in its proximity that she fell to her knees retching, and crawled, blind and sick, until she knew no more.

She awoke to the sound of feathers: an eyeless bird inches from her face, plucking one of the tight twists of her hair with its hooked beak. She flinched away with a cry, and at the sound it cupped its wings and rose silently. It was impossible to guess how long she had slept, but the retching sickness she had felt since approaching the seven-edged stone was gone. She ate and drank: food enough for five days if managed carefully, but only another two days of water. When she ran out, would she grow desperate enough to drink whatever flowed in the dark streams that crossed her path? And later: Would she eat the tiny many-legged things that collected in damp places, or would she turn to larger prey?

Shouldering her pack, she walked until stalagmites gave way to another forest of tall, sturdy-stiped mushrooms trailing shredded veils like willow wands. She began to forget that it had not always been like this. The cavern smelled of opened graves, decaying fungi, carrion. The interminable sounds of moisture became a bland gray noise that faded in her ears until she heard only her own footsteps and the breath in her lungs.

She came to the abrupt end of the not-woodland and, startled, looked up from her feet across a marsh to a meadow of lichens furled like ferns into waist-high coils: everything dim but entirely crisp and depthless. Far to her left was a patch of the faintest possible blue light reflecting up onto the swelling folds of the cavern's ceiling: a ghast city, for ghouls disliked the smell of the lichens that cast that light, and gugs avoided all light. To her right the cavern wall rose to the ceiling in slopes and ledges, perfect ghoul terrain. She hoped the crags were not too steep. She had been a great climber in her youth, but that had been long ago.

The marsh's surface was scummed over with a weed that seethed restlessly. She had no desire to touch that strange, writhing skin, and was contemplating her alternatives when she heard the meeping screams of a ghoul, too desperate or frightened for silence, and the splashing of bare paws racing through shallow water—and following, a low-pitched, horrid hooting. She had been carrying her machete; she limbered her wrist and stepped back into the cover of the mushroom trees.

A young ghoul stumbled into sight, terror written in every line of its shambling form, its sloping, long-jawed features. It had been running through scummy water that came only as high as its reversed ankles; it waded deeper, until the weedlike scum swarmed against its thighs. But it would go no farther and it turned at bay. Hooting with triumph, a dozen hippocephalic ghasts burst from the trees across the marsh: sport hunters, for the long barbed spears they carried in their bifurcated forehooves were too small-tipped to kill the ghoul, but would only cripple it. There was nothing she could do; but in the end neither ghoul nor ghast escaped, for the scummy surface of the marsh rose up and swept over them all, dragging them beneath the weed in a froth of frenzied struggles. She found another way past the marsh and into the meadow beyond.

It was not so long after this that she found signs of a ghoul troop's camp tucked under an overhanging crag. Half-gnawed bones, organs left to soften with rot, and horrible souvenirs were scattered among rumpled mounds of shredded corpse-clothes and the hair of dead women: nests. Everything showed signs of recent occupation, so she called out the passwords she had been given, adding a few stumbling glibbers of her own: that she had a gift for the eldest ghoul, and a request.

One and then five, and then in the dozens and scores, the ghouls emerged from their hiding places and surrounded her. Almost, she wished that she did not have the opalic vision, for they were the stuff of darkest nightmare, somewhat human in form and yet insufficiently so: the reversed hinges of their knees and ankles;

the long, many-jointed fingers; the soiled fur that covered their sagging, quasi-human torsos. Worst were the small, intelligent eyes set into their decayed, canine faces. They crept near, the smallest ones approaching closely enough to touch her clothing and skin with their own cold, small, rubbery paws. She set her jaw and repeated her passwords.

Eventually, the oldest of them approached, and Vellitt offered it—*her*; it was a female—the little black box Carter had supplied as a gift. The eldest snatched it from Vellitt's hands and slouched away clutching it to her empty drooping dugs. When she returned a brief time later, surrounded by a vile miasma yet smacking her chops as though at a pleasant remembered flavor, she meeped that Vellitt Boe was to be accorded every ghoulish courtesy.

They offered their choicest food and drink. She refused politely, indicating that it would all be poison to her, but that clean water would not be unwelcome. Though clearly thinking a little less of her for her fussiness, they supplied this and fell to the feast they had fashioned themselves.

As they ate, Vellitt explained her quest to the waking world but did not elaborate the reasons. They would not care whether Ulthar and the Skai valley were destroyed except as it afforded a bumper harvest of corpses, and she did not want them tempted. They expressed great excitement at the undertaking, for ghouls are a fervent lot. After much conversation, a number of the younger ones declared the intention of escorting her, as they had heard stories of waking-world graveyards and wanted to taste their dainties. The eldest sighed heavily and assigned an old female to accompany the party, for the young were always foolish and might get their honored charge killed, or even forget the sacred nature of the passwords and eat her themselves.

By the time they left, the party had swelled to twenty or so: the reluctant old female assigned to the task, a few middle-aged ghouls, and many youths, mostly female. Their goal was a cellar in a harbor city on the skirts of the ragged mountains that conceal the plateau of Leng from the Cerenarian Sea. In that cellar was a staircase only ghouls knew, which led up through the thick-walled chimney of an ancient inn and terminated in the waking world. No ghouls of their troop had climbed those stairs for a century, and there was no telling which graveyard of the waking world they might end up in. Vellitt Boe knew little of the dimensions of the waking world. She could only hope the graveyard would not be too far from Clarie Jurat.

The party moved faster than she would have expected, quickly ascending the cavern wall and passing through a great natural archway to enter a chain of smaller caves and tunnels. Each carried something—a pelvis to gnaw; an oversized club made from the ulna of a gug's arm; a thick-mossed gravestone—and loped tirelessly. Whenever there was water to cross, the ghouls plashed in, holding their gravestones and bones overhead as they paddled. Vellitt followed, there being no options.

There was a horrid festiveness to the young females' enthusiasm, and a grotesque familiarity as well, for they reminded her of nothing so much as the students of Ulthar Women's College—Raba Hust, Derysk Oure, Therine Angoli, and the rest. For their part, the adults might almost have been Fellows of the College, long-suffering and largely ignoring their charges except when they grew too loud. Seeing them all in this way would for a time decrease her ongoing horror until, listening to the younger ones meeping over some treat, she would remember that the bones they bickered over were human. And yet, why should it matter? The dead did not need those bones.

Ghasts and gugs were larger than ghouls but somehow less horrible to Vellitt. At least there was no hint of humanity in those monstrous forms, no glimmer of human intelligence in their eerie eyes. With the ghouls, it was hard not to see the possibility of her own degeneration in their almost-human forms, as though the only thing between her and ghoulishness was the almost accidental hinging of her legs. Vellitt felt her jaw sometimes, to feel whether it were narrowing, elongating into something sloping and canine.

They did not rest on any schedule Vellitt could determine so that she walked sometimes in a daze. She had not known she was capable of such traveling. When they did stop, she dropped to the stony floor as though in a faint, too tired even to find a wall to sleep beside.

Once she woke to feel a rubbery paw grasping her ankle. Had she been a little more awake, she might have spoken first; she might not have swung down with her machete and felt it connect, and heard the anguished cry of a wounded ghoul as it ran howling off, leaving behind an arm severed at the elbow. She was aghast, for it had been the ghoul she called in her mind Yllyn after a second-year Practical Government student at the College, because of a similarity in the way they tipped their heads when they were thinking. For a time, Vellitt could hear the wounded ghoul following them—lacking an arm she had grown clumsy—until two of the others returned from a private expedition carrying fresh bones and licking their lips. She was not heard again.

The caverns became more populated. These were ghast lands, so the wary ghouls stayed to the rough margins; ghasts usually killed ghouls, but they also captured them to add to their herds. The youngest of the females grew very concerned for Vellitt and patted continually at her hands and clothing. It was a grotesque version of the schoolgirl crush Vellitt had seen so many times in the College, yet she almost welcomed the attention. Watched over with such an obsessive regard, she would not be taken unawares.

At the center of one of the largest of the caverns was a gargantuan shaft leading downward, a quarter of a mile across and emitting a steady, hot, foul wind. They had entered high on one wall, and she could see a little distance down the shaft. A city had been carved into its walls, with broad, steep ramps and square openings, and she was a little comforted, recognizing it for a gug city. Gugs were horrible—elephant-sized, oily-furred, and immense-pawed creatures, their eyes staring from eyestalks on either side of the toothed vertical gash of their mouths—but less terrible to her than anything else in these lands. A gug city might

contain horrors but it held few surprises, for when she had been
lost in the under-realms, she had encountered an infant gug and
followed it into its city, where she had survived for a time. Neither
it nor any other gug had shown her kindness, but neither had they
killed her.

When the younger females saw the signs of the gug city,
they clamored to hunt one, for ghouls hated gugs, and killed
them whenever they had sufficient numbers. Experienced with
managing the enthusiasms of the young, the elder wagged her
greasy canine head. They might, certainly, and it *would* be a treat,
but gugs could be had any time, after all. Did they not want to taste
the delights of a waking-world graveyard? Then they must stay
focused. Regretfully they agreed, and soon enough forgot, finding
a place where some creature had fallen from a height, and fighting
to lick the shattered flesh from the lichens with their agile tongues.

Despite their vigilance, they were ambushed—and not by
gugs. The ghouls had been loping in their tireless way down a
thick-lichened defile when many ghasts—large as horses and
mostly quadrupedal—surged suddenly from concealed holes
beyond the defile's lip. Mêlée was instant and universal. Vellitt's
machete was out of reach, but she drew her long knife and fought
until it was slammed from her hand by the ghasts, buffeting her
with their heavy shoulders, grabbing with their strange, grasping
forehooves. The ghouls they did not treat so gently. She heard their
screams all around, and saw the young female who had declared
herself Vellitt's protector crushed beneath the hooves of the largest
ghast. But they did not injure Vellitt, only bumped her farther and
farther from the screams of the ghouls until, in the end, she heard
no more.

The ghasts did not cripple her (as was their way) nor bind her.
They clubbed her with their hooves until she was half-hoisted onto
the back of one of the ghasts. She tried to slide off, but the other
ghasts crowded close, until with a hoot from the largest of them,
they departed the blood-soaked defile. They maintained a fast,
swarming lope without pause and without sound. It felt a little like

riding a horse, if a horse's skin oozed the smells of carrion, and its mane were not hair but short writhing fleshy tendrils. After a time, she fell into a miserable trance that was neither sleep nor dream, a daze that did not end until they came to their city and bore her down its broad ramps, down until the very walls seemed to seep darkness. The ghost city shared the pit with the gugs' city she had seen before. She saw the gug arches and tunnels barely a stone's throw away across the shaft and shouted, hoping that in some miraculous fashion the gugs might hear and rescue her. But it was a ridiculous hope, and in any case the ghasts rammed her with their horrible heads, until she could do nothing but gasp for breath and struggle not to be crushed.

The ghasts stopped at last. She half-fell from her vile mount's back, and was forced through a small opening in a wall. A stone door closed behind her, and she heard the heavy sound of a ghast settling itself against it.

Vellitt Boe despaired. The ghasts did not intend to maim her and add her to their herds, but that meant they had another use for her. She was sure that they had learned of her from the night-gaunts, and were holding her until she might be turned over to the whatever god sought her, to be cast into the crawling abyss or to suffer some more immediate torment—that, or the ghasts might keep her in secret until they could find a way to better utilize her to their advantage, for ghasts are always aware of the main chance and respect only the highest of the Other Ones, despising the little gods that pursue their venal, foolish agendas across the upper lands.

The room was tiny, a cube scarce six feet across: nearly the size of her lovely little teak-walled cabin on the *Medje Loïc*, but too small to serve any purpose she could think of for the ghasts, who might perhaps push their heads and forequarters through the small door but no more. So: a cell. Her opalic sight showed her featureless walls, the sealed door, and two gratings carved into the

living rock. As she watched, a millipede the length of her hand
slipped from the upper grating, swarmed down the wall and across
the floor, and disappeared into the lower one. A moment later it,
or a different one, reversed the journey. In time, she realized there
were many millipedes, and that this cell was part of a highway of
sorts for them.

Her knife had been struck from her hand, and the ghasts had
torn her pack from her. All that remained to Vellitt was whatever
she had been carrying on her person: the red opal pendant, her
canteen (full, for she had passed safe water a short time before the
ambush, slinging it over her shoulder rather than returning it to
the pack), a single packet of pemmican, the leather pouch of gold
and coins, the remaining letters of credit and the Bursar's notebook
for keeping accounts (much stained now), the small black-
lacquered object from the waking world, matches in a waterproof
case. Useless, unless she could set a fire with the notebook and
somehow frighten the ghasts with it.

And so Vellitt wept. If it was not already destroyed, Ulthar
would be, as soon as the Clarie Jurat's mad grandfather awakened.
And Jurat herself, lost into the waking world; and the ghouls that
had accompanied her these leagues, dead or enslaved; and the
young female who had so foolishly fought for her—and Vellitt
herself, unable to save even her own life.

She wept until her tears dropped to the ground and the busy
millipedes ran through the moisture that fell on their path. They
scuttered through her tears and scattered along their many routes,
myriad feet tracing secret tracks through every corner of the ghast
city, and even into the city of the gugs.

There are many gods in the dream lands: the great gods,
Azathoth and hoary Nodens and the crawling chaos Nyarlathotep
that is their messenger; but also many lesser gods, meek and
mad, that carry in their hearts secret affections they cannot
acknowledge without exposing the things they love to whatever
sadistic torments the Other Ones might devise. Certain small
gods had lived once on the snow-peaked slopes of Hatheg-Kla,

and (though they dwelt now under the cruel eye of Nyarlathotep, on cold Kadath), still they remembered their old home and the pretty valley of the river Skai. Others, even less important, had lived in Ulthar's Temple of the Elder Gods, drinking the smoke of the sacrifices and gazing with senile affection on their city: the markets, the homes, the squares and fountains. They had watched the University with dim approval: ancient Eb'Taqar and many-halled Meianthe, New and Serran and Thane's-Colleges, Stë-Dek, and even the Women's College, humblest of the Seven.

The minor gods could not combat their masters, not directly. But they were not without resources. In a land defined by dreaming men and bickering gods, there were no sure rules, but there was also no certain randomness. Vellitt had once saved an infant gug that had fallen into a pit and been pierced by punji stakes. Already the size of a full-grown wolfhound, and already stocky, ugly, and fetid, the creature held no neonate attractiveness, but she had been alone in the under-realms. This pierced, crippled creature was the first thing that did not strike sick horror into her soul. By the faint light of lichens, she lowered herself into the pit and levered the young gug free. Though it must have been in great pain, it did not struggle or bite her, only held still, its vertical maw agape in silent panting, expelling a smell of carrion inches from her shoulder. At last she rocked back on her heels and said aloud, "There you go;" and at the sound of her voice, the gug leapt to its six paws and bolted. Only then did she see the other gugs gathered at a distance, adult, gigantic, alien, and terrifying. They had been watching her. She was sure that, had she made different decisions, they would have destroyed her. The infant ran between their feet and was gone. A moment later, the adults followed, and she had followed them, having no better plan for her deliverance.

The busy millipedes scuttered through the secret places of the gug city and left traces wherever they walked of Vellitt Boe's tears. And a certain gug, grown to full size and dwelling a thousand leagues from the flesh-lined den of its infancy, padded upon six paws each a yard across, along steep ramps and up wide stairs;

over a soaring stone archway that bridged the shaft shared by two cities; and stalked through the alleys of the ghasts, cracking apart such structures as stood in its way, following a scent it remembered from its earliest youth. For gugs forget nothing.

The first intimation of this came to Vellitt when she heard panicked hooting outside her cell door and a terrible sound, as of something fleshy crushed between great jaws. The door was smashed with a blow that threw stony shrapnel across the tiny cell, and a gug's great paw reached in, patting the cell's floor and then withdrawing. Because she had nothing to lose (and in any case, to die quickly was better than to be given to whatever gods sought to stop her quest), Vellitt crawled through the opening and stood. Its head was inclined as though it looked down at her from its unfathomable eyes, and she knew suddenly what had happened and why. It was splashed to its belly with the remains of the ghast that had guarded her cell.

"Now what?" she said aloud.

She could see with her opalic vision that ghasts were clustered everywhere, just out of reach of the gug. They began a great hooting at the sound of her voice, but the gug made no sound at all: only turned and padded through the ghast city, the creatures falling back as it approached and pooling to follow behind them. Vellitt walked beside the gug, one hand against an ancient scar upon its flank.

To her surprise, the gug did not leave her even after they had climbed back into the wide, low-ceilinged cavern, and the ghasts had relinquished their hooting pursuit. After a time, she realized it meant to stay beside her until she left the under-realms. Gugs made no sounds and did not appear to have ears, but she glibbered in the ghoulish tongue of her goal, to find the cellar in Lelag-Leng; barring that, to find another path into the waking lands. The gug gave no signs of understanding but walked off as though given an order. She followed it.

Time blurred. They moved quickly, for the gug did not hesitate to cross open terrain, though it avoided the cyclopean cities of its kind. It neither slept nor apparently did it grow tired. It did not eat. Whenever she collapsed from fatigue, she feared the worst, but she awakened each time to find herself untouched, the gug crouched like a gigantic six-pawed cat as though guarding her. The ghouls had taught her things she might eat, so she peeled sheets of rank lichens from the stones and devoured them as she walked. After her canteen ran dry, she licked the water that ran down the walls. She had been thin but grew gaunt, and felt ancient and inhuman, as though she were herself a monster, alien and unknowable. When she remembered Ulthar it was with an abstract concern, as though she had heard once of such a place, of daylight and greenery, crowds in bright colors, and voices.

They came to a cavern where she saw ghasts watching a great herd of blind, shuffling animals: humans scarcely less bestial than their keepers. She begged the gug to free them, but it kept to its silent route and did not even slow. Another time, the gug lowered itself to its knees beside a lake of dimly glowing fluid, which she took to mean she should climb its back, and it was thus they crossed, her face inches from the gaping vertical mouth that split its head in half.

At one point, she realized she was being followed by a small party of ghouls. She laid a trap and captured one, a cunning female of middle age with something more of intelligence in her eyes than was the rule for her kind. Vellitt asked questions, but the female refused to answer until the gug placed a forepaw upon her chest and pressed. She squealed and then the answers came, in short, wheezing, rubbery meeps: Vellitt Boe was sought by more than one of the bickering gods, each for his own reason. Some sought to cause mischief; ending her quest would guarantee this. Others hated the Old One that was Clarie Jurat's grandfather, and would delight in tormenting him by whatever means they might. For still others, she had herself become the goal. The gods could hate for no reason at all, and their malice had turned toward her.

The ghoul continued, though a thread of thick blood slipped from her mouth and her voice took on a wet, gobbety sound. One enterprising god had offered a village of new-made fresh corpses to any dweller of the under-realms that would deliver her to him. This ghoul and her companions had determined to earn the reward.

Were there routes where she would be safe? Vellitt asked. The ghoul gurgled: She would certainly be caught when she tried to reënter the upper lands. The gug pressed harder, and the ghoul added slowly, in gasps: perhaps, from the ancient ghoulish city beneath Sarkomand. There was a way that went directly from the under-realms to the waking world without touching the dream lands.

Vellitt opened her mouth to ask more, but the gug at least was done. It leaned forward and tore the ghoul's head free of its shoulders. Blood and brains gouted across the lichened stones. Vellitt fell back, sickened; but when she looked again, there was nothing left, not so much as a scrap of bone, only blood splashed here and there. The first questing beetles, pallid and soft-shelled, emerged from a crevice and pressed their mouthparts against the stains. Soon even those would be gone. It was as well. At least this way, Vellitt could not be tempted.

Gratitude and horror made a heavy mixture, but the gratitude outweighed the horror. The ghoulish passwords could no longer be trusted, and the gug was in its inscrutable way the only ally she had. If she had gone to Lelag-Leng according to her earlier plan, the gods or their bitter messengers would have caught her and her quest would have ended. There was another advantage that came from trapping the ghoul. It had carried a sliver of obsidian as long as her hand and sharp enough to draw blood. Vellitt slid it into the empty sheath beneath her jacket and nearly wept with relief: armed again at last.

After a forever of walking, she found they were in a series of vast, high galleries, crafted by huge, unknowable hands or paws. The rooms were all the same, many hundreds of yards long and fifty across, jumbled with ruinous structures, boulders, building stones, petrified wood—and beneath everything, icy water in fetid pools. The soaring ceilings had been carved into fantastic shapes: venous guilloché of incredible detail in one hall, irregular herati and botehs in the next, vining wormlike fretworks in a third. These were the sky, she realized suddenly: the sky interpreted by beings that had never seen its shifting patterns, but only heard them described. It was not a gug city, yet the gug knew it well enough for, in the seventh of these galleries, it turned aside into a carved passageway where gaps in the living rock had been filled with tight-laid courses of dressed stone. The passageway began to ramp upward and curved in a decreasing spiral. Occasional steps appeared, until Vellitt was ascending a great circular widdershin stair, the gug almost entirely filling the passage just behind her.

At irregular intervals, the staircase widened into circular chambers some twenty yards across and only just higher than Vellitt could reach with her upstretched hand. The gug hunkered low and crept awkwardly across these rooms. Each room had seven windows spaced equally around the perimeter. Those of the lowest levels looked down into the halls of the city beneath Sarkomand, but after that she found her opalic vision could not penetrate the veil of darkness beyond the sills, and by this she surmised that they did not look into anywhere in her own world—or perhaps, any human plane at all.

They ascended: stairs, chambers, stairs again. She lost count of the seven-windowed rooms. She turned and turned, always up and to the left, numb to anything but the sick burning of her muscles, the cartilage grinding in her knees, her heaving lungs. Drained of energy and then of volition, it became easier to lean against the outside wall and close her eyes as she ascended, only opening them when she felt the moving air in her face that presaged each chamber. She stopped looking from the windows.

Coming to the fiftieth or seventieth or hundredth chamber, she opened her eyes and felt them pierced by something harsh as a ragged blade. She fell back with a cry, bringing her hands up as a shield, and the gug muscled past her. But it was only interference between the opalic vision and a white light that was shining in all the windows, bright as sunlight. She lifted the red opal from her throat, holding it tight in one hand.

They were not alone.

A figure stood before her: apparently young and very male, amber-skinned and long-faced, with winging eyebrows and fine-sculpted lips tipped into an expression that mingled disdain and amusement and the inutterable boredom of the gods. He wore pleated robes and a headdress she could not see clearly, as though it vibrated in and out of the visible spectrum. If he had been dressed in tweeds and scholar's silks, he would have looked a little like a perfected version of the young men who attended her Third-Order Saddle Shapes lectures—except for his violet eyes, which were utterly mad. She knew him for a messenger of the gods.

"You cannot stop me," she said. The gug beside her had flattened itself to fit beneath the low ceiling, but in such a way that its four massive forepaws were free to strike. Its head was lowered, the eyes on each side of its maw slit against the searing light, but alert.

"Can I not?" the messenger said. His voice was musical, but his laugh was a clashing sound like lightning striking a temple tower to the ground. "The walls are thin just here, between your little world and this room. But very well, perhaps I cannot. Still, you would be wise to pause a moment and listen to me."

"I am listening." She sounded churlish in her own ears, but the less she said, the less likely was it that she would make some fatal mistake.

"There is no reason to ascend and retrieve this descendant of a meaningless god. Your quest has come to nothing, Vellitt Boe. Ulthar is destroyed, Skai's plains a new wasteland. Return to your world and pick up what pieces you can of your life."

Messenger of the gods or not, Vellitt Boe was not inexperienced in the detection of lies. She shook her head and said only, "No."

His violet eyes were sorrowful, though flickering in their depths was the eternal mockery. "You do not believe me. Take my hand and I will show you."

"No." She stepped forward, and the gug inched forward beside her. The messenger did not move, only tipped his head and looked down at her with mad violet eyes.

"*I* see. You cannot stop me," said Vellitt Boe. "If you could, I would be dead already, and this chamber would be a smear of black ash. And if Ulthar were truly destroyed, you would have brought me visions and shown me relics. You are just a shadow here. You have no power."

His smile contained every darkness. "Perhaps, or perhaps I merely choose not stain my hands with you. Others will. And perhaps I shall go now and destroy your Ulthar myself."

He vanished and in the same instant the brilliant white light in the windows winked out as well. Vellitt found herself in utter darkness, and glibbering all about her. Ghoulish cries of attack. She fumbled the pendant back around her neck and her opalic vision flared, flat and dim: the circular chamber filled with foes, the gug crammed between ceiling and floor and sweeping ghouls aside with blows of its enormous forearms. She pulled the obsidian blade and fought.

It would not have been enough if it had been Vellitt alone, but the gug was strong and, despite the close quarters, quick. It was clearing a path toward the upward staircase with its forepaws. She ran. A ghoul rose before her, and she struck it with the knife, which shattered into shards of black glass in her hand. She threw the broken hilt into its startled canine face and ran to the staircase. It was smaller than the others had been; there was no way the gug could follow her.

She paused and turned on the bottom step. The gug was surrounded by circling ghouls nipping in with stone blades and bone cudgels to strike wherever its back was turned. Trammeled by the low ceiling and slipping on the viscera-slick floor, the gug could not turn easily. It grasped in one of its four arms a ghoul, but as it bent down to bite off its head, another jumped, aiming a sharpened hipbone at the base of an eye-stalk.

"No!" Vellitt cried, and leapt toward the gug.

And the gug, perhaps hearing her voice, reared up against the stone ceiling of the seven-windowed room. The stones groaned against one another as it heaved, and then with a terrible shrieking they broke across the gug's shoulders. She had a sudden impression of plates of white marble, tumbling blocks of coarse gray stone, and rusting iron beams, before searing light broke through the shattering roof and blinded her. She cried out, and the gug surged forward. Something hit her in the head. Her last thought was a word that sorted itself into meaning as she passed out. *Wisconsin.*

Wisconsin. It was a place. It was where she was: a state in the United States, which was also where she was. It was *June*, which was Thargel—the sixth month of the calendar here. She knew the year, and why the years were numbered as they were. Shell Lake, Wisconsin. Midafternoon.

New information cascaded into her mind. Her head hurt as though she had been struck (it had, she remembered); or as though it were rearranging its pathways; and this vocabulary, these concepts, were also new. She could not get her eyes open, was not even sure she was breathing or her heart beating. There was warmth on her face, a rough, hard surface beneath her. She was lying down, she realized with a flicker of relief. Dead or alive, her body remained hers. There was a steady low growl close by that did not change in pitch or stop for breath. *Am I dreaming?* she thought, and started laughing—for that was the one thing she certainly was *not*, was dreaming—and it was this that opened her eyes.

She was lying on a broken, rough-paved lane—the word came to her, *asphalt*—that dipped through a hollow in a neglected cemetery beside a small temple—a *church*, a *Lutheran* church of brown brick and fieldstone, plain and unfussy. Concealing the sky were tall oaks and other trees, ones with pointed leaves, *maples*; and on the ground, *bluegrass* and *fescue* needing a mow, mixed with crabgrass and chickweed. Beside the lane, a mausoleum of moss-skinned marble with its lintel cracked, and a rusted iron gate gaping on its hinge.

The steady growl beside her was the gug, or what had been the gug. Words came to her for what it was now: *Buick; Riviera*—which was also a sea coast in a distant land, France. 1971, the year it was built. Almost fifty years ago. And then everything: how internal combustion engines worked and where the ignition key went and how to operate the windshield wipers; synthetic 5W-40 because Wisconsin was a winter land, R44TS spark plugs gapped to thirty thousandths—data tumbling into place until she knew the specs as though she had worked on the car herself. Swapping the points for digital ignition; adjusting the valve train. She understood. The waking world had no place in its schema for gugs as they were, so when the gug followed her into the little cemetery, it had been reshaped into a thing that *could* exist: a low, slope-roofed car with a jutting front end and vertical grille, and a long, tapered back window tucked between the split, slanted back bumper; everything golden-gray with dust, as though they had just come off a long gravel road.

She stood, a little shakily, aching and queasy from the—*adrenaline*—that had turned to toxins in her blood. She was wearing jeans—cotton trousers, but women wore them here—and boots, and a dark t-shirt. She put up her hand: the red opal was still around her throat, though it no longer affected her eyesight. She was, impossibly, clean. She felt her hair's tight twists, pulled one forward, and found it was silver and black still. There might be no admission point in this world for gugs; but for older women, apparently yes. She could feel it settling about her, what this world would expect of a woman her age and color. She fit scarcely more naturally here than in her own land.

She leaned against the gug's hood, feeling the steady rumble of the old V-8. The long haunch of the left rear bumper had been damaged in the past and repaired with Bond-o, where the infant gug had been transfixed in the ghouls' pit-trap so long ago. How did it feel about this transformation? Did it feel despair, trapped in steel, toothless and clawless, never to taste flesh again? Or did it delight in the bright taste of gasoline, the speed of its new muscles, the ways that clever warm hands would repair its ills?

Through the windshield she saw a jacket thrown on the bench seat and knew without looking that she would find the same things she had carried in her own world: the gift of Reon Atescre, matches, the gold and coins the Bursar had given her. This world.... Did she have a home, a job, a past here? Lovers and ex-lovers, a post at a university? *Harvard Yale UW Mizzou Minnesota Menomonie Baker Oxford Cambridge Sorbonne* riffled into place, like flipping through a stack of index cards. Did she have a physician—no, a *primary-care provider*; medications? No, these were all gaps. She had her gug and the things it carried. She had this knowledge of the waking world sifting into her mind. She had herself. This is how Randolph Carter said it had been for him when he first came to the dream lands. As a youth—*teenager* was the word here—he had known everything he needed, but there had been gaps.

Vellitt stretched her back (and that, at least, felt the same) and walked onto the rough grass to look at the nearest tombstones: *Voeller. Axtman. Halvorson. Johnson.* She placed her finger on *Anderson.* The moss filling the ornate *A* was dry and delicate as old paper.

She had in that first sweeping moment fully understood just how immense this waking world was. Seven billion people. How would she find Clarie Jurat in all these leagues, among all these people? Asking the question, she knew the answer. The small glossy box she had been given in Hatheg-Kla was a phone, lost or left behind by some dreamer in the temple of Flame. Hers now. She leaned into the window of the car that was once a gug, and pulled it from her jacket as more details slipped into place— password protection, GPS, maps, apps. The phone flared into life at her touch. There were no signs of the man who had once owned it. There was a single name in the favorites list: *Clarie Jurat.* She touched the name and the phone, hummed in her hand. She typed the name into a search field, fingers fumbling, and a tiny map zoomed onto a blue dot labeled *Clarie Jurat 789 miles.*

This was new, too: that distance here was a certain thing, unchanging.

She got into the Buick and shifted into gear, and the gug's voice changed pitch and volume. It was all ingrained in her, the clever coordination that changed gears or slowed down, the turn signals, the vents, the cranking windows. The rough lane turned into a winding road that led beneath dappled tree-shadow through the oldest part of the cemetery and to the main gate. She pulled into the street and stopped abruptly.

In the cemetery it had been largely hidden from her by the dense trees: the sky, blue and entirely empty, blue and blue and blue, without tessellate shiftings, without the massy swells of otherness that bloomed always in faint seething twists. Blue, featureless and weightless. A bird flew from a maple tree to the branches of an elm down the street. Beyond it, high overhead, she saw motes at the extremity of her vision, and then they swept down close enough to see that they were a flock of starlings, a cloud of them, changing directions as they flew, like a mist writhing, like gnats pillaring or herrings schooling. And behind them, the sky, empty, untextured, unmeaning, flat, and blue.

She stared until a pickup truck swung past, honking its horn.

Clarie Jurat was in Miles City, Montana. The phone offered suggestions for routes, and Vellitt Boe took the quickest of them. The land she drove through reminded her of the countryside behind Celephaïs, green with trees and bright with crops, save that the hills were gentler and there were no mountains behind them, only clouds and the hollow sky.

She passed through small towns of flat, unancient structures; houses with unornamented chimneys, wide-windowed gables, clapboard sides. The main streets were broad and faced with low buildings of brick and glass. There were larger roads lined with big boxes of concrete and steel filled with goods, cars for sale in glittering ranks. There were signs everywhere, white, black, green, and every color, on the highway and in the towns; street names, shop fronts, sales, warnings, advertisements. No place in the dream lands was so emphatically labeled. Streets and roads did not have signs, and shops had only small placards in their front windows. Even inns' signs were pictures only. Signs were promises that a thing was *here* or would be *there*, that rules would last as long as paint. Here, nothing changed at the whims of the gods.

There were no gods in this place. She could feel it in the same way she felt the vacuity of the massless sky. The air was empty except for the smells of June grass and recent rain, birds and the contrails of jets. There was an easiness, as though gravity here were in some indefinable way less onerous, but it was not a lesser gravity that made things lighter. It was the absence of gods, as though she had walked her entire life under a heavy hide and cast it off at last.

The gug's engine purred westbound and came to a many-laned freeway crowded with cars of black and silver and white and the colors of the jungle birds of Kled. When she came to a town of medium size, she stopped and converted some of the gold coins to paper money in a *pawn shop*. She stopped for gas. She ate chicken—which was new to her; there were no chickens in the dream lands—and drank cold tea. The gug growled steadily on, and the freeway swept her past stores, high-treed suburbs, and cluttery neighborhoods. She came late in the afternoon to a shining city of buildings tall as crags and gleaming with crystal and steel. She passed it, and the setting sun spread its wings before her, high cirrus clouds catching fire in the sky above the tree-clustered, rolling plains. The sun set and the first stars came out, Venus and Regulus, and then Beta Leonis and others: scores and then hundreds, more than she had ever imagined. She could not attend to the road, but pulled over and watched the sky bloom. Yes, millions. Billions.

Vellitt stopped for the night in a motel: no gossipy innkip or locals drinking in the taproom downstairs, and no encircling protective wall. She had no clothes but those she stood in, so she asked advice from a civil young woman in a gray trousered suit who stood behind the front desk, and was sent to a big box that was a store. Later, she slept in a room that was a rectangle, with a black-and-white photograph of a river gorge over the immense bed.

She dreamt that she stood upon a high marble terrace and looked out upon a hushed sunset city. Ulthar. It still existed. She was right that the god's messenger had lied to her. A long staircase of porphyry and jasper descended to a Gate, and beyond it, she could see the underground garden in the temple on Hatheg-Kla; but the Gate was locked. She shook her head, and shaking it awoke. She looked out the window and the moon was full, flat, and white. It moved slowly, almost imperceptibly, obedient to the geometries of gravity, of physics.

Millions of stars.

In the morning the tag on the GPS map read *Clarie Jurat 467 miles*. The country had changed in the hours Vellitt had driven after dark. The trees were gone, the land flatter. Only green-gold grasses remained, and rare tight folds in the plains that were waterways marked by thick bands of cottonwood trees, and every so often a cluster of buildings and signs and trees: a freeway exit. Otherwise, the land seemed as empty as a desert, a green desert alive with wind.

She drove, and the sun drifted behind her, up, and overhead. She felt she probably had sunglasses, and it turned out she did, in the glove compartment. The gug had no air conditioning, so she drove with the windows open, and her bare arm grew hot. The air tasted of concrete and motor oil, pollen and dust and sunlight.

The country grew rough and broke into badlands, great sections of rock shredded and tipped at angles as though they had been dropped when some unknown god's blind tantrum had ended; but it was no god, only volcanism, winds and rains and vast unmeasured eons of time. The badlands softened and became outcroppings among rolling hills of dry grasses and brush, pronghorns and cattle. She stopped for gas; stopped for bathrooms; stopped because she was thirsty, because she was hungry; stopped sometimes because she needed to stop and listen to the voiceless wind, and see the empty sky.

Clarie Jurat 217 miles. Clarie Jurat 84 miles. Clarie Jurat 12 miles.

Vellitt Boe found Clarie Jurat in a shop called Common Grounds, walls of brick and dark wood wrapped around the smells of baked goods and brewed coffee. She paused in the doorway and saw her behind a long steel counter. In Ulthar, Clarie had worn skirts, dresses, her University robes, square-heeled shoes, and her hair had been a smooth, tidy braid: discreet attire, appropriate to a University woman, though her charisma had shone through. Now—how long had it been for her here?—her black hair was a shaggy cropped tumble that fell to the nape of her neck, and there were silver hoops in her long earlobes. She wore narrow jeans with soft canvas shoes—*Vans*—a t-shirt, and a black barista's apron, and her left arm was marked with a tattoo that wrapped her from wrist to sleeve-edge.

There was a mirror behind the coffee bar and Vellitt saw herself for a moment reflected over Jurat's shoulder, and she looked as strange to herself as Jurat did: the ropes of her hair, the black blouse opening like a crow's wings about her throat. They were both changed, in this waking world.

"Can I help—" Clarie Jurat said in her familiar, music-filled voice and looking up with a smile, fell abruptly silent. "Professor—Boe?"

"Jurat," Vellitt said, and with the word, she felt as though a longed-for freshet of water had been splashed in her face; for this was the end of her quest, she thought. *At last.*

"How are you here? Is—is anything wrong? My father?"

"Yes," Vellitt said baldly. "—Not your father, no. But yes, there is something wrong. We have to talk."

The bell on the door jangled. "I can't talk right now," said Clarie Jurat, as two women walked in with a stroller, a toddler dressed in brilliant purple and green bursting forward beside them, shouting, *Choc! Choc!* "Come back at seven. That's an hour and a half."

Vellitt walked through Miles City: quickly done, for it was a small town but lovely, heavy with trees and grassy lawns and shade. This was the home Clarie Jurat had chosen. The schools were low brickwork sprawls and had grounds filled with slides, swings, climbing structures, as though children could be permitted to play. There were people everywhere, and half of them were women. The churches were silent, sleeping and godless; there was no smell of dried blood, no stains upon their calm altars.

At seven, she returned, and Clarie Jurat took Vellitt to a tiny house of blue and white clapboard, with a bedroom hardly larger than the bed it contained, a green-tiled bathroom, and the rest of the space a single room that was kitchen and dining room, living room and entry. Clarie talked as she poured iced black-currant tea, proud of the house, the little wooden kitchen table and matching chairs; the little laptop she had purchased the week before—"It does *everything*," she said reverently, and couldn't help laughing at herself—the thrift-store dresser on newspapers in the center of the room, which she was refinishing based on videos she found online. There were no signs of a man's presence. She showed everything to Vellitt Boe, and Vellitt said nothing, and wept inside for Clarie Jurat.

At last Clarie said, "Shall we order a pizza? Then we don't have to go anywhere. We can eat in the kitchen. I have beer."

"Of course," Vellitt said. "I was driving and I suddenly thought *Canadian bacon*, but I don't know what it is, except as something that goes on pizza."

Clarie's smile was golden and lovely as sunrise. "Yeah, so many things I woke up knowing without ever experiencing them."

She ordered pizza and brought two beers from her refrigerator. Vellitt tasted hers, bitter and fizzy. Perhaps she made a face, for Clarie said apologetically, "I know. It's not as good as the ale from the Pshent, is it? Beer here isn't very good, so far as I can tell. So, Professor. How, why?"

"You may as well call me Vellitt. Where is the man who brought you here?"

Jurat sighed a little. "Oh, Stephan. He didn't bring me *here*. He's from Missoula—that's west of here, it's all mountains and pine trees—so that's where we went, and when we split up, I came east. Four months ago, now. Wow, it seems longer."

"I'm sorry for the loss," Vellitt said, because that was a thing that should be said.

Jurat looked rueful but shrugged. "It was me. I got here, the waking world, and he was—just irrelevant. So small, compared to everything he might be. Everything I had imagined. I thought I was in love with him until I got here." She shook her head. "It's strange, how things are. People are together and then they're not, and you can't explain any of it."

Vellitt said, "It wasn't *him*, was it? That you loved. It was this." She gestured: the room, Miles City, the waking world. Adventure.

Clarie nodded. "Yeah. I mean, I work in a coffee shop. People here don't even see it; it's like this boring job for them—but every day people say hello to me; every day I meet someone new, who is round and bright and—scattery, made out of *parts*, plans and fears and love and worry and I don't even know what. I don't know how to explain it. Random and meaningful and beautiful. I know that doesn't make sense." She gave a little laugh, half defiant.

"I know," said Vellitt. "I *do* know. I arrived yesterday—in Wisconsin, so I've been driving. No one here tells people what they mean, what their world means."

Clarie picked at the bottle's label. "And there are women everywhere and people in different colors, and it's all amazing. Science. Geography. Do you know that math makes sense here? Look at this." She stretched out her tattooed arm. A number wrapped around and around her arm, beginning at her wrist and vanishing into the short sleeve of her t-shirt. *3.141592653589793* . . . "Pi," she said. "It never changes here. The rules never change, Professor. Vellitt. Here, physics is just cause and effect, and the moon orbits the earth on a schedule. They know *years* in advance where it will be."

Vellitt waited, a skill learned in decades of tutorials and classes. Jurat had been her best student. She would get to it.

Clarie continued, "And they have colleges everywhere, and universities, Professor. Vellitt. I can study Mathematics here. Or anything. They have sciences we've never even heard of."

Vellitt waited.

"Did you come to bring me back to Ulthar?" Clarie said finally. "Because I won't go."

"I am so sorry," said Vellitt, and she told her of a small god who tossed restless and rousing on his couch; that if he awoke to find Clarie Jurat gone from his world, he would destroy Ulthar and the Skai valley.

"That's ridiculous," Clarie said. "I'm nothing there, just a third-year at University."

Vellitt pulled Clarie upright and led her to the mirror of the dresser, and looked over her shoulder at the girl, radiant, long-eyed and narrow nosed and shiningly beautiful. "Clarie, you're not like other people. You know this, though you very properly take no advantage of the knowledge. You are the granddaughter of a god."

Clarie shook her head. "No. There are no gods."

"Not here. But there. Gods and gods and gods, and every one of them capricious, tiny, and powerful. Your grandfather is one."

"Fuck him," said Clarie Jurat. The word sat strangely in the mouth of a College woman. "When has he ever been anything to me? Fuck them all. I will not go back."

Vellitt waited. There had been an expression that would move across Clarie's face when she was working some difficult proof in a tutorial, intent and inward. She had that look now, and Vellitt waited. All the Ulthar women, the students and scholars and Fellows: Therine Angoli and Raba Hust, Derysk Oure and Yllyn Martveit, Gnesa Petso and the Bursar; the rest of the University and her father and every other man and woman and child of Ulthar, and beyond it Mir and Hatheg and the glowing green plains of the river Skai.

"This is what life is, then," said Clarie into the stretching silence. Mingled anger and despair filled her voice. "Doing things you hate. I thought if I came here, maybe it would be different, I could be something amazing."

"Clarie—"

Three little chimes rang.

"That's the doorbell," Clarie Jurat said. "The pizza." She started to cry and could not stop for a time. In the end, it was Vellitt who went to the door and paid the man.

Vellitt Boe and Clarie Jurat sat long, eating pizza and drinking the terrible beer. They did not speak much. Clarie was clearly full of dark thoughts—and Vellitt, as well, hating herself for her quest.

But Clarie put down her beer and said finally, with a small, twisted smile, "I'll do it. Of course. I should have said that earlier, right? That's what Ulthar Women's College women do, isn't it? The right thing. Except that I don't know how to go back."

Vellitt said, slowly, "It's not so hard from this side. You sleep, is all. I think your grandfather's blood will call you home."

"And you'll be with me." It was half a question.

Vellitt stood and crossed to the window, looked out on the sunset sky, her gug parked on the street behind Clarie's rusty Toyota. "I cannot."

Clarie's voice behind her was angry. "What? Why should I return if you will not?"

"Not 'will not.' Cannot. I've known since Hatheg-Kla. I hoped it would not be true; but as I climbed into this world—it's clear now. I can go back, and I would be destroyed and that would be the way of things. Or I might be spared so that I could watch Ulthar destroyed, after all." Vellitt turned. "I've lived in Ulthar for so many years, Jurat, and never thought of it as home. It was just an endpoint to my journeys—I could not keep traveling so I stopped. And it happened to be Ulthar. And now that I can't go back, I realize it became home, anyway." Vellitt exhaled something that might have been a laugh.

There was a silence. Vellitt watched the shadows collect beneath the trees.

"No," Clarie said after eternity. Vellitt turned, for her voice was changed, strong as steel. She walked to the window to stand beside and together they looked out: Miles City and the shadows, the cars. "It's not his blood that calls me home—not in the way you mean. Some people change the world, and I guess that's me. And some people change the people who change the world. And that's you. I'm one of them, Vellitt. I'm a god, right? So *I* can save Ulthar." She turned, and all the attention of this altered Clarie Jurat focused on Vellitt Boe, and she fought the impulse to faint from the stress of that regard.

Clarie went on, "I've seen a world without gods, and it's better. You: stay and live free of gods, and I will return and fix my world. There have to be ways to counter them. To fight them. I am one of them. I can do it." She laughed, and for a moment it seemed as though the little house was filled with thunder and the earth beneath them shuddered.

Vellitt stumbled backward. Clarie pivoted to look at her. Her eyes reflecting the kitchen lights seemed filled with flame. "Do you doubt me?"

"No," Vellitt said. "No."

They fell asleep at last, Clarie Jurat in her little bedroom and Vellitt Boe on the sofa, wrapped in a crocheted afghan Clarie had bought at a thrift store. Vellitt found herself on a marble terrace, but the terrace looked out on nothing but darkness, and the clustered urns were filled with black roses that smelled of dust. She knew how to read these signs. Clarie Jurat was beside her: brilliant, strong-willed, beautiful, with long fierce eyes and her hair a glowing crown. They descended together the seventy steps to the Gate—and just visible beyond was a cavern like a secret garden, with fungi like willow trees and mosses like grasses; and on the tessellated path was a man with violet robes and a heavy spade-shaped black beard: Reon Atescre who was now Nasht.

The Gate was secured with a lock, shining like gold. They had no key, but Clarie said in a god's voice, "I will enter," and the Gate burst open. "Live without gods," she said to Vellitt, and stepped onto the silver pavement.

"Wait—" said Vellitt, remembering a thing suddenly. She felt in her pocket for the Bursar's little lined notebook, filled with expenditures. "Take this back to Gnesa when you can." She extended her hand through the opened Gate and felt the dream realms buzzing at her skin. Clarie took it before turning back to Reon, who had fallen to his knees before her.

"Do not kneel," said Clarie Jurat in a voice like thunder, like earths breaking and stars forming. "No more gods."

And Vellitt Boe awoke, shoutingly awake on the couch in what had been Clarie's house, and she was alone.

She stood, feeling an ache in her lower back, too old to sleep on couches. A beer bottle on the unfinished dresser had left a white ring; at some point in their sleep, the mirror had broken into shards that lay scattered across the floor. She glimpsed movement in one, but it was only her reflection as she stretched and looked about.

Clarie Jurat was gone and already the rooms seemed as though they had been emptied of life, embedded in the impenetrable amber of the past. Would there be unanswered texts, an unfilled shift at the coffee shop in Main Street, a missing-persons report, and her Toyota rusting until it was towed? Or would the waking world reseal itself over the place that had been Clarie Jurat, and leave no signs she had ever been there?

She walked outside. Birds sang in the shrubs beside the door, and flared up and across the street as she walked down the steps. The sharp smell of gasoline came crisp from the neighbor's driveway, where he filled his lawnmower's tank from a red poly can, and he nodded a greeting. Light glowed from street and tree and lawn and house, and over everything shone the brightening sky, godless and unfigured. The Buick slept beneath the oak tree by the street, lean-haunched and gray and beautiful to her. On the hood, as precisely as a statue, sat the small black cat, her tail curled about her feet. When she saw Vellitt, she made a sound and stood in a complicated fluid movement that was back-arch and leg-stretch and tail-twist and head-butt into Vellitt's cupped hand.

"You're staying?" she asked aloud. The cat meowed again.

Infinities away, Clarie Jurat walked down the seven hundred steps into the dream lands to change her world. And Vellitt Boe picked up the cat and sat on the Buick's hood and said, "Well, this is us, then. Now what?"

Noah's Raven

Ten months after the ark first floated, and forty days after its keel snagged on a drowned mountain peak, Noah released a raven to look for land. Her name was ungraspable by humans, but might be translated as Bessary, plus a term ravens used for the taste of three-day-dead goat when the temperatures have stayed just above freezing, plus a color at the 327-nanometer wavelength, plus a sensation along the rictal bristles in a particular sort of cool air. Her feathers rustled like silk, and the arch of her beak was particularly beautiful.

The other raven had been called something roughly translatable as Arum/*the eleventh day of the moon/the taste of iron-rich water/ fourteen young raised to adulthood.*

If Noah had asked, the local ravens would have met and determined a good pair: old enough to have sense but still young, strong, and with a successful nesting history: smart ravens, good at problem solving. *If* Noah had asked—*and* if he had been right that the entire world even could be covered in water. But that was nonsense: even a young raven knew this. A flood only covered parts of things. Fly high enough, and you would see something, somewhere. And Bessary and Arum were not even paired. Arum had eased into a slightly tufty, late middle age with his partner, Tanipelis, whereas Bessary was flapping enthusiastically toward full adulthood, and spent her time with a crew of similarly light-winged adolescents who ate and played together, and slept in comfortable rows in the communal night-trees.

But Noah did not ask, not the ravens, not anyone. He had been told: *seven of each clean animal, two of each unclean*, which was a lot of work in a hurry. God had implied that the animals would come to Noah, but that's not how it worked out. *Some* did come, or maybe were just wandering past the ark site on their way to someplace else. Others had to be hunted out.

By the end, Noah was getting sloppy. If he didn't have enough of an animal, he killed what he did have, and hid the bodies in an ever-growing corpse pile on a hillside nearby. What, was God going to check up on every single vole? Would He even notice the absence of the rose-beaked wren or the ghost mouse? If He liked them so much, He should have made sure they showed up on time. Some animals, Noah never caught even one, and these he treated as children's tales and legends, even if in his youth he had thrown sticks at them and stalked their woodland nests.

The birds were a particular challenge. Noah did his beleaguered best: set snares in trees and beside marshes and in fields, then assigned his daughters to sort and cage the captured birds. There were mistakes, of course. They could not always tell the difference between this sparrow and that, plus females and males often did not resemble one another. Noah's daughters tried their best, but in the end, they caged what seemed a reasonable number of small brown birds all together and left them to sort it out amongst themselves. If they got more than they needed of something, they freed the extras, but any birds injured in the nets were killed and their bodies tossed into a sinew- and feather-threaded heap.

The bird-corpse pile was how Arum and Bessary were caught. The vultures and other carrion birds went to Noah's larger corpse pile, but the ravens were curious. So much carrion in a single place was surprising, but all birds? It was not at all a known thing and surely merited a look. And so it was that Arum and Bessary were squabbling over the corpse of a white-capped nightfisher when a concealed net snapped closed. A few yards away, Tanipelis had been plucking the feathers from a dead red-tailed hawk. Rattling with fear, she tore at the net, and when Noah's daughters approached, she attacked them. Protecting their heads, the daughters shoved the tangle of birds and net into a bamboo cage painted with tar and fled. A day later, when they at last risked returning to where they had dropped the cage in the birds' staging area, Bessary had bitten the net into shreds, and the ravens now huddled in opposite corners of their cage. Arum was silent; Tanipelis was gone.

Cages and coops, stakeout lines and fences, nose twitches and goads, ever more noise and smell. The largest cages were pushed up the long ramps on cedar-log rollers, then lowered into the ark's deep hold. The animals that could be led were dragged into the stenchy dark and tied, struggling, into their stanchions. Noah had plans for which animals went where, but by the end, there was no order to any of it: antelopes stacked atop cheetahs beside newts, beavers by wolves by a dirt-filled crate for the star-nosed moles; and smaller cages crammed into every crevice and corner.

Bessary and Arum were placed on deck, part of a stack of cages tied down tightly beneath an oilskin tent, where the larger birds were kept.

The rain started; the rain kept on. In a series of shuddering jolts, the ark lifted at last from its blocks and was afloat. It had been hastily made, and water came in everywhere, seeping up through the ballast, down from the hatches, and between the planks of the deck and hull. Noah's sons set the oxen to the treadmill pumps that would keep the ship afloat. As long as they were here they might as well make themselves useful.

The rain kept on and kept on. Water soaked through the oilskin, down past the skysweeps in the cage above. Bessary and Arum crouched on the rotting remnants of the net until the shreds slipped through the floor onto the giant petrels beneath them; then they slept on the cage's bare bars. So much water rinsed the tar from the cages, and after a time, Bessary saw it would be possible to bite through the cords that secured the bamboo. But why? The rain kept on and kept on. Where would they go?

At least there was plenty to eat.

Every so often Noah or one of his sons staggered along the rain-swept deck to slop a rank stew that changed every day into wooden bowls in the cages. The stew was delectable, Bessary thought, but Arum only picked at it, sunk into a lethargy she could not stir him from. She *prruk*ed and rattled and knocked and sang at Arum, but he would not speak, just gave the sound that meant *back off*, and after a time, not even that. When he slept, she groomed him delicately, so as not to awaken him.

Nothing at all, until a day when he said: *The snow markhors are gone.*

What do you mean? she asked, but he said no more. And she in any case knew, because now that he *had* said it, she could taste their death. Somewhere in the ark's reeking belly, the male snow markhor had died, coughing. And in the cold counting-game of the ark, one of a species was the same as none of a species, and so the female was killed as well, and both thrown together into the stewpot.

The rain kept on. Four days later, Arum said: *the reticulated honeydrinkers.* After that: *the crested aurochs.* Arum collected each name like a shiny object found on the ground, then dropped it into Bessary's mind. *The giant pangolins.*

Bessary, with all the time in the wet world and the taste of the dead on her black tongue, thought it through. She knew what Noah believed was going on: the world swept bare by water and wave, this fat floundering ark containing the last creatures in all the world. But that was nonsense: No flood could *cover* the earth. So Arum must mean that all the reticulated honeydrinkers *here*, on the ark, were gone. There must be others, on high lands Noah had no notion of.

The rain kept on. *The paladin shrews. The speckled skinks. The fieldcats.*

Ravens had a practiced palate, but Bessary, each day tasting a mix of creatures she had neither seen nor known of, was becoming an expert at fathoming the truth of what she ate. That's how she knew that the fieldcats were *really* gone. Floods might not cover the earth, but they *had* covered all the fieldcat ranges. These two fieldcats really had been the last two, until they were dead, and it was all perfectly clear in the taste, as clear as the alpha-keratin of fur, the iron of blood. The fieldcats were *gone*. Extinct.

The hemippes. The monkeyface wallabys.

The rain stopped, and the wind began. The ark was a graceless vessel, toiling across the waves in juddering heaves. *The great gnippans.*

The skysweeps. Their cage above the ravens was taken away, and now Bessary and Arum were the top of the stack, and the tent pressed against their cage. Bessary tore free a piece of oilskin that she pulled in through the bars, giving her a patch of coarse cloth to sleep on, and incidentally leaving a hole through which she could see the world outside: red-eyed Noah or his sons when they staggered along the heaving deck; beyond that the broken gray sea; and beyond that the sky: a sharp thin blue, layered with stratus clouds and high, thin cirrus like a ragged veil.

The gray efts. The cryptic treehunters.

Arum had always taken their situation harder than Bessary. After his molt his feathers grew in ragged and raw-edged, no longer smoothly nestling into their places. He ate so little that Bessary wondered how he knew who had died.

She was afraid. They were not even friends, let alone mates. But if he died, into the stewpot he would go. And then so would she—and it would not matter whether there were other ravens in the world, because there would be no more Bessary. Extinction can be as global as *all*, or as personal as *me*.

The sea starlings. The scimitar oryxes. The bennū herons.

The rain and then the wind, the cage and Arum dying beside her and the growing list of lost animals. It had been going on forever when the ship gave a deep wooden shout and staggered to one side, like an ox leaping away from a wasp sting. The waves changed gait, and instead of tossing the vessel, they slammed against it. It had been so long that even Noah did not understand immediately that the ark had grounded, on a crag a few fathoms beneath the waves. The waters were dropping.

The sea otters sensed the kelp and young shellfish on the other side of the hull, and squealed and writhed in excitement. They could survive—if anyone could have gotten to them to release them. For everyone else, land underwater was no land at all, and waters dropping were not waters gone. And the waters, they stayed and they stayed, perhaps a little lower each day but still, not land.

The queen vultures. The passenger pigeons. Gone: gone from the ark or gone entirely, and if not this time, then the next.

By the fortieth day of the ship's grounding, Noah was nearly mad with exhaustion and despair. Plus winter was coming again. He came on deck. The tent over the bird cages had been worn thin by sun and wind and rain, so it was no great labor to pull the oilskin away and unveil his biggest birds. He looked them over. Gone: the skysweeps, the ordinal phalaropes, the desert condors. The remaining birds were a draggled lot, many ill, others hard to rouse from their anomie or despair.

The ravens' cage was eye-height. Noah contemplated Bessary, clinging to the side of the cage, disheveled but alert, and watching him with one bright eye. Arum lay flat on the scrap of oilskin, unmoving except for an occasional flick of ragged feather, but that might have been the wind.

Noah said, "Well, he's dead, but you look strong enough." He pulled out a small hand axe and began to chip at the bamboo of their cage.

Bessary said, "He's not dead." This is before the Tower at Babel fell and words between tribes and species failed, but anyone could have read the mantling of her wings and her fierce stance for what it said.

Even so, he misunderstood. "Don't worry, it's not about *that*." He meant the stewpot and the taste of Arum—and Bessary—in tomorrow's meal. "I need something."

She waited: wings still half-mantled, a skeptical eye.

He said, "There's land somewhere. I know it. I need someone to fly high, look around, and then come back and tell me whether this is almost over." Even to a raven, he sounded weary and sick at heart.

"Why would I do that?" said Bessary.

He had returned to breaking open the bamboo cage. "Why *wouldn't* you? It's what animals are *for*, doing things." He meant: *doing things for us*. "You're worried you'd come back and be killed since the other one's dead? I swear we won't." He looked solemn; he thought he spoke the truth. "Come back, and even if you don't find any land, we'll keep feeding you. We'll feed you *extra*, so you can try again in a week or two. In fact, you could even stay with us, after." He put down the hand axe and bent back a wall of the cage. "You're smart and good at things. You'd be useful."

Bessary tried to jump out, but it had been a long time since she had moved more than a wingspan in any direction, and she stumbled. Noah caught her and placed her on the deck, then stepped back quickly—for she was as high as his thigh, a hook-beaked, taloned shadow, the black of an oak tree killed in a lightning strike.

She looked around. Even from his safe distance, he towered over her. But *beyond* him, and past the railings and structures that had hemmed her in for so long, the sky was enormous. She cupped her wings to the tiny drift of air along the deck, flicked them out to full extension and then preened, settling each feather into its right place.

He was still talking, still thinking it out. "You'd be as good as a dog. Better. Smarter, and you can fly. You could herd, or guard, or even just keep an eye on things. Maybe you could have young with someone else, a crow or maybe an eagle? *That* would be something."

She hopped to the railing and extended her wings experimentally. They were weak but good enough.

"Bring us good news, raven," said Noah.

"I'm gone," she said, and she was.

At first, Bessary was clumsy. She stepped off the railing and, where her wings should have caught her fall and lifted her without thought, she dropped instead, fast toward the water. But her muscles remembered their work in time. Her wingtips flicked out and she powered her way up past the railing, past gaping Noah and the tower of cages, past the birds as they blinked in the unaccustomed light and called to her.

When she was clear of it all, she hovered, tipping from side to side as she read the bright particularities of the air until she located the ark's updraft, shaped by cookfire, the effluence of a thousand breathing lungs, and cedarwood hot in the morning sun. Slanting across, she slipped into the sweet spot and began to ease upward in tight circles.

Up and up. When she had been on the ark, her existence had contracted to the single point that was the cage, but now it unfolded and unpacked, until she flew in a three-dimensional foam of air, rich with variations in texture and temperature. The horizon climbed as she climbed, a pale thin line, infinitely distant now. The world beneath her looked like a vast bowl brimming with water. Blue sky and clouds stuttered on the rough waves so far below, but she could also see through, *into* the water, and *there* she saw the land that Noah craved and would eventually claim: the puckers and wrinkles of mountains, paler where the water was shallower, the valleys still only deep blue mysteries.

Such a pointless errand: a month or two from now, the flood would have receded anyway.

From this height, the ark was the size of a wood chip, a thing so small that a pebble might crush it. A disk of soiled water ringed it, jetsam and effluvium half-concealing the mountain on which the ark had snagged. In the northeast, a vague discoloration still dirtied the water over which it had passed; to the west, a current dragged a broad stain from the ark, extending as far as she could see.

If Noah was right, this flood had been God's judgment on humans as a species, and the very last of them lived on that flake of bark below her. *If* he was right—but of course that was nonsense; even a young raven knew that. Of course there were others. The humans would keep doing what they do: the quaggas, the thylacines, the burrowing boas. But Bessary had grown expert at tasting the dead. Eventually the humans also would be gone, she knew: if not this time, then the next.

And the world would rebuild itself along new lines, without golden toads and without warrahs and without humans.

And without Bessary—but that time was not yet. She was very high now, the sun hot on her wings. She saw a dark fleck in the air a little distance away, so she flicked her wings to slide across and inspect it. It was a small brown spider, suspended from a thread a thousand feet up, sailing the sky to a home it had never seen. Another time, she might have eaten it. But today, Bessary slanted away, and flew back along the wind, toward a green moment barely visible on the horizon.

Crows Attempt Human–Style Riddles, and One Joke

"Have you guessed the riddle yet?" the Hatter said,
    turning to Alice.
"No, I give up," Alice replied: "what's the answer?"
"I haven't the slightest idea," said the Hatter.

Lewis Carroll

Q: How many jays is too many?
A: Whoever gets there first.

Q: Six crows find a dead dog. The dog kills them. How?
A: The dog was poisoned, and they eat it.

Q: Cats have four legs. Why?
A: To slow them down.

Q: What is a car?
A: Meat-maker.
A. Wind-maker.
A: A can full of people.
Q: What is a beak?

A: Meal-maker.
A: The direction you go.

Q: What is the best food?
A: Whatever I have that you don't.
A. Whatever you have that I don't.
A: [Long answer involving directions to a nearby fast-food taco restaurant where the dumpsters do not close properly, which also includes a pun on the crows' term for good luck.]
A: Deer.

Q: What do mice eat?
A: Who cares?
A: Judging by the way they taste, mostly seeds.
A: Nothing important.

Q: What is a tree?
A: Seven crows, ten discussions.
A: The first place.

Q: Fast as a car but never faster. What?
A: The shadow of the car.
A: People inside the car.

Q: The jay finds eggs in her nest. What does she think?
A: Someone left food!

Q: The chicken crossed the road. Why?
A: It was a strong wind.

Q: The difference between a crow and a human?
A: The human has to walk everywhere.
A: A human's head only goes this high [hops]. A crow's head goes
  this high [flies].

Q: The difference between one mile and five miles?
A: The dumpster behind that food store there.

Q: Dirt outside, meat inside and rocks inside that. What?
A: A dead hawk [and its crop].

Q: A human put food on the ground.
A: The squirrels ate it.

Q: What opens doors?
A: Humans [roundly criticized as too obvious].
A: Waiting.

Q: What is a human?
A: Dog-maker.
A: The changer.

Q: A crow mates with the rain. Why?
A: The first bluejay was lonely.
Q: Ever annoying, ever present, ever delicious. What?
A: Feather mites.
A: Food wrappers.

Q: What is a nest?
A: Crow-maker.
A: Six stories.

Two crows walk into a bar.
Crow One: We should have ducked.
Crow Two: No, ducks are assholes.

The Privilege of the Happy Ending

This is a story that ends as all stories do eventually, in deaths.

When Ada's parents died in the winter of her sixth year, she was sent to the neighboring parish to live with her aunt, Margery. Margery was a widow with three daughters, all older than Ada; and their names were Cruelty, Spite, and Malice. They lived in a narrow cottage with a single room, and rain came in where the thatch had grown thin beside the falling-down chimney. Margery had a garden and a pig and some piglets, and three sheep, though one was old. There was also a coop full of hens with a single rooster. There was no room for an orphan in Margery's narrow cottage, nor in her narrow gray life, so Ada slept in the coop surrounded by the chickens: their feathers and fluff, their earthy smell, their soft nonsense gabbling—and of everyone in that household, Ada's food was scantest but her bed was softest.

Ada loved all the hens, but her favorite was Blanche, white as a pearl and sturdy as a peasant's ankle, with five bright white nails on each ivory foot, and a beak the pink of tender rosebuds in May, and a flat little comb and wattle the crimson of full-blown roses in July. She was as pretty as an enameled jewel made for a duke, yet her golden-black eyes were clever as clever. Blanche's egg-laying days were past, but it was Ada's task to collect the eggs and tell her aunt who was laying and who was not; and so Blanche was not eaten.

There was a day after the hay had been brought in but just before the fringed golden wheat was ready for the sickle. After Margery and the sisters broke their fast, the porridge pot had been nearly empty (and the rest needed for dinner); so once Ada had fed the hens and collected the eggs, she went into the old forest to find something from which she might make her own meal. But she knew it was dangerous to go alone, and so she took Blanche.

The road became a path as it crossed into the shadows of the old forest. Ada was gleaning sweet musty blackberries and bitter-bright burdock greens (too late in the season, but there they were, and thus worth trying) until Blanche saw the feathery little leaves of kippernuts tucked close to an oak tree's roots. Ada squatted to dig the tiny tubers from the ground, and carefully brushed them free of dirt. She had two for each one Blanche took. They agreed this was only fair, for she was bigger and had done the work.

Ada had eaten six-and-twenty kippernuts (and Blanche thirteen) when they heard someone running along the path-that-was-a-road. The news that comes on fast feet is seldom good but is always important, so Ada leapt up, and Blanche scurried from her bug-scratching to press close, peeking around her legs. But it was just a boy that burst into sight, heaving and panting and out of breath: older than she, thin and dressed poorly (for *he* was an orphan as well), and running on bare feet beaten hard as bootsoles.

When he saw Ada, he paused, gasping until he could speak at last. "Where. Is your father? I have. News that is. Worth. A penny or more."

"I have no father, but I have an aunt. She lives that way." Ada pointed along the path.

"Is there a. Village? I don't want to. Waste my time."

"There's a church and a miller *and* a blacksmith," said Ada, looking up at him. "What news is worth a penny?"

"Do you *have*. A penny?" said the boy.

She shook her head. "I have a chicken, and I have this pin. My mother gave it to me before she died." She pulled it from her collar to show it to him: fine as a hair and straight as a thread pulled tight, with a tiny silver knob at one end.

"A chicken's too heavy," he said but plucked the pin from her fingers, though she had offered neither. "It's wastoures! They came through Newton and Blackhill and killed everything. And then they split into two big groups and one turned north, and the other's coming here. I stay ahead of them and earn pennies by warning people."

Wastoures. Perhaps you have not heard of them, you people born a thousand years after Ada and Blanche and this runner— whose name is Hardourt, though his part in this story is nearly over: His name will not matter to you, though it matters to him. In your time they are gone, but in the twelfth century, every child knew of them, and adults as well. Wastoures: scarce larger than chickens but unfeathered and wingless, snake-necked and sharp-beaked and bright-clawed, with little arms ending in daggery talons. For long years there would be no wastoures (except in memory and dread), and then a population bloom, like duckweed choking an August pond, or locusts after a dry spring, or cicadas rising from the ground each seventh year. For reasons unknowable, they emerged in their scores of thousands from some secret cave or forgotten Roman mine, and seethed like floodwater and plague across the land. Eventually they died off, plunging heedless from cliffs or drowning in waters too deep to cross; or else autumn made them torpid, then dead—but not before they had eaten every breathing creature they encountered. They were in everyone's nightmares. Small children feared them more even than wolves or orphanhood. These were dark times, wastoure summers.

Wastoures. At the sound of the word, Blanche had fluttered into Ada's arms. The girl shivered and said, "Take us home! Please, I'm too little to run fast enough by myself."

He eyed her. "You're too big to carry. How far is it?"

"Very far," she said sadly. She had walked all morning and now it was early afternoon. If she ran home—if she *could* run so far—she would not get there before the midwife's cow began complaining to be milked. And Margery would not notice her absence until dusk, when there would be no one to chivvy the chickens to their coop. The wastoures would catch her before that.

"Then I can't take you," he said. "You're too slow. They'd catch us both and eat even our bones."

Ada knew hard truths. She was raised in them. "Take Blanche, at least."

Blanche clucked and tightened her feet, pinching at Ada's arms. The boy snorted. "What, that? It's just an old hen."

Ada fired up indignantly. "She's the cleverest chicken that ever was! And she talks."

"Lying is a sin!" said the boy. "You're a crazy little girl"—though he was not so much older than she.

She freed one hand from Blanche and pointed down the road. "At least go to my aunt and my cousins and tell them? And the priest and the blacksmith. I'm sure there are *many* pennies there."

"Good luck." The boy took off running and did not slow nor look back. And now he is gone from this story.

Ada stood in the path-that-was-a-road, holding Blanche tightly. When the patter of running footsteps had faded, there were no sounds save the humming insects and the air soughing in the trees. She looked back the way the boy had come, but there was nothing to see yet, only trees and plants, and high above them all the towering clouds of August, uncaring about the tiny affairs of people and hens and wastoures.

"What should I do?" asked Ada aloud.

And in her light, sweet, gabbling voice, Blanche said: "We must climb the highest tree and wait 'til they're past. He told the truth. They're coming."

Did you think that Ada had lied to the boy to save Blanche? She is a very honest girl. Because no chicken has spoken within *your* hearing, do you assume none ever has?

Ada put down Blanche and they looked about. The old forest was dense with staunch oak and shivery beech, saplings and shrubs, coiling ferns and little low groundling plants. Everything was either too big to climb or too small to save them. Ada hopped for the nearest branch of a low-slung oak, but it was much too high.

Blanche said with decision, "Not here, but there will be Somewhere."

Was that a sound? Yes. It was the ripple of running water where a brook ran along the bottom of a clearing clotted with grasses and encircled by young trees. Across the clearing was a pile of stones that had once been a house: French or Saxon or Roman or any of the races that had swept across England's face. Gone now, all gone: absorbed into Englishness, into legend and folktale.

Was that a sound? Yes. It was a rising wind in the trees, from the east. Ada carried Blanche through the head-high grass to the pile of stones. It was ringed by nettles but she paid no heed, only pushed through and heaved Blanche over her head to the top of a fallen wall—for Margery had clipped each hen's right wingtip, and Blanche could not fly but only flutter. Ada crawled up after and hoisted Blanche onto an overhanging elm-tree branch, but she could not reach it herself.

Was that a sound? Yes. It was a great red buck crashing through the underbrush. Ada saw him flash across the clearing, wall-eyed in panic, heavy-footed and careless of sound. Blanche said, "Stack the stones," and so Ada did, scrabbling together the biggest she could move atop the wall, until she could climb to the top of her teetering mound. She jumped for the branch and scuffled her feet up the trunk to sit at last beside Blanche on the rough gray bark.

"Higher," said Blanche. Ada climbed up and up, and the hen jump-fluttered along. Up and up, until the branches creaked ominously and bobbed like osiers from their small weight.

Was that a sound? A scream, or sudden wind, or a cart's wheel complaining? Ada looked but there was little she could espy, only elm leaves and a bit of the clearing, and one glimpse directly down, of the pile of stones and the ground a great way below that.

Blanche said, "Let me see what *I* may see." She hop-fluttered to the tippiest branches of the tree.

Ada peered after her. "What *do* you see?"

Blanche said: "I see sky and clouds. I see the sun setting, and the steeple of our own church. That's the west. I see a flock of birds rising where something has frightened them. That's the south. I see trees moving in the wind and I see smoke from chimneys. I see trees moving, and it is *not* the wind. *That* is the east. I see smoke from a thatched roof burning. I see a meadow covered with darkness, and the darkness is coming toward us."

She hopped back to Ada. "I see wastoures. Use your shawl to tie us to this branch so that we don't fall in the night. They are coming."

Was that a sound? Yes. A low wail, a storm-sound, a surf-sound of chattering nattering shrieks, louder than crows in their murders and rooks in their parliaments, louder than ten thousand hawks fighting for blood. A thousand talons pounded the ground. Blanche ruffled her feathers and buried her face in Ada's arms, but still the sound.

The wastoures came. The trees shook and the tall grasses shivered, first from animals fleeing, every deer and mouse and marten and vole running for its life—but then from the wastoures themselves. They trampled the grasses as they poured like a flood across the clearing, eddied wherever they found some living thing to eat, crashed against the trees and scoured the bark with their claws and talons, until swarming they at last swept past. But always more.

The night was bright-mooned, alas. Ada saw a fallow doe pulled down in her flight (for she would leave her fawn behind) and skeletonized quicker than a hen lays an egg, and the fawn even faster than she. The wastoures swirled around a pile of stones in the clearing until they unearthed a fox den and ate the kits. There was a great anguished roaring in the forest, which Blanche whispered surely was a bear pulled from her hiding place and killed. The wastoures could smell Ada and Blanche, and some spent the night leaping at the elm tree's trunk. But wastoures cannot fly, nor could they jump high enough to reach that first low branch. After a while Ada saw that they could not get to her.

Hour after hour; the moon set and still they churned below, a seething darkness in the dim starlight. Ada feared she and Blanche would fall, for she was not very good at knots yet, but nothing bad happened. She was only rocked gently like an infant in its cradle, far above the tossing sea of wastoures. At last she slept, for a child cannot always be awake even in a time of terror.

But Blanche did not sleep, watching from her bright golden-black eyes.

By first light there were fewer wastoures. The crushed grass was red with dawn and more than dawn. The lingering wastoures bickered for the chance to pull the blades through their beaks, for the blood.

Ada whispered to Blanche, "I have to do water."

"So?" Blanche had no great opinion of the things people worried about.

Ada wrinkled her brow. "They'll smell it."

Blanche tipped her head as though listening through the feather-edged pinholes of her ears, though what she listened to was not the air. "By now, most are far to the west. These are the little lame ones that cannot keep up. They'll leave soon enough."

"They don't seem any littler than the others," said Ada, dubious, but she peed over the side of the branch anyway. One came sniffing over and looked up, eyeing them from its sideways-tipped head before it ambled off to the west. The others followed.

Ada was very hungry (for bitter burdock and blackberries and a handful of kippernuts had been yesterday's dinner and supper, and today's breakfast, too). But still she waited until Blanche said at last, "We can get down now."

"Are we safe?" said Ada.

"We are never safe," said Blanche.

It was worse descending. Blanche flutter-jumped from branch to branch, but Ada had to lower herself carefully, and the bark that had seemed so sturdy under hands rushing up now broke away under the same hands creeping down. The lowest branch was higher than she remembered, and it was a long time before she could bring herself to drop to the tumbledown wall.

At the sound, one final wastoure emerged from a pile of fallen stones. Not all the blood drawn in the long night had been that of forest creatures; this wastoure had been slashed accidentally by a fellow and itself become prey. It limped toward them, hungry and curious, but Blanche spread her white wings and snapped her short rose-pink beak. To her surprise it turned away and limped westward into the forest.

And now *it* is gone from this story as well. Imagine its ending as you would. If you are kind, see it dead quickly in the jaws of a hungry young wolf a short league from this place. If you are as cold as the world, then see pain, infection, hunger, and death a mercy at last.

Ada picked up Blanche and recrossed the clearing to the path-that-was-a-road. The wastoures had crushed the ferns and trampled the shrubs, gouged the beeches and staunch oak trees with claw marks, scattered blood and shards of bone everywhere—but the road home was clear, for the deep-trenched ruts were more permanent than any horde.

It was afternoon when they came at last to the forest's edge and saw their little church across the trampled fields and its handful of houses and huts, but the chimneys were unsmoking and the doors agape or gone. There was no sound: no churn or quern or clattering loom, no hammer on iron or chisel on wood, no oxen or horses, milk-cows, sheep, or chuckling chickens. Ada had always been a little afraid of the village's big dogs and even more afraid of the geese, but neither came buffeting down the lane to bowl her flat.

Margery's cottage was at the far end of the village. Three wastoures had clustered there around something gray and red in the lane. They did not look up.

"Will they eat us?" whispered Ada.

Blanche said, "I think they are not hungry."

Perhaps she was right, for at their approach the wastoures sidled into the woods, leaving their dinner half-eaten: Father Alfred's donkey. Blanche fluttered from Ada's arms and ran across to peek through the gaping door of the nearest cottage, where Ada's only friend Giles lived, with his siblings Armand and Geoffry and Natalie and Marie, their mother and father and aunt, five goats and a dog, two cows, and the chickens and ducks.

"Is anyone there?" asked Ada.

But Blanche said only, "Do not look inside the huts. Do not look closely at anything."

Everywhere was the same. There were corpses or parts of them. Sometimes they could tell who it had been. Other people were just not there and there was no telling where they had gone, or how. The donkey was partially eaten, but his short gray face was for some reason untouched, and his eyes were closed as though he were sleeping. Ada had always longed to stroke his nose but she had been scared to put her hand so close to those long yellow teeth. Now she stroked it at last, and it was as soft as she had guessed, like kitten ears.

You ask, Where is her grief? Why does Ada not scream and wail, as you might, or I? Why does she not fall to the ground in despair, run weeping in circles, scream and tear at her hair? It is a cold answer. She has seen horrors before this, horrors at six, orphaned and alone. She has been here before. She has learned that adults always fail you, if only by dying. So what's new? At least she has Blanche. Not every lost child does.

The door to Margery's cottage was closed but the thatch had been torn through, and the oiled oxskin that glazed the window was in shreds. When Ada reached for the door, Blanche pushed her white head between hand and iron latch. "Best not," she said.

The door to the coop was agape, and the sunlight streaming in filled the air with golden flecks. The chickens were gone, dead or fled or hiding deep in the hearts of trees they had managed somehow to ascend. Here, there were only torn nests, broken eggshells, and splashes of blood clustered with flies, but the air still smelled comfortingly of them, feathers and fluff, millet and shit.

And what of Blanche's grief? Do you think she feels none? I have known a chicken who pined to death, waiting by the gate for a dead coopmate until she starved. Can you know what she feels if you have not lost what she has, if you are not yourself a hen? But Blanche is practical, and there is Ada to look after.

Ada's little bed of hay and rags had been ripped apart. She plumped it back together and cuddled down, with an eye on the open doorway. Blanche tucked herself carefully onto her favorite roost just above (and no one to fight her for it, alas, alas) and said: "We must plan."

They could not stay. Wastoures did not come every year, but when they did, it was in waves. Tomorrow, the day after, next week—they would come again, and keep coming until winter froze the dew and they died or found secret caverns to sleep in. Also, there would be scavengers, foxes, rats, and others on two legs, scrounging through whatever was left behind. Ada would not be able to hide here.

There was no point to following the wastoures' path, for everywhere they had been would be the same: ruin, loss, and the clustering scavengers. And the lands they had *not* yet touched would be overrun with fleeing people and animals, lost or afraid to go home. No one would care for a small bare-footed girl and a clip-winged white hen.

"What *can* we do?" Ada asked. She was drowsy with eating. They had gone out again and found food everywhere, in lavish and unguarded profusion. The wastoures ate only flesh, so there were tarts and turnips, cabbages and tender new carrots. Ada had filled her skirt with apples and bread (nibbled, for some mice had survived) and carried them back to the coop.

Blanche said, "Wastoures cannot swim. If we cross a lake or a river without a bridge, we'll be safer. Maybe. A town with a moat would be best."

"What's a moat?" Ada knew what a town was; it was more people than she had ever seen in her whole life, all in a place.

"A river that runs all the way around a town. A ring of water," said Blanche.

Ada nodded as though she understood. "What do we do?"

"Find a new home. Find a family and make ourselves part of that."

"I suppose," said Ada dubiously. Her experience with families was not so happy as Blanche's.

"First you must do a thing for me," said Blanche.

Ada nodded; she was so very tired.

Blanche dropped to the floor beside Ada and stretched out her right wing. "Pluck the clipped feathers."

Ada sat up. "But you won't be able to fly!"

"I cannot fly now. If you pluck them, they will grow back whole."

"How long will that take?" Ada asked.

But Blanche did not know, for it had never happened to her. It was only a sort of legend in every henyard.

It was an uncomfortable business, for Ada was afraid to hurt Blanche and it required a strong pull, and Blanche could not help twitching away. But at last it was done and there were two feathers piled beside Ada's bed. By that time it was dark. And, because Ada was after all a very small girl (and Blanche a chicken), in spite of the dead, the smell of blood, and the loneliness, they slept. They could not have in any case kept their eyes open, not even if the wastoures had run ravening in and devoured them down to the bones.

In the morning, Ada filled a basket with white bread, a hard cheese wrapped in a cloth, and butter in a little wooden tub she had found sunk into a pail of water at the midwife's house, all finer than anything she had eaten since coming to Margery's cottage. She did not think to bring a knife nor money until Blanche reminded her (Blanche was old for a hen and accordingly wise), and then she took a dirk and eleven silver pennies from the blacksmith's house, and put on a blue gown that had belonged to his middle daughter—for her own was ruined and there was no sign of his family, no sign at all. They walked south into the new morning.

A small girl and a hen are not built to travel fast nor far, especially when they must often hide. Their path crossed the wasteland the wastoures had left behind: ruined fields and orchards, collapsed huts and trampled copses. Pillars of ravens and rooks circled above the wastoures' leavings—but even amid all the ruin were places that had not been damaged, as though the wastoures had been a wildfire, razing one field and leaving the next untouched.

They passed a village the wastoures had missed, but there were men with bows and short swords everywhere about it. "Leave it," said Blanche. "That is no home. We'll find somewhere better."

They saw other people like themselves (but adults), lost and stumbling, or moving with fierce purpose. Some carried food, but others carried things that made no sense: a mirror, a silver candlestick, a roll of vellum, a fine cape too warm for August. Once there was a woman with her head uncovered and her hair a tangled mat down her back, cradling a bundle and weeping; she saw Ada and folded to her knees, reaching out, and the bundle dropped forgotten from her hands: not a babe in arms but a crumpled wad of rags. Later a man chased them, snatching for Blanche until she attacked, flapping into his face; and he stumbled back with a scream, hands laced over his eyes and blood seeping past his fingers.

And now *they* are gone from this story as well, the blinded thief and the grieving woman and these other hard-faced or frightened roamers. I have not told you their stories. They do not matter. They die alone, unremembered, pointless except to make a point.

All authors leave a swath of destruction. We maim and move on. The privilege of the happy ending is accorded to few.

That night, Ada and Blanche slept in an empty sheepfold under the bright-mooned sky. In the morning they went on, though the soles of Ada's feet burned with the friction of calluses on dirt. In time they came to a brook. Ada lay down on the bank, paddling her feet in the cold water as Blanche scratched for worms.

"What do we do now?" Ada asked.

Chickens do not take much note of the expressions of people, but even to Blanche she looked pale and tired. She dropped beside her and rubbed her small feathery face against Ada's arm. "There will be a place for us. I know it."

The wind shifted, and as though she had summoned the sound, they heard the distant sound of church bells: a single low bell rung nine times, then a pause, then nine more.

And nine, and nine again. Blanche said, "Nine for a man, and seven for a woman"—the distant bell was tolling seven; seven; seven—"and three for a child of more than four years."

Ada was six. "What if you are smaller?"

Blanche's voice was a soft clucking. "For an infant, a single bell to remind men of the soul reaped early, and to comfort the mother."

Three, three, three. A long pause, and then a single toll.

Blanche said, "Someone still lives, to climb the church tower and pull the rope. There is order there. *That* is where we must go."

"Will they want us?" Ada asked, for Margery had not.

Blanche smoothed a feather with her beak, heaved herself back onto her sturdy claws. "We will find out."

They followed a sunken lane, smooth with use and pounded smoother by the recent four-toed prints of wastoures. They hid from a youth limping the other way, and from two hard-faced men dragging a high-piled handcart. They hid from a double file of silent monks bearing a dead man on a litter, and from a half-grown wild boar so lost in the pain of its torn flank that it stumbled unseeing down the middle of the lane. In the afternoon, Ada shared the last of her bread with Blanche, leaving the pot with the remains of the butter at the base of a beech tree, for even ants grow hungry.

They were still trudging along the lane when the bell tolled again, so sudden, close, and loud that all they had to do was turn left and climb a hill.

And there was the Unlucky Village.

Perhaps the wastoures' numbers had been greater here, or their hunger. From the breast of the hill the village looked no more than huddled ruins: houses and cottages destroyed, stone walls and chimneys toppled, roofs collapsed. The outbuildings were torn apart entirely, and only piles of stone, thatch, wood, and withy marked their sites. The fences and gardens had been trampled into the ground. A wasteland of stained, crushed grass was all that was left of the common green. Only the little parish church looked intact, though the lead roof had buckled in one corner. The bell had fallen silent again.

Blanche scuttered a few steps down the path to the village, but Ada did not follow. Seeing this, Blanche said, "Come," in the tone that had once brought her chicks running (grown now, grown to hens and cocks: grown, gone, and dead).

Ada chewed her lip. "No."

What is the hen's equivalent of a sigh? A puff of breath and an impatient shake of wattle and comb? Blanche gave it. "It will be night soon, and there will be wolves and bandits and perhaps wastoures, too."

Ada's head shook, *no no no*, though she did not realize it. "There's nobody here."

Yet there was white smoke rising from a chimney, and the sound of iron on wood, and the drifting scents of an oakwood fire and barley porridge on the boil. Blanche sighed again, that complicated act, then chivvied Ada down the path, the girl stumbling and her lip trembling. But what choice did they have?

They passed the first fallen fence, and at last they saw someone, a woman leaving one of the ruined cottages to hurry across the green.

Ada did a very brave thing then. For all her fear, she called out, "Wait!"

The woman did not stop, only averted her face as she ran past, vanishing around the corner of a paling half-erected to surround the church. Blanche fluttered into Ada's arms, and they tumbled after her and saw other people now: a woman stacking wood salvaged from a ruined house, a man digging a grave. Another, holding a paling upright in its hole, looked up grim-faced, but he also said nothing, and turned back at a sharp word from the man trying to set the post—as though that would stop the wastoures when they came again, as though anything would.

Ada stood uncertainly in the middle of the claw-flattened lane. "What should we do?" she whispered, though she knew that Blanche would not speak in front of these hard-faced people. The hen in her arms only shook her head.

"Who are you?" asked a voice, unexpected and very close. Blanche fluttered to the ground squawking, but Ada looked up into the face of a man they hadn't noticed. He had been rehanging a nearby cottage's door; he still held a mallet and the new-forged pin for its hinge.

Ada looked at Blanche for advice, but the hen said of course nothing. "Are you ghosts?" she asked at last.

The man put down his mallet and stepped back from the door. He was very tall and wore dusty black shoes. "We look it, I guess," he said. "Are you?"

Ada shook her head. "No, I am a girl, and this is Blanche. She's a hen, not a ghost either."

"You're alone?" The man came close.

"No!" said Ada indignantly. "I have Blanche. But we don't know what to do."

The man looked down from all his great height for a moment, then knelt and reached out a hand to her. "You might stay here with me and the boy. I'm Robert. I have room for you if you want it."

After disaster, when we are adults, we survive if we can. We are hungry, we are cold, we are sick or injured. We save what and who we can. There is fear, loss, and crippling grief, but we do not have time or energy yet to fully reckon our dead. We must think about tonight and tomorrow: portioning out the phone's charge and our only bottle of water, tallying the last seven doses of our heart medication, now six, now five. Periods start whether we have tampons or not. Diapers need to be changed even when there are none. But someone will come. We will hear helicopters, trucks, see red crosses and crescents. We will be safe.

When we are children alone in the heart of horrors, we do not know this.

There had been no warning for the Unlucky Village, no boy earning pennies until he felt the wastoures' talons scything the air at his heels. Robert had been a farrier (but the horses were gone) and a husband (his wife, as well: walking back from the Egendon market where she had gone to sell her weaving and eggs) and a father (daughters dead with their mother, and his son in the churchyard's fifth new grave). Robert was an old man, though he had not been so a week ago.

He gave Ada the loft his children had shared. "But no chickens indoors," he said. Blanche slept in the henhouse, which was empty except for her own quick heartbeat, for the wastoures had found them all. Each night Ada crept out to cuddle with Blanche until Robert brought her back in.

There was another child that he had found: a boy a little older than Ada. The day after the wastoures had passed, Robert had gone searching for his wife and daughters, though he found no signs of them but a ribbon that might once have been blue. On his way back, he heard a hopeless, unaware moaning from within the hollow trunk of a fallen oak tree and opened the trunk with his axe. There was a boy, wedged as deep as he had been able to get. His right foot was shredded where the wastoures had worked for a while at pulling him out. Robert brought the boy home and laid him in his own bed. The boy's name was Ulf, though Robert will never learn this.

This, then, was Ada's family in the Unlucky Village: grieving Robert substituted for bitter Margery, raving Ulf for the cruel sisters, and Blanche. There was plenty of food (though no meat) and blankets enough for everyone who was left. Robert was gone all of each day, trying to set the fields to rights without oxen, guarding against looters, and working on the paling—for always the Unlucky Village worked in fear of the next wave.

It was Ada's job to watch the porridge pot and the fire, and also to watch the boy. When Robert was not by, Blanche crept in and sat with her. Her plucked feathers were growing back, little sharp quills so delicate she could feel air currents like fingers on them.

Watching Ulf was not an easy thing. He was feverish and kept reaching down to paw at his leg above the ruined foot, mottled the color of marsh water. He gabbled *Mother* and *Father, Jesus* and *Mary*; the names of his sisters and brother, his dog, and his family's cows.

On the second day, he started up in his fever and grasped Ada's arm with a hot hand like a claw. "You don't belong here," he hissed. "He's *my* father now."

Blanche flared her wings and snaked her white neck forward, but before she could peck him, he had released Ada and fell back delirious again, crying and repeating, "The Lucky Village, the Lucky Village."

Blanche settled on Ada's knee, one wary golden-black eye on the boy. Ada whispered, "What's the Lucky Village?"

Blanche contemplated, in the way she had. "It's a true thing. There is a village where the wastoures don't come."

"Is it a town with a moat?" asked Ada.

"No," said Blanche. "It is just luckier than others."

"Where is it?"

"Somewhere near." Blanche kept no maps in her head, though she could find places once she knew they existed.

"Your chicken talks?" said the boy abruptly. He had a habit of sudden lucidity.

Ada said, "No."

"I know it did! I'm sick but I'm not deaf." He pushed himself upright in the bed.

"You dreamed it," said Ada fiercely, "and if you tell Robert, I will stick you with a pin"—for she had forgotten that the running boy had taken the pin her mother had given to her. But when Robert returned at dusk (and Blanche in the yard, meek as a nun, as though she had never seen the inside of a house), the boy had fallen back into terrors and seemed to remember nothing of their talk. A line had begun creeping up the boy's leg like oak-gall ink spilled ankle to calf.

"He's going to die," Blanche said softly once when they were together, and Ada nodded. She remembered the smell from when her parents had died.

But Robert did not know that smell, or chose to ignore it. The boy would be fine. He needed time. He needed herbs. He needed charms hung over his bed, and painted upon his leg. He needed to be kept cool, to be kept warm, to be poulticed with nettle infusions, to sleep, to be prayed over. The line crept up and up. When Ada could not sleep for the sound of the boy's sobs, she crept into the henhouse and cuddled Blanche close, nose deep in her sweet, earthy fluff.

On their third day in the Unlucky Village, there was news: a boy not running but trotting loose-kneed with exhaustion, who told them that a wave of wastoures had passed in the night, to the north. "Is Woodend safe?" asked a woman whose daughter had moved there to wed. But the boy shook his head.

"I started in Berton, and I ran through Tirborne and Nutley and Chatton and I hid in a tree when they went past, and now I'm going back. I came past Woodend last night. There was nothing left." He thought. "Nothing to recognize."

But the woman was screaming already, and she beat him with her fists until two of the men pulled her still screaming away; and instead of staying for the night as he had hoped to, the boy left—though with a wallet full of fried porridge-cakes and new apples slipped to him secretly by one of the other village women; for it was not *her* bad news he carried, and it might have been.

Now this boy also is gone from this tale. He will return safely to Berton with thirty-two pennies, apprentice himself to the blacksmith (who has lost all his sons), and in time become blacksmith himself. He will have three daughters and two sons, and mourn his first wife when she dies in childbirth, but not so much that he will not wed again. He will not have nightmares. He will not dream.

Horror does not strike all equally.

That night Robert said, "The boy needs meat."

He and Ada sat at the little crooked table beside the fire, eating porridge stiff from a day's cooking, with hazelnuts and some lettuces that had survived the garden's ruin, and drinking small beer. Ulf had rejected everything. He tossed in the corner bed, moaning in his sleep.

"There is none," Ada said sadly. Her mouth watered as she thought of stewed beef, duck meat pressed until it was tender, trout fried and sizzling, the sweet flesh of such chickens as were not Blanche.

Robert gestured outside. "We have the hen." Blanche was pecking for insects just beyond the cottage door. She looked up, her white feathers aglow in the sunlight, plump, bright-eyed, and hale.

Ada shook her head.

He rubbed his eyes. "We have to be reasonable. It isn't laying and it'll have no chicks. And the boy needs to eat. A good broth, some stewed meat—"

"No."

"He's *sick*, girl. We need to get him better."

"He's not going to get better," said Ada: too young to know what should not be said. "He's going to die anyway."

Robert slammed his fist on the table and stood, and the room loomed with his shadows, cast from firelight and the late sun shining in through the door. "The boy will be fine!" he said.

Ada began to cry, and Blanche scuttered through the door and flutter-hopped ground to bench to table, and launched herself at Robert's face. Robert threw up his hands to protect his eyes and grabbed Blanche by the throat. She hung, fluttering and squawking.

"You can't eat her," Ada cried. "She talks."

"Lies are the Old Gentleman's work," Robert said sternly.

But Ulf had been awakened by the fight, and said, in the quick feverish voice that came in his moments of clarity, "It does! I heard it yesterday. And *she* said she would stick me with a pin if I said anything." He raised a thin finger at Ada.

"Hens do not speak," Robert said, and held up Blanche to look at her, no longer struggling but hanging loosely in his hands. Blanche gave a sudden writhe and dropped to the table, and said:

"If I did, would you not eat me?"

This was the end of Ada's family in the Unlucky Village.

Robert stopped his ears against Blanche's words and Ada's tears, and dragging the girl to the coop, threw her inside, the hen scuttering protectively after her; slammed the door shut and left them there. A talking chicken *must* be some trick of the Devil. It might even in some fashion attract wastoures, for hen and horror were likewise two-legged and claw-footed, snake-necked and bright-eyed. In any case, Robert had no room in his life for things he did not understand yet could not ignore. The hen would be killed and made soup of, that was understood—though first the priest must expel any demons, lest they enter the boy. That would be a task for the morning. The girl would get over it. What choice did she have?

But in the night, as Ada clutched Blanche tight in her arms, the hen said to her, "We must go."

"Where?" asked Ada. "Everywhere will be like this."

A chink in the back wall admitted a blade of steel-colored moonlight. "The people of this village see nothing but badness. The Lucky Village will be different."

"Will it?" said Ada dubiously. "Shouldn't we go to the Town with a Moat?"

But even a talking hen that sees truths may ignore them, and decide instead that the easy path is the only one. Blanche said, "The Lucky Village will be fine."

The coop had been built to keep chickens in and foxes and weasels out. Still, fear and fingers found a way to pry loose a board in the back. It was noisy but no one of the Unlucky Village (not even Robert) opened their tight-sealed doors to learn what new ill thing the sounds augured.

Ada squeezed out, and Blanche after her. For the rest of the night, they hid in a ravaged cottage nearby. At first light, they started to walk. There was no food and no blankets, only the eight remaining silver pennies and a shawl that had once belonged to Robert's oldest girl, which he had given to Ada, soft as a chick and blue as an August sky.

The raving boy, Ulf, will die in two days and be buried on the third. Robert will die later, and it will not matter when or why or how, even to Robert.

Blanche and Ada walked for a day and another, and in the night between, they slept in the house of a woman who said not a single word, only wept steadily as November rain, even as she put out fresh-baked oakcakes and honey and arranged a blanket into a little nest beside the fire. Though there was room enough and the walls were firm, neither girl nor hen spoke of staying. In the morning, the unspeaking woman gave them the last of the oatcakes and a skin to carry water in.

Things happened, horrors and little beauties.

When it seemed prudent, Ada asked after the Lucky Village, but no one had heard of such a place until an ancient man mumbled past his five remaining teeth, "That'm Byfield." He pointed with a finger so bent it seemed to turn back on itself. "Along o' there. An' east o' the Hangin' Cross an' west at the River Bye an' on for five, six miles. But they don' like strange folk"—and he pointed to a scar on his arm, many decades old.

On for five, six miles. They ate worms and honey cakes, purslane and dandelions and berries from inside a bush where the birds had not gotten to them. They ate beetles and a loaf of barley bread that Ada purchased from a blank-faced man with one of her pennies. They grew hungrier. They hid. They hid. They hid.

At last they came to a narrow lane with a signpost Ada could not read, but—"This way," said Blanche. They turned and came down through a copse of oak trees between fields amazingly untrampled.

And there it was. The Lucky Village was cradled in a curve of a clear, swift-moving stream, and the green before the gray stone church was clustered with fat sheep—for in these troubled times, it seemed safest to keep them close. There were chickens (though none who spoke) and geese and even a farrowing sow. There was a parson and a miller, a blacksmith and a harness-maker, a baker and a woman who gave herbs and treated injuries, a man who rented out his strong back and a woman born foolish who could not speak—and what was her use in the village none would say (though we guess and do not guess wrong).

The Lucky Village had never been attacked by wastoures. They did not understand what accidents of landscape and circumstance protected them, so they interpreted their safety in their own way. They were lucky because they were good—but they also had to be careful: virtuous, discreet, cautious, slow to change, swift to assess sin and exact punishment. They were wary of strangers at all times, but during a wastoure summer, the Lucky Village turned everyone away, with weapons if need be.

Ada and Blanche were intercepted by a man scything a field, and brought to the steps of the church to stand before the parson and the blacksmith. The rest of the Lucky Village gathered around them. They asked questions: What did a very small girl in a sky-blue shawl, carrying seven pennies and a chicken as white as a pearl, have to offer that they could not simply take from her, had they not been good men? Was *she* good? Did she know her prayers? Did she honor the Church? Did she work hard?

Ada, confused and tired and hungry, wept.

The Lucky Village said, Well, we don't need more of *that*.

Ada scrubbed her eyes against her shoulder (for her arms were filled with Blanche) and said, "My chicken is magic. She does tricks." Blanche gave a sudden start.

The Lucky Village said, What sort of tricks?

Blanche was looking as wary as a chicken can look, head tipped sideways to observe Ada fully from one golden-black eye. Ada only lowered Blanche to the stone stairs.

"Blanche, count to nine." Nine was a lucky number.

Blanche tapped the stone delicately with one ivory-nailed foot. Nine times.

It's a sham, said the Lucky Village. You always say nine, or you gave her some secret signal.

"What is three plus four, dear Blanche?" said Ada.

Blanche spread her wings and resettled them. Arithmetic was hard until she imagined beetles scuttering across the ground and snapping them up, first three, then four. Seven.

Exclamations; a spattering of hands clapping.

"And she can dance, and she can talk, and she can tell the weather. But she will only do it if you let us stay."

The woman who gave herbs to the Village knelt. "Poor little things!" she said. Her voice was kind. "You may stay with my husband and me. We have never had children."

"And no one will eat Blanche?"
No one, promised the Lucky Village.

It all looked very much as Ada's little home had looked. Her new mother and father were kind, if stern. They gave her much to do and were very serious about her prayers. In her home with her own parents (before they died), Ada had not yet learned the church-word prayers, just little English rhyming versions. After their death, Margery had not cared much about Ada's eternal soul, but now her new father demanded she learn the proper *Pater Noster* and *Ave Maria*, and he beat her when she was slow—though not hard: a swat merely, to keep her alert. Blanche, who was always close by, ruffled up at this but did not peck or claw.

Even on the warmest afternoons, Ada wore the blue shawl and carried with her the seven pennies, her little knife, and some bread—for after leaving the Unlucky Village, she had learned to keep close everything that was hers, plus whatever food she could. Her new mother gave her an ancient leather pouch for this purpose, to reassure her until she settled in.

There was a bed for her inside the cottage, but Ada slept with Blanche in the coop. "It's not right," said her new father, but her new mother only said, "Peace, husband; she has seen things. Give her time." And so it was permitted (for now), and in the meantime Ada learned the church-word prayers and worked hard.

There were other chickens. None of the chickens of Margery's flock had ever spoken save Blanche, but who knew the natural rules of talking among chickens? Not Ada. When she asked Blanche, the hen disdained them all as silly creatures saying nothing worth hearing. But Blanche knew this was the price for staying in the Lucky Village: sleep safe, surrounded by fools who are not even kin.

In the long blue August dusks, the Lucky Village brought out a rough table from behind the ale house and placed it on the green, and Blanche hop-fluttered onto it and answered questions. At first she only added numbers for them, tapping the worn wood with one white toe.

Then the Lucky Village asked, You said it talks? That it tells the morrow's weather?

Ada and Blanche looked at each other. Robert had cast them out for speaking at all, let alone foretelling anything. Why should the Lucky Village be any different? For Ada had not lied: The weather *was* one of the truths that Blanche knew, though she had never bothered to speak of it before the wastoures came. It could not be changed and she'd had her coop to retreat to, so why bother? But it had been useful as they wandered, since the wastoures.

"Yes," said Blanche finally. Her voice was a sweet gabble that cut through the rattling twilight insects and the never-quite-gone murmur of the Lucky Village's talk. "Tomorrow will start foggy down by the stream, but it will clear, and after that it will be hot and bright. The trout will stay cool in the hollow below the willow tree. The bees will cluster on the goosefoot and the meadow saffron. Beetles will hide, but the little grass-snakes will lie in the sunny lane and be easy to catch."

Exclamations, uneasy laughter, surprise. Some thought Ada spoke for Blanche through a clever trick, though she was very young to have such skill. A few groused that anyone could predict all that at this season. One or two wondered whether this was the Devil's work. But on the whole, the Lucky Village was pleased. Knowing the weather was indeed useful, and perhaps this hen was yet another proof that they were not lucky but blessed.

Days passed. On the Feast of St. Alcmund, wastoures seethed across the countryside a few miles to the south. Jesu preserved the Lucky Village, yet again.

A few days after that came a running boy, warning of another wave from the west, half a day away and headed straight toward them. He made no pennies from the Village for, safe in God's arms, it knew it owed him none; and in any case he was a coarse, ill-favored child who stirred no compassion. Cursing them for heartless, he turned to go, but Ada ran after and gave him one of her pennies. Now she was down to six.

His name is Piers, this running boy. He has a birthmark shaped like a hare on his face, and an expression in his despairing eyes that no child should bear. His ankle hurts, from when he stepped on a rock and it shifted underfoot, but he still can run. How likely is it that he survives? How real do you want your fiction?

In the indigo twilight after vespers that night, the Lucky Village crowded close to Blanche. The nights were growing cold, so there was a bonfire that cast a shuddering light across them all. The Village would be fine, of course it would—though there were some who thought they might have shown more compassion to the running boy, given him bread at least.

Naturally we trust our benevolent Lord, said the Lucky Village. But. Is there anything we should be doing, anything more? Are we failing at anything?

"I am a hen. If you want sermons, go to Parson John," Blanche said, a little tartly, for her new-growing flight feathers were itching. Parson John paused from sweeping the first fallen leaves from the steps of his church, just in earshot though not a part of the ring of listeners. He was one who believed Blanche was a temptation instead of a reward, but he trod warily. His flock's willingness to be led was inconstant in wastoure summers. They might cast *him* out.

Well, say *something*, said the Lucky Village.

With what was very near a sigh, and knowing they found comfort in such things, Blanche spoke the church-words Ada had been learning. "*Ave Maria, gratia plena, dominus tecum. Benedicta tua in—*"

"Profanation!" Parson John cast down his broom with a clatter that startled Blanche into Ada's arms where she stood beside the table. The Lucky Village exclaimed, murmured, and looked uneasily between man and hen.

"Did she get them wrong?" asked Ada. She was not as good with the church-words as Blanche.

"Abomination!" he bellowed, and the Village's murmurs grew louder, became mutterings. Ada's new mother stepped forward, but her new father placed his hand on her arm: safer to wait and see how this would arrange itself. The ring of watchers parted to admit the parson as he stomped to the table, stabbed a finger toward Blanche. She eyed his pointing finger rather as though she might bite it, feathers ruffled in the hot wind of his shouting. "A beast must not speak the words of angels!"

"She's not a beast!" said Ada, looking up, indignant. "She's a *chicken.*"

The parson towered over her. "A soulless beast!"

Outcry; exclamation.

Parson John looked around the ring, and shouted, "Our Lord gave us dominion over such! And we throng to this beast, like the Israelites in the desert before the false idol of the Calf, and we listen to heresy. *He* will not forgive!"

Ada's new mother stepped backward, into the circle of her husband's arm, and turned her face away.

This is how Ada and Blanche were cast from the Lucky Village that very night, into the path of the ravening wastoures.

What of the Lucky Village, cradled in a fluke of geography and conditionally cruel? You blame them for sending children to die alone. But they have their own. They must be prudent; they must be reasonable. They must make a choice, and so they do what is right for their own children and not these strangers—though of course there *are* some that are merely cruel, or selfish, or too absorbed in their own fears to spare thought for others.

Their God does not seem to mind, but we little gods that are readers and writers: we mind. Imagine the Lucky Village destroyed at last, if it comforts you. Or, if you are kind, imagine it learns its lesson and is rewarded with long lives and rich harvests. Imagine there is a lesson here. Still, why is fiction held to a higher standard than reality?

Dusk was fading into darkness. Ada fled headlong, for the men who had driven them away were still outlined by the bonfire with their cudgels and staves, and they scared her. Blanche scurried alongside, calling in her distress. They ran over the curve of the hill and then farther, until they were in a lane between trees, where not even starlight could reach them, for the crescent moon was not yet risen. It was utterly black.

They ran until Ada stumbled, fell headlong into the unseen lane and sprawled there, grizzling and crying. Blanche huddled close.

"Hush," said Blanche, with the soft chuckling of a hen soothing her chicks; but her ears were open.

Ada wailed. She had hit her chin and was seeing stars, green flaring bursts behind her eyes, though it was so dark.

"Hush," said Blanche, but it was no longer a chuckle: It was a sharp, snapping cluck.

Ada wept. She was six.

"*Hush,*" said Blanche, and this time it was a terrified whisper.

Ada's breath caught in her throat.

They heard it over their own hurrying heartbeats: still distant, the storm-sound of chattering nattering shrieks, the thunder of clawed feet.

"Not under the trees. Not like this. We must get into the open," said Blanche.

They stumbled through utterful, utter darkness—and still the sounds, behind them and to their right. There were other noises now: splintering wood, branches torn, an animal's scream so tormented that it could not be identified as man or beast or bird. They tumbled on until they saw a lightening ahead, and suddenly they were out of the trees and running beneath a star-scattered sky. The lane ran between fields too dark to see as more than textures, but rich-smelling, barley to one side, scythed hay to the other. No houses, no lights, no shelter, no convenient tree; and still the sounds. Closer, louder.

There was a ragged wall on one side of the lane, a bit taller than Ada's head. "Here," hissed Blanche, and terror pushed them up the rough stones.

They crouched on the wall's top course, which was scarcely wider than Blanche's body. Everything was dark still. The gabbling sounds came from across the lane and beyond the barley field. As much as they could for the darkness, they watched the trees there. But now sounds came down the lane as well, a thundering of hooves and alarm-calls. A herd of fallow deer raced heedless in their hundreds, so close that Ada could have reached out and touched their heaving flanks as they passed. The wind of their flight smelled rank and peppery.

They could not see what pursued at first, but they heard them: the gabbling and screeching of wastoures. It was not the main wave, only a few score that had smelled the deer and broken from the larger group to stampede the herd. They hurtled past, and above them Ada and Blanche crouched, frozen, soundless, and as flattened as they could be on so narrow a perch.

The wastoures' heads were lower than the wall's top edge and perhaps they would not have bothered with Ada and Blanche, or even noticed them. But an adolescent bringing up the rear hesitated as it passed. It rocked back on its haunches, listening. Its head was a long dim wedge anchored with flicking eyes so pale they seemed to glow in the starlight. Ada was still as wax, yet it swiveled suddenly toward them. It scrabbled at the wall but couldn't get purchase, then opened its long muzzle to bare a fringe of sharp teeth and a hot rotting smell, and gave a call that was a cross between a kestrel's screech and the *tuk-tuk-tuk* of a hen calling others to food.

"Jump down on the other side of the wall," said Blanche. "And run." But Ada did not move: calcified in fear, trapped tight as a chick in its shell.

After a moment, a larger wastoure joined the first. The smaller one sidled away, lowering its weight on its narrow hips and twisting its head to the side: a silent language unlike that of chickens, and yet Blanche understood it well enough. The higher-ranked wastoure clawed at the wall, long neck stretching up. Closer, but it could not reach, either. It lifted its head and called that screeching *tuk-tuk-tuk*. Others loped back: perhaps twenty of those chasing the deer. Looking down, Blanche saw a swarm of backs and reaching necks and snapping long jaws. Ada still did not move, though her eyes were open and gazing at the milling wastoures.

They scraped and jumped at the wall. One, longer-necked, used its chin as a balance point to scratch its way upward, forelegs scrabbling along the stones. Blanche flared her wings and stabbed with her beak at its nearer eye, and it fell screaming down among the others, leaving a sticky smear of vitreous humor on the wall and the taste of slugs on her tongue. The swarm attacked the fallen wastoure, but the leader still watched Blanche, as though thinking something through. It made a sound, an abrupt clatter rising from its throat.

Blanche understood it well enough: no longer a sound that summoned others to food, but something like a hen's challenge-call to a strange pullet brought into her flock. She had not been lead hen of Margery's kitchen yard without reason. She growled a chicken's growl, an angry rattle she had not had to make since her laying days. "*Back away*," it was, and, "*Who are you to use that tone with me?*"

The wastoures went silent and retreated a little, leaving the shredded remains of the fallen one humped against the foot of the wall. Every wedge of a face angled toward her, smeared with blood that looked black under the moonless sky. Every pale eye gleamed flatly, like a silver penny rediscovered in a dark corner. The leader snapped its head from side to side and chittered a clattering throat-sound: a clear challenge.

Blanche growled again, louder, and this time it was, "*Go.*" She opened her wings and stood tall: a rooster's stance. The leader reared in its turn, slashed the air with its gaping jaw, and chittered.

Was she afraid, fierce Blanche, facing down these monsters? The wastoures were taller, toothed, smelling of fresh blood; with claws sharper than a fighting cock's spurs and forelegs that reached and grasped in a way that wings could not. More: There was something of cunning in the leader's eyes. But Blanche was clever, too—and she was so angry that her fear was a mere background hum in her heart.

"Go," growled Blanche, and she snapped forward with her beak, though the leader was too far away to peck. Nattering, the swarm recoiled. The leader lowered its weight a little on its narrow hips, still looking up. The dialect of its posture was unfamiliar yet understandable: confusion, wariness, skepticism.

Blanche looked down, small and sturdy and strong as a queen with a naked sword in her hand; and, hunched low, the wastoures peered back at her. She said, in words and hen-sounds and manner, "*Turn. Turn and run. Run until you drop in your tracks, run until you die. Do not return.* GO."

The leader stepped backward, swiveled, and ran arrow-straight across the barley field. The others collected into a ragged mob behind it and vanished under the trees. In a moment even the sounds of their feet were gone. The only noise was the rustling of leaves: a night wind rising.

Ada still did not move, and when the hen pressed against her hand, it was cold as death. "It's all right, dear one," Blanche crooned. "They're gone."

The wastoures run, twenty-three of them, driven by a strange compulsion. They run and do not deviate, past farmhouses and villages. And when they come to the ford in the Wendle, where the water breaks knee-high on a riding mare, they run into the water, lose their footing, and are swept away. Dead, as she demanded of them.

As for Ada, Blanche will not tell her that the wastoures have died. She is a child. She should not have to imagine how they fought the Wendle as it pulled them down, how their lungs filled with weed-foaming water, how their fear was as great as the world.

"What was *that,* hey?" said a voice behind Ada and Blanche.

His name was Pall, he told them: an orphan who with certain fellow spirits had cobbled together platforms in the trees where they could sleep safely. They were seven in number, and they scavenged for food and other things. "Why, we're rich!" he boasted to Ada, who had roused at his voice, begun crying, and now followed him, still grizzling, across the cut hayfield with a somewhat limp Blanche in her arms. "I have a silver candlestick, and three shillings and a lady's fine gown and a gold piece with a lion's head from some foreign land and a bridle for a horse and—"

The list was a long one, long enough to take them to the beginning of the forest. He stopped at the foot of a tree as he ended, "—an' I'll go to the King and he'll make me a lord, I'll be *that* rich—Here."

He pointed to a rope leading up into the boughs.

"I can't." She started to grizzle again. Ada was a brave girl but she had just seen terrible things. Also, she was tired and hungry—and she could not climb like this in any case: six and small for her age.

"Rules are, you have to climb to be one o' us Dead Squirrels," said he. "But still, that hen o' yours . . ." He gave a low whistle and a loop of rope dropped from the heights. "Put your arms through an' hold tight. I'll carry that hen."

"No," said Ada and held Blanche tighter, squeezing from her a squawk.

"I can take care of myself," said Blanche. Presumably, the boy had heard her speak already, so there was no point to concealment.

And so it was that they were lifted into the treetops, Blanche clinging to Ada's shoulder (and trying not to dig in too hard); Ada spinning and bumping until she learned to walk her feet against the trunk as they ascended. Pall shinnied up the other rope so quickly that he was already at the top to hoist her onto a rough platform scarcely bigger than her own little bed had been, back when there had been such things as parents and homes. A single candle in a horn-paned lantern cast grimy light onto the faces and hands of the boys as they sat in the crooks of branches or leaned back into the boughs. The oldest might have been twelve; the youngest was scarcely older than Ada.

"Why'd you bring 'em up?" said the Oldest. "We could've talked to 'em below;" and the Youngest wrinkled his face, adding, "They're not Squirrels!"

"There're still wastoures about," said Pall. "Seemed safest. They got *skills*, men. From right up here with your own eyes, you saw it. She sent 'em all away somehow, that hen."

"How'd you do that?" said a Squirrel, as another asked, "Where?" and the Youngest said, "Make them *all* go away!"

"I didn't send them away," said Blanche, who was literal-minded. "I only sent the chiefmost of them. The others followed her. I think that's their way—like chickens, only not so clever." She preened a little.

Surprise at her soft, gabbling voice. "You talk?" said one; while, "But what did you *do?*" said the Oldest; and the Youngest shaking his branch in excitement until leaves cascaded down into the darkness, crowing, "I saw! You stood up tall and flapped and shouted and they got scared and ran away."

"That hen," said Pall to the others. "She's got *skills*, see."

The Oldest Dead Squirrel looked down at them: Ada, curled tight in the exact center of the platform and still crying; and Blanche standing beside her, small, round, and sturdy, her head tipped so that she could look back at him with one appraising eye.

"*Can* you send them away?" said the Oldest.

Said Blanche, "Yes."

"Well, then," he said. "You can stay—but not if that'n's gonna cry all the time."

And after they tied Ada loosely onto the platform (so that she would not fall off in her sleep), each Dead Squirrel tucked himself into whatever nest he had fashioned in the branches close by, cradled in such wealth as he was able to rescue from the ruins of the world. The Oldest blew out the candle, for candles were scarce (wastoures ate tallow and wax), and in the darkness, the Dead Squirrels spoke. They had names from before or that they had given themselves: Pall and Red Paul, Stibby and Renard-the-Fox, Weyland and Edmund Blue-Toes and Baby Jack. Ada was half asleep and Blanche did not care about such things, and yet the names stuck in their minds and were not forgotten.

And they had stories: a monkey from the Holy Land that Stibby had seen at the last but one Michaelmas Fair (but maybe that was a lie); baby pigs that came when you called and swallows that slept snug as housecats at the bottoms of mill ponds for the winter ("I saw it myself, so it's true as true," said Red Paul); digging out a badgers' cete in the spring (when sisters and parents still lived) and finding a scrap of tile old as old, painted with a single half-closed eye like a wink. As Squirrels nodded off, stories became whispers, became wishes. Family, family; home, home. No one said *safety*. They knew there was no such thing. As for the Youngest, he told no tales at all, nor wished, but only cried silently now that he could not be seen.

Soon all were asleep save Blanche, tired as she was and late as it was.

It seemed that she could keep the wastoures away from Ada. Knowing this was like November sunlight in her feathered breast. And Pall *was* right: she might be able to preserve these boys as well. A roost in the trees might become home to hens, but people were not suited to it. Come soon, come late, they would need to come back to the ground where their flat, sturdy feet served them so well, and when they did, she could keep the wastoures away from them, also.

Ada, safe. The Squirrels, safe.

What of the others? The boys who brought news, running for pennies until their feet or their hearts failed them. And all the others, alone, crowded with family into brief havens, defended by parents who died before their eyes—and even the ones who would live long lives without seeing a wastoure, but were hunted across the decades in their dreams. (But not the silent children already underground and feeding worms in the churchyards. For them it was too late.)

The only way to protect them *all* was to stop the wastoures altogether. Was that possible?

There had been a leader among the wastoures she had sent away. Blanche's understanding of hierarchies was subtle in ways no human can fathom, but call it *alpha*. If the swarm that had trapped them at the wall was led by an alpha, then all swarms had alphas. Bring two swarms together, and there would still be just one alpha, for the lesser would fall back. So: gather all swarms together, and there would a chief of all chiefs, an alphamost alpha. Send that one away and the others would follow.

Where would it be, such a leader of wastoures? And once she knew what to ask, this was a thing she knew without learning, like the weather. She *felt* her, as iron filings feel a magnet: an aged uttermost queen whose cunning was as sharp and strong in Blanche's mind as the smell of yew in a churchyard. And the way to the queen was as clear as *home* to a salmon in June: some leagues, south by southwest. She ruled in a cool, damp cave of limestone that breathed the salt smell of a sea dead and gone long before hens or wastoures or any air-dwelling thing. Her court surrounded her, all the other egg-laying females, also grown old; and beyond them, the last lingering juveniles still too egg-tender to collect and ravage forth.

All of this sensing thrummed with the uttermost queen's demand to her flock: *grow/go forth/find caves and flourish/there is no returning.* It was hard to comprehend but not impossible, in the way a traveler in a foreign land can pluck meaning from signs by their shape and placement, and it thrummed like a pulse, like surf on a shingle beach.

Could she stop this uttermost queen? Blanche knew truths but not all truths. Still, what choice did she have?

The night sky brightened as the crescent moon rose. It found a way through the leaves and shone onto Ada, who jerked upright, looking about wildly.

"Hush," said Blanche in her gentlest soft chuckling-to-chicks voice. "We are in the trees."

Ada nodded. "Are we safe?" she whispered.

"We are never safe," said Blanche. "But from the wastoures, perhaps. I know what to do."

Ada would not stay with the Squirrels, despite all her fear. She had been afraid since the day her mother had died (and the baby with her), which had been five months after her father had died in the fields, cut almost in half by a plough. The people you loved failed you in a thousand ways, not least by dying out of your sight while you were doing what they told you to do, collecting walnuts in a basket or pulling weeds in the garden. After such lessons, who would not keep her eyes fixed on her last loved one? So Ada would not stay behind—and she would not again freeze in fear.

The Dead Squirrels did not want to let them go, but Blanche had a certain voice they all remembered, though their mothers were dead, and in the end they lowered Blanche and Ada from the tree with gifts: a stale honey-cake they had been saving and a water-skin that was just barely manageable if Ada filled it only halfway.

The Squirrels: three will die, one by a fall, one of the flux, one killed by a man driven mad by this world. Which live? Which die? You have your favorites. Pall, because he is named and has shown kindness. Baby Jack because of his tender sobriquet, and we are sentimental about the young, though the world is not. The Oldest, though you do not even know which Squirrel that is, whether Weyland or Renard-the-Fox or even Edmund Blue-Toes. And if you knew that Stibby used to beat his little sisters and steal their food, and that Edmund once threw stones at a kitten until it died, would that change things?

The remaining four will live for a while, and then die, like everyone else.

Are you counting the deaths in this story, keeping a roster? Is it higher or lower than *The Wizard of Oz*? There are more than I have told you.

Things happened, and other things.

Blanche and Ada backtracked along the path the wastoures had carved, past St Giles's and Coombe Pastor and what was left of Rufford. Everything was lush where blood had soaked into the ground, and flies clustered like clouds at the thickest-growing places. Blanche scratched for her own food, but Ada needed more: bread at least (there was no meat or milk), and someone to help her when she got a sliver in her heel that she could not reach. She gave more of her pennies away, and soon there were only two.

At midafternoon on the sixth day, as the sky darkened with rain to the northwest, they came over the shoulder of a raw-rocked hill and saw a ruin in a clearing of the forest below them: the pale crumbling walls of what had once been a Roman villa, destroyed not by wastoures but by weather and centuries of people stealing its stones for their own chimneys and fences—though it had been long centuries since any had come to this place.

Blanche shivered. The uttermost queen was stronger now that they were so close, and her demands scratched at Blanche's mind the way growing feathers prickled in their sockets: */grow and go forth/eat/do not return/do not stop until you find new grounds/if you can/*. Walking into the compulsion was like wading against flowing water, but Blanche marched on, and Ada close beside her.

They picked their way down the slope toward the villa. There were no plants beyond a few dusty shrubs, for anything smaller had been trampled flat by the waves of departing wastoures. There was no sound of living creatures, not so much as a fly; but when a rumble of thunder made them look up, they saw two birds circling against the heavy clouds. Blanche cast one golden-black eye on their braiding flights and knew them for carrion crows, but Ada only wondered whether they had babies and how they kept them hidden.

A lone wastoure came suddenly around a collapsed wall, gawked, and gave a stuttering cry that was fierce cousin to the *tuk-tuk-tuk* of a hen summoning her chicks. A second popped from a hole in the leaf-covered ground. A third. More poured around corners and up from holes, and loped toward Blanche and Ada, calling. *Tuk-tuk-tuk.*

"I wish had not brought you," said Blanche, but Ada laid her hand on Blanche's broad back and said, "Where would I go?"

The first wastoure paused some paces away, wary and weaving, twisting its neck to peer from each eye in turn. *Tuk-tuk-tuk.* The others streamed past it, until—

"*STOP*," Blanche said, with her rattling growl.

The foremost wastoures halted as though they had slammed into a wall, so abruptly that the rest crashed into them and they all fell together in a shrieking, bickering mass. Blanche flutter-hopped on, Ada alongside, and the wastoures scrambled out of reach—but more kept appearing, and more, until chicken and child walked through a horde of them, in a clearing an armspan across.

The wastoures were a cohort not yet full grown and mostly the same size, a little taller than Blanche and waist-high to Ada. The only thing like this in Ada's small experience had been coming into Margery's kitchen yard in the morning, when the hens would swarm toward her, hungry and loud. This was so much worse: she could smell their hot breath, a mix of sweetness and rank meat, the smell of flyblown bacon hanging in a chimney before the smoke has cured it. Their claws beat on the hard-packed earth. She felt a touch on her heel and though she wanted to be brave she gave a little scream.

Blanche said, "*BACK.*"

The wastoures stumbled away but they still kept pace. Blanche fluttered up into Ada's arms.

Down the hill, and into the tumbledown villa itself. Blanche's eyes were on the wastoures, but Ada was watching her feet, for it would not do to fall. A single perfect little circle appeared on the dust: a raindrop, and then another. The ground changed as she walked, claw-pounded dust to rain-spattered dirt to flagstones, and finally to a ruined mosaic peeping through the leaf-litter, of a gold-green fish against waving blue lines. The rain-wet colors were startling.

Ada tightened her grip. "We found it!" she whispered. "The Town with a Moat!" Blanche only ruffled a little, a hen's equivalent of a frown.

They crossed the pavement to where two ruined walls met. "Here," said Blanche, and dropped from Ada's arms.

The wastoures stopped, a tight chattering circle that blocked all ways. All ways but down: there was a triangular hole at Ada's feet, where a flagstone had broken in half and left a gap.

A wastoure popped up its head, a quick lunge away.

"*Go,*" said Blanche, and it fell back as though it had been struck.

Ada did not like holes: not cellars, not caves, not even the thought of safe happy busy burrows full of baby rabbits and their mothers. And this was none of those, but a gash, a ragged breach fringed with dirty broken mosaic that looked like teeth. (She did not think, like monsters' teeth. She knew what the teeth of monsters looked like.) She could see through the hole a second floor some feet beneath the first, heaped with leaf-mold and sticks, and the fallen flagstone, tipped at an angle that made it look like a wet, pale tongue.

The young wastoures jostled closer, snake-necked and sharp-beaked, narrow heads weaving and bright claws curling. Their eyes were hungry and curious.

"*BACK,*" hen-growled Blanche, and they recoiled.

Ada looked into the hole.

Blanche said, "I know. But we must go there."

Ada knew hard truths: had been raised in them. They dropped together.

* * *

In another version of this story, they do not come to the ruined villa, but instead find the Town with a Moat. Ada is collected into the heart of a family with three daughters, whose names are Charity, Kindness, and Patience. Blanche is given a gold collar and lives to a great age. Stop here if you like.

It was not a long fall, and there was a pile of litter at the bottom, pounded into a cushion by the claws of wastoures. Ada landed awkwardly, but Blanche fluttered down, white wings outstretched, and guarded her as she clambered off the leaves. They were in a broad, low space as large as the room overhead would have been, and just tall enough for Ada to stand upright. Irregular piles of rock served as pillars to hold up the . . . floor, it had been when they walked above; but here it was their roof. Daylight and silver rain filtered in through holes where the floor-now-roof had fallen.

A thousand years before, this space would have been heated by a furnace, and the villa's owner would have walked through his rooms overhead, warm-footed and smug; but neither Ada nor Blanche had ever imagined such things as hypocausts. Nor had that owner (whose name was Fabricius, who died of cancer; at the end, he wore a red cloth concealing the tumors on his neck: not a vain man but tidy) imagined such things as wastoures, for they came down from the mountains only long after he was gone.

The general darkness and the pillars made it hard to see far clearly. Wastoures dropped through the holes and crowded closer, more with each moment until—

"*BACK*," hen-growled Blanche.

Just out of arm's reach, the circle re-formed. The uttermost queen's demand vibrated in Blanche's hollow hen-bones, trembled in each feather like a maddening itch: */grow/go forth/waste the way/find home and hole/do not return/*.

A young female pushed forward into the circle of space: clever and assertive, alphamost of those present. It reared tall and looked down on the hen, first with one eye, then the other, and Blanche read the challenge clearly enough. To gain the high ground, she hopped onto the fallen flagstone, though peering faces fringed the hole just overhead. Now she could see more clearly across the hypocaust. Ada still as a stone, in a dirty shawl that had once been the color of sky. The sharp challenge in the young alpha's eye as it swiveled to view her, the reflexive clench of its foreclaws. The wastoures in their scores, a milling chaos in rain-wet darkness striped by streaks of light glancing down through cracks from above. There was a rough gash in the far wall of raw rock that led down into deeper darkness. It was there they must go.

Blanche opened her pearl-white wings and stretched her neck and hen-growled, "*Leave. Die. Be gone.*"

Her order beat against the queen's demand. To the young wastoures, it was like the throb of two great bells tuned a quarter-tone apart: a thrumming in their teeth, in the fluid of their eyes, in their hearts as they struggled to keep the beat. Some dropped to their haunches shivering and clawing themselves, but most attacked whatever was closest, pillar or kin—though never Blanche and Ada. Some seethed toward the holes and, swarming over their fighting broodmates, fled into the rain. A hard-willed few did not seem much affected, the young alpha among them. They still encircled Ada and Blanche.

"*Go,*" Blanche said, with wing-mantle and head-thrust and hen-growl. In the end, the alpha snapped her jaws but stepped aside, and the remaining wastoures dropped back. Blanche and Ada crossed to the broken place in the hypocaust floor. Rank cold air breathed up at them. They crawled through.

A thousand years before Ada and Blanche, when the villa's builder had selected his site, the laborers had discovered a hole. There was no telling what caves or hidden rivers might be there to undermine the villa's foundation, and the hole was too small for an adult to pass through, so they sent down a child of eight. An orphan. The child did not return. They built there anyway, sealing the hole with a great flat stone.

The child's bones are gone. Should I tell you how he died?

Blanche and Ada stood on that fallen stone. They were at the highest point of a limestone cavern, a long, sloping-floored space barely touched by a rain-silver glow that filtered from two places, the hole behind them and a single high crevice off to one side.

Ada saw only glints and movement; faint light touching the curve of what might be an egg, the sudden spark of a kindling eye. She heard pattering claws, a dislodged stone, the breathing of the young ones clustered in the doorway behind them. She smelled water and earth and the memory of salt. And wastoures.

Blanche saw even less than Ada, but she understood more. The eggs of the uttermost queen and her court had been laid here across decades, collecting until a current ran through them like the chemical change that pulls a cicada brood from its shells, each seventh or seventeenth year. The eggs hatched and the young grew, then left in their legions, seeking new caves that would meet the needs of so stringent a reproductive strategy. This wastoure summer was waning, so only a few hundred eggs remained, clustered at the cavern's far end. Beneath the queen's demand / grow/go forth/find caves/and flourish/ Blanche could feel the weak, unformed impulses of the restless unborn, pressed against their curving walls.

A score of females stood between Blanche and the eggs: the court. She felt the currents of their thoughts, as well: fear and anger, ambition for themselves and their eggs, but above all, pervasive and unstopping, the desperate hunger for wastoures to thrive. They stepped forward, silent and snaking-necked. And among the eggs stood the uttermost queen, the alphamost alpha: ancient, crumpled as wet linen, and marked with sores where her skin was shredding—for she was dying, her task nearly completed.

She did not advance: did not need to. Her underlying demand did not change, but there was another thread now, tenuous (for she had not changed her demand in long decades) and specific: / *kill this unflock unthing/do not let it be/.*

"*Die*," Blanche said to the uttermost queen, though she knew that she would not be stopped so easily. She was right. The queen only shivered as though shaking away a spiderweb; but the rest were confused—the court, the half-awake eggs, the young fighting overhead in the hypocaust, or scattering outside in the gray rain: even the seething hordes long leagues away.

The queen above her eggs stretched her neck, stance broad, tail twisted high and lashing—*/kill/unkind unkin/unfriendly unflock/.* Even the strongest of the juveniles could not enter the cave against the ancient demand, */go hence/,* but the females of the court were cleverer, stronger. They advanced.

Ada made a sound in her throat like the squeak of an infant mouse.

"BE GONE," Blanche growled. Two of the court broke and ran in a great curve around Blanche and Ada to the hole, but it was blocked with fighting juveniles. Ada saw none of this, only heard shrieks and claw-nailed feet running, and then smelled the bright fresh thread of new blood.

And Blanche said: "DIE. KILL YOUR EGGS. KILL YOUR QUEEN. KILL YOURSELVES."

The court's advance fell into chaos. One attacked another and they rolled screaming down the long, sloping floor toward the eggs, and as they tumbled past, others turned to fight one another, or dropped convulsing to the ground. Deaths and more deaths, wastoures laid waste and wasting. At the still center stood the queen, splashed with the blood of her people, her eggs, and herself: too strong to fall but not able to counter Blanche's demands.

/you/kill all/ said the queen—*/who kills me/they cannot/*

"Well, then," said Blanche. To Ada she said, "Cover your eyes, dear one."

But Ada did not.

* * *

The uttermost queen is gone. The humming voice in the remaining wastoures' narrow skulls is now Blanche's: *DIE. Kill the eggs. Kill yourselves.*

The final eggs are ripped open by the last member of the queen's court, uttermost queen by attrition. She is too weak to kill herself before she tears open the eggs. The yolk-slick infants slide free and writhe in the cold air until she bites open their throats. Her death when it comes is a mercy.

DIE, BE DESTROYED.

And everywhere the wastoures die. They throw themselves from cliffs. They bolt into lakes. They ram headfirst against stone walls until their jaws dislodge, and still they do not stop. They tear one another to pieces, frantic and babbling with the blood of their broodmates in their throats.

Some hordes are driven by stronger-willed alphas, but even their strength fails. A few manage to avoid Blanche's demand, alphas and their bands that have gone far enough that the humming lies less heavily. The hypocaust and the chamber of eggs are gone—but the task was always to find a new cavern and begin the long task of producing enough eggs to start a new brood.

One young, strong-willed female does find an apparently suitable cave, though it is chalk, not limestone. She is now the uttermost queen by default. She goes to ground with the band she has been able to save. It is not as good; eggs collecting in a chalk cave are softer-shelled than those laid in limestone. */grow and grow strong/* she demands, but the shadow of Blanche's humming voice also sifts into the proteins of their yolks.

When after long years there is at last a new brood, many do not hatch. Some kill themselves or one another before they leave the nest. A few survive, raven forth. Still fewer, the next time there is a brood. There are five last wastoure summers spread across a century, until they die off entirely and dissolve into memory. Such documents as recorded their ravages are lost, rotted or turned to endpapers and razor strops, mouse nests and tinder.

But in that last century, in those last broods . . . The ever-smaller courts and their weakening queens tell tales of horror to the dwindling eggs and the diminishing young. Pearl-feathered Blanche spreading her wings is a nightmare that everyone shares, stained into their genes, feared more even than skin rot or water. Hers is a name too dreadful to utter in daylight without blood spilled to wash it away. She is a monster, *the* Monster, Destroyer of Worlds. Waster.

Who calls a thing genocide? Not the aggressors. Blanche is monster and savior, depending on who you ask.

Here is where we stop, if you want a happy ending, for Blanche and Ada anyway. At the moment, Blanche and Ada are alive, triumphant. The wastoures are defeated.

If we go past this, things complicate again. Blanche is already old, a hen past laying. Ada will also die: plague or childbirth, an infected knife wound from cutting mutton, dysentery, grief. Even should she die at ninety, safe in a goose-feathered bed and surrounded by loving descendents, she is dust.

Or, turn back to the first page and read their story again. Now they live on, though in darkness and fear. A happy ending depends on when "The End" is written, by whom and for whom. For purposes of this tale, then: The End.

Publication History

"Tool-Using Mimics," *Clarkesworld Magazine*, 2018.

"Mantis Wives," *Clarkesworld Magazine*, 2012.

"Butterflies of East Texas," *The Golden Ticket* (privately printed), 2017.

"Five Sphinxes and 56 Answers," *DIAGRAM*, 2020.

"Ratatoskr," *Sunday Morning Transport*, 2022.

"Coyote Invents the Land of the Dead," *Clarkesworld Magazine*, 2016.

"The Ghastly Spectre of Toad Hall" is published here for the first time.

"The Apartment Dweller's Bestiary," *Clarkesworld Magazine*, 2015.

"The Apartment Dweller's Stavebook," *DIAGRAM*, 2020.

"The Apartment Dweller's Alphabetical Dream Book," *Conjunctions Online*, 2019.

The Dream-Quest of Vellitt Boe, Tor.com, 2016.

"Noah's Raven," *Lightspeed*, 2020.

"Crows Attempt Human Riddles and One Joke" is published here for the first time.

"The Privilege of the Happy Ending," *Clarkesworld Magazine*, 2018.

Acknowledgments

James Gunn and Ursula K. Le Guin were two writers I was very lucky to know. Between them, they showed me how and what and why to write, and they inspired me to be courageous and disciplined. I could never thank them enough what they gave me, and now I can't—but I hope they knew. Or know.

These stories were written across a decade, which of course means a lot of places and people were part of my process. I especially want to mention:

- my family: my mother and my wonderful brother Rich and his equally wonderful clan.
- my friends, coteachers, and writing partners, Chris McKitterick and Barbara Webb. I would not be the writer I am without their regular presence in my life.
- the friends who kept me thriving. There were many, but I especially want to name Elizabeth Bourne, Marti Dell, and Jay Fraser, Bruce Frey, and Paul Scott who were almost daily parts of my life.
- all my grad students, but especially Jason Baltazar, whose kindness extended to designing teeshirts and illustrating a story for me.
- artist Laura Christiansen for the amazing invitation to be part of *Then and Again,* the inspiration for my first story in this collection.
- the editors who selected these stories: Neil Clarke, Joe Hsien, Ander Monson, Julian Yap, Jonathan Strahan, Bradley Morrow, John Joseph Adams, and Gavin J. Grant.
- the coffeeshops that sustained me: Alchemy, 1900 Barker, MacLain's, and Sunflower, all in Lawrence KS; and Badger Brew in Rice Lake WI.
- the Raven Bookstore, the Dusty Bookshelf, abebooks, and Wonderfair: sources of all delight.

About the Author

Kij Johnson writes speculative and experimental fiction, and has won the Hugo, Nebula, and World Fantasy Awards, among others. She also writes gaming material and teaches creative writing, novel idea generation, and science fiction and fantasy lit. She was the associate director of the Gunn Center for the Study of Science Fiction and the Ad Astra Center for Science Fiction and the Speculative Imagination, both at the University of Kansas; now she assists with the nonprofit Ad Astra Institute, exploring the intersection of speculative fiction, STEM fields, and creativity. (kijjohnson.com)